Jesus' Island of Dreams

The Legacy of Apostle Thomas

How Christianity Survived
the Second Century

Island-of-Dreams Series

By Stephen Thomas White
With Rev. Dr. Charles G. Jenkins, PhD.

Library of Congress Cataloging-in-Publication Data

Stephen Thomas White
Jesus' Island of Dreams / Stephen Thomas White with
Rev. Dr. Charles G. Jenkins, PhD.

After, LLC ISBN 978-0-615-51735-3

Printed in the United States of America

This is a work of historical fiction. Unless footnoted, names, characters, places and incidents either are the product of the author's imagination or are used fictitiously, and any resemblance to actual persons, living or dead is entirely coincidental

While the author has made every effort to provide accurate telephone numbers and Internet addresses at the time of publication, neither the publisher nor the author assumes any responsibility for errors, or for changes that occur after publication. Further, the publisher does not have any control over and does not assume any responsibility for author or third-party websites or their content.

Index

Exhibits

✝ Part I ✝

✝ **Chapter 1** ✝

Death, Dreams and a Birthday
Monday, December 12, 118 A.D.[1]

Thomas slept and dreamed he was standing next to a large rock. In front of him he saw a forest of dark green pine trees, with wind blowing on his back. As he turned around, he realized he was high on a hill. He noticed the forest ended and land slopped down with green grass waving all the way to flat rocks near the sea. To his right was a sharp drop off. At the bottom was a flat meadow with yellow blooming grass waving in the breeze from the sea. He could smell and taste the sea water in the soft wind blowing in his face as he turned. Something touched his shoulder ever so lightly. It tingled. He slowly turned around.

He could not see the source of the touch on his shoulder, then suddenly he was blinded by bright white light. Ever so slowly his vision began to clear. He blinked several times and looked at a man in white robes walking

---

[1] Authors' note. Dates noted in this book are in the years 118, 120, 124 and 125 A.D. and are based on the Gregorian calendar which became effective in 1582 A.D. by the decree of Pope Gregory XIII. The Gregorian conversions back to 118, 120, 124 and 125 A. D. were completed using the Gregorian calendar converter at www.fourmilab.ch.

towards him only a few feet away. Thomas became fearful, but a voice told him to be calm. The face gradually came into focus.

"Can you see me now?" He asked. "I am Jesus. Your great grandfather was my brother and one of my apostles. He was a great friend. I'm here to warn you and tell you of important work you must do."

They were now standing face to face. Thomas stared at Jesus with awe, and asked, "What must I do? Where are we?"

"Thomas, you are eighteen today. You have finished your schooling. You are living in Arimathea in a home near our great uncle Joseph of Arimathea's home. When he was driven out of Israel, he left his property in Arimathea for family members who needed remoteness. You and your family members have lived here safely away from Jerusalem in this mountainous area. Many descendents of the House of David have been hunted by the Romans and many of those who lived in Jerusalem have been denigrated and killed. Luscious Quietus, a Roman ruling the land of Israel, has been removed and a new ruler will be replacing him."

"This is unbelievable news," Thomas said. "We have not dared to leave for the past few years because of this odious tyrant, but You say Lucius Quietus[2] has been removed? Last night Abba, my father, died. We want to bury his body in the family tomb in Jerusalem. Are you saying it is safe to go there?"

"Yes, it is now safe," Jesus said. "Your great grandfather's homes in Arimathea and in Jerusalem have been passed down to you with the death of your father. The great home in Jerusalem was rebuilt by your grandfather after the Romans destroyed Jerusalem and it now stands vacant awaiting you. The home has a burial tomb which is shared with our families' descendents; the tomb has two rooms. In the second room are stone ossuaries. One of the stone ossuaries contains Apostle Thomas' written records he prepared during my ministry. When I talked with my Father in Heaven, Thomas wrote a record of those conversations."

"In that ossuary are gold and silver bars as well as silver coins to allow you to buy a ship and build a house of worship on this island where we now

---

[2] The Jewish Encyclopedia, Lucius Quietus. (Roman general and governor of Judea in 117 C.E. Originally a Moorish prince, his military ability won him the favor of Trajan, who even designated him as his successor. The Talmudic accounts imply that a cruel persecution took place under Quietus.)

stand. You know you have further resources provided to you by Apostle Thomas which are on deposit with the bankers in Damascus and Alexandria. You have visited them."

"In the tomb's second room are other ossuaries containing our people's documents removed from the temple before the temple was destroyed. I encouraged two priests, Dan and Guy, to take the documents out of the temple before it was destroyed. They also made maps showing a cave with two rooms where they found other documents and relics made by God. You must find these documents and relics. Take only the documents and items made by God. Everything must be brought here to this island to be stored in a stone vault you are to build."

"Why have you chosen me? Thomas exclaimed. "I am too young. How can I do what you ask?"

"Walk with me," Jesus said. "I want you to remember this island for you must be able to find it. I was here with Joseph of Arimathea before I started my ministry. He and I agreed this unknown island would become an ideal building site for the storage of records. The island is isolated and away from the cities. Look at the slope of the grassy land; it is a perfect location for gardens and vineyards. The flat rocky area by the sea is where you will build the granite vault in a house of worship."

"I want to show you where you can quarry stone for your buildings. To our left as we are walking, you see the forest; use it to supply wood for building materials. Here we are at the end of the forest. As you can see there is this large outcrop of stone. It can supply you with stone you will need. I will visit you again to show you how to build the vault. This slope has very tillable soil. Bring grape vine starts and plant them up here to give them an early spring start. There is a flowing spring at the top of the hill. Water them and let them grow while the construction is done."

"Look again into the forest. You will find resources in there for you and others to use to promote and develop the religion of the Nazarenes that I founded. Many are now calling the religion of the Nazarenes by another name. They are calling themselves Christians to honor me."

"You and others will develop leaders and an organization for my Christian religion. Find a way to work with friendly Romans to protect you in this mission. Get them to protect you, the island and the house of worship. They protect many places they control. There will be good Romans to help you. You must find them. Learn their ways to bind them to you. Dine with them and appreciate their ways. Have faith in them. They will frighten you, but you must be bold and learn to deal with them. Some day your mission will become a vital life-changing option for Rome."

"How will I know who are friendly Romans that will help me?" Thomas said.

Jesus looked firm and said, "I was rejected in Israel by the leaders and they taunted the Romans to kill me. Simeon ben Kosiba is a new leader who is out of control now. My people of the lost tribes are in Britain, Ireland, Gaul and Espania. They are with me. The time has come for you to take my Good News to the lost tribes. Before you, Joseph of Arimathea and many others took my Good News to the lost tribes. They will welcome your family and friends when you move them."

"I visited Saul who was persecuting my apostles, disciples and Nazarene members. I asked him to stop his harassment, change his name to Paul and spread my Good News. He changed his ways and successfully converted many. He wrote wonderful letters which have been preserved. He had success because he was of the gentile world; he knew them and their ways. You must follow his work in whatever way you can. Continue his work of bringing my Good News to the gentiles. I caution you. Apostle Paul, the Greeks and the Romans used Sunday as the Sabbath. This is different from the Jewish religion which has always observed Saturday as the Sabbath. It is fine to observe Saturday or Sunday as the Sabbath. Do not try to make the Romans change their Sabbath to Saturday."

"Honor the Jewish religion, but be careful of many current leaders. They are on a foolish mission to gain freedom from the Romans. They will eventually lose and most if not all of them will be destroyed. There soon will be terrible times ahead for Israel. The Nazarenes need to leave. Nasi[3] Judah in Jerusalem is the great grandson of my brother Apostle Jude. He will duplicate the writings of my apostles and disciples so that you will have copies to use in spreading my Good News. Take these with you."

"Be warned, there are people in Israel who will learn about the temple records and they will try to take them from you. You must stop them and protect the records and relics. Keep very secret what you find in the rooms in the cave."

---

[3] Authors' note: Nasi means leader of the Nazarene's founded by Jesus. Nasi Judah was the last Nazarene Nasi. Bishop became the normal title outside of Jerusalem.

"You must trust Me and do as I command. Remember this island. You have four important missions. You must remove the documents and relics from Israel, spread my Good News to the lost tribes and the gentiles, move Nazarenes out of Israel and use the resources on this island and some you inherited to develop and further the organization for my religion. I will visit you again to tell you more. I will be with you."

Thomas woke up and lay in wonderment. "Jesus and the island seemed so real," he whispered to himself. "Could I really have been there? Was the dream real? Yes, it must have been real; I am sure I will recognize the island when I see it again. Jesus has ordered me to do these things. I do not know how, but I will do as he has commanded me. I must find these records, the gold and silver and become a Nazarene priest. Nasi Judah in Jerusalem can help me. But why did Jesus select me? He could have selected my grandfather or my own father if only he had lived. There were others, such as Nasi Judah."

Thomas lay mumbling to himself, "Have I been set up to do this with the gold, silver, records, instructions and maps in a tomb on my property I inherited from my father? If all goes well, I will know if it's true. But it is terrifying to think of the magnitude of doing what Jesus has ordered me to do. Jesus is prescient about the events to take place in Israel before they happen. All four of His instructions are huge projects. There are so many things I must learn. I must find others to help and advise me, but they must be trustworthy. This is indeed an earth shaking challenge."

Thomas fell back into a deep sleep again dreaming he saw rolls of documents where he was trying to find one that would tell him who wrote them. He awoke in darkness, groaned and rolled over, going back to sleep. After a while, he was on a sailing ship. It was raining and the wind was fiercely blowing the ship out of control. He and the men around him were terrified of the rain, wind and intensity of the storm. He felt the bitter wet cold and tasted the salt from the sea water. He and the others were screaming and listened to the wrenching of the ships' wood hull being twisted by the roaring waves and howling wind.

He awoke again with a start. He lay awake thinking about those two strange dreams. It was just a weird night. Anyway, he had never had access to rolls of printed documents and had very little experience on the sea. He had a feeling the dreams were a prelude to many major future challenges. From what he knew, everything was in disarray in Jerusalem and everyone must be having sleepless nights. He could not fathom the magnitude of the dream with Jesus.

Thomas laid thinking, "I am the great grandson of Apostle Thomas. I am living in my father's estate in Arimathea. The estate was originally purchased by Apostle Thomas. Here in Arimathea I have been neighbors to other descendents of the rich men Nicodemus and Joseph of Arimathea[4] who was the richest person in Judea during the lifetime of Jesus."

Both Joseph of Arimathea[5] and Apostle Thomas were businessmen working together in the trading and caravan business. Joseph was known throughout the Roman Empire as the Tin Man being the Nobilis Decurio in the Roman army. Apostle Thomas became known as the Caravan Man trading tin ingots and gold for silk and spices in India. These were sold in Parthia, Damascus, Israel and Egypt. My great grandfather's knowledge of the languages spoken in India and Parthia had made him the perfect candidate to eventually teach the Good News of Jesus in those countries.

Joseph of Arimathea was forced out of Judea after Jesus' death and resurrection, but his estate in Arimathea was retained for his extended family. Apostle Thomas' estate in Arimathea provided protection from Jewish persecution for his children when he went to India.

"Now I have inherited his estates in Arimathea and Jerusalem, as well as, large amounts of silver, gold, coin and banking deposits in Damascus, Syria and Alexandria, Egypt. Jesus knew I helped my father manage the deposits and lending done by the Jewish bankers in Damascus and Alexandria.

---

[4] The New King James Version Bible, Matthew: 27:57-60; Mark 15:43-46; Luke 23:50-55; John 19:38-42; St. Joseph of Arimathea at Glastonbury, by Lionel Smithett Lewis, page 94. (Joseph of Arimathea was previously known as Joseph de Marmore as he lived in Marmorica in Egypt before he moved to Arimathea.)

[5] The Drama of the Lost Disciples, by George F. Jowett, page 17-18. (Joseph of Arimathea was reputed to be one of the wealthiest men in the world at that time. He controlled the tin and lead mining in Cornwall Britain. He owned one of the largest private merchant shipping fleets afloat used in the transportation of tin and lead. He was in the employ of the Romans as a "Nobilis Decurio." He was an influential member of the Jewish Sanhedrin and a legislative member of the provincial Roman senate. According to the Talmud, Joseph was the younger brother of Joachim, the father of the Virgin Mary and great uncle to Jesus.)

"My father died after a long illness early in the evening yesterday, Thomas thought. "My Uncle Cleophas, Aunt Ada and Ada's handmaiden, Grace, helped me prepare my father's body for burial. We dressed him in his finest robe and laid him on a wood carrier in the great room. We wanted to take him to Jerusalem to bury him in the family tomb, but we thought it was too dangerous to go there. We went to bed to wait until the next day to decide what to do with my father's body."

Thomas looked around his room in the twilight and realized the sun was about to come up over the mountain to begin a new day. Two roosters in the yard began to crow.

"Stephen, my cousin, should be here soon from Sebaste," Thomas said quietly. "My uncle Cleophas, Stephen and I will transport Abba's body to Jerusalem. I must get up."

He climbed out of bed, washed his face and went out to sit on the steps to watch the sun rise. His uncle Cleophas came out to sit with him and said, "Your Aunt Ada and Grace will have some breakfast soon."

Ada came out with a quilt and put it over the shoulders of Cleophas and Thomas. She sat down and took the end over her shoulder and said, "You silly men. Both of you looked cold out here."

Grace came out and said, "Thomas, are you all right. You were talking and yelling in your sleep. With the death of your father, I was concerned about you. You are the only one left in your family, but we are here to comfort you."

Grace lived as a handmaiden, working for Ada and the household for the past three years since her divorce. She had married at age seventeen, but could not get pregnant and her husband divorced her. Her parents were dead and she had no family. Since she could not get pregnant, no man wanted her even though she was a pretty woman with dark brown hair and hazel eyes. Ada gave her a job at the request of the bishop in Capernaum. She was twenty four now and a devoted servant to Ada and the Thomas household.

"He's alright Grace, he had some wild dreams," Cleophas said, "He will tell us all about them. Thomas, you look concerned. Are you feeling alright this morning?"

"I feel fine, but alone. I'm so lucky to have all of you living with me," Thomas said. "Cleophas, I know you told Ema, my mother, you would take care of me. She asked you to do that for her. You are my second father and Ada you are my second mother. Grace, you're like a sister to me."

"You are like one of our sons," Cleophas said. "But you have been the one who has taken care of us. You managed the household and the farm property even when Ema and Abba were alive. You grew up quickly and took responsibility. You have proved you are very capable and have the experience of an older man. You have been managing the family banking business with your trips to Damascus and Alexandria. You and your father have always been generous to me, Ada and our family."

Thomas broke down and cried. Between sobs he said, "I'm so sad Abba died last night. When he lost Ema, he became sick and wanted to die. We hoped he would get well and live more wonderful years, but he did not want to live. Now he is gone. We talked last night about plans to take Abba's body to the tomb in Jerusalem, but we were worried about the Romans. Just in case we decided to go, I sent a friend on horseback when we went to bed. He traveled to Sebaste to request my cousin, Stephen, to leave as soon as possible to travel here. He should be here soon."

Ada said, "You did all you could for your father."

Thomas smiled now and said, "Thanks, Grace and please sit down. When I went to sleep, I began to dream some very strange dreams. That must be when I was yelling. I awoke and lay thinking about the dreams, and about some of the events after the death and resurrection of Jesus who appeared to me in the first dream. He told me that it is now safe for us to go and move to Jerusalem. He said that the terrible and odious Roman ruler, Luscious Quietus, here in Israel has been recalled by Rome. He feels it is now safe for us to go to Jerusalem. Jesus told me the house in Jerusalem is mine and is vacant. What do you think?"

"Thomas, I must hear all of the details of your dreams," Cleophas said. "I am not surprised that Jesus talked to you now. You may only be eighteen today, but you are wise beyond your years. Does he have work for you to do?"

"Yes, I will tell you when we eat."

Ada smiled and said, "Thomas dear, you are so tall with beautiful blue eyes, auburn hair and beard. You have this aura that causes people to look up to you. Since you were little, you displayed leadership skills. Your father told us long before your mother died that Thomas should be master of this house. In the future you will be tested, but we have faith in you. We will do whatever we can to help. I am anxious to hear the other details of your dreams."

Thomas sat up and said, "Uncle, should we move to Jerusalem now along with our transport of Abba's body?"

"Thomas, it is your decision but if you do move, I think Ada, Grace and I will wait a few days."

Thomas nodded. "After breakfast go talk to your children. I will get the wagons and horses ready. Ask your son, Adam, to come with us. After Stephen gets here we can load my belongings and then pack Abba's body for the trip. It will be very late when we arrive in Jerusalem. We will be tired when we get there, but as late as it may be, we must inter Abba's body in the tomb before sunrise tomorrow. We can then rest for a couple of days before you return back here."

Just then his cousin, Stephen, rode in on his horse with Thomas's friend close behind. Stephen hugged Ada, Grace, Cleophas and Thomas."

"I knew I should get here as soon as possible," Stephen said. "I told my parents goodbye and told them I would be gone for several days. My father told me, you're only seventeen, but I guess you can go. He said to express their condolences for your father's death and wish you happy birthday, Thomas."

After the friend left, Cleophas said, "Let's have breakfast. Thomas has some important information to tell us."

"I had three dreams last night," Thomas began. "I'm still in awe by the dreams."

Thomas talked through most of their breakfast. He started with the last dreams. After drinking some juice, he started in on the experiences in the first dream. "Jesus commanded me to find this island, build the house of worship and vault and spread His Good News to the lost tribes and the gentiles. He warned me terrible times for the Jewish people are coming, so I must help Nazarenes to leave Israel."

Thomas omitted moving the records. Only he knew about them and thought he should keep it that way. "Jesus specifically said there are sources of wealth on the island which I must use to build the Christian religion. I don't know what he meant, but he said he would visit me again to go over my missions. I feel overwhelmed. His commands are explosive and monumental. I am frightened and anxious about His instructions to locate and become friends with good Romans. He said I must find them for our protection in our efforts and the safety for the house of worship. I must learn their ways. I believe they can become true Christian believers and help start a true nascent of growth."

"How are you going to do all that?" Stephen said. "You will need a lot of help. I can't let you do this alone, let me be part of it. I am seventeen and finished my schooling at the Torah school. Father has been asking me what I'm going to do. Until now I did not know. I have been considering becoming a Nazarene for a long time. I didn't because of my father. Now I want to be baptized in Jerusalem. Thomas, you just described the most incredible adventure. You will have to fight off the men who will want to join you. You need me just to teach you how to say no. Many men will want to leave our nation."

"I am very grateful that you want to help," Thomas said. "I want you to be with me in this challenge and arduous undertaking. Why don't you move to my Jerusalem estate? It's great that you want to be baptized to become a Nazarene. I want you to meet Judah who is a great grandson of Apostle Jude and is now the Christian Nazarene leader, the Nasi in Jerusalem. We'll need to continue our education and training to become priests, teachers and missionaries. We need to recruit men to help us acquire a ship, supplies and tools to take with us. Remember, Jesus is pushing me to get started, but I must be prepared. Time will become a critical part of our effort."

"Yes, Thomas," Stephen said. "I have to be part of this adventure with you. We have a lot to learn and do. It will take some time. We must be organized and keep from getting killed in this turbulent time."

"I will be coming back driving the two wagons with my son, Adam," Cleophas said. "When we return you can ride back to Sebaste and pack your things. Ada, Grace and I will pack our belongings and will bring my son with us to pick you up."

"Could it be dangerous to be on these trips back and forth to Jerusalem?" Ada asked.

"Yes, I'm frightened about your move," Grace said. "I've never been to Jerusalem. It's a big city. I will be nervous until I get there. I'm sorry but that is the way I am."

"Both of you are right," Cleophas said. "I will have our two son-in-laws, Carmel and Gad, accompany us on horseback. They should bring their swords and short knives. We should do the same. Thomas you have your bow and arrows. Bring those along with your sword and knives for you and Stephen. Right now I will go visit Adam, Carmel and Gad," Cleophas said, as he walked out the door.

"Stephen, let's go hitch the horses to the two wagons for loading," Thomas said.

Thomas and Stephen went out and bridled the horses, attached the tackle, hooked the horses to the wagons and drove them to the house, chasing the chickens and goats out of the way.

When the wagons were moved, Ada and Grace made a bed for Stephen in the front wagon. Thomas packed his personal items and came out with three bags, his sword, two short knives and his bow and arrows. He felt nervous and knew it could be perilous if he had to use them. He placed them in the wagon where he and Stephen could reach them quickly and put the bow and arrows under the seat. Ada and Grace came out with the food and Cleophas returned and packed a few personal items to take with him. Carmel and Gad arrived on horseback.

"It's time to bring my father out," Thomas said.

The shrouded body was laid properly in the wagon and tied down so it would not move around while they traveled.

Cleophas took the reins for the wagon carrying the body. Thomas took the reins to the other wagon and Stephen climbed in beside him. Carmel and Gad mounted their horses and adjusted their swords to be easily removed. Thomas drove his horse forward with Cleophas following, waving to Ada and Grace. They had not gone very far when they came across Adam. He climbed aboard next to Cleophas. They traveled steady into the dark and until they were getting close to Jerusalem, but were stopped by Roman soldiers on horseback. "Who are you?" one of soldiers asked.

Cleophas said to the soldiers, "We're taking the body of Thomas's father to the family tomb in Jerusalem,"

"We're friends of Nasi Judah of the Nazarenes," Thomas said. "We have homes in Jerusalem and Arimathea. The tomb is in the upper city and we must inter my father before daylight."

"It is dangerous for you to be out here in the dark," the soldier said. "We will lead you."

They followed the Romans and before long they passed through the Valley Gate and rode to the higher neighborhoods. The Romans stopped and said, "We will leave you here."

Thomas encouraged the horses forward passing houses with light in their windows. They soon came to the Thomas estate and pulled into the lane leading to the house. Cleophas pulled out torches he had packed. His lighter flared and he lit the four torches. Walking to the tomb, Thomas said, "My father showed me when I was twelve how to open the door to the first room and how to open the door to the second room. I hope I can remember."

Thomas went to the post with the handle attached. He felt around, located the handle, gave it a pull and the stone door started to roll. Stephen gave the door a push and it rolled further back to reveal the opening. Thomas took a torch into the room. It was large with several niches to store ossuary boxes and shelves to inter the bodies to decompose. The bones would be placed in their ossuary later. Cleophas and Thomas selected the shelf way back to the left for Thomas's father.

Cleophas and Adam pulled the handles of the wooden carrier back until Thomas and Stephen could grab the front handles. Carmel and Gad held a torch in each hand, walking in front of them. Once inside, the torches were placed into the room's torch holders and they carefully removed the blankets from the body, then lifted the body onto the ledge.

Thomas kneeled down by the ossuary holding the remains of Ema, his mother, who had been interred four years ago.. Cleophas took a lid from an empty bone box outside for later engraving of the father's name. The torches and blankets were removed after Thomas gave a prayer, touched up his father's clothes and kissed his check. As Thomas stepped outside, he was crying.

"You are a brave son," Cleophas said. "I know you loved your father and mother very much."

Stephen and Cleophas rolled the door shut while Thomas locked the handle. Thomas took one torch and led everyone to the house, opening the door and locating the torch holders. Cleophas set the ossuary lid on the side table, showed everyone the great room, the storage room and servants' quarters.

"Let's get the torches, go to the wagons and bring our belongings," Thomas said. "We need to unhitch the horses and tie them and your mounts to the olive tree until morning."

Coming back into the house, Cleophas took the downstairs bedroom, Gad and Carmel went into the servants' quarters and Thomas led Stephen and Adam upstairs and showed them each a bedroom to use. Thomas went into his room and was asleep as soon as he got into bed.

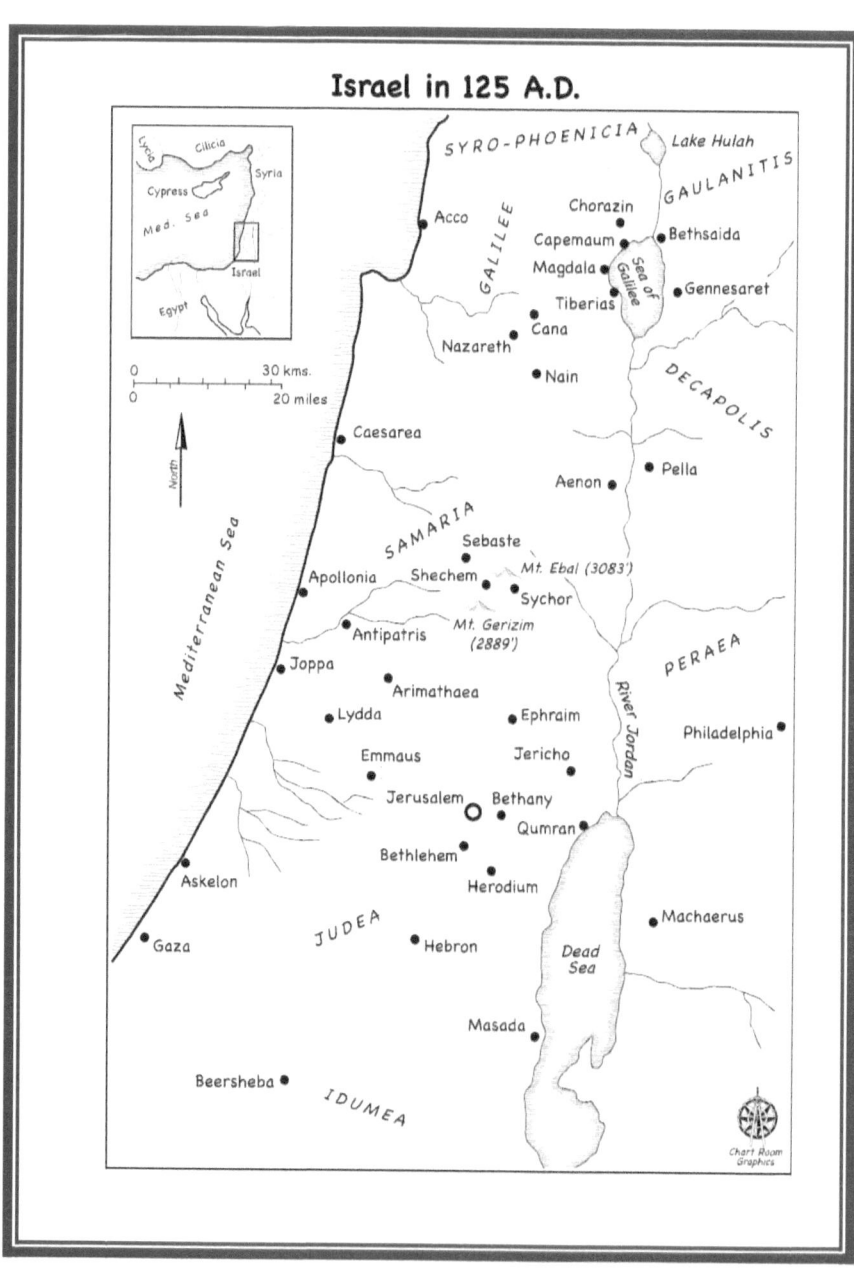

Israel in 125 A.D.

✝ Chapter 2 ✝

Morning in Jerusalem
Tuesday, December 13, 118

Thomas awoke first and wondered what part of the day it was. It seemed too quiet, but then again there were no chickens or goats around the house. He got up and walked out of his sleeping room. He could hear Adam in one room and Stephen in the other. He crept down the stairs and slipped quietly out the front door.

He looked out to see how the two mares and two geldings were doing. He walked over and threw more hay in front of them. He noticed their coats were dirty and muddy. They looked haggard and tired. He pulled out a bucket from the wagon and went to the outlet from the cistern to get water. Taking a bucket full of water, he brought it back for one of the mares who drank all of it. She picked up her head, snorted and blew wildly through her nostrils spraying water all over him. He laughed and rubbed her ears and forehead.

"Thomas, you're busy for just getting up," Stephen said laughing, as he walked up. "Your mares and the geldings need a good dousing with water and a scrub."

"Stephen, you're pretty chipper," Thomas said. "What part of the day is it? I can't tell with this cloud cover."

"I don't know either, but it feels like mid-day," Stephen said. "I'm just glad to be here."

They walked to the cistern outlet and retrieved two more buckets of water. As they were walking back, Cleophas and Adam came out of the house.

"I heard you asking the time of day," Cleophas said. "I think we are in the mid-afternoon. We need to go to market and fetch some food and supplies before it gets dark."

Thomas was watering the second mare and Stephen was scrubbing the first mare when Cleophas came out with Adam, Carmel and Gad. "While you two are doing this good work, we will walk over to the upper market by Herod's Palace. I hope we don't encounter any problems."

"If we keep these horses here very long, we will need to build a watering trough," Thomas said.

"While you are thinking about the watering trough, let's get the water to take inside," Stephen said. "Getting all this dust off us and putting on a clean robe is appealing."

"We have a guest," Thomas said, as he looked at the man walking up the lane towards them. "Hello and welcome," Thomas said.

The man walked up to them. "Are you Thomas?"

"Yes, I am Thomas and this is my cousin Stephen. Who are you?"

"I am your neighbor," the man said. "My name is Jacob. My grandfather was Simeon ben Cleophas. How is your father?"

"It is very nice to see you again," Thomas said. "It has been a long time and I did not recognize you. I apologize. To answer your question, my father passed away two days ago. We came directly here from Arimathea and interred Abba in the tomb very early this morning. My uncle Cleophas, his son and two of his son-in-laws came with us. They have gone to the market."

"I am sorry to hear about your father, although I didn't know him very well. When Governor Luscious Quietus was recalled by Caesar Hadrian last spring, we decided to come back to Jerusalem. Your father and I hired a caretaker for our properties here several years ago. Do you plan to stay?"

"Yes, I moved here, but I will keep my apartment in the Arimathea estate so I can go back once in a while."

"Judah Kyriakos is the new Nasi," Jacob said. "Judah is the great grandson of Apostle Jude. He was elected to succeed Nasi Joseph who was executed by Quietus last January. Judah is busy all the time now at the Nazarene Synagogue, which is higher up the hill above our homes. He has recruited several men to make copies of the apostle's and disciples' writings so they can be distributed to all the bishops away from Jerusalem."

"I met Judah three years ago," Thomas said. "But I'm sorry about Nasi Joseph. Wasn't Nasi Joseph married? I heard his wife passed away and he'd married a young woman."

"Yes, his wife did die and he married a woman named Rebecca about a year ago," Jacob said. "She was seventeen then and has not remarried. She lives in Nasi Joseph's old home a few houses from here."

"What has happened to Akiva who owned the third house here," Thomas asked. "He was the grandson of Apostle James."

"Akiva was killed last January when Nasi Joseph was executed," Jacob said. "Two of his sons were also executed. They should have lived in James' Arimathea estate. Akiva's daughter, Sahar, owns this house now. She inherited the house here and James' home in Arimathea. She is living in Shechem with her aunt which is a very unsafe place to live. My guess is she will come back here now that it seems safe in Jerusalem again."

"Amira is my wife and she is doing fine," Jacob said. "She'll be pleased to hear the news about you and the others. Please come over and visit us tomorrow. I thank heaven you are doing well and moving here. It'll be a pleasure to get to know you, Stephen, Cleophas and his wife. I know you are busy now. I'll let you get back to work."

Jacob walked down the lane and disappeared as they took water into the house to clean up. Cleophas and the boys came in carrying food they had bought at the upper market. Two young boys were with them carrying part of the load. They were dismissed with a coin each and they ran back down the lane.

"You did well," Thomas said. "Most of that is for me, I guess."

"The boys and I decided while we were walking over to the market to return to Arimathea in the morning," Cleophas said. "The boys are anxious to get home. We'll need to drop Stephen off in Sebaste."

They prepared dinner and found dishes, utensils and pans in the pantry.

"This house is well equipped," Stephen said. "It is going to be fun living here."

"I believe we are ready to have dinner," Thomas said. "May I pray? Father in heaven, we give thanks to thee for protecting us on our journey from Arimathea. We pray for our safety here in Jerusalem and a safe trip back to Sebaste and Arimathea for those that must leave again. Please bless this food we have prepared that it may nourish and strengthen our bodies. We pray this in the name of Jesus Christ. Amen."

They ate, enjoying the new beer[6] Cleophas had bought. After dinner they had a small amount of wine[7] from an amphora in the pantry. They sipped the wine in the great room in front of a fire in the large fireplace before going to bed.

Wednesday, December 14, 118 A.D.

In the morning, Thomas saw Stephen, Cleophas and the boys off on their return trip to Arimathea as Cleophas said, "We will go straight to Sebaste to drop Stephen off then on back to Arimathea. I will return with Ada, Grace, Stephen and the boys within a couple of weeks.

Thomas visited with Jacob and Amira by himself. He went to meet with Nasi Judah and arranged with him to baptize Stephen when he returned. While there he arranged to begin a training program for both of them to become teachers and missionaries. Thomas wanted to keep secret the mission to move the records to the island in the Mediterranean.

Friday, December 30, 118 A.D.

Stephen, Cleophas, Ada, Grace and the boys arrived after sixteen days. Grace moved into the servants' quarters, Cleophas and Ada took the downstairs bedroom and Stephen took a bedroom upstairs.

Ada said, "I've been in a panic to get here. Poor Grace was frightened and lay under the covers in the wagon all the way here."

"I felt safer under the blanket in the wagon," Grace said, "I'm so happy to be here. This house is larger and nicer than I thought it would be. Thomas, thank you for letting me come here with all of you and work for this household."

---

[6] Biblical Archeology, September/October, 2010, "Did the Ancient Israelites Drink Beer?" By Michael M. Homan.

[7] Author's note: During this period people drank wine, watered wine, watered vinegar, beer and other sweet alcoholic drinks. Water was either not available or distrusted.

"My folks seemed pleased with my plans to help you," Stephen said. "They wished me luck in becoming a Nazarene. They are still very fearful to become Nazarenes. Hopefully, we can convince them to convert, be baptized and be saved."

**************Over the next two years***************

Ada and Grace became good friends with Amira. This helped them become more settled. Cleophas and Jacob were like old friends frequently discussing James the Just, Simeon ben Cleophas and Apostle Thomas. They talked to Judah about the crucifixion of Simeon ben Cleophas at the orders of Caesar Trajan. They could not imagine the audacity and malevolence of the Romans to crucify a man that was documented to be one hundred and twenty years old. How could they?

Nasi Judah baptized Stephen and started their training. Thomas and Stephen met many people in Jerusalem. "I hear many people talk about both of you," Cleophas said one Sunday morning. "You are not yet perceived to be humble servants of Jesus."

Thomas found an engraver and had the lid from the ossuary bone box engraved with Abba's name and stored it. They were active in the Nazarene ecclesia. The months went by during which Thomas and Stephen took periodic trips back to Arimathea to hunt and fish in the Sea of Galilee with Adam, Gad and Carmel.

Thomas found a carpenter to build a watering trough in front of his estate. He inquired of Nasi Judah about the House of Prayer in Bethany.[8] It was in poor repair and parts of it were destroyed by Titus's forces when Jerusalem was destroyed. Thomas began the effort to restore the House of Prayer which was the former palace of Lazarus, Margret and Mary Magdalene. He paid to have it rebuilt with new stables. Finally Thomas bought ten horses for the stables to be used by Nazarene members. He and Stephen brought their horses over from Sebaste and Arimathea.

When in Jerusalem they frequently walked around the city and stopped to heal people and pray for them. They continued to be amazed how their advice and prayers improved the lives of people they met. They converted

---

[8] The Coming of the Saints: Imaginations and Studies In Early Church History and Tradition, by John W. Taylor, Page 88.

many Jews, Greeks and even Roman soldiers. It was surprising how many people wanted them to tell about the life of Jesus Christ and discuss the Good News Jesus taught. They learned all they could from Nasi Judah. He gave great lessons and they used those teachings to teach others. They hoped to obtain copies of the writings of Jesus' apostles and disciples, as soon as possible.

✝ Part II ✝

✝ **Chapter 3** ✝

Ossuary Box and Room Two
Monday, March 28, 120 A.D.

Just after breakfast, Thomas was talking to Cleophas and asked, "How long should we wait to enter the tomb and place Abba's remains in the ossuary? Abba only waited a year for Ema."

"It has been two years," Cleophas said. "We could do it today if you would like."

Grace looked concerned and said, "Can I help you. Let me fold his clothes and bring them in the house for you."

"That is very thoughtful of you, Grace," Thomas said. "Please come with us."

The four of them went out to the tomb. Stephen carried the engraved ossuary bone box lid, linen straps and a bag. When Thomas rolled the door open, he peeked in but couldn't see anything. He expected a strong smell, but it just smelled musty.

Cleophas lit the torches. He and Thomas stepped through the doorway and placed all four in the torch holders. Stephen came in with the bone box lid. Grace went with Thomas and Cleophas to remove the clothes Abba had worn. She took them into the house. Thomas carefully removed the bones and placed them in the bone box. The lid with his father's name engraved on it was placed on the box. Thomas wrapped two linen straps around the bone box and lid. They slid the ossuary into one of the niches beside his wife.

"Now that Grace is back in the house, could we go into room two and read the moving instructions for the records and see how much gold and silver is there," Stephen asked. "I know that has nothing to do with your father, but we should know."

"Sure, that is a good idea," Thomas said. "He found the lever to release the door to the second door and gave it a sharp pull. The round door rolled open. They brought two lighted torches and placed them in the holders in the second room.

"I have waited for a long time to see what is in these ossuary boxes," Thomas said. "I must say I'm excited. Look how the boxes are lined up. Which would be Thomas' box? Maybe it is the one on the left end. It seems to be set aside and is larger than the others."

Thomas removed the straps of linen from around the box and took the lid off. Here is a note that says, *"There is gold and silver at the bottom of this box, but be careful with my writings. Take these sheep skins with the writing I made while accompanying Jesus. These are words Jesus told me that came from talking with our Father in Heaven. They must be preserved and taken to an island visited by Joseph of Arimathea and Jesus in the Mediterranean Sea. Their map is included in this box."*

"The note is signed by Apostle Thomas, brother and Follower of the Way of Jesus Christ," Thomas said.

Thomas handed the note to Stephen and removed the package of leather pages and set them aside. He picked up the map and another note. "Let me read this note," Thomas said. *"I, Joseph from Arimathea, visited this island with my grand nephew, Jesus. This is a fairly small island in the Balearic Sea. There are larger islands, but Jesus and I selected this uninhabited island as the best solution for storing the writings of Apostle Thomas and other records to be stored there. Jesus and I were surprised when we found a treasure there and buried any access to it. I drew this map on our way to Israel. I have given this note to Thomas for him to include with his writings. We want Thomas' writings to be taken to this island and stored there."*

Thomas laid the map and note on Thomas's package. He pulled out nine silver bars and found nine gold bars below them. He pulled out the gold bars and found the bottom covered loosely with silver Roman coins. "Stephen, hold the bag open. I will gather about half of these coins and load them into the bag."

Thomas replaced the gold and silver bars, and then he gently replaced the package of sheepskins with the two notes and the map back on top. He tied the linen straps together and stood up.

Thomas removed the lid from the next ossuary and laid it by the wall. On top were two notes and two maps. He pulled out the first note and read,

"There are four ossuary boxes with records brought from the temple record room by Dan Hannan and Guy Kadros. Both men are Sadducean Priests and Dan told me he and Guy were concerned with the possible destruction of the temple. In a dream Dan had with Jesus the Christ, He told him to remove the records and bring them to James and me for storage. Jesus told Dan to leave the attached maps showing where ancient records and artifacts are stored in two rooms in a cave below the temple. The records and the artifacts are to be taken to the island in the Mediterranean Sea and stored there. James and I do this in the name of Jesus Christ. I have written this in my name, Simeon ben Cleophas."

Thomas laid the note down and picked up the second papyrus note and began reading, *"We are Sadducean priests. Our names are Dan Hannan and Guy Kadros. We are leaving the Sadducean priesthood to become Nazarenes, as followers of the Way of Jesus. We will be leaving Jerusalem with the other Nazarenes to avoid the danger that will be rampant in the devastation and destruction of Jerusalem. We removed these records from the record room in the temple and brought them here to preserve them. The records include Moses' records he brought from Egypt, records from King David, King Solomon and genealogy records."*

"On the back is more writing," Thomas said and began to read, *"I, Dan Hannan, was given instructions by Jesus Christ in a dream. We have prepared two maps which are attached showing the location of ancient records and artifacts in two rooms in the cave south of the temple mount. We found them when we explored the cave when we worked as temple stone masons before we became priests. We do this in the name of Jesus Christ. Amen."*

"Let's take the maps, locate the records and artifacts hidden in the two rooms in the cave, Thomas said. "We can bring them back and store them in this room. That way when we get ready to leave Jerusalem, everything will be here."

Thomas put the notes back into the box and replaced the lid. They took the bag of coins, the maps, doused the torches and sealed the two rooms.

In the house the three of them sat staring at each other. "You don't want to go to the cave alone," Cleophas said. "You need some protection and help. We don't know the volume of the records or the size of the artifacts in the rooms in the cave or who may try to stop you. Why don't you and Stephen ride over to Arimathea and get Adam, Carmel and Gad to ride back with you? If they come over here for a few days, there will be six of us with swords and knives to protect ourselves."

Cleophas took them into the great room where he walked into the fireplace and stepped over the hearth to a space on the left side, reached up and pulled a handle down. The side of the fireplace had a door made of stone and it swung inside. Thomas pulled out four handfuls of coins out of the bag they brought from the tomb and placed them on a table. He took the bag into this small safe area and set the bag down on a shelf. He came back out, closed and locked the door. "I did not know that was there," Thomas said. "Thank you, Cleophas."

"I helped your father take some coins and gold out of there three years ago," Cleophas said. "There are a couple bags left in there from your grandfather. Your father had paperwork in a room in Arimathea for deposits held in Syria and Egypt. Some of the deposits in Damascus, Syria and Alexandria, Egypt were made by King Akbar in Edessa when Thaddeus went there at Thomas's request and healed him."

"Uncle Cleophas, I knew about those deposits," Thomas said. "The amounts are sizable. My father told me my grandfather went to Damascus, Syria and Alexandria, Egypt and verified the amounts and obtained new paperwork and wax sealed clay tablets. The amounts are in measurements of silver. I went there and talked to those bankers. We discussed freeing up some of the amounts for me to use if I need any."

"There are bags of coins on the shelf in there," Thomas said. "Have we used any of those since we have been here?"

"Yes, I thought you knew," Cleophas said. "You kept enough out to last us for a while. You and Stephen each take some. Ada and I will hold onto the rest for shopping."

Most of the day had passed, it was late afternoon when Stephen and Thomas set out extra robes with their swords and knives. They got their sleeping mats and blankets and tied them with leather ties. Ada collected enough food for two days and put it in a bag.

Grace placed the food bags by the door and said, "Thomas and Stephen, please be careful. I worry for both of you when you leave. I especially worry for us, because I feel much safer when both of you are here."

Thomas smiled and said, "I know you worry Grace, but Cleophas is here. We will be careful and will only be gone for a few days."

They decided to have an early dinner and go to bed. Tomorrow would be a long day.

Tuesday March 29, 120 through Friday, April 1, 120 A.D.

Thomas and Stephen walked over to Bethany to ride their horses from the House of Prayer's stables. They rode to Arimathea in less than two days and returned in two days with Adam, Gad and Carmel. They left their horses at the stable and walked back to Jerusalem arriving in the late afternoon on Friday.

They had dinner with Cleophas, Ada and Grace. While they were eating, they talked about the trip from Arimathea. Grace expressed her happiness they were back and said, "I'm frightened all the time you and Stephen are gone. I worry bad men will come here."

"Grace, we will be gone more and more," Thomas said. "I know you are concerned, but you will be fine. Cleophas is here and will take care of you."

After dinner, the men sat around in the great room in front of the fire for a while. They talked about the trail to the cave. Would the cave entrance be open or covered with the debris from the destruction of the temple? Thomas reminded everyone to keep quiet about why they were going to the cave and about what they may find.

Adam and Stephen went to bed upstairs first, but Carmel and Gad followed them and slept in the vacant bedrooms upstairs. Thomas told Cleophas, Ada and Grace good night and went to bed.

† **Chapter 4** †

The Cave with Two Rooms
Saturday, April 2, 120 A.D.

The next morning Thomas came down followed by Stephen and the other men. Soon everyone was eating breakfast. "I have put out the shovel, bar and the hammer," Cleophas said. "Do we need anything else?"

"Let's take a rope, a blanket, and some torches," Thomas said.

"Will you tell us what you find in those caves," Grace asked. "It must be really important."

"Grace, we won't tell you for your own protection," Thomas said. "We must keep this a secret and whatever we find hidden. Even you and Ada must not know. Someday we can tell you, but not now."

The six men walked toward the temple mount. Passing by the rebuilt Herod's theater, they turned right to walk down to the lower city. They passed the pool of Siloam and went out the road to the Dead Sea. They turned left and descended the hill into the Kidron valley. They walked below the backside of the City of David. As they passed Gihon springs above them, the pathway started to be littered with debris and covered with building blocks from the destruction of the temple. Thomas was following one of the maps that Dan and Guy had made to lead to the cave opening.

"The temple mount was built over Mount Ophel," Thomas said. "Gihon springs are about a thousand or more cubits south of the Temple Mount. The cave we want is below and north of the Gihon Springs which we have already passed. It's pretty close to the south end of the temple mount. Those blocks ahead of us are in front of Dan and Guy's cave entrance."

"I can see a cave entrance in back of these pieces of broken limestone," Adam said.

Thomas unwound the rope he was carrying. He and Adam tied the rope to the block. All six of them got hold of the rope and at the count of three they gave a giant pull. The block did not move. Adam looked in back of it.

"There's a fragment of the block sticking out at the bottom. He unwound the rope and squeezed down the back of the block and tied a loop around the fragment. They grabbed onto the rope and gave another pull, tipping up the block, rolling it over towards them. Adam turned with a smile. "We can enter the cave."

Thomas looked at the opening as he wound the rope. "The cave entrance is about twenty cubits (thirty feet) below us," he said. "It'll be a job to bring whatever we find up here."

"We'll have to slide down this rubble to the entrance," Stephen said

Cleophas flashed the lighter flint and soon had three torches lighted. He gave one to Adam who slid down the rubble to the front of the cave. "We can stand up and walk when you get down here," he shouted. "Thomas, come down with the map."

Thomas slid down the rubble and stood up. The others followed. The cave opening became larger and higher as they walked further in from the entrance. The interior was a large room. Thomas walked to the back of the room to a cave which led into the mountain on a slight incline.

"This is an old natural limestone cave," Thomas said. "We can walk in it if we stoop over some and hold the torch down low. The map says the first storage room is three hundred paces from the big room. Let's leave our swords, the rope and the blanket here."

They entered the cave and walked forward with every other person carrying a torch. The roof became a little higher, making it easier to carry the torch. They rested, looking at the floor, the higher ceiling and flat walls.

"Cleophas, Carmel and Gad, I think it'd be good idea for you to go back to the big room and wait for us in case we encounter a cave-in or a problem," Thomas said. "If everything looks safe, one of us can come back to get you. Give me the shovel. Gad, hand Adam the pry bar."

Thomas started forward, looking for a side cave. He walked through a couple of turns and stopped when he reached three hundred paces. To his right a chunk of the wall was missing.

"I hope this is the place," Thomas said. "It sure looks like the side of this wall collapsed. Obviously, someone cleared the walkway where we are standing. The map shows this to be an entrance to a room with a door behind this rubble. Stephen, start moving this rock and dirt out with the shovel."

When most of the rubble was moved, Adam scraped the pry bar down the left side, then scraped down the right side and encountered some metal almost at the bottom. Thomas held the torch closer and noticed a tarnished flat copper plate down close to the floor. He slid the pry bar between the plate and the wall. He pulled it further out and heard a snap. The panel opened slightly. He pulled on the top edge and Adam pulled on the bottom. The rough slab pivoted until Thomas could get inside.

The room's rough hewn ceiling was higher than the cave and about ten paces across each way. Near the back were four clay jars. There were brass lanterns and large piles of rotting material that looked like drapery. It was piled on top of a large object. He moved the drapery and under it was a gold box with winged personages standing on top. It lay on a wooden carrying tray. The gold box had its own golden carrying rods through gold rings on each side. Its height from the floor to the top of the box measured to just above Thomas's knee. It was about the same width as its height and was twice as long. They stared at it in awe and Stephen asked, "Could that be the Ark of the Covenant?"[9] Why didn't Dan and Guy say what this relic was?"

"They were probably afraid to say what they thought it was," Adam said. "Maybe they didn't want anyone to know until now."

"If it is the Ark of the Covenant, it has been missing for several hundred years," Thomas said. "This must be the relic Dan and Guy wrote about."

Thomas got down and rubbed his robe on the flat gold surface. It shone brilliantly in the light of the torches. "This top with the two cherubim is the mercy seat," Thomas said. "It is separate from the box, but it fits in the top perfectly."

---

[9] Ibid, Exodus 25: 10-22. (This reference describes how to build the Arch of the Covenant.)

"How could the Ark of the Covenant[10] have been here for several hundred years without being found?" Stephen said. "I guess the cave-in and the tight fit of the door made it invisible."

"Jesus told Dan and Guy to make the map for us. Jesus told me to find these records and only take relics made by God," Thomas said. "I guess Jesus knew this box was here. He had to know it is the Ark of the Covenant?"

"These jars have plugs in the top of them," Stephen said. "They seem to be sealed with something that was sticky, but is now dried hard. It must be pitch."

"Stephen, would you go back and ask Cleophas, Carmel and Gad to come here," Thomas requested. "Don't tell them what we found."

Thomas, Stephen and Adam continued to look at the items in the room. Thomas picked up a rod with an object on the end that looked like a white pomegranate. Cleophas, Gad and Carmel came in through the rock door. Cleophas examined each item.

"We think it is the Ark of the Covenant," Thomas said. "In my dream with Jesus, He said to find the relic made by God. The Ark of the Covenant contains the second set of stone tablets made by God with the Ten Commandments. The Ephod and Breastplate[11] should be with the Ark of the Covenant. Let's unfold this rotting drapery material. Look, there is a bag."

"I believe this is the Ephod,"[12] Thomas said, holding a garment. "It was worn like a vest. Please hold this Cleophas. I bet this other item in the bag is the Breastplate of Judgement."

Thomas pulled the next item out and held it up for everyone to see. It had four rows of settings with twelve different stones. It had gold rings on each side of the Breastplate. Beaded gold chains hung from the gold rings. It had two gold rings on the shoulder straps. There was an object above the rows of stones over the left side.

"This is the Breastplate of Judgement[13] with the Urim and Thummim[14] worn over Aaron's and his descendants' hearts," Thomas said. "They wore it

---

10 Authors note: The Ark of the Covenant has not been seen since 586 B.C. when the Babylonians destroyed the temple which was built by King Solomon and completed about 986 B.C.
11 Ibid, Exodus 28: 6-29.
12 Ibid, Exodus 28: 6-14.

over the Ephod and these shoulder gold rings attached to the rings on the Ephod. The Breastplate was worn to protect Aaron from the danger of the Ark of the Covenant when he talked to God. Talking to God must have been dangerous. Right now it looks harmless enough."

Thomas carefully folded the Ephod and the Breastplate and then he tucked them back into the bag.

Thomas and Stephen unfolded the drapery material until they were satisfied it held no other objects. Thomas took off the top of the Ark of the Covenant and Stephen placed the bag with the Ephod and Breastplate inside. Thomas looked around and said, "Let's take the Ark of the Covenant and the clay jars. Leave the rest here."

Cleophas took a clay jar and a torch and went out first to light the way. Thomas and Stephen each picked up an end of the wooden carrying platform lifting the gold box. They struggled to get out the door and turn into the tunnel. The others picked up the other clay jars and walked to the cave entrance.

They went back to the room. Stephen and Thomas pushed on the door until it slid shut. Thomas closed the copper plate against the wall. He could hear it lock the door in place. He made sure it was flush with the wall. They took turns lifting the rocks and shoveling the dirt back like they had found it. They arrived back at the big room and laid everything down.

Adam went outside to see what part of the day it was. He then slid back down the slope and walked into the big room. "It is mid-afternoon," he said.

Thomas said, "Let's go back in the cave and try to locate the other room on Dan and Guy's map. Take the tools and torches. Follow me. I will count the steps described on this map. The distance is one thousand six hundred paces. It'll take us a while to walk in there."

Thomas started walking, counting his paces. The cave sloped higher, passing two sharp turns until Thomas had counted to eight hundred. They stopped and looked at a smaller cave going off to their left.

"This small side cave is noted here on the map," Thomas said. "We are to ignore it and go on past it."

---

[13] Ibid, Exodus 28: 15-29.
[14] Ibid, Exodus 28: 30.

Thomas walked, counting, saying out loud every time he reached one hundred more. When he announced one thousand five hundred, they stopped to look at tunnels going off in three directions.

"The cave we are to follow goes straight ahead and appears to be manmade," Thomas said, moving his torch around. "Everyone wait here while Stephen and I go forward. We'll call you if it is safe."

Thomas walked until they came to a waist high drop in the floor. He gave the torch to Stephen and climbed down. "Call the others to come here."

Stephen shouted for Adam and the others to come forward, the echo rebounding back. He heard Adam shout, "We're coming now."

Stephen climbed down the drop-off. They both looked around and decided the door must be on the right side, although it looked like an unbroken wall. The others arrived and Adam climbed down and walked around. The area they were in was like a large room with a high ceiling and a flat floor. There was a small cave going off to the left, next to the ceiling. There was a small hole in the corner below the cave in the ceiling.

"My guess is they built this to be used for storage, but never finished it," Thomas said. "They probably changed their mind when they opened that small cave next to the ceiling. That hole in the floor must keep any water drained that comes in from the cave above. I wonder where it goes. At any rate, the map shows the room we are seeking to be on the right. Adam, take the pry bar and scratch around. See if you can find any cracks."

Adam scraped down the right corner where he ran into a small hole near the floor. Next to the door, he could see an indent. He reached in with his fingers and pulled out a rod with a handle.

"I think this rod goes in that hole to unlock the door," Adam said. "The rod is square on the end. Let's see what happens."

Adam pushed the rod through the hole, but at first it went in only about half way and stopped.

"It doesn't engage anything," he said. "Turning the key a little more, it slid in further and engaged. He twisted the handle but it didn't do anything."

"Take the pry bar and put it through the handle and twist it with the bar," Thomas suggested.

Adam put the bar into the handle and pried the rod to the right, but nothing happened. He reversed the direction and pried gently again, then twisted the rod a little firmer. A crack appeared and then the edge of the door.

"There's a handle built into the side of the door about waist high," Thomas said. "Pull the key out and stand back."

He got his hand on the notch in the rock door and pulled hard. The door slid open with the bottom scraping along the floor. Thomas stepped inside and Stephen handed him a torch.

The others looked at the room's high ceiling. It was much larger than the other room, being square and about twenty paces deep and wide. There were four beds on one wall and two benches. Copper pans and bowls were in the back. The wall next to the opening of the door had a dozen clay jars along the wall. They looked in them and found they had sealed stoppers. There was a high table in the back left corner with more clay jars on top.

"This room looks like a hiding place for a few people," Thomas said. "It also was used for some storage. Let's pull out the stoppers. I bet some of these hold grain or corn."

Cleophas leaned the unlit torches on the left wall by the drop-off and noticed the remains of a fire on the floor with smoke burns up the wall. "Whoever stayed in this room must have done their cooking out here," he said. "The smoke would have gone up through that small cave acting as a vent near the ceiling."

Thomas examined the first bed which had legs made of ivory[15] with a mat lying on ropes tied to the wooden frame. He lifted up the first bed and found a couple of robes and some sandals. He slid the first bed against the wall by the door. He went to the second bed which was made like the first and slid it against the first bed. On the floor where the second bed had stood he found blue and purple material. He held it up and found that it was a little decayed, but had been finely woven. He laid it on the second bed and looked down at what was under the material. There were five gold painted poles with gold hooks on the ends. Tied to each hook was a tarnished socket.

"Everyone, I think I have found the screen for the door to the tabernacle,"[16] Thomas said. "We talked about this in Torah school. It hung in front of the Arch of Testimony."

Gad and Carmel used their knives to take the stoppers out of the clay jars. Cleophas was holding a torch over them so they could see into the clay

---

[15] Ibid, Amos 6: 4.
[16] Ibid, Exodus 26:36-37.

jars. The first three clay jars contained corn. The next five jars contained papyrus scrolls and the last four contained more corn.

"Gad and Carmel, put the plugs back in the jars with papyrus rolls and set them up on the drop-off," Thomas said, then gave a sigh. "I don't know if I am happy or scared to death by what we have found," Thomas said. "Before the temple was destroyed everything we have found was so important."

"You have instructions from Dan and Guy," Stephen said. "They were visited by Jesus telling them to prepare the notes, the maps and get them to Simeon ben Cleophas. Then you were visited by Jesus, told to find what was on the maps and take what was made by God to the Island-of-Dreams. How can you question what we have found and what we should take?"

"You're right," Thomas said. "I just get nervous at times. I feel like we are removing the guts of the Jewish religion, but Jesus says we must do this, so let's get busy and see what else is here."

Thomas went to the third bed and found it was just like the first two. He slid it next to the second bed. Lying on the floor were clothing items. Stephen picked up two tunics with sashes. Thomas picked up two pair of linen trousers. They folded them and set them on the third bed. Stephen picked up two turbans and laid them with the other items. Thomas stooped down to see what had been under the turbans. Lying there was a gold object on another linen tunic. Thomas picked up the gold plate and showed it to Stephen.

"I believe this is a plate of pure gold to be worn on a turban by Aaron or a priest who was a descendent of Aaron," He looked closely at the plate. "It has blue cording under it.[17] It was worn as a Holy Crown. These other clothes must have been worn by sons of Aaron.[18]"

Stephen folded the last tunic and placed it on the turbans. Thomas laid the gold crown on top clay jars on the top of the drop-off. They moved the fourth bed, made of gilded wood poles with a mat lying on ropes tied to a wood frame. Thomas looked at a blue robe on the floor. He picked it up and little bells attached to the bottom tinkled. It had blue pomegranates hanging on it.

---

[17] Ibid, Exodus 28: 36-38.
[18] Ibid, Exodus 28: 39-43.

"You have the Robe of the Ephod,"[19] Stephen explained. "It was to be worn by Aaron or his descendents when they went into the Holy of Holies."

Thomas found a grinding stone and thrasher to crush corn and grain. Stephen found four more clay jars standing empty on top of a table. He noticed the table was made of wood covered by copper or brass. As he looked at the table further, he saw each corner had a horn. The table was square and the top was even with the middle of his chest. It was large, being wider than he was tall. It had rings attached to the four corners with tarnished poles through each side so it could be carried."

"This is the bronze temple altar,"[20] Thomas said. "It's too large to take with us and besides it wasn't made by God. I think we have now seen everything in here."

"This place is creepy," Stephen said. "All of this clothing is rotting away."

They talked about what may have happened to those who slept and ate here. There were no human bones, so they could not have died in the cave or the room. The torches started to flicker. Thomas grabbed a spare torch and lit it.

"I wish we could establish whether these relics came from the first temple here in Jerusalem," Thomas said. "The Samaritans built a replica of the Jewish first temple on top of Mount Gerizim, so these relics could have come from the Samaritan temple on Mount Gerizim, which was destroyed by the Seleucid Governor John Hyrcanus when he captured Shechem and destroyed the temple and its facilities on top of Mount Gerizim two hundred and fifty years ago.[21]"

"I don't think the Samaritans had time to hide their copies of these," Cleophas said.

---

[19] Ibid, Exodus 28: 31-35.

[20] Ibid, Exodus 27: 1-8.

[21] Biblical Archaeology Review, November/December 2010 – Volume 36 Number 6. The Samaritans became a separate Hebrew sect in the Persian period in the fifth century B.C. The Jews returning from Babylonia rejected the Samaritans and considered them to be gentiles even forbidding Jews from marrying Samaritans. The Samaritan temple on Mount Gerizim has been under excavation for twenty-five years by Yitzhak Magen and others.

"I think all we want to take is the gold crown," Thomas said. "We'll leave the cloths, altar, beds and stored corn here."

Thomas put the gold crown in a pocket in his robe. Cleophas brought out the burning torch. Adam and Thomas closed the door and heard it snap. Adam twisted the key to lock the door and replaced the key in the hole in the rock frame. They climbed up the drop off and took the five clay jars with the documents.

Thomas started back down the cave with the others following. They were breathing heavily when they were about halfway back. They stopped for a short rest. Cleophas led them forward again. They came into the big room.

"It is going to be a job to take the gold box up the slope," Stephen said. "I guess four of us can carry or drag the box up the slide."

Gad and Carmel picked up one end of the wood carrier. Thomas wrapped the blanket around the box while Adam tied the rope with the knot on the end to pull. Thomas and Stephen carefully climbed the hill with two jars each. Cleophas and Adam dragged the box up the hill, digging a small trench with Carmel and Gad pushing. Gad slipped and the box slid down the slippery slope. Carmel yelled and Cleophas and Adam lost their grip on the rope. Gad grabbed the box riding it down the slope. Everybody panicked. Thomas walked over to see if anyone was hurt. Stephen got the men regrouped. Carmel scurried down to help Gad. They agreed to go slower. At the top they took the box around the block and set it down. They returned to the big room, donned their swords, smoothed their robes and decided who would carry the tools.

"Stephen and I will carry the gold box," Thomas said. "The tools and torches can be tied on it. The rest of you will carry the clay jars. We have a full moon to light our way. Cleophas and Adam, please lead us. Let's move out."

They carefully walked through the debris led by Cleophas. When they reached the road to the Dead Sea, they stopped and everyone put their load down. They looked up the road through the lower city. Very few lamps were burning. A detachment of Roman soldiers on horseback came down the road. They stopped to look them over.

"What are you fellows carrying?" The soldier asked.

"We've been gathering some berries and olives to take back to process," Thomas said. "We bought some wine in these clay jars from some friends. We ended up later than we expected."

When the soldiers were gone, they picked up their load and continued on until they reached Herod's theater. They stopped to rest. Some couples were out walking in the moonlight but ignored them. They picked up their load and continued on to the Thomas estate. They walked along the lane and went directly to the tomb. Thomas found the handle and pulled it, allowing the door to roll open. They entered room one. Thomas found the brass rod and pulled it to release the door to room two. He and Stephen went back out, picked up the Ark of the Covenant and carried it into room two. They stopped while Cleophas came in to remove the torches, tools and rope. Thomas took the gold crown and placed it on top of the blanket over the Ark of the Covenant.

"Let's leave the blanket on the Ark of the Covenant for now," Thomas said. "We can remove the blanket and examine it at another time. We should not tell anyone what this box is. No one needs to know. Let's stick with the story of a relic. We need shipping boxes for the Ark of the Covenant, the clay jars and the records in these stone ossuaries."

Thomas took out a quill and papyrus paper. Stephen and Adam gave dimensions for each box that was needed to Thomas for him to record. Thomas gave the list to Adam. They brought the clay jars in and stood them behind the ossuary stone boxes. They locked the doors to both rooms and took the tools and rope into the house. The six of them, tired and hungry, walked in the house and sat down on the benches around the table. The food with goblets and amphoras of beer, wine and juice were set out. They ate and told Ada and Grace of their hike, but didn't describe what they found. They didn't say they brought anything back."

"I guess you had to go look," Grace said. "I had hoped you would find something important, but at least you satisfied yourselves there was nothing to be found. I'm going to bed."

"It's very important that none of us talk about what we did today, Thomas said. "If the Jews or others thought we found anything, we could be tortured; we could even be killed. Mum is the word. Can I count on all of you to keep this secret?"

Everyone said they could, as Thomas looked at each person.

Finally, everyone said goodnight and went to bed.

Stephen Thomas White

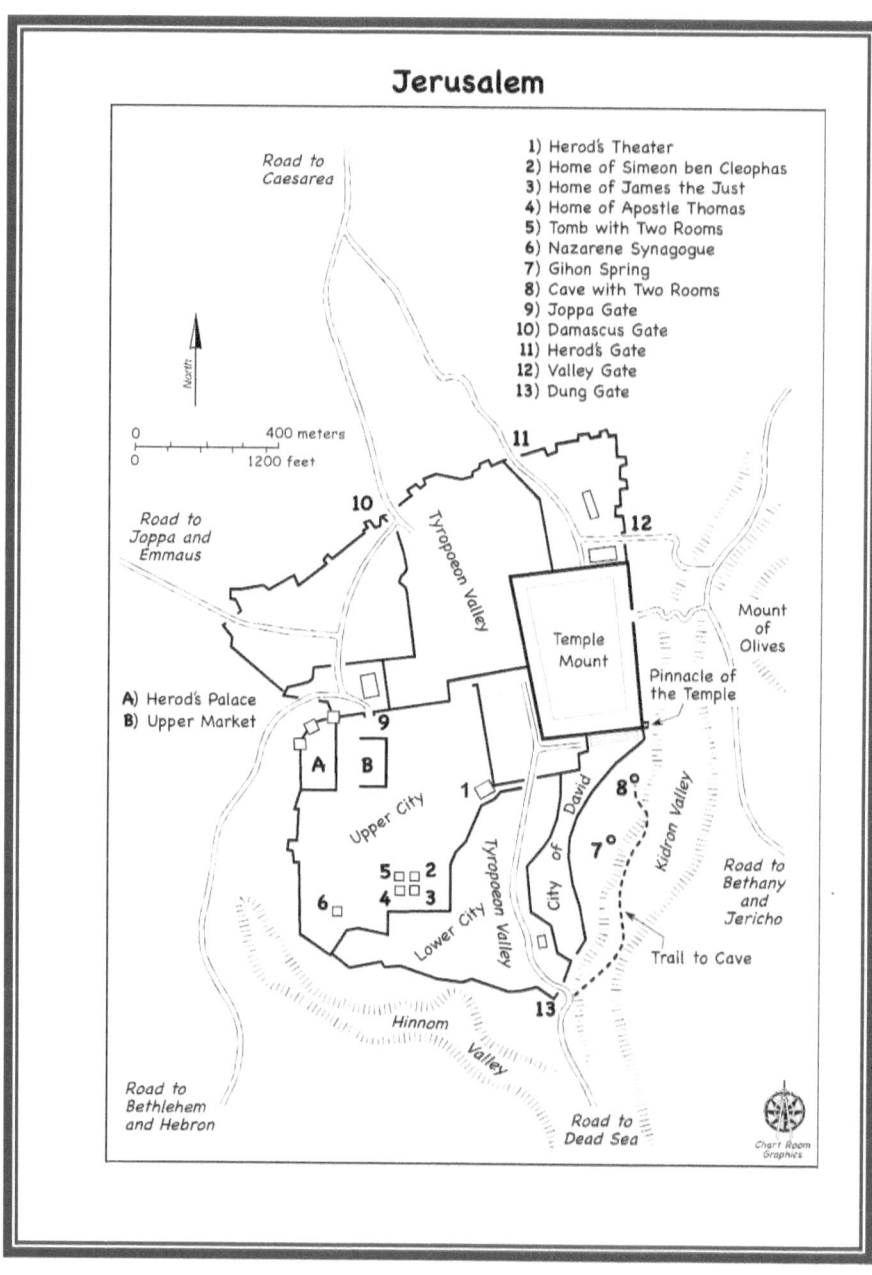

Jerusalem

1) Herod's Theater
2) Home of Simeon ben Cleophas
3) Home of James the Just
4) Home of Apostle Thomas
5) Tomb with Two Rooms
6) Nazarene Synagogue
7) Gihon Spring
8) Cave with Two Rooms
9) Joppa Gate
10) Damascus Gate
11) Herod's Gate
12) Valley Gate
13) Dung Gate

Road to Caesarea

North:

0   400 meters
0   1200 feet

Road to Joppa and Emmaus

A) Herod's Palace
B) Upper Market

Tyropoeon Valley

Temple Mount

Mount of Olives

Pinnacle of the Temple

Upper City

City of David

Kidron Valley

Road to Bethany and Jericho

Lower City

Tyropoeon Valley

Trail to Cave

Hinnom Valley

Road to Bethlehem and Hebron

Road to Dead Sea

Chart Room Graphics

✝ Part III ✝

✝ Chapter 5 ✝

Recruiting Three Missionaries

Saturday, October 7, 124 A.D.

It was early Saturday morning. Thomas talked to Stephen about the day being his twenty-fourth birthday. "Over the past two years, we have traveled with the caravans making two trips to Damascus, Syria and two trips to Alexandria, Egypt. We met with the Jewish bankers that managed my investments that originated with Apostle Thomas. The bankers managed my investments and are now second and third generation family members. I am their client. They have been successful and made good fees lending my money. My funds have grown nicely with both of them. I told them I wanted at least half of the loans liquidated. I want my money to be transferred to me within a couple of years. I instructed them to gradually get half of my funds liquid. My instructions were that I would send papers in advance of any withdrawal. As you know I want the gold and silver to be delivered to my estate in Arimathea."

"Our trips have been very instructive for me," Stephen said. "You wanted me to meet the bankers in case I needed to see them for you or if something happened to you. Now it is no longer safe to go on these caravans since Simeon ben Kosiba started building his rebel army last year. He is waging guerrilla warfare against the Romans and kidnapping men to be in his rebel army."

"Stephen, you are right about this guy who calls himself the messiah, Bar Kokba.[22] We have made these trips and had a good time getting ourselves ready to begin our missionary work. But Simeon ben Kosiba is forcing us to get out of Israel as soon as we can. It's time to plan how to find the island. For simplicity, I'm going to start calling it the 'Island-of-Dreams.' We need to buy a ship, recruit some men to go with us and find tools and supplies to take. The men we recruit must be able to speak and write Aramaic, Greek and Hebrew, and be Nazarenes."

"We may need to convert some of them to become Nazarenes or Christians, as some people are now calling us," Stephen said. "I agree they should be educated and able to speak and write Aramaic and Greek. But we won't be here in Israel, so not all of them need to speak Hebrew. You've talked about the buildings we are to build on this Island-of-Dreams. Let's find a strong man with building experience."

"We need someone familiar with Roman rules," Thomas said. "And obviously, we need a man to captain our ship. The other men just need be unafraid to help us do our missionary work, which may include standing before a group to talk or make presentations. We need unmarried men who are willing to leave Israel. Who do we know that can fit all of those criteria?"

"Possibilities could be members of our congregation," Stephen said. "Paz attended Torah school and has trained to be a document preparer. He's the son of a high priest who wants him to also become a high priest as well, but he has become a Nazarene and wants to leave Israel."

"I know where Paz lives and I like his name," Thomas said. "Paz means shiny pure gold. Let's go see him."

Thomas and Stephen left, walking down the lane to the road. The olive trees were bare and the day was bright and sunny. The air smelled of smoke from many cooking fires in nearby homes.

"Paz lives in a recently restored home that had been burned by the Romans when they destroyed Jerusalem fifty-five years ago," Thomas said, as they walked along.

"There it is over there," Stephen said. "It's a pretty nice place."

---

[22] Authors' note: Simeon ben Kosiba became known as bar Kokba the messiah. He began his rebel army in 123 A.D. He directed his rebel army to conduct guerilla warfare against the Romans until he declared war in 132 A.D.

Thomas knocked on the gate in front of the courtyard. A man came out with a dog. "Thomas and Stephen, it is nice to see you," the man said. "You must be here to see Paz?"

"Yes, we would like to talk to him," Thomas said.

"Please sit on these benches while I go get my son."

Thomas walked around admiring the carpentry work of the house, the new courtyard and the tastefully planted trees and bushes. Soon, Paz came out with a tray of cakes and goblets. "Sit down and refresh yourselves."

"We've recognized your clear and concise thinking in congregation meetings," Thomas began. "Stephen and I are planning to acquire a ship to sail across the Mediterranean Sea to find a special island I was shown in a dream. We'll be doing missionary work wherever we can along the way. We also will be building a house of worship on this island. There will be homes to build along with planting vineyards and gardens. We'll return here to take some records with us to store in a vault we will build in the house of worship. We'd like to invite you to go with us."

"I am very flattered that you have asked me to do this," Paz said, looking stunned. "My father will be angry if I say yes. But I'm worried about Israel with this illegal rebel Jewish army that began last year. I think it is a good time to leave. I believe very strongly in Jesus Christ and I would love to do missionary work with you."

"Thank you, Paz," Thomas said. "Please keep this to yourself for now. I'll have some periodic planning meetings you should attend. Stephen will give you a days' advance notice. We'll need others, but we want them to be educated. Can you recommend someone?"

"Yes, I know two others you'll like," Paz said. "The two men I have in mind are Mark and David. Mark is a big man, a tax collector for the Romans, and David's father is a friend of Jacob, your relative and neighbor. Mark reads talks and writes Hebrew, Aramaic and Greek, fluently. He is used to working with the Romans and the priests in the Temple. Mark went to Torah school and became a Nazarene a few months ago, though he wants to keep that secret. He is twenty-eight and worked building houses for a few years before he became a tax collector. I went to Torah school with David and he's also a Nazarene. Both of them are anxious to leave Israel for the same fears we all feel."

"I know David and I like him," Thomas said. "It sounds like Mark fills the bill for someone who could supervise the buildings we will build on the

Island-of-Dreams. He'll also be useful in our dealings with the Romans. You arrange a meeting and we'll see you in the morning."

Sunday, October 8, 124 A.D.

The next morning, they walked back to Paz's house. When they knocked on the gate, Paz greeted them and invited them into the courtyard. Mark and David were standing there. Paz introduced them. There were cakes and goblets of juice on a table. They sat down and served themselves.

"I have told Mark and David why you want to meet them," Paz said.

"My father has been after me to decide what I'm going to do," David said. "I want to leave Israel because I am afraid of the future with the rebel Jewish army battling the Romans"

Thomas looked at Mark who said, "The rebel Jewish army is growing and I understand the fierce will of the Romans. Paz probably told you that I recently became a Nazarene and was a home builder before I became a tax collector."

"Good," Thomas said. "Six years ago I was living in Arimathea and had a dream. I was on the Island-of-Dreams and had a visit with Jesus. I walked with Him and He told me I must find that island, build the house of worship, the homes and plant vineyards and gardens. He told me I was to take Apostle Thomas' writings and some old temple records that had been removed before it was destroyed. He clearly said I was to take his Good News to the lost tribes and gentiles. He instructed me to follow the work done by Apostle Paul."

"That was quite a dream," Mark said. "The old temple records are really interesting."

"I grew up in Arimathea," Thomas said. "My great-grandfather was the Apostle Thomas and he made a lot of money trading silver and gold for pepper, spices and silk before and after he became an apostle. Simeon ben Cleophas and James the Just received wealth and property here in Jerusalem from Joseph of Arimathea, who was Jesus' grand-uncle. I have inherited the estate in Arimathea and here in Jerusalem. I have enough wealth to buy a ship, pay for our trips, and build the house of worship and the homes on the Island-of-Vision."

"I'm excited now," Paz said. "You did not tell me all this yesterday."

"David, you look angry," Thomas said.

"No, I'm not angry," David said. "I'm just afraid you won't invite me to go with you. I want to go. This is everything I have dreamed of doing and much more."

"Paz, have you been invited to go," Mark asked as he finished his juice.

"Yes, I was invited yesterday," Paz said. "I said I very much wanted to go."

"I think this is a most exciting adventure, Thomas," Mark began. "I would love to go with you. I'll supervise the building work and will certainly enjoy missionary work with you or alone. I'm eager to go. I don't think any of us are going to feel bad about leaving Jerusalem."

"I'm delighted," Thomas said. "I invite both of you to go with us. But don't talk about what I have disclosed to anyone. Stephen and I have not talked about this, but I plan to go over to Joppa to buy a ship and find a man to be our captain. We'll probably need one more man besides him."

"I'll let you know when we will meet for our first planning meeting," Stephen said. "We will meet at Thomas' home after we return from Joppa."

"Mark and David, if you change your minds before our first meeting, let Paz know," Thomas said. "Once we've divulged our full plans, you can't walk out. Again do not tell anyone about what we plan to take to the island. Any news of what we plan to take could be disastrous for us and our work."

Thomas and Stephen left and walked up the roadway. The wind was blowing and the trees were bending. The weather showed signs of the beginning of an early snowstorm.

"I can still taste that cake," Stephen said. "The grape juice was a little tart, but I liked it."

"Yes, both were good," Thomas said, holding his robe. "Sorry I sprang that trip to Joppa on you. I have heard about a representative for a boat manufacturer in Joppa. It's critical that we find a boat captain to recruit while we are there. The captain can advise me on buying a used ship or having a new one built."

"I think your idea of finding a ship captain to help us decide on buying or building a ship is a very high priority," Stephen said, as the wind blew his hair into his face. "Being desert and mountain men, we don't know anything about ships."

✝ Chapter 6 ✝

Multipurpose Trip to Joppa
Monday, October 9, 124 A.D.

The next morning Thomas and Stephen walked over to Bethany carrying their swords and got there in mid-morning. They saddled their horses. They were back at the house at mid-day. When they had tied their sleeping mats, robes and food on the horses behind their saddles, they were ready. Hooking the sword-scabbards onto the saddles, they rode out through the Jaffa gate.

There were many people walking on the road. A Roman detachment returning to Jerusalem stopped to talk to them. "Sir, we're on our way to Joppa," Thomas said to the soldier in charge. "Do you think we'll meet any thieves or recruiters for the illegal rebel Jewish army?"

"We've heard reports of recruiting activity," the soldier said. "You'll need to watch for any suspicious people, for we have heard of men carrying knives and robbing people. You two will be prime targets. Are you going to sleep overnight on the way?"

"Yes, I'm sure we will," Thomas said. "Do you have any suggestions where to stop?"

"Yes, we stop by the stream that goes over the road," the soldier said. "You can see and hear people approaching you on foot or by horseback. Are you Thomas, the Nazarene?"

"Yes, I am Thomas and this is my cousin, Stephen," Thomas said. "Who are you?"

"I'm Principale Bardo," the soldier said. "You may not know it, but many of us have heard about you. Some of our men have become Nazarenes. You baptized a couple of my men. When you get to Joppa, go to the fort and ask for Centurion Markus. He will be helpful to you, but ignore his gruff manners. Tell him I sent you to him. You can leave your horses in the stable at the fort."

By late afternoon they came to a stream running across the road in a large clearing at the top of a hill. There were other people camped there. Thomas selected a spot away from the others where they could see both directions. It had a grassy area next to a tree where the horses could graze. They rolled their beds out and laid their swords along side. They took their food, went across the road and sat around a fire with the other campers. They talked to those who were of the Jewish faith and going to a synagogue in Jerusalem.

"Where are you going," a camper asked. "You seem to be rather wealthy with your fancy robes, horses with saddles and swords. Do we need to fear you?"

"No, we were concerned about you," Thomas said. "Do we need to fear you?"

The campers laughed and thought the question was funny.

"We mostly fear the rebel army," Thomas said. "Have you encountered them?

"No, we have not, but you should be careful of them."

Nothing more was said.

Tuesday, October 10, 124 A.D.

The next morning was cloudy and cool. They got up at daybreak and ate soft bread and cheese. After getting ready to leave, they said goodbye to the campers and rode on, enjoying the cool sweet air, hoping it would not get windy. As they rode along, Thomas said, "I've been thinking about Cerrone's help and advice on buying a second ship. I'm buying two ships for the price of one. I guess this is the beginning of Roman support. What will be next?"

They rode into Joppa arriving at the Roman fort in early afternoon. A soldier came out to challenge them. "Who are you to ride over here," the soldier asked. "This area is for soldiers only."

"I apologize for riding into the fort area," Thomas said. "We are looking for a stable to board our horses for a few days. We were told by Principale Bardo to ask for Centurion Markus. He thought he would allow us to use your stables."

"I'm Centurion Markus," the soldier responded. "How do you know Principale Bardo?"

"He knew of me before we met him," Thomas said. "We talked to him on the road yesterday."

"Principale Bardo left here two days ago," Centurion Markus said. "Why did he think I would help you? We never do what Jews ask. Who are you?"

"My name is Thomas and this is my cousin Stephen. We are Nazarene missionaries, and some of Principale Bardo's soldiers have become Nazarene members. Stephen and I baptized several of them. I did not know you never boarded horses other than for your soldiers."

"Principale Bardo talked about the Nazarenes," Markus said. "He thinks we could benefit having more Christians here. Are Nazarenes and Christians the same?"

"Yes, Nazarene is the original name, but we are called Christians outside of Jerusalem," Thomas said. "I guess since we are out of Jerusalem we are Christian missionaries."

"Based on Principale Bardo's comments to you, your horses can stay here in our stables until you leave," Markus said. "You'll be our guests. Stop in to see me for a visit before you leave. You may want to try one of the imported wines I have in my private stock."

"It is a pleasure to meet you, Centurion Markus," Thomas said. "Stephen and I would be delighted to take you up on your kind offer."

"The stable is over there. Tell them to let you enter your horses and hang your bridles and saddles."

"We've never been to Joppa," Thomas said. "We have swords and knives. Will we need them here? If we don't, we will leave them with our saddles."

"You should be safe here. I recommend you leave them with your saddles. Where will you stay?"

"I understand there is an inn here for travelers," Thomas said. "Could you direct us?"

"Yes, follow the path from the fort and it will lead to the pier," Markus said. "The inn faces the pier. The innkeeper is a good man. I have seen his rooms and they are satisfactory. He and his wife prepare great food."

"Thank you, Centurion Markus," Thomas said. "I have two more requests of you. Do you know a representative for the boat manufacturer, and do you know of a man that has experience as a ship captain?"

"The boat manufacturer's representative is also a fisherman," Markus said. "Ask at the pier where his fishing boat is. As for a ship captain, I do know of a man who comes by the pier every day who recently left employment on a Roman ship. His name is Peter."

He grinned, "Ask any girl you see about Peter and they'll know where he is. He is a remarkable judge of women, but I think he is a very capable ship captain."

"Thank you for the information. We'll come by later tomorrow."

Thomas and Stephen walked down the path and came to the pier. Thomas asked at the first ship if they knew which fishing boat belonged to the ship manufacturer representative. The man looked at Thomas and said, "He's out fishing now. You will want to come back at sunset. Can I tell him who you are?"

"Yes, if you see him tell him we will be staying at the inn," Thomas said. "Tell him to ask for Thomas. One other thing, do you know a man named Peter?"

"Why, yes I do," the man said. "Walk down to the end of the pier and you will likely find him sitting there."

When they got to the end of the pier, two men were sitting with their feet hanging over the water. "We are looking for a man named Peter," Thomas said. "We were told that one of you may be he."

"I'm Peter," one man said, as both men stood up. "What can I do for you?"

Peter was the taller of the two men. He had a well-trimmed beard and mustache. His hair was long and pulled into a braid. Anyone would conclude he's a handsome man with green eyes and a friendly grin. His clothing was more like a Roman's uniform: a leather blouse and a leather skirt. His sandals were well used. He was very tan.

"We're looking for a man with experience to be the captain of my ship," Thomas said.

"Where is your ship?" Peter asked. "And who are you?"

"My name is Thomas and this is my cousin Stephen. We are Nazarene missionaries. I'm in Joppa to buy a used ship or more likely to order a new ship to be built for me."

"You are Nazarenes," Peter said. "I was baptized in Rome to be a Christian. Are Nazarenes and Christians the same?"

"Yes, they are the same," Thomas said. "What are you doing here in Joppa?"

"I was working for the Romans, but I didn't like the captain of my boat," Peter said. "He told me good riddance when I quit. I've been looking for the right job, but nothing has been of interest to me so far."

"What type of sailing experience have you had?" Thomas asked. "You look young, but you appear to be a salty sailor."

"I worked sails, rowed when needed, and have been the first mate on several ships," Peter said. "I've loaded and unloaded many ships, repaired sails, rudders and leaks and have even been the captain on five voyages. I'm twenty-eight and that's not so young. I'm probably older than you."

"Yes you are," Thomas said. "I'm impressed with your experience. It sounds like what we need. I'm delighted that you're a Christian. What languages can you speak and write?"

"I can speak and write Greek, Aramaic and Latin. There were times when I needed to keep records in each of those languages. All three languages are important. I can speak enough Hebrew to get by. Why do you ask?"

"I need educated men to go with me," Thomas said. "If you captain my ship, would you enjoy being a missionary with us?"

"I'm a new Christian," Peter said. "You'll need to be patient with me, but I can learn if you have Jesus' Good News stories. I'll enjoy reading them. How many missionaries will be going with you? Where would you want to sail?"

"We have three others besides Stephen, you and I," Thomas said. "I think we need one more missionary so we have seven to manage the ship. We'll be sailing across the Mediterranean Sea to find an island. There might be several trips."

"You'll normally need more than seven men to manage a sailing ship," Peter said. "I could design a ship to be run by seven, but you would need to have it built. Where in the Mediterranean would you be going?"

"It's in the Balearic Sea," Thomas said. "We refer to it as the Island-of-Dreams on a route going towards Britain. We have a map produced by the great uncle of Jesus. His name was Joseph of Arimathea. He traveled those waters for many years."

"I've heard of him," Peter said. "He and his son Josephus owned a fleet of ships. They sold tin and lead ore to the Romans and any other buyer they could find. Joseph of Arimathea was known as the tin man. The family still has the fleet of ships and the trading activity. Was he a relative of yours?"

"Yes, he was Jesus' great uncle," Thomas said. "My great grandfather was Jesus' brother and his name was Apostle Thomas."

"That's very interesting," Peter said. "I never thought I would meet a descendent of one of the Apostles. I can see why you want to do missionary work. How can you afford this effort you are contemplating?"

"For now let's just say I can," Thomas said."Do you want to be my captain and be a missionary with us?"

"Yes, you've intrigued me," Peter said. "Why do you want to find this Island-of-Dreams?"

"It would be a long story," Thomas replied. "I'll tell you at a later time. Can you keep a secret? We need to keep our plans to ourselves until we leave Israel."

"I'm honest and loyal," Peter said. "You take me on and I'll keep your secrets."

"Who is your friend here," Thomas asked.

"This is my good friend, Ben," Peter said. "He just turned eighteen and writes letters for people. He writes and speaks Greek, Aramaic, Hebrew and Latin and has been to Torah school. He's an orphan and lives with his uncle who is after him to decide on a career to be able to support himself."

"Ben, you have heard my conversation with Peter. What do you want to do with your life?"

Ben was a sharp looking young man with his long brown hair and matching brown eyes. He looked intense, but lively. His beard and mustache were very thin, but arched nicely from each check. He had a friendly and positive look about him.

"I would like to leave Israel," Ben said. "I'm afraid of the illegal Jewish rebel army. They're recruiting men like us against our will, fighting against the Roman army and risking our way of life. Peter has told me what he learned about Christianity in Rome and I'm now a believer in Christianity. I would be happy to become a Christian and sail with you. Doing missionary work would be interesting. I listened to your conversation with Peter and was hoping somehow you would ask me to go with you. I know I really don't know you and Stephen. I think I like both of you and your adventure sounds challenging. I know I'm young, but I can work with people quite easily. As you can see I like to talk."

"I like you too, Ben," Thomas said. "Could you and Peter come to the inn with Stephen and me?"

They walked together to the inn. When they entered the innkeeper came up, asking, "What can I do for you?"

"We need two rooms and a table for the four of us," Thomas said.

"I can get you two rooms, but they must be paid for in advance."

Centurion Markus came into the inn. He walked up to say hello to Peter and Ben. He asked the innkeeper if he had gotten rooms for Thomas and Stephen.

"No, we were just going to talk about price," the innkeeper said. "Do you know these fellows?"

Yes, I know all of them," Markus said. "Thomas here has come to buy a ship. I would hope you will take good care of him." He walked over to another table and sat down.

The innkeeper stared with surprise at Thomas.

"I'll have two of my best rooms prepared for you. You can pay me when you leave. Can I show you to a table over there in the corner? You must have important matters to discuss."

"A goblet of beer for each of us to start will be satisfactory," Thomas said. "Could we also have some sliced cheese and bread? Do you have any raisins, nuts or olives?"

"Please be seated and I will attend to your wishes." The innkeeper scurried away.

"Let's be seated," Thomas said. "I have something important to tell you, but it must be kept a secret. You need to know how important our mission and work is to me and to someone very important you've heard about."

The innkeeper brought their beer, cheese, bread and nuts. Thomas told them of his visitation with Jesus. Then he went on to talk more about the island and the commandments of Jesus. He emphasized the importance of the records and the missionary work. "I do not know where we will spend most of our time," Thomas said. "It remains to be seen how much missionary work we will do once we leave Israel."

The four of them talked, laughed, ate dinner and got to know each other during the evening. At last, Peter got up and said, "Ben and I should let the two of you go to bed. Can we finish our conversation in the morning?"

"Come back to the inn at mid-morning and we will talk some more," Thomas said. "I'm sure both of you will fit in nicely with our group. Ben, please let your uncle know we would like to talk to him tomorrow."

After Peter and Ben left the inn, a fisherman came to their table. "Are you the men who were looking for me?"

"Are you the ship manufacturer's representative?" Thomas asked.

"Yes, I am, but I just got in and need to finish cleaning my boat. I can come here earlier tomorrow. Could we talk then?"

The fisherman left the inn. The innkeeper came over to Thomas and said, "I have your rooms ready. Please follow me."

Thomas went into a deep sleep and dreamed of Jews who had learned of the temple records being taken. They were angry and wanted to get them back. A voice in his dream warned him to be careful of these men. He awoke in the dark and lay thinking about the dream. "I wonder who might have disclosed our secrets. If it has been disclosed, it has to be Paz, Mark or David who leaked the knowledge of the temple records," he said to himself. "If one of them did, it shows a lack of maturity and dependability. But worse, it could be a crisis. We won't know until we get back to Jerusalem."

✝ Chapter 7 ✝

A Captain, a Design and a Recruit
Wednesday, October 11, 124 A.D.

It was early, but Thomas got up and pounded on Stephen's door. "Good morning. "I had a dream I would like to talk about it."

"I also had an alarming dream," Stephen said. "Let's go downstairs and talk about our dreams while we eat."

They seated themselves at a table in the corner. The innkeeper's wife came out with some breakfast for them. When she left, Thomas said, "I dreamed some Jews heard about the temple records we have. A voice in the dream warned me to be careful of them. I'm concerned that Paz, Mark or David did not keep our secrets."

Stephen said. "I woke up wondering if Paz was unable to keep the secret because in my dream he was yelling at his father."

"It's troublesome," Thomas said. "We could have an impossible situation. If a large group of Jews come after us, we'd have no chance."

Peter and Ben walked up to the table. "A hearty good morning to you," Peter said. "But you look very concerned. Is there a problem?"

Thomas smiled and said. "I'm just anxious to return to Jerusalem."

"My uncle is very pleased with the idea and wants to meet you and Stephen. I'm very excited."

"We are ready and excited to go with you," Peter said. "If we do go, where will we stay in Jerusalem until we get ready to leave Israel?"

"You will stay at my house," Thomas said. "You will each have your own bedroom. The four of us will sleep upstairs. My aunt and uncle live with us in their own bedroom downstairs. Grace is my aunt's handmaiden and stays in the servants' quarters."

"It sounds like you have an estate," Peter said. "I'm anxious to see it."

"We met the representative for the shipbuilder last night after you left," Thomas said. "He is planning to come here in the early evening to discuss our needs. You said yesterday you might have some ideas for a ship that seven men could sail or at least manage."

"Yes, I got up this morning early and lit a candle, got some sheepskin, quill and ink. After you said we could have a ship built with three inner storage levels. The six of us couldn't row it very far, but we could use the oars to maneuver around piers and next to land. It would be a true sailing ship. I have designed a top deck that is complete with a step down area for ten seating positions on each side. We would just spread out three to a side to work the oars. I also have designed three sailing masts to give the ship more speed. With my design, we can even learn to almost sail it into the wind."

Peter laid out the piece of sheepskin. He pointed out that the design was incomplete but showed some key design features. It had three cabins and a galley on the second level. "If I could stay here working on this design, I'd have it completed by early afternoon." Peter said. "You could go with Ben to meet his uncle."

Thomas, Stephen and Ben left Peter drawing on his sheepskin. Ben led them out onto the pier and headed towards the fort and then made a right turn into a small neighborhood. They went into a nice house that overlooked the Mediterranean.

"I want you to meet Thomas and Stephen," Ben said. "This is my aunt and uncle. They have been so kind and loving to let me live here since I was twelve. My parents were killed by the Romans in a riot in Bethlehem."

"Yes, Ben has been our responsibly these past six years," the uncle said. "He talked to us last night and this morning about your offer to baptize him to become a Christian and be a missionary in other countries. I believe it to be a wise decision. I'm glad to meet you and Stephen. I appreciate you coming to talk to me. Ben will be a strong and dedicated asset for you. He's honest and hard working. We're proud of him and will miss him. What you are offering is a blessing for Ben. We also approve of his new friend Peter. I must say Thomas, you impress me as an outstanding teacher and leader."

"Thank you," Thomas said.

"I have some thoughts for you to consider in your travels," the uncle said. "We Jews have been expecting the messiah since the time of David and Solomon, but we have been unable to accept Jesus as the messiah. Since Jesus was crucified there have been many men who have come forward in Cyprus, Mesopotamia, Egypt and Cyrene claiming to be the messiah. Each of those men led their people into killing and mayhem. In the end, these pretenders were killed and most of their followers died with them. I fear this nonsense will continue into the future. Right now this Bar Kokba movement and its leader Simeon ben Kosiba is saying he is the messiah. He will die along with his followers and ruin what is left of our great nation and religion. Jesus was a loving, law abiding man with great powers and wisdom. At this time, you are wise to leave Israel."

"Thank you for your perspective," Thomas said. "It has been a pleasure."

Thomas and Stephen waved as they left, agreeing to see Ben back at the inn for lunch. They walked out to enjoy the view from Ben's home and the sparkling Mediterranean. They turned and followed the path back to go to the fort. At the entrance, they were met by a soldier who demanded to know what they wanted.

"We left our horses in your stable yesterday as approved by Centurion Markus," Thomas said. "Is he available? He invited us to meet with him today."

The soldier looked surprised and walked into the fort leaving them standing. Shortly, Centurion Markus came out to greet them. "Please follow me. They walked in the fort and out into a lovely flower garden.

"Wait here while I retrieve some of the sweet wine I told you about yesterday." He came back carrying a small amphora and three small goblets. He offered a goblet to each. "This wine is made from raisins grown in Crete and is called Passum. It is very tasty by itself. Please sip it while we talk."

The wine was luxuriant with body and blended with the caressing sweet smells of the flowers near them. Markus smacked his lips, making Thomas chuckle. He seemed to be in the throes of pleasure. "Markus, you have splendid taste in flowers and the best of unique wines," Thomas said. "Do you know very much about the inhabitants of this city and the area around it?"

"Joppa has a fine mayor by the name of Ezra, who is away today," Markus said. "Citizens include many Jews, Christians and Greeks. Christians are prone to say we have mostly gentiles. I'm one of those. Disaster befell

Joppa sixty years ago. Vespian sacked this town and the Jewish and Christian population was devastated. It has been rebuilding. If you do any missionary work here, there will be crowds who will want to hear you. I know I would. There is a need for some good news."

"We've enjoyed your flowers and this very special sweet wine," Thomas said. "But we need to return to the inn. We've recruited Ben and Peter. We'll come by at daybreak to saddle our horses and leave."

"Both of you have horses," Markus said. "How will Peter and Ben travel?"

"We had planned to take turns walking and riding the horses," Thomas said.

"We have extra horses here that Centurion Baroni ordered us to take to Jerusalem," he said. "Principale Bardo brought Baroni's orders. You could take two of these extra horses for Peter and Ben to ride. My soldiers will catch up with you with the other horses where you stay overnight. I suggest you stay at that place where the stream goes over the road."

"Centurion Markus, we can't thank you enough for how you have accommodated us," Thomas said. "You have removed the uncertainty of our return trip to Jerusalem. Maybe there will be some way to repay your kindness."

Thomas thought, "Here is more proof of Jesus' assurance that the Romans will help."

"You'll be back and I'm looking forward to the changes you could bring to Joppa," Markus said. "I look forward to seeing you in the morning."

Thomas and Stephen followed the trail back and entered the inn and found Ben talking to Peter. They sat down and requested some lunch from the innkeeper's wife. Peter finished designing the ship as they ate their lunch.

"You will want to order a design from the boat manufacturer and a cost estimate," Peter said. "Here's what I am designing. It'll have a full top deck and three sails. There are two lower decks. I'll call them sub-decks one and two. Sub-deck one is under the main deck and has the galley in the rear, storage cabinets for personal and food storage and three sleeping rooms with three bunk beds in each. Sub-deck two will be used as the main storage deck for supplies, tools and equipment. Most Roman ships have incomplete top decks and one sail. They may want to charge extra for my added design features. I hope not. I'm now convinced you do not want to buy a used ship. You're better off with new sails, rudders, lines and anchor."

The sun had gone down. The innkeeper was lighting oil lamps throughout the inn. A percussive hush came over the inn as the boat manufactures' representative entered. He came to Thomas's table, his smile pushing up his ruddy jowls. "Hello Peter and Ben," he said. "What are you doing with these men?"

"These men have hired us," Peter said.

"Please sit with us," Thomas said. "Peter has a rough drawing with dimensions for the ship I hope to order."

"This design is a bit of a departure from some of the Romans' ships," Peter said. "It has a different design for the drop down area for the rowers. It has a complete top deck and three sails."

"You are right about it being different," the representative said. "Your drawings and my letter explaining what you just told me is enough. I can send these to the ship manufacturer and request their final design before you order it. They will give you a cost estimate. You'll need to return to approve it and pay half of the cost after the first of the New Year."

He got up carrying the ship design on the sheepskin and left the inn.

"We need to be at the fort stables at daybreak," Thomas said. "We have made arrangements for the trip to Jerusalem."

† Chapter 8 †

A Kidnapping Attempt
Thursday, October 12, 124 A.D.

Stephen arose before sunrise, freshened up for the day and went outside to walk along the pier in the predawn light. Most of the fishing boats had already left. Thomas walked up behind him and said, "I knocked on your door but you were gone. I asked the innkeeper's wife to prepare four bags of food. She is working on that now."

They walked back to the inn to the carrressing light of the oil lamps. Taking their places at the table, they watched Peter and Ben walk into the inn. After breakfast, the innkeeper and his wife were bowing at the door as they left to walk briskly to the fort and out to the stable. Centurion Markus stood with four soldiers who were holding the reins to four horses. "A good morning to each of you," he said. "Your swords have been attached to your saddles. My men have tied down the halters and your sleeping mats. These two horses are for you Peter and Ben."

"I'll be leading my men with the extra horses," the soldier said. "My name is Principale Benito. "We will see you tonight late at the crossing of the stream over the road."

"I look forward to your return," Markus said. "Have a good day"

Markus turned and walked back into the fort. The four rode out of the stables with Thomas leading the way. They traveled at an even walk, giving Peter and Ben time to get acquainted with their horses. They traveled steadily until Thomas found a good place to stop for lunch, but Stephen spotted a small pond through the trees. After tying the horses to some trees where they could feed on the grass, they sat on a fallen tree to eat their lunch.

They had just started eating when about one hundred men in formation marched by on the road going towards Jerusalem. Sitting quietly and not moving, they watched the men. They continued eating and were surprised to see twenty men on horseback gallop along the road towards Jerusalem. They went back to their horses and tied their food bags and took a couple of hearty swallows from their water bags. Thomas showed Peter and Ben how to tighten their saddle girths. Retying their water bags, they mounted and cautiously returned to the road. They could see nothing of concern and started walking their horses along the road.

It was early afternoon when they reached the top of the hill where the stream ran over the road. There were a few campers setting up for the night. Thomas selected the same spot they had used on the way to Joppa. They were invited over to a fire. They talked about the rebel army soldiers they had seen marching and those ridding their horses hard along the road. One of the campers thought the rebel army had a camp nearby.

They invited Thomas and his men to eat with them. They enjoyed a delightfully pleasant meal watching the campers, smelling their garlic sauces and how they poured it over their food. After they finished eating, they walked back to their camp site to hang up their food and water bags. Suddenly, ten men ran at them from each direction, grabbing and shouting, "You are now a part of the Jewish army."

They forced them along the road, going back towards Joppa. They had just gone over the crest of the hill when about twenty Roman soldiers on horseback with halters on ten more horses galloped up to them.

"We are taking these traitors to Hadar for they have stolen temple records," one man said, holding Thomas.

Benito recognized Thomas who had the kidnapper's hand over his mouth. Benito rode in and stabbed the man with his sword. He screamed and ran. The other kidnappers ran, leaving Thomas and his companions panting and sweating.

"You were almost too late," Thomas said. "But we thank you for freeing us. You and your men are an answer to our prayers."

Benito led his men over the hill and set up camp along the road, away from the campers. The campers enlarged their fire and invited the soldiers to join them. One of the soldiers brought three loaves of bread, bags of grapes and a block of cheese. The campers brought in an outer row of log seats. Benito sat next to Thomas and Stephen.

"I have known you less than a day," Benito said, grinning. "And I have already had the opportunity to save your necks. They would never have let you go. The rebel army kills those who try to get away. They consider escapees to be traitors. Who is this Hadar they shouted about?"

"I've never heard of Hadar," Thomas said. "Whoever he is, he thinks I may have stolen some old temple records. I hope to find out about it when we get back to Jerusalem."

When the fire died down, Thomas and his men excused themselves. The soldiers did the same and went to their campsite. It was soon quiet as the fire went out.

Friday, October 13, 124 A.D.

The soldiers were up before dawn, awakening Thomas and his small band of missionaries. Benito marched over to Thomas and said, "You and your men should ride with me up front of my men. We can talk and it'll keep you out of our dust."

The horses walked at a steady pace. Thomas enjoyed the sunlight caressing his arms and face. They passed lush sweet smelling verdant areas and then saw arid places with a musty smell. By early afternoon they entered the Jaffa gate. Benito led the missionaries and the soldiers to the stables at Herod's Palace.

✝ Chapter 9 ✝

The Attack on Thomas' Estate
Friday, October 13, 124 A.D.

Peter and Ben left their horses at Herod's palace. They walked with Thomas and Stephen who held the reins of their horses. At the Thomas estate, they walked up the short lane and tied the horses to the olive tree by the new watering trough. Next to the tree were four men standing in front of a leather tent. One man asked, "Is one of you Thomas?"

"Yes, that is me," Thomas said. "Who are you and why have you set up a tent on my land?"

"Your uncle Cleophas hired us to give you and your estate protection," the man said. "He's waiting to tell you more about the tragedy that occurred when you left on your trip. He'll tell you about us and the danger. My name is Neta."

They walked to the house. Cleophas stood out front to greet them.

"I would like you to meet two new missionary companions," Thomas said. "Meet Peter and Ben. Peter is our new ship captain."

"I'm delighted to meet you," Cleophas said. "We have one of the upstairs bedrooms set up and ready to accommodate both of you. We have kept the fourth bedroom upstairs free for any additional guests."

"It's a pleasure to meet you," Peter said. "It sounds as if you have taken good care of our modest needs."

"You will find that Thomas does not live on modest needs," Cleophas said.

They followed Cleophas into the kitchen where he turned and said, "The day you and Stephen left, this house was attacked. I was over to Jacob's house, when several men broke in through the front door and grabbed Ada and Grace. Ada said a big ugly brut held her while the others searched the house. He whispered to her while the other men were searching that she and Grace would be next."

Cleophas started to cry and continued, "When they could not find what they were looking for, they started questioning them about the temple records. They said over and over between blows with their fists that they did not know. They then beat them more and tore off their clothes and repeatedly raped them. Thomas, Ada said the men were especially vicious with Grace because they thought she was your woman."

Cleophas wiped his eyes and went on, "I came back to find the house a mess. Ada was naked, bruised, bleeding and crying in our bedroom. Grace was naked and she had bled excessively from the beatings and knife wounds. Her nose had been broken and one of her cheeks were smashed. One of her arms was also broken. She must have put up quite a fight, but she lay dead on her bed. I cleaned and prepared Grace's body which I wrapped in linen strips and then in a white shroud. I still can't believe I was gone? I believe Ada will recover, but she is still in shock right now. She is sleeping. We must try to be quiet."

"How many men did this?" Thomas asked wiping his tear stained eyes.

"There were four of them," Cleophas said. "They said they would do worse things to you."

"Cleophas, I am so sorry about Ada and Grace," Thomas said. "Ada is such a wonderful lady and should never be disgraced and violated like they did to her. Grace was always afraid when we were gone. Maybe she had a premonition something like this was going to happen. I feel so bad. Cleophas, you know you would have been killed if you had been here. This is odious, intolerant behavior. It's alarming that Hadar would have his men do this to innocent women. I want to kill that Hadar and the men who did this."

"I've never heard you say anything like that," Stephen said.

"Even in my Christian heart, I'll never be able to forgive this brutal attack and murder," Thomas said. "But Cleophas, I'm glad you hired those four men camped out front? Does this have anything to do with Paz?"

"It has to do with Paz's father," Cleophas said. "It seems that Paz told his father in confidence about the temple records you have. Paz's father was alarmed and told a man in confidence; he thought was a friend, about the temple records. That man is a rich Jew by the name of Hadar who is from Syria with a mission here."

"We dreamed about Jews learning about the temple records and a fight between Paz and his father while we were in Joppa," Thomas said.

"Paz found out what his father had done and got into a fight with him," Cleophas said. "Paz and his father came here to warn us after the men had attacked here. Paz's father learned too late that Hadar is a Jew on a mission to restore the temple. He wants those records back for when and if the temple is rebuilt. Hadar is connected with Simeon ben Kosiba who is recruiting for the rebel Jewish army. Paz's father did not know about this connection, but Paz did. Paz also knew that Hadar is shipping swords, knives, horses and supplies to the rebel army."

"Will four men be enough?" Thomas asked. "This is a very dangerous turn of events for all of us."

"The only good news is that Paz's father didn't know where the records are kept," Cleophas said. "I didn't take any chances and talked to Nasi Judah who knew Neta very well. He and his men had been protecting Nasi Joseph, but the Romans drove them away when they arrested Nazi Joseph and crucified him. They're good Nazarenes and trained to fight. You met Neta, who is the leader. He can get more men if we need them. From what I pay him, they will buy their own food and cook for themselves. I showed them where to wash their clothes and where to deposit their waste pots. They will only contact us if there is a problem. I have introduced them to Jacob and Amira."

They went out to take care of the horses. Neta led his men over to introduce them. Back in the house, Thomas talked to Cleophas about meeting Peter and Ben in Joppa. Stephen talked about Peter's ship designs and the meeting with the representative. Thomas talked about Principale Benito and how he and his men saved them from the kidnappers.

"I believe those men who tried to kidnap you were men working for Hadar," Cleophas said. "I fear they will keep trying to capture you to find out where the temple documents are hidden."

"They said they were, so we'll need to be careful," Thomas said. "Stephen and I will take the horses back to Bethany in the morning. We'll attend services at the house of prayer and then walk back together. I hope we will be safe."

"I'll have Neta bring in three more men and watch you on your trip over to Bethany," Cleophas said. "They'll wait for you and watch you on the way back."

"Thank you," Thomas said.

"By the way, Adam, Gad and Carmel will be here in the morning," Cleophas said. They're bringing the wooden boxes to pack everything in room two in the Tomb. It will be good to have them on hand in the first room, but no one can see us bring them here. I told Adam to cover the boxes with blankets when he delivers them. They will be really angry when they find out what happened to Ada and Grace. By the way, as I mentioned I have Grace's body wrapped in a white shroud lying on her bed. We should put her in the tomb today. Only you know how to open it."

Peter said, quietly, Cleophas I am so sad and angry about what happened to your wife and Grace. We're going to be staying here and I hope we can be of help around the house and with security. Ben and I will try to stay out of the way."

Cleophas said, "Thank you Peter. But I forgot to tell Thomas, I have hired three ladies recommended by Nasi Judah. There is enough room in the servants' quarters for them. They will be here tomorrow. One woman is older and will stay long enough to nurse Ada until she recovers. The other two are younger women. Both will stay until all of you leave to find the Island-of-Dreams. After that we'll see. For now they will do the cooking, cleaning and washing. There will be nine of us now, including them."

Thomas looked pleased and said, "I am still saddened by what Ada suffered, but the loss of Grace is horrific. She was so anxious and nervous about us being gone. They hurt her so badly. She must have been terrified for her Christian soul. The rapes defiled her and Ada so."

Cleophas and Thomas took Peter and Ben up to show them their room. "We are delighted by the luxury you enjoy," Peter said.

"We are humbled by your grand estate and family," Ben said. "I feel like Jesus himself picked us to help you."

"We have it nice now, so enjoy it," Thomas said. "You'll earn your way in the days ahead. Now let's take Grace out to the tomb. I would like to say a prayer for her."

Saturday, October 14, 124 A.D.

At dawn Thomas heard a knock on the front door. Thomas threw on his robe and ran down the stairs meeting Cleophas at the door. When Thomas opened the door, Neta stood with three women. He said, "These women have been sent over by Nasi Judah. I know them. They are fine Nazarene women. This is Elizabeth whose husband and his brother were kidnapped into the rebel army. This is Leah who has an injured foot and walks with a limp, but she is a hard worker. Mary lost her husband two years ago and her children are grown and married."

Elizabeth was sixteen. She was shy and held her head down. She had light brown hair and soft brown eyes. Leah was twenty and had a determined look on her face. Her limp had toughened her. She had long medium brown hair, an overly large nose with rosy lips. Her eyes were blue with a twinkle. Mary had long grey hair pulled back and held by a ribbon. She had on a nice robe, new sandals and was friendly and outgoing.

The women came in and Cleophas introduced them to the four men. Cleophas took Mary into see Ada. Thomas took Elizabeth and Leah into the servants' quarters. "You can arrange the room and decorate it however you like," Thomas said. "Come in the kitchen and have breakfast with us. I will show you the pantry and how to get water."

After breakfast, Neta knocked on the door. "There are three men here with a wagon with something covered in blankets. They would like Thomas to come out and tell them where to put what they have brought."

Thomas went out and greeted Adam who was driving the wagon. Gad and Carmel had already dismounted.

"Adam, please pull the wagon up by the olive tree." Thomas said. "Neta, will you send for some more men to come here to secure the neighborhood. I don't want anyone near the estate while we unload the wagon. Be careful because it is the Sabbath. We will wait until you are sure we are secure. Adam, Gad and Carmel, go into the house and see Cleophas. Ada has been injured and Grace has been killed."

Thomas went in and Ada had come into the kitchen and sat in her chair. The boys were very angry at what had happened. Everyone was so relieved to see Ada doing so well. Mary had hand bathed Ada and was rubbing some lotion on her face. The other women were scurrying around fixing some breakfast for the boys.

Later Neta returned and said, "We will make sure no one comes near the property."

The men walked to the Tomb and Thomas opened the door. Cleophas placed two lit torches inside the first room away from the nitch where Grace lay. The men came in one after the other with a box and stacked them where shown. Finally the largest box was brought in by two of the men. Cleophas and Thomas removed the torches. Stephen rolled the door shut and Thomas locked the handle. No one saw what was on the wagon, not even Neta. Thomas walked back to Neta and told him all was secure. He gave Neta Roman coins for each of the six extra men. Everyone went back in the house.

✝ Part IV ✝

✝ Chapter 10 ✝

Kidnap Attempt in Lower City
Tuesday, January 2, 125 A.D.

Mary had gone home before the New Year, after Ada insisted. Leah and Elizabeth were up fixing breakfast. Cleophas and the missionaries ate early. When Paz, Mark and David arrived, Thomas and the six companions held the seventh planning meeting. Each of the men had disagreements with how to find the Island-of-Dreams and why they were finding an isolated island. The design of the house of worship led into a particularly emotional dialogue. Finishing, they needed a break and went out to walk around.

They greeted Neta and his men, telling them they were planning to go the lower city. Heading past Herod's theater, they turned to go to the lower city of Jerusalem. Thomas looked over his shoulder to see Neta watching them. They encountered several people begging for blessings. Thomas blessed a man to cast out the unclean spirits in him.

Thirty men walked casually up to Thomas and the missionaries. All at once they grabbed each missionary forcing them to go with them. With knives to their throats, they were half dragging them towards the nearest gate out of Jerusalem. Thomas and the missionaries made vociferous cries for help. Most of the people begging for blessings ran away. A frail old man and two teenagers tried to help Thomas, but were stabbed repeatedly with short knives by the kidnappers.

"You can stab us or cut our throats," Thomas yelled. "All of you are cowards. We do not support your cause. You will lose and destroy Israel."

"Leave me alone," Mark screamed. "I don't want to join your illegal army. We will not go. You can't kidnap us."

"You're Nazarenes," one kidnapper shouted. "You don't have the temerity to stand against us. You'll fight for Israel and Simeon ben Kosiba, just like the rest of us. If you do not, we'll kill all of you Nazarene deserters. The true Messiah is Simeon ben Kosiba not your lousy Jesus the Christ. Hadar has ordered us to find you, Thomas, and your missionaries, because you have our Jewish records."

The kidnappers pushed and pulled them. They struggled and cried out.

"You are callous and rotten men," Stephen yelled.

"You're cutting my neck and wrenching my arms," Thomas screamed. "You stink like animals."

"This is criminal what you're doing," David shouted. "You cannot plunder and lay waste the way your leader does in the name of God."

"You uncouth miserable Jewish misfits," Thomas shouted. "We will not accept this treatment. Hadar is a curse. I will show you idiots."

Thomas whispered to Stephen, "I'll make a diversion. These men are going to kill us if we do not tell them where the records are. If we tell them they will kill us, anyway."

Thomas pushed his robe above his head and ducked down, slamming those around him, and fled away. He screamed as loud as he could. He ran towards some Roman soldiers coming in through the gate. They stopped. There were twenty soldiers commanded by an officer. They gawked at Thomas, running naked.

"Those men are kidnapping us to go into their rebel Jewish army," Thomas screamed. "Stop them."

"Catch them," the officer yelled.

Shortly, the missionaries were surrounded by soldiers and the kidnappers had run like cowards. Stephen handed Thomas his robe. He pulled the robe on, and grabbed the six missionaries, hugging them.

"How did you get out of the robe and run so quickly?" Ben asked, with a lipless smile. "Didn't you feel embarrassed running naked to the Romans?"

"I was too frightened to be embarrassed and I was praying too hard," Thomas said, laughing. "I don't know how it happened. One minute several kidnappers held my robe in the back and front. When I ducked, they kept the robe and I ran. It was like a miracle to see the soldiers coming through the gate."

The Roman officer scowled as he marched back to Thomas. "You were lucky we were on our way back to the Palace," he said. "You were dangerously close to being kidnapped or killed. They are fearless to come into Jerusalem and try to take the seven of you in broad daylight. They killed one poor man and two teenage boys. They cannot be good Jews to use such abusive and slanderous language. They were debasing Jesus Christ. I was insulted by what they said and I'm not even a Christian. My name is Principale Bardo. We've met on the road. I must report this to Centurion Baroni. He will be furious."

"They are terrible people," Thomas said. "They are a band of miscreants. As you recall, my name is Thomas and these are my missionary companions. Tell Centurion Baroni we are Nazarene priests and four of us live at my estate."

As Thomas led the way home, they all talked about how close they came to being taken, and killed.

When they arrived at the lane to Thomas' estate, Thomas asked Paz to come in for a talk. Mark and David left to go home. Thomas and the other missionaries greeted Neta's men and went on into the house.

He invited Paz into the great room for privacy and said, "All of our lives continue to be in danger because you told your father about the temple records. I am sure you are aware of what this is doing to our plans and safety."

"You told me to tell no one about your plans or the temple records," Paz said. "I know I made a terrible mistake telling my father. Both of us are very sorry, but I swear that I learned to trust no one, including my family. I hope you can trust me in the future."

"We have a lot of risk to face in the future and you must promise to keep my faith."

"I swear and pledge to be faithful to you in the future," Paz said. "I beg your forgiveness."

"As you know you have risked all of our lives," Thomas said. "I will hold you to your pledge. Now go on home and I hope we will not need to talk about this again. We can't go far enough away from them to be safe. This problem will follow us wherever we go."

Wednesday, January 3, 125 A.D.

The next morning it was a cold winter Jerusalem day. The four missionaries came in and sat in the great room enjoying the glow of the oil lanterns. After breakfast they worked to distill future plans. Thomas twisted the collar on his gold and brown robe, the kidnapping weighing heavily on his mind.

"Thomas, it's time to see the shipbuilder's plans, but how will we travel safely to Joppa?" Stephen asked. "We've heard reports of bandits. We narrowly escaped being kidnapped by Hadar's men last fall. Look at what happened yesterday right here in Jerusalem."

"I agree it is dangerous, but it's time we returned to Joppa," Thomas replied. "We have to get the ship ordered now so it will be ready before summer. But how can we travel safely? Maybe the Roman Commander can advise us, or provide protection. Jesus advised me in my dream to find good Romans. The Commander lives in Herod's Palace next to the three towers."

"Principale Bardo talked yesterday about Centurion Baroni," Stephen said. "I wonder if he is the Commander."

"No, there's a new senior officer here in Jerusalem," Thomas said. "I've heard he's a fair man with the gusto of a daring young adventurer. Come on, let's hurry over and see him."

As they came out, Neta stuck his head out of his tent flap. "Keep an eye on us," Thomas said. "We're going over to Herod's Palace."

Dark clouds hung overhead with a cold wind blowing their robes out in front of them. Thomas' feet were cold; his sandals kept sliding on the walkway. They entered the gate at Herod's Palace and met a soldier who introduced himself as Principale Pardi. He was dressed in a heavy leather uniform, a shinning helmet with a centered red brush, belt and scabbard for his sword. His brown eyes matched the color of his uniform. He was short and handsome. His stern expression jolted Thomas in his gut and Stephen was taken back. They knew they wouldn't want to cross him for the glimpse of his chilling power would not be forgotten.

"We request a meeting with the garrison commander," Thomas said.

"State the business you wish to discuss," Pardi ordered.

"We need to travel to Joppa, and it's very dangerous. We need advice on how to make the trip with less risk. Can you help us?"

"I will need to arrange for your meeting," Pardi replied, his expression softening. "Are you the ones who were almost kidnapped yesterday and were rescued by Principale Bardo? Who is the naked leader?"

"Yes, we are," Thomas said laughing. "And yes, I was the naked one."

"Slipping out of your robe and running was very clever," Pardi said. "As to your meeting, please return tomorrow at mid-morning."

† Chapter 11 †

Miracle at Herod's Palace
Thursday, January 4, 125 A.D.

The next morning was a dark and cloudy day again. After enjoying a late breakfast, they went out to let Neta know where they were going. Both Stephen and Thomas were dressed well with a light shirt under blue robes which had some dark fringe around the lower part of their neck. They quickly left to make their appointment at Herod's Palace.

Thomas trudged along, at first excited, but then he became nervous again.

"It's foolish to think they will help us or care," he said. "Think how quickly things can explode here without notice. Jesus was happily teaching in the temple when Caiaphas, son of Ananas the Elder ploted to create a false trial to kill Jesus. He blackmailed Pontius Pilate, bribed Judas Iscariott and pushed Jesus' trial and crucifixion to be completed in less than twenty-four hours. The Romans were aware of all that, but were fearful of Caiaphas and did nothing. Why then would they help us now? They may see us as trouble makers. I hope they are different than Pontius Pilate or the officers who were here when Lucious Quietus was governor."

"You're being pesimistic again," Stephen said. "You were told by Jesus to find good Romans."

They slowly approached the gates to Herod's Palace. It was just before mid-day, and they were met by Pardi again. He smiled but kept formal military protocol, walking ahead of them into the reception area at the palace. He saluted a tall imposing man with fine blond hair and no beard. He was a serene man with a natural smile. He was manly and had a pleasing way about him beneath his tough exterior. He had shinny armor over a leather shirt and skirt. There many gold medallions hanging each from gold chains around his neck. His sword scabbard was gleaming and his short knife was in a gleaming carrier on his left hip.

"Centurion Baroni, these are the two I told you about yesterday," Pardi said, bowing.

"Yes, I know who Thomas and his missionary companions are," Baroni said. "I heard you were nearly kidnapped yesterday. Principale Bardo said he and his men were startled when you ran naked towards him. Was that you?"

"Yes, that was us, and the naked one was me," Thomas said. "Being naked was the least of my problems."

"Why have you requested a meeting with the area commander?" Baroni asked.

"We are Christian missionaries," Thomas explained. "We're having a ship built and we need to go to Joppa to approve the design and make a payment. I want to have the ship built and delivered before summer. We will be taking the payment for the ship with us. The journey is dangerous with the rebel army recruiting young men. We know there are bandits on the road, and our lives will be at risk unless we have protection. We were assaulted on our last trip."

Centurion Baroni grinned, and then gave them a stern look. He walked them into a large room off the reception area and introduced them to Tribunus Laticlavius Cerrone, the area commander for Jerusalem. He stood tall in the purple stripes of his position, even taller than Centurion Baroni. He had fair skin and pale blue eyes. His hair was light brown and his face was clean-shaven. When Thomas looked into his eyes, he had the feeling you could see right through them. He was imposing but friendly.

"They need to go over to Joppa and are in fear for their safety," Baroni explained. "These are the men that almost got kidnapped yesterday. I think they need protection even in town."

Cerrone nodded. "Please tell me about your trip to Joppa and what you may need from me."

"We are Christian missionaries and have permission from our Nasi to leave Judea to do missionary work, find an island and build a house of worship. I have recruited missionary companions and need to have a ship built."

"Now explain why you are leaving to do missionary work in the Mediterranean, when help is needed right here in Israel."

"We appreciate your concern for Jerusalem and Judaea," Thomas replied, humbly. "I am worried about the escalating violence and the attacks by the illegal Jewish army will lead to harsh consequences from Rome."

"You are very wise and realistic about the terror and tension around here," Cerrone said. "I'm also concerned about those problems. We're going to double the Roman Legions in Israel. I hope that will be enough, but this could go on for many years.[23]

After studying them, Cerrone said, "Thomas, I am impressed with you; but I'm also worried about your ambitious plan. I have heard several people talk about you. Although you are young, you are a dignified, fine-looking man, but where are you weak? Where might you fail? You'll face enemies everywhere you go. There is no doubt you are doing the right thing for your God, but knowing your weakest link is more important than knowing your strengths."

"Thank you for that compliment," Thomas said. "I'm surprised you have heard people talking about me. I don't think of myself as being known well enough for others to talk about me."

"I know the mayor, the Nasi and others who know you very well. You would be surprised what I know about you and Stephen. You have become two of the city's outstanding citizens and I have wanted to meet you. Could you join Centurion Baroni and me for lunch out on the terrace to have further discussion? We have many heavy issues to explore."

---

[23] Authors' note. Tineius Rufus had the X Fretensis under his direct command (Most of those transferred to Judea from 119 A.D. to 132 A.D. were probably killed in the Jewish uprising of the Bar Kokba War. (In December 133 or January 134, Julius Severus superseded Tineius Rufus as governor of the war zone. He commanded a large army. Three legions were deployed: VI Ferrata, X Fretensis (already there) - hastily strengthened with marines from Italy- and XXII Deiotariana. No less than seventeen auxiliary units of two to three thousand each are known to have fought in Palestine. Legion XXII consisting of five thousand men was probably annihilated by the Jews at the start of the war, since there are no indications of its existence after this war. See www.ancient-warfare.com)

"Stephen and I will be happy to accept your invitation," Thomas replied, surprised by Cerrone's interest. "But why do you think of me as one of the outstanding citizens of Jerusalem?"

"You're one of our wealthy citizens and you do good work like restoring the House of Prayer in Bethany and building that stable used by your Nazarene members. We know you and your uncle have hired Neta and his men for protection. I heard about the attack on your home and the blatant rape of your aunt and the murder of her handmaiden, Grace. This Hadar, who is after you, is a very dangerous man. We are after him because he is bringing swords, knives, horses and supplies to Simeon ben Kosiba for his illegal army. I have heard he believes you have temple records and wants them in a rebuilt temple. I don't care about the records, but I do care about his supplying Kosiba. Your efforts could be fruitful in capturing Hadar."

Thomas looked grim and said, "You have raised my fears. You're saying it's a major fear for you as well. We'll do anything we can to help. I want to kill this Hadar and the men who attacked my home and family."

"Good," said Cerrone. "I was in hopes you felt that way. I know I would if I were you."

Following Cerrone and Baroni out to the terrace, Thomas noticed that Cerrone limped and wondered what caused it. Was it an injury?

"Notice the surroundings from the terrace next to the fountains," Cerrone explained. "There's a spectacular view of Merriam's Tower, named after Herod's wife that he killed just before he died. In this area, we will enjoy the warm sunshine without the wind."

A servant appeared with four goblets and a small amphora on a tray. He poured watered wine for each and Cerrone gave him lunch instructions.

"You look surprised by Herod's Palace and these fountains and gardens," Cerrone replied.

"Who would not be amazed? Stephen and I had no idea what was here. We've only lived in Jerusalem a few years. None of the people I know could have even dreamed of such grand and opulent areas. I haven't even seen a play in the restored theater."

"I'm surprised," Cerrone said, bending forward. "You should see a play before you leave Jerusalem; I could get you invited. I attended a play recently with the mayor, his wife, Ruth, and some of their friends. I had the pleasure of meeting the current Nasi leader, Judah, his wife and Rebecca, the widow of Nasi Joseph, who was killed eight years ago by our former Governor Luscious Quietus.[24] As you know, Luscious Quietus was a very successful Roman General from Mauretania. He was successful in quelling the Jews in Mesopotamia and here in Israel. Some say Caesar Trajan considered making him his successor. When Trajan died seven years ago, Hadrian became Caesar; Governor Quietus was recalled that summer and was executed."[25] So his being a winner led to his disaster."

Thomas nodded. "Because of Governor Quietus, Stephen and I did not dare to move to my home in Jerusalem until he was removed. We know Rebecca, Nasi Joseph's widow. The loss of Joseph was very tragic. Rebecca is young, beautiful, vibrant and very passionate. Joseph didn't have a brother to take care of her, so Rebecca has stayed single."

"Thomas, several years ago my wife died during childbirth," Cerrone said. "Now I have met Rebecca and can't get her out of my mind. The night I met her I had a dream. We went on a walk in the palace and she was warm and greeted everyone we met. She's so social and gregarious. At the play, everyone wanted to know where she came from. I need to understand her religion better before I approach her. She seems reluctant. I guess it is because I am so different from her. I need to know more about the Nazarenes. Thomas, tell me more about Christianity and about her deceased husband, the previous Nasi."

"The Nasi is the leader of the Jerusalem Nazarene organization," Thomas began. "The Nazarene ecclesia is headquartered here and has been trying to coordinate Christian bishops, schools and missionaries throughout the Roman Empire. The Nasi is a very important position and also serves as our local bishop. The Romans and Jews have made the job of the Nasi very

---

[24] Procurators: By Gotthard Deutsch and Samuel Krauss. ("Luscious Quietus (c. 117). After suppressing the uprising of the Jews in Mesopotamia, he was appointed governor of Judea (Eusebius, "Hist. Eccl." iv. 2, § 5). Dio Cassius states that he administered Palestine subsequently to the consulate (lxviii. 32).

[25] JewishEncyclopedia.com, Luscious Quietus-Roman general and governor of Judea in 117 C.E. Originally a Moorish prince, his military ability won him the favor of Trajan, Luscious Quietus was recalled by Hadrian and executed shortly afterward as a possible rival (Spartianus, "Vita Hadriani," §§ 5, 7; Dio Cassius, lxix. 2).

difficult. Nasi Judah has a number of scribes copying the books and letters of the apostles and disciples."

Thomas put his hands on his knees and continued, "I first need to tell you about Jesus and his life. Mary, Jesus' mother was visited by the angel Gabriel, who told her she would be impregnated by the Holy Ghost and would give birth to a son, and call him Jesus.[26] Jesus was born in Bethlehem,[27] a descendent of the House of David from both his mother, Mary, and his adopted father, Joseph. Herod the Great heard of the birth of the new king of the Jews in Bethlehem and ordered the death of all children two years old and younger in Bethlehem. God told Joseph to take Mary and Jesus[28] and flee to Egypt which he did. Later, God told Joseph when Herod died and he should return to Israel."[29]

"They returned and settled in Nazareth because that was out of the reach of Herod Archelaus[30] who was still looking for Jesus. Jesus grew up attending Torah school. Joseph died when Jesus was twelve. Joseph of Arimathea was the richest man in Israel and was the youngest brother of Mary's father and Jesus' granduncle. Mary married Joseph's brother, Cleophas, and became very close to Cleophas's wife who was also named Mary. Jesus moved into Joseph's Arimathea estate, but often stayed in either his Bethany or Jerusalem estates. Jesus and Joseph of Arimathea went together on trips to Britain where Joseph managed the production of tin and sold it to the Romans and others. Because of this, Joseph was a Nobilis Decurio, a high and important position, in the Roman Army. He was also a member of the Sanhedrin being the Prince of David and was a member of the local Roman and Jewish Senate."[31]

"Joseph of Arimathea was good friends with Lazarus's father, Theophilus, who was a Syrian Prince and Governor of the maritime country. Theophilus was married to a Jewish woman, Eucharia, who was a descendent

---

[26] Ibid, Luke 1: 26-38 and 2: 21.

[27] Ibid, Luke 1: 4-7.

[28] Ibid, Mathew 2: 13.

[29] Ibid, Mathew 2:19-21.

[30] Ibid, Mathew 22-23.

[31] St. Joseph of Arimathea at Glastonbury or the Apostolic Church of Britain by Lionel Smithett Lewis, late Vicar of Glastonbury, page 73.

of the House of David.[32] He owned a fish smoking and pickling facility in Magdala. When he died, Martha was the oldest and became the executor of the estate. She liquidated parts of the estate and divided the proceeds between Lazarus, Mary Magdalene and herself. They retained the estates in Magdala, Bethany and Jerusalem. Mary Magdalene was involved in the fish smoking and pickling business at Magdala that bought fish from Mary Salome, Zebedee and sons, James and John. Fish were bought from brothers, Peter and Andrew. Lazarus moved to Jerusalem and became a member of the Sanhedrin and the Senate. Martha lived at the Bethany palace."

"Jesus became very good friends with Peter, Andrew, and his cousins James and John. Peter married Perpetua who was a wealthy daughter of Aristobolus, a son of Herod of Chalsis. Jesus became acquainted with Aristobolus, his brother Barnabus and their sister, Mary, who later married a Roman and lived a few years in Cyrene and Egypt where John Mark was born. Mary and John Mark returned to Jerusalem and bought the house in the upper city with the large meeting room upstairs where Jesus and his disciples had his last Passover dinner. That house belongs to the Nazarene ecclesia now and somehow survived the destruction by Titus' army."

"When Jesus started his ministry, He was in his late twenties and went to his cousin, John the Baptist, to be baptized. John the Baptist's mother, Elizabeth, was advanced in years before he was born, but her husband, Zacharias who was also advanced in years was visited by Angel Gabriel to let him know she would become pregnant by him and she did."[33]

"Jesus asked his friends Peter and Andrew and his cousins James and John to become his apostles. He invited his brothers, James, Judas Thomas and Jude to join them. He wanted other representation in his apostles so he chose Judas Iscariot. He needed a scribe, so he chose the tax collector Mathew Levi.[34] He chose Simon the Zealot from Capernaum. He selected two Greek men, Philip and his friend Bartholomew, from Bethsaida in Galilee."[35]

[32] Ibid, John W. Taylor, page 83.
[33] Ibid, Luke 1:11-25 and 36.
[34] Ibid, Mark 2: 14-16.
[35] Ibid, Mathew 10: 1-4.

"Jesus formed his own Sanhedrin of seventy members[36] and was able to get Aristobolus and Barnabus to help recruit his seventy disciples. They were sent to begin ministry work in many cities and later to many countries. John Mark went with his uncle Barnabas to several countries teaching and doing their own ministry work for Jesus."

"Jesus taught that the Jews should abandon the Law of Moses because it had become a wedge between God and the Jewish people. He taught the law of love your neighbor.[37] This teaching of baptism eliminated the sacrifice of animals which was the source of wealth of the House of Ananas. The Romans kept one member or another of the Ananas family as head priest for before Jesus was born until Jerusalem was destroyed by Titus. Jesus taught that man could be saved by belief in Him[38] and baptism for rebirth of the spirit, forgiveness of sins and leading eventually to resurrection of the body. He taught the Jews to obey the Romans and love themselves and their neighbors. Above all they were taught to love him and God."[39]

"Jesus started his ministry, choosing to live a life of austerity. He had many things to teach people and won the respect of the Essenes, the Zealots, the peasants of Israel and many Pharisees. He was able to convert water to wine,[40] walk on water[41] and feed thousands[42] with only two loaves and a few fish. He had great powers to heal the blind, the lame and bring the dead back to life, such as Lazarus who died and was dead for four days. He cast out demons from victims to bring them to good health."

"Caiaphas, the son in-law of Ananas the Elder had been appointed by the Romans to be the Head High Priest when Jesus was thirty-three. He decided to kill Jesus when he was preaching in the Temple at the beginning of Passover. On the night of the day before Passover, he had Jesus arrested by the temple guards as identified by a kiss from Judas Iscariot. Jesus was tried all night, first at Ananas the Elder's home and then at Caiaphas'

---

[36] Ibid, Luke 10:1-24.

[37] Ibid, Mathew 7: 12 and Galatians 5: 14.

[38] Ibid, John 3: 15-17.

[39] Ibid, Mathew 22: 36-40 and Mark 12: 28-32.

[40] Ibid, John 2: 6-10.

[41] Ibid, John 6:18-21.

[42] Ibid, Mark 8: 1-21 and Mathew 15: 32-39.

house.[43] A session before the Jewish Sanhedrin was conducted with Joseph of Arimathea and Lazarus testifying to defend Jesus."

"Early in the morning Jesus was taken before Herod who questioned and mocked him. He was then taken before Pontius Pilate at Fortress Antonia. Pilate could find no fault with Jesus. In the end, because Caiaphas was blackmailing Pilate, Jesus was scourged[44] and sentenced to be crucified.[45] He was crucified and died on the cross for all of mankind's sins. He died on Wednesday, the beginning of Passover, a special Sabbath day.[46] Pilate released Jesus' body to Joseph of Arimathea who washed and treated his body with the help of another rich man Nicodemus[47] and secured Jesus' body in Joseph's Garden Tomb."[48]

"On Friday, Nicodemus and Joseph of Arimathea were arrested by temple guards and taken before the Jewish Sanhedrin. Nicodemus was released and Joseph was locked in a cell that night and all day on the Saturday Sabbath until late that night when Jesus resurrected and came and took Joseph out of the cell and delivered him to Arimathea.[49] On Sunday morning, the day after the second Sabbath, Mary Magdalene with other women went to the tomb only to find the very heavy stone door blown away lying ten cubits from the tomb.[50] A Roman centurion was standing back in awe and the temple guards ran away. An angel came out of the tomb and told the women Jesus resurrected and was gone."

"Later, Jesus appeared to Mary Magdalene and asked her to set up a meeting with the apostles so he could appear to them which he did. Thomas was not there but he came to another appearance by Jesus and felt Jesus' wounds and declared 'My lord and my God.'[51] Jesus appeared to Joseph of Arimathea and Cleophas as they walked to Emmaus.[52] Jesus continued to

---

[43] Ibid, John 18: 13 and 24.

[44] Ibid, John 19: 1.

[45] Ibid, John 19: 15-16.

[46] The Day Jesus Died, A Koinonia House Publication, by Chuck Missler.

[47] Ibid, John 3: 1.

[48] Ibid, John 19: 38-42.

[49] Gospel of Nicodemus, Chapter 15.

[50] I, Joseph of Arimathea, A Story of Jesus, His Resurrection and the Aftermath, by Frank C. Tribbe, page 9.

[51] Ibid, John 20: 28.

[52] Ibid, Luke 24: 13-53.

appear before many others for forty days at which time he ascended into heaven."

Thomas enjoyed these several minutes telling the story of Jesus in an emotional dialogue.

Cerrone was quiet, staring at Thomas as he finished. "You have told me many parts of the story I had not heard," he said. "I heard Jesus came from a wealthy and well educated family. Jesus truly was an amazing man among men. I have been fascinated with Jesus' resurrection. My religion does not have any belief about an afterlife. I heard a lot of this story about Jesus Christ when I grew up in Rome. Later I learned more in Cyprus about how you Christians live and love everybody."

"Cerrone sipped from his wine goblet and continued, "You may not know, but about ten years after Jesus' resurrection, Caesar Claudius made a declaration in the Roman Senate. He declared it was a criminal offense punishable by death to be a Christian or a Druid and that all Jewish descendents of the House of David were to be put to death.[53] Every Caesar that followed Claudius continued to pursue that declaration[54] up through Caesar Trajan. Today we seem to have a lull in some locations regarding the attitude towards Christians. However, we Romans continue to crucify and kill Christians in Rome and many other places in the Empire. Today those of us here in Israel and in Cyprus, quietly, do not agree with that decree and you are safe with us. We see value and strengths in the Christian movement as they become settled and peaceful. The problems start with the gentiles, as you call them, including me. There is fear of the Jewish religion and the mayhem they caused in the Kitos war in Cyrenia, Cyprus, Egypt, Mesopotamia and here a few years ago. The Romans took massive actions to stop them. These prior problems with the Jews fifty-five years ago and recently with the Kitos war causes fear of Jews and Christians. The gentiles need to be educated about Christianity to stop the fear and distrust of them."

"Stephen and I know some of that history of crucifixion and other forms of killing. As I mentioned we stayed out of Jerusalem up until about eight years ago until the replacement of Governor Quietus allowed us to move to Jerusalem. Never the less, we were fearful about your attitude when we came here today."

---

[53] Ibid, George F. Jowett, page 89.
[54] Ibid, George F. Jowett, page 93.

Cerrone studied the face of Thomas and then Stephen. "You noticed that I limp and sit awkwardly with this stiff and painful knee. I had a wound that will not heal."

"I wondered about the cause," Thomas said.

"Cerrone leaned back and stretched out his limber leg and said, "I have a hard time believing the stories of Jesus' miracles, so I would like to test you. My knee was run through with a spear. I have been limping and experiencing constant pain for several months. For some reason it will not get better. Would you pray for it to heal?"

"Stephen and I will gladly pray to Jesus for your healing."

They stood up and placed their hands on his injured knee and Thomas prayed, "Jesus, heal the injury that plagues this man and restore the normal use of his knee and leg. Amen."

As he finished the prayer, Cerrone said, "My leg feels hot. Could that be the healing?"

A moment later he shouted, "A burning heat just hit my leg like a hot piece of iron."

A flash of light came down upon him. Baroni was so surprised by the light, he dropped his pottery goblet and it shattered on the stone floor. Cerrone jumped up and limped around. He finally walked back after some time and sat down with ease.

"I don't know what to think," he said. "My pain is almost gone. Could this be a miracle?"

Thomas looked at Stephen, a little surprised by the rapid healing. A new goblet was brought out for Baroni and the spilled drink was mopped up. Everyone sat silently finishing their lunch.

"You were healed because I asked for healing in the name of Jesus Christ," Thomas said. "Jesus is the one who healed you. You believed he could do it if we prayed and requested the healing. Your faith provided the tool to heal your leg."

"You are too modest; I am healed and I believe your god did the healing," Cerrone said. "I didn't realize I believed before you prayed. I'll never forget the feeling of burning heat hitting my leg. The flash of light was startling when it came down on me. If my leg had healed over a few days, I would have debated who healed it. But, it happened so quickly. It has to be a miracle."

"There probably will be some pain for a while, but certainly not as severe as before," Thomas said.

"You don't understand," Cerrone said, brushing back his fair hair. "The pain is gone. There is only a tingling deep inside."

"That's great news," Thomas said. "The light that descended on you reminds me of something Jesus said, *'I am the light of the world. He who follows Me shall not walk in darkness, but have the light of life.'*[55] You now have the healing of His light, because you believed."

"If I may, there is another comment Jesus made to his disciples before his betrayal," Stephen said. *'While you have the light, believe in the light, that you may become sons of light.'*[56]"

"I met many Christians in Cyprus before I came here, and I thought they were strange," Cerrone said. "I saw so much mixed love and hatred of Christians in Rome. But my own religious beliefs seem weak compared to what I have seen and heard about Christianity. I remember the Romans who became Christians were so excited. They felt and displayed joy in their lives. Your visit today has convinced me that I do believe in your God and the story of Jesus. I would be very pleased if you would arrange to baptize me. I also would like to join your congregation. I could use a little joy in my life, especially with all the hatred and killing here in Israel."

"We're very pleased you've decided to become a Christian," Stephen said. "We'll enjoy your participation in the Jerusalem Nazarene congregation."

"Thomas, I've heard about baptism, but tell me how it is performed," Cerrone inquired, with a concerned look on his face. "Rituals have always bothered me."

"You should have no need for concern. All we do is walk into a body of water," Thomas said. "I will say a baptismal prayer. Part way through the prayer I will have you submerge your whole body under water and then I will complete the prayer. You will only be under the water a moment. The submersion in water and the prayer gives you forgiveness of your sins, and your spirit is reborn."

"Could the baptism be done in the River Jordan the day after the Jewish Sabbath?" Cerrone requested. "I understand Jesus was baptized there by John the Baptizer. I would be pleased if we could get there by mid-day."

---

[55] Ibid, John 8:12.
[56] Ibid, John 12:36.

"You provide the transportation and I will perform your baptism the day after the Sabbath," Thomas said. "I have walked there, but a ride would be nice."

"Please meet me here at daybreak, the morning after the Jewish Sabbath and we will go together," Cerrone said. "The day after my baptism, I will have thirty soldiers accompany you and Stephen for your trip to Joppa and return with you when you have ordered the ship."

Everyone sat quietly for a while sipping their wine. The weather had become warmer. The cloud cover had moved past the City and the sky was sunny. Birds flew through the trees next to the terrace. The view of the gardens and ponds along the walkways and terrace with the tangible fragrances was a delight.

"We have some business to discuss," Cerrone said, leaning forward. "Thomas, tell me more about you, Stephen and your project."

Thomas smiled confidently and said, "I am a descendent of Jesus' brother, Apostle Judas Thomas. Stephen is a descendent of Lydia,[57] a sister of Jesus. I had a dream of an island in which Jesus told me we must build a house of worship. In the dream, I was on the island with him looking carefully where he pointed for the location to build the building. He told me I must take certain records and store them in a vault in that house of worship. He emphasized taking His Good News to the lost tribes and gentiles. I asked him why me? He said I could do what he asked. I feel called because Jesus has ordered me."

"We need a ship with unique design requirements," Stephen said, continuing for Thomas. "We slipped over to Joppa and ordered a ship design based on our requirements some time ago. Now, we must review the cost and approve the plans before the ship can be built. Approval of the plans has to be done as soon as possible to allow the shipbuilder enough time to complete it before summer."

"We'll be lugging the silver to Joppa to pay a deposit when we approve the design," Thomas noted. "It could ruin our lives and our dreams if we were robbed or kidnapped into the Jewish Army. Hadar is after me so we could be killed."

"Yes, I would hate to see you in the rebel Army," Cerrone said, then laughed. "Sending my soldiers with you provides us a good patrol for that

---

[57] Gospel of the Nazarenes, 5:23.

road. As to the Cyprus shipbuilder, I know him and the ships he builds are durable, strong and sea worthy. I have talked to other officers in Israel, including Tribunus Laticlavius Pasquali in Sebaste, Tribunus Laticlavius Mascaro in Caesarea and Governor Rufus. We are very concerned about this Hadar and since he is after you, we believe you can help us."

"What can we possibly do?" Thomas asked.

"We want to catch and execute him and his followers," he said. "We want them to attack you and your companions, and we might get lucky and catch him. Principale Benito told me last year he let twenty of Hadar's followers go when they tried to kidnap you on your way back from Joppa. We will not let them go if they attack you again. I believe you can help us in other ways but we need to evaluate what you can do."

Thomas nodded, "Since my security needs may fulfill your need to catch Hadar, We'll do as you ask."

"I have had experience with work being done on islands," Cerrone said. "My fellow officers and I heard about your desire to find a Mediterranean island, as reported by Centurion Marcus. Benito told me you ordered plans, and we have been in touch with the shipbuilder. We are impressed with your ship design for use in our own fleet. We can arrange for you to purchase two of those ships for the price of one. Why would we suggest you purchase two? You will be helping us and we will help you. When you are building on an island, you will be sailing regularly to bring in material, men and supplies. This means one ship should be dedicated to the construction. You will need another ship to travel to Israel and other places we may ask you to go."

"I'm impressed with your experience and forward thinking on our project," Thomas said. "Yes, I can see the need for two ships."

"If you agree, purchase two ships when you are in Joppa," Cerrone said. "But there is much more; we will supply you with security, at your home, your trips within Israel and on your trip to find your island. Here in Jerusalem, I want your security-man, Neta, to contact Principale Bardo. He will assign at least four of our soldiers to assist him with his protection of you, your companions, your family and your home. They will not wear Roman uniforms in this assignment, but they will be able to call on Bardo for additional support."

"I'm breathless with what you want us to do and your level of support," Thomas said. "I'll order two ships and talk to Neta."

"I'm excited for you, your missionary work and that you will act as bait to Hadar," he said. "I almost feel like a missionary myself with my new found belief. I wonder what you can accomplish in missionary work and catching Hadar."

"I'm enthused with Jesus' command for us to do missionary work," Thomas said. "I keep wondering how we will carry it out."

"There is another element you need to understand," Cerrone said. "We have a custom in the Roman Empire which we have established between us. This relationship is independent of our religion or country and we call it a client and Patron[58] relationship. You are my client and I am your Patron. This is more than friendship; it is set of obligations. You agree to do what I ask of you and in return I agree to help you and look out for your protection as needed. Our relationship is the first of many such relationships you will enter with me and other Romans. Over time you will develop a maze of relationships with many. Have you heard of this Roman custom?"

"I've had no relationships with any Romans," Thomas said. "Jesus told me to develop relations with Romans. Maybe he knew of this custom. Personally, I like this practice and will hold each Patron I encounter with the type of obligation you described. Thank you for telling me about this practice. I knew I would be in your debt, but this brings new meaning to our relationship."

"Stephen," Cerrone said. "This relationship is the same between you and me. Is that understandable and acceptable to you?"

"I think I understand," Stephen said. "You are expecting some loyalty in this relationship and I like it. I will always be available to help as you request."

Baroni smiled looking from each man to the next and said, "Both of you should understand that this same relationship Cerrone described is the same with other officer positions such as between you and me, if I get assigned to work with you. Likewise, you will have this relationship with Principale officers and likely with the governor. As Cerrone says, it becomes a web or a maze."

---

[58] Hadrian, and the Triumph of Rome by Anthony Everitt, page 27. ("A powerful Roman was a *ptronus*, or protector, of many hundreds or even thousands of "clients," not just in Rome or Italy but across the Mediterranean. A patron looked after his clients' interests.")

"I must leave you now," Cerrone said, standing. "Thank you again for coming here today. I'll see you Sunday. I'll pray to thank Jesus for my healing."

They stood and watched Cerrone go back into the palace with no limp.

Baroni replaced his short knife and led them back to the entrance. "It appears we'll be spending some time together," he said. "In the future, when we're not in front of my men, I would be happy for you to call me Baroni. I will talk to Cerrone about doing the same thing with his title. You'll be with Principal Pardi for the trip to the River Jordan and to Joppa. I'll talk to him. The healing was so incredible. I never expected that to happen."

"God works in mysterious ways," Thomas said. "And I'm overwhelmed again. Jesus is so far ahead of us, it almost scares me to death."

As Thomas and Stephen walked back from their meeting, they talked about the healing and

Cerrone planned his baptism. "Cerrone demonstrated so much faith after his healing," Thomas said. "It reminds me of the faith that the centurion expressed to Jesus as he entered Capernaum. He said, *'Lord, my servant is lying at home paralyzed, dreadfully tormented. And Jesus said to him, 'I will come and heal him.' The centurion said, 'Lord, I am not worthy that You should come under my roof. But only speak a word and my servant will be healed.' When Jesus heard, He marveled, and said to those who followed, 'Assuredly, I say to you, I have not found such great faith, not even in Israel!' Then Jesus said to the centurion, 'Go your way; and as you have believed, so let it be done for you.' And the servant was healed that same hour.'*"[59]

"You're right Thomas, I was thinking about that passage while we were still with Cerrone."

"I'm concerned and excited at the same time for the role he wants us to play with Hadar," Thomas said. "His offer to provide us with all of the security he described is so much like what Jesus described to me in my dream."

---

[59] Ibid, Mathew 8: 5-13

✝ Chapter 12 ✝

Baptism Arrangements
Friday, January 5, 125 A.D.

"What do you think of Thomas and Stephen?" Cerrone asked Baroni. "I never expected to encounter anyone like them. I was taken with both of them the moment they came to me. I felt comfortable, I guess because they talk and act like our fellow Romans. They were well respected in Joppa by Centurion Markus and Principale Benito. Principale Bardo encountered them twice and liked them."

"I felt comfortable with them when Pardi introduced them to me," Baroni said. "There's something about Thomas, that makes you want to know him. He has those blue eyes and he does not blink. I had a hard time looking him in the eye. He is self-confident, yet humble at the same time. He has unique leadership skills and appears to have signed up a quality group. The experience with Hadar will tell the real story."

"I was surprised when they blessed my leg and that hot heat hit it," Cerrone said. "It made me shiver when that light came down over me. Did it scare you? You dropped your goblet."

"You cried out and the light came down at the same time," Baroni said. "Yes, it did scare me. I'm pretty sure it startled Thomas and Stephen too, because they both jumped."

"My leg feels fine, but it's still tingling," Cerrone said, smiling. "I'm looking forward to the baptism. I will be comfortable with Jerusalem for the first time. I haven't ever felt that way about the Jews here. With Thomas and Stephen helping me, perhaps I will stand a good chance of courting Rebecca.

I think she is going to be a delight. Maybe marrying her could be good for me and her."

"What about Thomas and his ship?" Baroni asked. "Their project is full of problems. Do you think we need to help him?"

"Yes, I feel in my bones that we must help him," Cerrone sighed. "I think Jesus called on me today to help Thomas with his project, but just as important we need to capture this Hadar. In any event, I feel as committed to Thomas' success as he obviously is."

"What do you think Caesar Hadrian would do if he heard what you and the other officers are planning? Baroni asked.

"I needn't remind you that we're told to use our own judgment in these matters," Cerrone said. "We're all adventurers and out for our just rewards as we find them. He expects us to use tactics that work to further our control. Believe me he'll not say a word unless we fail."

****

"Look at how Cerrone has saved us," Thomas mused. "We didn't do anything to earn it. He just gave it to us after Jesus healed him. I think Jesus will always open doors when we're in danger. But really Cerrone has covered our weakest link with plans to see that we're protected."

"You know Caesar Hadrian's predecessors, Trajan, Domitian and Nero, hated Jews," Stephen said. "Hadrian is building heated pools here in Judea and he got rid of that terrible Luscious Quietus. I wonder what he knows about the Nazarene Ecclesia. I hope he won't hate us for baptizing Cerrone."

"We know that some Romans have become Christians outside of Jerusalem, but none are members of the Jerusalem ecclesia," Thomas said. "That's good for us and Cerrone. He is a powerful Roman and it appears he might be a wonderful friend for us and the Jerusalem congregation. I hope he understands that the Nazarene ecclesia is really Christian. The only place the terms Nasi and Nazarene ecclesia is used is here in Jerusalem. If we start any congregations outside of Jerusalem, we will be appointing a leader and should therefore call him a bishop."

"We're going to leave Israel and subject ourselves to the risk of being martyred either by Jews or Romans like many of Jesus' apostles and disciples were," Stephen said. "The risk is great."

"Stephen, we've an important mission to move the records and artifacts. If I'm martyred: I'll die for what I believe. I'll never deny my faith in Jesus. I may experience fear but it will not deter me."

"Thomas, I was named after a Christian martyr. I would gladly die rather than deny my beliefs."

"As we go out into the world, what would you say if a Roman soldier asked you if you're Christian?"

"Why do you ask?"Stephen inquired.

"It's bound to happen and you won't know why he is asking," Thomas said. "You could go to prison and even be killed if you refuse to worship Roman Gods. We need to be very careful how we talk to Romans once we leave Israel."

As they arrived at the Thomas estate, Thomas and Stephen strolled up the lane, greeting Neta's men. Thomas said, "Neta, I need you to go to the palace and talk to Principale Bardo. He'll arrange to supply you with four or more plain clothed Roman soldiers to assist you with our security. He will assign the men to you and they will not wear Roman uniforms. He will explain the reasons to you."

Peter and Ben were out front by the olive tree waiting for them. They all greeted one another and went into the house to the great room. Cleophas was appreciating a fire and said, "Thomas and Stephen, both of you look happy. You must have good news."

"We do have great news," Thomas said. "Stephen and I prayed to heal the commander's knee and Jesus healed it. We'll baptize Cerrone on Sunday at the River Jordan and he wants to marry Rebecca. He told us Hadar is supplying Kosiba with armament, supplies and horses for the illegal rebel army and believes we can help remove Hadar. He's talked with other officers and Governor Rufus and will allow us to buy two ships for the price of one which we will do. In return for what he asks, they will provide us with security here, on our trips in Israel and on the ships when we leave. He's supplying Neta with four soldiers and I sent Neta to go over to the palace to talk to Principale Bardo. I'm concerned and grateful at the same time."

"The protection to go to Joppa is what you went to see him about," Peter said. "You and Stephen got what you wanted and a whole lot more. This will lead to other help from the Romans. I have seen them do wonderful things, but they can do dastardly things just as quickly. Cerrone is a Tribune and likely a senator. He has wealth and power and now he appears to be your friend. Don't forget they are also fortune hunters."

"This is great news and calls for a celebration," Cleophas said. "Let's have some sliced cheese and nuts. I will get some special wine I bought for this kind of occasion. Thomas keep talking, we can hear you."

"Stephen, we should talk to Nasi Judah tomorrow. He'll be visited by Baroni on Cerrone's behalf. I want the Nasi's advice on this baptism so I perform it just right. We must also pray to Jesus. He told me in my dream that I should become friends with some Romans. He said they can frighten men, but I must be bold. I was nervous at first, but I guess I was bold enough. I'm pleased with the visit."

"I was there," Stephen said. "Everyone, Thomas was bold; he just didn't know it. Cerrone was a little gruff at first, but he soon began treating you as an equal. He knew all about you and was anxious to meet you before we arrived. I watched Baroni and he seemed to be surprised."

They enjoyed the treats. As it got colder, Ada joined them. The fire was comforting. Everyone pulled their seating closer to the fire to enjoy the flames and the aroma. Leah and Elizabeth came in to enjoy the heat. The wine was fruity. The small amphora only contained enough for half a goblet each which was just right. They sat around enjoying the snack, and talking the rest of the afternoon about all that had happened and what needs special attention.

Peter became enthused about the palace story, but then turned to tell about his time away from Israel and about the time he spent in Rome. He met some strange people who said they were Christians but had different ideas. "I listened to some of the discussions and wondered if they were really talking about the teachings of Jesus or something they heard or made up," Peter said with disgust. "One of the ideas being preached was the concept fostered by Cerdo, that the God of the Jews was a lowly God who created evil matter. They were saying the God of Jesus is good. Since matter is evil Jesus could not have lived a physical life and was here in spirit only.[60] Do not believe any of this. This was nothing like the stories Jesus told or his references to his heavenly father. Those people sounded like lofty intellectuals."

Thomas looked angry and said, "I heard that Cerdo lives north of Israel in Syria and preaches that the Jewish Torah should be discarded since the Jew's God created evil matter and is the God that demands obedience. Cerdo was a student of Simon Magnus who was a magician from Sebaste. This

---

[60] Christian Classics Ethereal Library, Cerdo, Gnostic Teacher: www.ccel.org

Simon tried to bribe Deacon Philip to obtain the power of 'laying on of hands.' Simon Magnus[61] ended up in Rome performing levitation for Caesar Nero, competing with Apostle Peter. Peter prayed to Jesus to stop Simon while he was levitating in the air. Simon fell to the floor breaking both of his legs. Cerdo believed that Jesus taught as a loving, good and merciful wholly spiritual God. Do not let this confuse you. We know that Jesus and all of us are descendents of Abraham. We know Jesus lived a real life and my great grandfather Judas Thomas was his brother and traveled with him. It's not evil or delusional. People want to carve out their nitch in whatever comes along. Those teachings are ego trips for intellectuals. Several of us grew up in the apostles' families. We heard the good news Jesus shared with everybody in his short ministry of three years. The world will long remember that ministry."

Stephen nodded, "While you were describing Christianity to Cerrone, I was thinking about the idea of faith alone. Thomas, what do you think about the words spoken by Jesus to his disciples regarding his second coming? He said he would award each according to his good works. Good works will not save you, but Jesus thinks your good works are important expressions of your love for him."

"If you are right about what Jesus said, then our good works are important," Thomas said. "But we still don't know what He meant by good works. We should think about this and pray for guidance."

"I agree, we all should pray about this," Ben said. "I know I need clarification."

"Speaking of faith," Stephen Said, "I'm troubled about the story of Jesus walking on water. Everyone I talk with about that story expresses the same doubts. Nasi Judah says to keep the faith."

"Not to change the subject," Thomas said. "But did we tell you included with Apostle Thomas' records is a note that recorded a trip taken by Joseph of Arimathea. The note described how he and Jesus were returning by ship from a trip to England for his management of the tin and lead mining there as Decurio for the Roman army. In my dream Jesus said he had been there with Joseph of Arimathea on a voyage back to Israel when they went on the island because of a leak in his ship."

---

[61] James the Brother of Jesus by Robert Eisenman, page 413.

"I worry about that problem sometimes, when I am at sea," Peter said. "The ships leak too often."

"The ship had been near the end of a deserted small island," Thomas said. "Joseph of Arimathea suggested a place to build a house of worship. Jesus said build a vault inside the house of worship for storage of records. That was the same place Jesus showed me in my dream. Joseph gave the map and note to Simeon ben Cleophas, after he described the island to Apostle James the Just and Apostle Thomas."

"Thomas, what happened when you had your dream?" Stephen asked.

Thomas looked serious. "In the dream Jesus appeared to me on the Island-of-Dreams. Let me paraphrase something he said to me, Look at this island. I want you to find it and build a house of worship here. The vault you are to build for the records and artifacts will be right under where you stand. Return to Israel for the records and artifacts. Take them back to the island and store them in that vault. We will do as he instructed me to do."

"Because of Joseph of Arimathea's' map and your visitation from Jesus in your dream, we can find the island," Stephen said. "As you recall, we petitioned Nasi Judah to give us leave to build a house of worship on an island in the Mediterranean. Nasi Judah was happy and said, 'It's an area where we want priests to recruit new members.' It'll be an exciting challenge."

"Xystus ,[62] the Bishop of Rome, wrote to us congratulating us on our objectives and offered help. His letter said, 'Apostles Paul and Phillip along with disciples Lazarus, John Mark and Barnabus made conversions in Cyprus, Malta Crete and Sicily, but there are many more Mediterranean islands you can visit to make more conversions and build houses of worship.'"

"Stephen, there is an area in Gaul where there are descendants of Christian converts of Mary Magdalene,[63] Mary's sister Martha, her brother

---

[62] The History of the Church from Christ to Constantine, by Eusebuis, as translated by G. A. Williamson, Page 157.

[63] The Catholic Encyclopedia: Mary Magdalene ("The Greek fathers, as a whole, distinguish three persons; the sinner Luke 7: 36-50; the sister of Martha and Lazarus, Luke 10: 38-42 and John 11; and Mary Magdalene. ...the Latins hold that the three were one and the same. The Greek Church maintained and the Roman Catholic Church has preferred the story of Mary Magdalene traveling to Ephesus with Jesus'

Lazarus, Maximus and several others," Thomas said. "Martha lived in Tarason. Lazarus was the bishop and built the house of worship of Marseilles. Mary Magdalene went into isolation and lived in south Gaul in a cave.[64] The descendents of those original Christians and those they converted are a strong base to expand our missionary work. I believe the Island-of-Dreams is near that area of Gaul. They could be helpful to us with our building projects."

"We must visit their descendents," Stephen said. "Once we find the Island-of-Dreams and get the construction of the vault and house of worship under way, we should visit Gaul. Mark will be very capable of managing the building projects. We also should visit Britain where Joseph of Arimathea and Aristobolus went as the first and second Bishops of Britain. Simon Zelotes and Apostle Paul also went to Britain to preach.[65] We can look for workmen and new members for our congregation in Gaul and Britain."

I know Martha, Lazarus and Mary Magdalene created a very large following. Maximus and a number of others became bishops in several other cities in Gaul," Thomas said. "Lazarus, Martha and Mary Magdalene were of the House of David and were very wealthy when they lived in Bethany.[66] They sold the Magdala castle and the Jerusalem estate before they moved to Caesarea."

"What are we doing tomorrow?" Ben asked.

"Good question Ben. Stephen, take Peter and Ben, let Neta know where you are going and walk down to Paz's house," Thomas said. "Ask Paz to

---

mother and the Apostle John. The French tradition is that Mary Magdalene, Martha, Lazarus and some companions came to Marseilles").

[64] The Catholic Encyclopedia: Mary Magdalene (" Magdalene is said to have retired to a hill, La Sainte-Baume, nearby, where she gave herself up to a life of penance for thirty years").

[65] Ibid, George F. Jowett, pages 80, 158, 185, 186 and 191.

[66] The Legend of Mary Magdalene, by The Nazarene Way of Essenic Studies ("Mary Magdalene was of the district of Magdala, on the shores of the Sea of Galilee, where stood her family's castle, called Magdala; she was the sister of Lazarus and of Martha, and they were the children of parents reputed noble, or, as some say, royal descendants of the House of David. On the death of their father, they inherited vast riches and possessions in land, which were equally divided between them").

contact Mark and David and invite them to come here in mid-morning tomorrow."

Saturday, January 6, 125 A.D.

In the early dawn, Thomas and Stephen came into the kitchen to say good morning to Cleophas and Ada. Peter and Ben came in to sit. "Good morning everyone, it is the Sabbath," Cleophas said. "Good work, Leah and Elizabeth. Let's all pray and have our breakfasts."

After breakfast, Thomas asked Leah to get a fire going in the great room. Thomas, Stephen, Peter and Ben went into the great room to wait for the other missionaries to arrive. Elizabeth was fixing some small cakes and juice to serve everyone. Paz, Mark and David were welcomed by Cleophas and shown into the great room.

"Let's talk again about details for the trip to the Mediterranean island," Thomas said. "We have been making lists of building tools and supplies to take on the trip."

Peter got up with his juice and walked around looking unhappy.

"You look sad," Ben said.

"I miss the open sea and the ships," Peter said. "I'm anxious to see our ship and get out on the water."

"Very soon we will order our ships," Thomas said. "On another subject, I must remind everyone; today is the Sabbath for our Jewish neighbors. We have some work to do but let's be careful not to offend anyone. We need to go out today, but be sure that it looks as if we are not doing any work. You all know the rules around here."

"We'll do our talking and work inside. I'm well aware of the problems the neighbors can cause us," Stephen replied. "They don't care that we are Christians and have a different view towards the Sabbath."

"Let's talk about a subject important to all of us," Thomas said. "When Stephen and I were walking back from the meeting at the palace with Cerrone and Baroni, we made a confession to each other. We each agreed that we are not afraid of being martyred for our faith in Jesus Christ."

The others squirmed and looked uncomfortable.

"I want to remind you how so many of Jesus' apostles and disciples were martyred. I have a list that Nasi Judah has accumulated. To just name a few, Stephen, James the Just and Barnabas were martyred by Jews. Thaddeus, a brother of Jesus, John Mark, Timothy and my great grandfather,

Apostle Thomas, were martyred by pagan worshippers in Armenia, Alexandria Egypt, Ephesus and India. By the way, Apostle Thomas was in India for seventeen years and converted thousands before he was martyred. Those martyred by the Romans were apostles Peter, Andrew, Philip, Bartholomew and Paul, disciples Simeon ben Cleophas, Barsabbas, Ananias, Onesimus, Crispus of Chalcedon, Urban of Macedonia, Herodion of Patras, Linus of Rome, and Aristarchus of Thessalonica. Of course Apostle James was martyred by Herod Agrippa I. There were many others, but we need to be sure that we appreciate the danger we are entering."

"Thomas, people are killed all the time," Mark said. "If I am martyred, at least it will be for something I believe in deeply. I refuse to fear being martyred; it is not going to stop or slow me down."

"We all know that being martyred is a real possibility," Ben said. "We could also be killed by a mob or mistaken by a Roman for being a thief. But thank you for that list. It really is surprising when you hear it. All of those people were chosen by Jesus to do his work and they did it with joy and love. I find it amazing that Jesus chose seventy disciples and twelve apostles and sent them to more than eighty cities all over the Roman Empire and several cities outside of areas controlled by the Romans."

"You are right Ben," Thomas said. "Now let's get back to our planning. We don't need to take everything with us on the ship on our first trip, because we'll return to get the records and relics."

Thomas stood up, stretched, and continued, "I'm really concerned that the Romans might destroy Jerusalem before we return. But, I have this feeling that Jesus will warn us before any tragedy comes to Jerusalem."

"I heard that Caesar Hadrian is planning to restore Jerusalem and the Temple," Paz said. "If he does that it should calm everyone. The concern is will the temple be a pagan Temple?"

"I've heard about Hadrian's plan, but I am not optimistic about it," Thomas said.

"I hope Jesus' warning will give us enough time to return and remove the records and relics," Stephen said. "You know the timing is also important for another reason; some say we may be in the end days. That could be another reason why Jesus is pushing you to get these records removed and stored."

"You're right," Thomas observed. "I'm happy we have been planning for our departure from Israel. It's exciting to be developing final plans. Who knows when the end days will come? That will be the time Jesus returns.

Changing the subject, I'm so glad we arranged with Nasi Judah to have all of you ordained as priests. Being authorized to do missionary work and baptisms means the seven of us now have equal authority as we travel. Nasi Judah was very proud of our plan to find the island and do missionary work as we travel. He prays for our plan to be successful to build the house of worship on the island. Judah thinks we will be doing more missionary work than we thought. He has his scribes preparing copies of the apostles' and disciples' writings for us to take with us. I hope copies will be ready before we leave."

Thomas got up and walked around thinking, then turned back to everyone. "Remember I told all of you, we are going to be doing missionary work as we travel. I went on to say our future presentations must be different for Jews and non-Jews. What I meant was Jesus freed the Jews from the Law of Moses, which is meaningless to gentiles. For Jews and gentiles, we will emphasize Jesus' power over Satan and his followers. Jesus, also, has forgiven us and eliminated our guilt, so we can be closer to God. Animal sacrifice is history. We will be touting the Good News. This Good News is our freedom from evil, guilt and that we will be saved by believing in and loving Jesus. The most important points are to love Jesus with all your heart and love your friends and neighbors. We will emphasize these points and tell the complete story. I want everyone to be part of the baptism ceremony tomorrow. Let us pray and thank Jesus for Cerrone's healing miracle."

They all kneeled and Thomas prayed. "Thank you, Jesus, for the healing you gave to Cerrone. Bless us that we may baptize him into your congregation. Please bless the soldiers and officers that they may be able to make the trip safe for themselves, the invited guests and us. Amen."

Thomas and Stephen walked a few blocks and met with Nasi Judah Kyriakos.[67] Thomas told him about the healing and conversion and then went over the baptism he would perform.

---

[67] Jesus and his world: an archaeological dictionary by John J. Rousseau, Rami Arav. According to Epiphanus (Panarion 66:20), the Jewish Christian Bishop (Nasi), Judah Kyriakos (from the family tree of Jesus) lived until the eleventh year of Antonius Pius (148/149 A.D.).

† Chapter 13 †

Cerrone's Baptism
Sunday, January 7, 125 A.D.

The missionaries left in the early dawn. The morning was quiet, warm and beautiful. The birds were out singing, adding to their enjoyment. When Thomas and his group arrived at Herod's Palace, Baroni came out.

"Most of the soldiers went ahead last night to the River Jordan by foot," Baroni said. "They were ordered to stay overnight in Jericho."

Thirty soldiers rode up on horseback and positioned themselves in front of the wagons. Cerrone, other Roman officers, Nasi Judah and his associates boarded the wagons. The soldiers on horseback led the way. Five wagons were followed by three supply wagons.

The mounted horses and wagons traveled through the Jerusalem streets. Some people had heard about the conversion and came out to watch. Some Jews jeered them. The soldiers traveled towards the Damascus gate and the soldiers at the gate saluted the officers.

The downhill trip to Jericho was sunny, but breezy. It was delightful, taking almost half a day. Soldiers lined both sides of the street with spectators standing behind them. The wagons went through the town and arrived at the River Jordan. More than one hundred soldiers were lined up. There were more than three hundred citizens standing around. The mounted soldiers separated to let the wagons pass through and then circled around close to the river. One of the soldiers came up to Baroni and told him several

Jews from the high priesthood wanted to talk to him. Baroni and Thomas walked to the edge of the soldiers and were met by a group of priests who seemed quite disturbed.

"This is a private affair," Baroni said. "You can watch but you will be escorted away if you interfere."

"You're baptizing an uncircumcised person into your Nazarene ecclesia," one priest said. "You are not permitted to do this in the Jewish faith."

"I am sorry, but the Nazarene ecclesia is a Christian faith now, not a Jewish faith any longer," Thomas said. "We are baptizing uncircumcised persons into our faith throughout the world."

The high priests were shocked and horrified, backing up to get away from them. Baroni and Thomas walked back down to where Cerrone was standing.

Thomas led Cerrone down to the water's edge where both looked back at the audience.

"Centurion Baroni," Cerrone said. "Please make a request that the missionaries, Nasi Judah and his group circle around at the water's edge."

When everyone was in place, Thomas kneeled and prayed, "Thank you Jesus for the safe journey. Please bless Tribune Cerrone and give him strength. Bless the Nazarene ecclesia, Nasi Judah and his leadership. Amen."

"Tribune Cerrone, please remove your uniform down to your tunic," Thomas requested for everyone to hear.

"I will do as you say," Cerrone said smiling.

He took off his armor and equipment, handing them to Baroni and Pardi. Thomas led him into the water but stopped and stared up at the sky. Strangely, a flock of white seagulls were flying over the River Jordan.

"Tribune Cerrone," Thomas said, part way through the prayer. "I will submerge you in the water and complete the prayer."

He put his hands on Cerrone' head and guided him under the water while completing the prayer. He then pulled Cerrone back up out of the water.

"May I present Tribunus Laticlavius Cerrone, our newest Christian? We rejoice in his belief in Jesus and God the Father. HE HAS BEEN SAVED."

A great cheering and yelling came from the audience and the soldiers. The high priests stormed off for the return trip to Jerusalem. With the high priests gone, the rest of the audience cheered even louder. Baroni brought a dry tunic from a supply wagon. A circle was formed around to let Cerrone change, dry himself and put on his uniform, armor and equipment. Thomas changed his robe.

When Cerrone was completely dressed, all of the officers, Nasi Judah, his associates and the missionaries lined up. One by one they congratulated him on his entry into the Nazarene Christian ecclesia. He smiled with an obvious joy. The white seagulls flew back and fluttered down to the water's edge, as if also rejoicing.

"Does that mean the Holy Spirit came here for my baptism?" Cerrone asked, staring at the birds.

"Yes, it does," Thomas said. "This is a very blessed part of the baptism of the spirit."

"Everyone, please get back in the wagons," Baroni announced. "We'll return to Jericho. After a brief stop in Jericho we'll proceed to Jerusalem."

The soldiers on horseback rode in front of the wagons and one hundred foot soldiers followed. In Jericho, the mayor and other officials were lined up to greet Cerrone. He waved and they traveled on to Jerusalem. The sun went down just before the procession reached the Damascus gate. It was crowded with soldiers and Christians waving and congratulating everyone. Cerrone stood and saluted as he passed through the gate. A group of soldiers stepped in behind the mounted soldiers and in front of the lead wagon with torches to light the road to the palace. Upon the arrival at the palace, Baroni stood in his wagon.

"All missionaries, Nasi Judas' group and all officers are invited to come into the palace for a special dinner."

He led them through the palace and out onto the terrace. Torches had been set afire. Food was on one large table, goblets on another. Further out were five tables and cushions for seats.

Baroni stood and announced, "The tables each have a colored ribbon. The red ribbons are for Roman officers, the blue ribbons are for the Nasi and his officials, the gray ribbons are for the missionaries and the purple ribbons are for Thomas, Stephen, Tribune Cerrone and me. Will the officers pick up a goblet while the rest of us line up for our food. Officers can then proceed to get food when we are through the line."

They went through the food line and sat down at the appropriate table. Waiters came to each table and poured watered wine or juice into goblets. Cerrone said with a smile, "Thomas and Stephen, you have made me feel honored today."

"Would everyone stand," Baroni requested. "The Jewish priesthood lights the torches on the top-edge of the Temple Mount. This gives our soldiers the signal to light the torches on the palace walls and towers."

At that moment, soldiers came along the walls to light the torches. A Roman soldier climbed each tower to light one or more torches. The ceremony was performed with impressive military precision. The heat of the day was cooling when they sat back down to finish dinner.

"Thomas, will you stand and say a few words?" Cerrone asked.

"It's a privilege to speak tonight," Thomas said. "I'd like to thank Tribune Cerrone for his hospitality. We have witnessed his special happiness gained by faith in Jesus the Christ. I pray your faith will continue to grow ever stronger. You've been saved today. Others will be awakened by God's word in your life and faith."

Thomas sat down to applause. Cerrone stood and waited for silence. He smiled and looked about the terrace. The waiters had crowded around the service entrances.

"I've been blessed today. Becoming a Christian was the last thing I thought I would do when I came to Jerusalem from Cyprus. Thomas and Stephen performed a miracle for me with a blessing and the healing of my leg. The blessing renewed my hope for us in this troubled world. I have faith in Jeshua who is called Jesus Christ. To you, Nasi Judah, I plan to attend your services in the future. To those of you who are officers who report to me, thank you for the respect you have shown me today. Thank you, Thomas and Stephen, for indeed I have been saved."

Nasi Judah walked over to whisper in Cerrone's ear, "Could two of my scribes come in from outside?"

"Centurion Baroni," Cerrone said. "Would you go out and escort the Nasi's scribes to his table?"

Baroni went out and returned shortly followed by three men carrying scrolls and leather cases. They stood by Nasi Judah's table.

"I'm especially pleased, Tribune Cerrone, with your faith," Judah said. "We feared you when you first entered our City. Your predecessor was brutal, but you have proven to be a trusted and honorable leader. We look forward to having your attendance at our services."

"I have gifts for Thomas and you," the Nasi said, after it became quiet again. "My scribes have prepared copies of the gospels for each of you on several scrolls. The first set of scrolls has words written by the John Mark and apostles Mathew, John and Peter. The second set of scrolls has letters written by the Apostle Paul, including his epistle to the Romans. Paul wrote these epistles as letters to Christian leaders he worked with in several cities. The next scroll has words written by Luke in his "The Acts of the Apostles" and "The Gospel According to Luke." This last scroll has the Gospel of Barnabas, The Gospel of Mary and The Gospel of Thomas. The Gospel of Thomas has The Secret Sayings of Jesus."

Nasi Judah looked around at the expectant eyes, and then said, "Let me recite for you a couple of examples from these scrolls. This is the first gospel written by Mark. It is appropriate for today. Mark talks about John the Baptist and his words say: *'---John came, baptizing in the desert region and preaching a baptism of repentance for the forgiveness of sins. ---After me will come one more powerful than I, the thongs of whose sandals I am not worthy to stoop down to untie. I baptize you with water, but he will baptize you with the Holy Spirit.'*"[68]

Judah looked around at the rapt faces and went on, "Mark continues: *'At that time Jesus came from Nazareth in Galilee and was baptized by John in the Jordan. As Jesus was coming up out of the water, he saw heaven being torn open and the Spirit descending on him like a dove. And a voice came from heaven: You are my son, whom I love; with you I am well pleased.'*"[69]

Thomas looked at Cerrone who had an awed smile on his face.

Next Nazi Judah quoted Barnabas, a member of Jesus' quorum of seventy disciples, who said: *"--consider how Christ has joined both the cross and the water together. For thus he saith: Blessed are they who put their trust in the cross, descend into the water; for they shall have their reward in due time; then, saith he, will give it them.'*"[70]

Nazi Judah gazed around the room to expectant faces and at his aides. "Apostle Paul said to the Galatians: *'You are all the sons of God through faith in Christ Jesus, for all of you who were baptized into Christ have clothed you with Christ. There is neither Jew nor Greek or Roman, slave nor free, male nor female: for you are all one in Christ Jesus.'*"[71]

He was quiet for a few moments thinking. All of those on the veranda sat quietly. The servants stood around to listen to what the Nazi would tell

---

[68] Ibid, Mark 1:4.

[69] Ibid, Mark 1:10-11.

[70] The Lost Books of the Bible, Chapter X: 11, 12.

[71] Ibid, Galatians 3:26, 28.

them next. The Nazi then smiled, looked up and continued, "Consider this too. Paul gave this advice to the Philippians: *'Finally, brethren, whatever is true, whatever things are noble, whatever things are pure, whatever things are just, whatever things are lovely, whatever are of good report, if there is any virtue and if there is anything praiseworthy-mediate on these things. The things which you learned and received and heard and saw in me, these do, and the God of peace will be with you.'*[72]

Everyone stood and quietly but respectfully clapped. The Nasi threw his hands in the air. Everyone abruptly became quiet.

"Wonderful words are written on these scrolls, and I hope each of you will be able to study them in time," the Nasi said. "Thomas, as you go forth, abide by these words and they will guide you and your missionary companions through the trials and travails of your journey of faith. There will be many challenges. Remember that telling the story of Jesus' life helps lead people to become believers."

Nasi Judah and his aides walked over to Cerrone. One aide gave him a number of scrolls. They then handed a number of scrolls to Thomas. Stephen took Thomas' scrolls and rolled them up together and inserted them into a leather tube. Baroni rolled up the scrolls for Cerrone and inserted them into a leather tube. Each tube had a round top with a round leather cap with the words in gold on the cap, "Fellowship with Jesus Christ." On the sides of each leather tube were the names Thomas and Cerrone.

Thomas stood and hugged the Nasi.

"These words will be very important as you leave this City," Nasi Judah said. "Go out to do your missionary work and find your Mediterranean Island."

"I'm proud to accept these words, and you can be sure I will read them more than once," Cerrone said. "Your gift and the words you have spoken are very special to me on my baptism day."

As everyone left, Cerrone said to Thomas, "Come by in the morning with your wagon and the thirty soldiers will be ready to lead you to Joppa."

"Since you have a feed bin and a watering trough, I had Principale Pardi take a wagon and a team of horses over to your estate for you to load and ride to the palace in the morning," Baroni said.

---

[72] Ibid, Philippians 4:8, 9.

Thomas and his missionary companions left Herod's Palace and walked back to the Thomas estate. Paz stopped Thomas and said, "I want you to know I've learned a great lesson and greatly appreciate your forgiving love. I promise there will be no more concerns about me. While you are away, you can trust me."

"Good," Thomas said. I'm counting on you."

Paz, Mark and David broke off to go home. The remaining four walked by the soldiers who were camped by the olive tree, their horses tied to the water trough. The soldiers had erected a third tent placing it so they could share the fire pit with Neta's two tents. They greeted Neta and the soldiers then went into the house.

† Chapter 14 †

Trip to Joppa to Order the Ships
Monday, January 8, 125 A.D.

Thomas, Stephen, Peter and Ben came down and ate breakfast quickly. They went out to load their sleeping mats and personal items onto the wagon. It was cold, and the extra shirt under their robes was welcome. The silver for the ship order was placed in a metal box built into the floor of the wagon. The soldiers had loaded their tent and extra gear onto the wagon. The horses and soldiers were cold and ready to move. One soldier took the reins with the missionaries seated in the seats behind the driver. Ben wished the three of them good luck and went back in the house.

They arrived at Herod's Palace in the dark. The soldiers removed the tent and gear from the missionaries' wagon and carried them away. The soldiers on horseback came around to line up in front of their wagon. Four more wagons came up the hill.

As it started to get light, Pardi came out to greet them. "I'll ride with you for a little ways then switch with one of my mounted soldiers. I want to talk to you."

He climbed in, announcing, "We'll leave through the Jaffa gate."

"Pardi, what's in the four wagons that follow us?" Thomas asked.

"Those wagons have food, wine, water, tents and supplies for five days for the soldiers and us," he said. "The drivers will be our cooks."

Cerrone walked out to wish them safe travel. He asked Thomas to step aside with him and said, "I have to express a concern. The Roman army can be your protection, but nothing more. If people took you to a judge about the goods you plan to take out of Israel, I fear the judge may declare the goods to belong to the Jewish nation. I don't want to know what goods you have. We'll protect you, but your business is your business. You will encounter hardships, threats and attacks that can lead to certain death. I'll be praying for your safety and success."

"Thank you for your concern and warning," Thomas said. "I hope we can avoid the possibility of what you just described. I'm counting on Jesus to watch over us and the safety of your men traveling with us."

The sun came up with some cloud cover. Wind blew dust around and smelled like rain. They started down the streets and went through the Jaffa gate. Soldiers at the gate saluted as they went under.

"Thomas, I'm from Sicily and grew up outside of Palermo on a vineyard," Pardi said. "When I was seventeen, I was asked to join the Roman army. I'm now forty and have been to many countries in the Roman Empire. My tour in Jerusalem started two years ago. I'll retire back to Sicily soon. I envy you missionaries and the adventure you're planning. I feel you're going to be wildly successful in your missionary work. One day maybe I can help with your Island-of-Dreams. Building a new house of worship, several homes, gardens and vineyards on virgin land is exciting to me. I wanted to tell you that I grew up in a family that produces wine. I'm sure my brothers control the family vineyards now. I would like to produce your wine, so don't forget me."

"I have wondered who we would recruit to plant and manage our vineyards and gardens," Thomas said. "I did not know where we would get our vine stock. Jesus, in my dream, showed me where to plant the vineyard. He instructed me to do that first, so we need to stay in touch somehow."

"I'll stay in touch. The Roman army will be able to contact me."

After some time, they stopped for lunch and a short rest, and then set off again. Peter and Pardi discussed various islands and cities they had visited. None of the islands they described sounded like the Island-of-Dreams.

"I worry about future Jewish wars," Pardi said. "Hadrian may get tired of this nonsense with the Bar Kokba movement and send in an army to quell the violence. If he does, it could be very severe and destructive. We all would be in danger. I hope you know, Hadrian has built spas in Israel, Cyprus, Britain and other countries because of his skin problems. While he was here he learned about the Jewish practice of circumcism and hates it. He considers it to be a savage practice. There is word that he will declare the practice of circumcism illegal. You don't want to be here if he makes that declaration. This may be the final straw to set off an all out war with the rebel Jewish Army and the local people joining the fight."[73]

They came to the stream that crossed the road. "We will camp here for the night," Pardi said, standing up in the wagon. "We've gotten here before any other travelers."

A soldier came to Pardi and said, "Ten people have walked up to the rear guards and want to know if there are any Christian priests from the Nazarene ecclesia with us."

Pardi walked back to talk to the people. He returned shortly to Thomas to say, "Two people want to be healed."

Thomas, Stephen and Peter walked back with Pardi following with torches. When they arrived all ten people knelt down. One of the men looked up and pleaded. "My wife has become blind. Could you help her to see again?"

Another man said, "My arm was stabbed some time ago and it will not heal.

"How did you know there were Christians with these soldiers?" Thomas asked.

"We saw you on the wagon," the man said. "We guessed you were Christian priests and something convinced me you were from the Jerusalem ecclesia."

"Do you believe we can heal these people?" Thomas asked. "Do any of you know Hadar?"

"We really do believe you have the power to heal," the man said. "Who is Hadar?"

"Pardi, bring these people to the fire," Thomas said. "Have the soldiers gather around and keep an eye on them."

"Clear a path," Pardi said. "Watch the people for weapons or aggression.

---

[73] Ancient Warfare Magazine. (In 130 A.D., when the emperor Hadrian visited Judaea, he ordered the construction of a new city to replace the town that Titus had razed to the ground, Jerusalem. It was to be a Roman city, with a Roman temple dedicated to the Roman supreme god Jupiter. Two years later, Hadrian forbade castration and circumcision, making a law against a practice that had offended Greek and Roman sensitivities for a long time. At this time, the Jews started the Bar Kokba war.)

"All of you line up and walk to the fire," Thomas said. "Please have the two people that need healing stand together in front of the fire."

Pardi led them through the soldiers. Thomas directed the blind woman and the man with the injured arm to take their positions and pointed to where the others should stand.

"Can you see at all?" Thomas asked the woman.

"I can only see some light with my left eye," she said.

"Do you believe we can heal you through Jesus the Christ?"

She bowed down and cried. "I believe in Christ and his power," she said. "I believe in you as a Christian priest and your ability to call on Jesus to heal me."

"Only your faith can heal you," Thomas said.

"I do believe you and Jesus will heal me," she cried out.

Thomas and Stephen placed their hands on her head. "Jesus, look upon this woman who believes," Thomas prayed. "Please heal her sight. We ask this in thy name. Amen."

They removed their hands and stepped back. The women put her head down briefly. When she raised her head, her eyes opened wide, and she started talking in a language they did not understand. She went on speaking for a short time. Her husband stepped around the fire and asked, "Do you know this language? What does this mean?"

"She is speaking in tongues," Thomas said. "The Holy Ghost has entered her, but do not worry. She is filled with the joy of Jesus' love and faithfulness."

After a moment she stood. "I don't know what I just said, but I can say more in my own language."

"Rest your eyes while we bless this injured man," Thomas said.

"Hold out your injured arm," Stephen said to the man.

"He has pus and swelling around the injury," Stephen said, after examining the man's arm.

"The wound must be drained," Thomas said.

Principale Pardi produced his knife and wiped it on a towel.

Stephen took the knife and said, "Ask someone to step around to hold your arm."

His brother complied. Stephen heated the knife blade in the fire and then made a cut through the swelling, and it burst and drained. A soldier poured water over the draining wound.

"Let the wound drain tonight," Stephen said. "We will now say a blessing for you."

As they knelt, they placed their hands on the man's arm above the wound.

"Father-in-heaven, please heal this man's arm through the power of Jesus Christ. Amen."

They stood and stepped back to the woman, "Open your eyes," Thomas said.

She slowly opened one eye and then the other. She looked up to Thomas. "I can see you," she said.

"How many fingers have I held up?" Thomas asked.

"Two," she said.

"That's good." The crowd murmured.

"Sleep here tonight and pour water over your eyes in the morning," Thomas said.

"Take some cloth from your robe and wrap your arm for the night," Stephen said to the man with the injured arm.

The husband of the woman, who had been blind, fell to his knees. "Thank you and Principale Pardi," he said and then confessed, "I was very afraid to approach you."

"We are people serving those in need," Thomas said.

A murmur of thanks came from all of the guests. Thomas walked back to their fire. Pardi was ordering four soldiers to feed the guests and to watch them in two shifts during the night.

"What about the other guards?" Thomas asked.

"My two other guard squads will also take shifts during the night," Pardi said. "Let's all prepare our beds and go to sleep."

Tuesday, January 9, 125 A.D.

They awoke to crying from the guest fire. Thomas walked over to find the husband comforting the woman who had been blind. The man looked up at them. "My wife has recovered most of the sight in both of her eyes."

"I'm pleased, but the healing will continue for days," Thomas said, as Stephen came over.

"The two of you have healed her," the husband said.

"No," Thomas said. "God has healed her through Jesus the Christ. God sent the Holy Spirit last night to heal your wife because of her faith."

"My arm is much better this morning," The man with the injured arm said to Stephen. "I believe it will heal because of my faith in Jesus. All I have heard is true. I'm so grateful you made it happen. Thank you both for these miracles."

The horses were saddled and the riders mounted up. The missionaries climbed aboard the wagon with Pardi now on horseback. He gave the order to move out. Waving to the guests who were walking on the road back to their homes, they traveled without stopping and made good time to Joppa. At the end of the harbor, Peter, Thomas and Stephen left Pardi who agreed to make camp there and protect their wagons. They went to the pier where the representative kept his fishing boat. His boat was gone.

"He's out fishing; he'll be back at dark," said another fisherman.

When they arrived back at the camp, a crowd had approached the soldiers guarding the camp. Apparently, the crowd thought they were an advance unit of the main Roman army. They would not believe Pardi when he told them they were a guard unit for Christian missionaries.

"We have our small Roman unit here and they did not expect you. I have never heard such lies," the leader said.

Thomas walked over to the leader who backed away fearfully. He was in a white robe with gold thread. His full beard was well trimmed.

"Who are you?" The man asked.

Arms in the air to quiet the crowd, Thomas stood motionless until everyone became silent.

"We are here under the protection of Tribune Cerrone, the Roman commander in Jerusalem. Do not fear us for we have only come to order two new ships. Three of us are part of a missionary group. Please return to your work or homes."

"I have never heard of Roman soldiers protecting Christians before," the leader said. "You must be very important. If you need help or assistance, let the harbor master know. I apologize for not believing you."

"Who are you?" Thomas asked.

"I am the mayor of Joppa."

"Thank you, mayor; we do have one more request."

"We will do whatever you request."

"We will be back after the change of seasons to take ownership of the two ships we are having built," Thomas said. "When they are docked at the pier, we would like them to be protected until we arrive."

"We'll put them in a special pier that we save for important guests," the mayor said, smiling. "I will inform the harbor master and the boat representative. Please allow me to meet with you and the representative tonight to be sure you are receiving the appropriate price and service."

Thomas thanked him. "I know where the representative dines each night and I will meet you there at sunset,"

The mayor turned to the crowd. "All is well, we can leave now."

At the camp, Thomas and Peter picked up their lunch and sat on the pier to eat. As Thomas was finishing his drink, Pardi came over and sat down. He seemed lost in his thoughts as he looked out to the Mediterranean. He finally turned and looked at Thomas.

"You talked about this Hadar who wants to take the old temple records away from you. Why are those old records important to him?"

"The Jews have been careful through the millennia to keep good records. They are careful about the descendents of Abraham and the twelve tribes. They are important to me and Stephen, also. I know why he wants them, but if he got them, they will surely be destroyed in the next destruction of Jerusalem. I must save them. Hadar and Simeon ben Kosiba are leading the Jews astray. Both of them are hungry for power and Hadar has the wealth to go after it. Either one would be a ruthless dictator, the opposite of Jesus. They are a danger and menace. My fear is that they will leave Jerusalem in worse shape than after the revolt put down by Titus fifty-five years ago."

Pardi walked back to talk to some of the soldiers. Later, Stephen, Thomas and Peter found a comfortable spot and took a nap. They awoke to hear talking and laughing. They went back to camp to find the mayor had returned with several men who brought fish from a fishing boat that had just returned.

"Principale Pardi, please accept these fish as our desire to have good will with you and the missionaries," the mayor said.

As the mayor left again, Pardi turned to Thomas and looked amazed. "How do you affect people the way you do? You have such a positive affect that people want to do you favors. I'm glad to be at your service and watch what comes next."

"Thank you for your compliment and confidence in our work," Thomas said smiling.

As they left to meet the boat representative, the sun was setting and Pardi's second in command wished them good luck.

"They don't need luck because they have God with them," Pardi said smiling.

As they approached the inn, a crowd had gathered outside the entrance.

"What's going on here?" Thomas asked.

"The mayor has gone inside to meet important people, and we are curious to see who they are," one man said.

"May we enter? Stephen asked.

The crowd backed up to let them walk into the inn where they saw the mayor at a table with the representative.

"May I introduce the mayor?" the representative said.

"Thank you, but we have met," Thomas said." It's nice to see you again, mayor."

They sat down around the table and watched the waiter set the table.

"I want to apologize to you now that I understand how important you are," the reprehensive said. "I have your plans. I think you will like them. The mayor told me I must give you our best price and protect the ship when it arrives."

Thomas smiled and thanked him.

"May I see the plans?" Peter asked.

The representative gave the plans to Peter who studied them, then said "This looks like what we requested. I assume it will be tested and corrected for any design errors."

"I will request they do a detailed review," the representative said.

"Could we see the cost of the ship?" Thomas requested.

The representative smiled and quoted a price. You have important friends.

The price is low?" Peter said.

"Yes, I have discussed the pricing with Roman officers," Thomas said. "I want you to order two ships with this design to be built for me. Can we trust you if we pay half the cost for both ships in advance?"

"With all of your new friends, I would not dare to cheat you," the representative replied. "I've a reputation I also must protect."

"We'll pay you half the cost for both ships at sunrise tomorrow," Thomas suggested. "We will pay the balance when both ships are delivered."

"We'll come to your camp at sunrise with our wagon to receive payment," the representative replied, smiling. "The builder has a ship here to take the payment directly back to Cyprus."

"We look forward to seeing you then," Thomas said. "I thank you, mayor, for your assistance."

They left and met the crowd out front and one man asked, "Who are you?"

"We represent Jesus the Christ," Thomas said. "We bring the Good News."

"Would you tell us the Good News?" Several people asked at once.

"We will return when the new season comes. Ask the mayor to set up a place for us to present the Good News."

"We will do as you request," the man said. "I believe many will want to hear your story. We will look forward to hearing about Christianity from you. I believe we have not heard the whole story of the life of Jesus."

The four of them walked back to camp. "It has been quiet while you were gone," said the second in command. "Our cooks are very pleased with the fish, bread and berries supplied by the people here in Joppa. We've roasted the fish. Come partake with us."

Thomas looked at the serving; it looked like a wonderful feast. They were surprised to learn the town had also brought Mulsum for their dinner. It was fruity and fresh with honey. The missionaries and solders sat around enjoying the meal and the Mulsum.

"We have enjoyed this meal like no other," Thomas said to the cooks. "You performed a miracle with the food and Mulsum supplied by the people here in Joppa."

The cooks bowed. All of the Roman soldiers laughed and cheered.

"Thomas, you and Stephen are not the only miracle workers," Pardi said.

The soldiers cheered again.

"I sent word to the Roman legion officers here in Joppa to inform them of our assignment and to expect us when the new season has arrived," Pardi said. "Apparently, Centurion Markus and Principale Benito are down the coast and will not return until tomorrow."

"I'm sorry we missed them." Thomas said.

"Could we take a few minutes to discuss a question raised by one of my men?"

"Certainly," Thomas said.

"Men, please listen to my question and the response," Pardi said. "Thomas, we have lived our lives believing in many gods. Our God Jupiter is our supreme god, but we have others like Mars, Neptune, Juno, Venus, Diana and Bacchus. Venus is the goddess of love, Mars is our god of war and Bacchus is our god of wine. We are confused by you, proclaiming Jesus is the Son of the one true God. How do we deal with this confusion?"

Thomas thought for short time and looked into the faces of the soldiers. "I know you and your men have believed in many gods, but they don't give you plans to live a good life, be saved when you die and go to God in heaven. If you look at Christianity, the Good News is to know your belief in Jesus gains you his good grace. Through his grace you will then be saved. Jesus told us the most important thing we can do is to love him with all our hearts, body and mind. We are to love our neighbors. You must compare what is offered by your belief in your many gods, who have no plan for your salvation, eternal life, forgiveness of sins and finding love in your life. I hope you and your men will be able to hear more about Jesus and his Good News as we travel together. Thank you for listening."

Walking over to the wagon Stephen said, "Thomas that was a simple straight forward answer."

"I hope they understood it just the same," Thomas said. "I didn't tell you what Cerrone said to me before we left the palace. He is concerned about the goods we are planning on taking out of Israel. If a complaint is taken to a judge, anything goes, but we could be required to turn over what we have to the Jewish nation. Being a Christian will not help us. Jesus said he will help us secure the goods for posterity. Cerrone may not be able to help us, so I pray Jesus can help us through this risk."

Wednesday, October 10, 125 A.D.

They awoke to the sound of a wagon coming their way. They got up and came out to find the ship manufacturer representative with five other men standing by a wagon and a team of horses. Thomas and Stephen greeted the representative and went to the wagon and counted out into three bags the silver for half the price of the two ships. The representative's men took the three bags of silver to their wagon.

"Count it before we leave," Thomas requested.

"I don't need to count it," the representative said. "I trust you and besides it's just a down payment. Thank you."

"I want you to know that I will take good care of any other missionaries that may want to buy a ship," the representative said when he returned. "I'll see you at the start of the new season."

They sat down and ate breakfast with the soldiers. Pardi ordered the soldiers and cooks to get ready to leave. When they had boarded their wagons, Pardi gave the signal to start back toward Jerusalem.

They were about to ride up the hill towards the camp site where the stream ran over the road, when a group of at least forty men carrying shields and spears came over the hill. Thomas and the Roman soldiers were still some distance from the men. Pardi shouted for his men to bring out their swords. The missionaries and cooks pulled out their swords and battle axes. The mounted soldiers, the cooks and missionaries grabbed their shields.

"Men on foot stay here to guard the wagons," Pardi yelled. "Those of you on horseback follow me up to those men coming down the hill towards us. Listen for my commands."

As Pardi and his men came near to the men coming down the hill, they stopped. "Who are you? Why are you ready for battle?"

One of the men stepped forward and lowered his shield. "You are transporting Thomas and his missionary companions. We want them."

"Why do you want them?' Pardi asked.

"Thomas has stolen temple documents which we want from him. He needs to be tried for his crimes."

"Who are you to make these charges," Pardi asked.

"We represent Simon ben Kosiba and Hadar."

"Simon ben Kosiba and Hadar are criminals," Pardi said. "You have no legal standing to make any charges or stand here ready to do battle."

"You Romans are the illegal occupiers of our country and we want you all dead."

"Charge and take them out," Pardi yelled.

Pardi and his men galloped into the group of men trampling down the men as they swung their swords. There was screaming and the clang of the swords and shields. Several of the soldiers received cuts, but nothing serious. Half of Hadar's men ran down the hill towards the wagons. Pardi and his men turned around trampling the dead and dying again as they pursued the running men. The soldiers and cooks at the wagons were in front with shields, with Peter behind them. Thomas and Stephen were off to each side with three spears each. As the running men approached the wagons, Stephen and Thomas threw their spears in quick succession. Five of the spears hit five of the men who went down screaming. By then Pardi caught up with them and they took out another eight. The remaining seven ran into the soldiers with shields. They hit the shields and then swords came around the soldiers' shields to imbed in the enemy shields, wounding most of them.

One man lost his shield and headed for Peter yelling, "Death to you." He stabbed at Peter with his sword; Peter ducked and turned around to stab the man. He collapsed screaming and Peter pulled his sword out making a wet sucking sound. Another man got up and ran to the side of the soldiers, swinging his sword and yelling. A cook with a battle ax brought it down on the side of the man's head and shoulder killing him instantly.

"I want half of you to go back up the hill to the dead and dying and dispatch any who are still alive," Pardi said. "The rest of us will take care of these men. Everyone watch out for others who may be waiting to attack us."

Pardi and several soldiers dismounted and grabbed three who were only wounded. The other men were quickly checked for life and dispatched if they were. The soldiers dragged the three live men to the side of the road holding them.

Thomas walked over to the men. "Where is your camp? How many are nearby."

"It is none of your business," one man said. "You are Thomas and you should die."

"Death to all Romans," the second man said.

Pardi promptly stabbed both men with his sword right through their chests. He pulled the sword out each time with a slick sound and the men fell over on their faces.

"I will tell you," the third man said. "We are camped a short way from here. Most of the men in the camp are on maneuvers half a day from here. We're new recruits and we're out practicing. When we saw you coming, we were under orders to get Thomas."

"Tell your leader that Thomas is under Roman protection," Pardi said. "We will pursue those who come after him and his companions. You will be targeted for death. Now get going."

"Leave the dead where they lay," Pardi said. "The rebels can clean up this mess. Gather their weapons."

When weapons and shields were loaded, the soldiers remounted and the cooks and missionaries boarded the wagons. When they got to the stream running over the road, Pardi stopped to say, "We are near the rebel army camp. We'll keep going, but be alert for possible encounters with them."

They stopped at dusk where the pond and stream were below the road. "We will camp and have dinner now," Pardi said.

Everyone was dead tired and in bed right after eating.

Thursday, January 11, 125 A.D.

During the night the wind blew and it rained. At dawn there was mud everywhere. The wind was howling. The cooks passed out bread and dates for breakfast. When all was packed, they set off for Jerusalem.

At mid-day they approached the Jaffa gate. The guards saluted as they rode through. The road was crowded on their way to the Palace. As they pulled up to the gates, Cerrone was there to meet them. He seemed very regal with his light brown hair, dark leathers and gleaming full armor. "Welcome back. I hope your trip was successful."

"It was," Thomas said. "Principale Pardi will report to you on the encounter we had with Hadar's men."

"Pardi will report to me and Centurion Baroni," Cerrone said. "I'm anxious to hear about this encounter."

Peter took over driving to make their way back to the Thomas estate. Two soldiers rode with them to bring the wagon back to the stable.

Ben was talking to Neta when Peter pulled the wagon up to the olive tree. They took the balance of the silver and personal belongings out of the wagon. The soldiers turned the wagon around and went back to the palace. Thomas and Stephen took the silver back to the tomb and returned it to the stone box from which they had taken it. While eating lunch, they told Cleophas, Ada and Ben about their trip, ordering the two ships and the encounter on the way back.

Paz, Mark and David knocked on the door. All seven missionaries went into the great room. Mark talked to them about his list, which included axes, log splitting wedges, heavy hammers, trimming lathes quarry equipment, etching tools, heavy hammers, iron bars, large rolls of rope and other carpentry, mortar and stone finishing tools.

"We have many Christian friends who will help us acquire these tools," Thomas said. "We have a few weeks to locate and bring in these tools on your list back here."

Afterwards, they relaxed in front of the fire in the great room.

✝ Part V ✝

† Chapter 15 †

Gone to Joppa to Accept the Ships
Monday, April 8, 125 A.D.

Thomas and Stephen strolled back home after meeting with Cerrone. Thomas noticed Neta stop two men and motioned to some Roman soldiers to help him. Thomas wondered if they were Hadar's men.

Arriving at the lane to the estate, Thomas was pleased to see the missionaries and Cleophas out organizing and inventorying the tools and supplies to take to Joppa. They were deciding which items would be taken now and which would be taken on the ultimate departure from Jerusalem. By late afternoon Paz, Mark and David went home. Thomas, Stephen, Ben and Peter went in the house with Cleophas to relax.

A knock on the door was answered by Cleophas, who called for Thomas. "Neta wants to talk to you."

Thomas stepped outside and listened to Neta for a few moments and then excused him. He came back into the great room. "Neta told me he had two Jews arrested by the Roman soldiers. The men had been sneaking around the cisterns and walking by the front of the property. These men were looking for ways to break into the house. They followed Stephen and me over to the palace and were trying to catch us on the way back. This is the third group he has caught and turned over to the Romans."

They talked about this danger until dinner was served. As they were eating, they heard shouting. Thomas got up to look out the door. "There are several men attacking Neta and his men. Get your swords. We have to help them."

The men ran to their rooms for their swords and short knives, and then ran out of the house. Two men had Neta cornered between his tent and the olive tree. Thomas stepped around and stabbed the side of one man who screamed and collapsed. This distraction allowed Neta to yell and stab the other man who toppled onto the side of the tent. Two of Neta's men and two strangers lay bleeding and moaning on the ground. One man in Neta's group and the four soldiers on loan were chasing four men up towards the cisterns. Stephen, Ben and Peter ran to the back to help them surround the attackers.

Thomas kneeled down to talk to one man who was lying on the ground bleeding. "Who paid you to come here," Thomas yelled. "Are there others in Jerusalem working with you?"

"We came in here following you from Joppa," the man whispered. "There are many men besides us. Others will succeed where we have not." The man died.

Neta's men were dead. He closed their eyes. The four invaders lay back with their eyes wide open. Screams were coming from the up the hill on the back of the property. Thomas told Neta what the dying man had told him. They looked up to see four men being dragged down the hill towards them.

Neta's man and the soldiers dragged three men to the lane. Peter and Stephen pulled another invader next to the others. They walked over to Thomas and Neta. "We cried out for them to stop and surrender," Stephen said. "They yelled obscenities at us and charged us with their swords. Ben threw his short knife and hit one man in the throat. He dropped his sword and pulled out his short knife. Peter stabbed him through his chest with his sword, killing the man instantly."

"One invader ran at Neta's man, who stepped out of his way," Ben said. "I dove down to catch his legs. The man flew over me and landed on his own sword."

"One of the soldiers said, "These men acted like they wanted to commit suicide."

"Go have our men bring a wagon," Neta said. "Let them know what happened. They must take all of these invader's bodies to the canyon, then take our dead men for burial tonight. Two men will replace our lost friends who died nobly tonight."

"This was terrible," Thomas said. "Neta, I am sorry about your men. I appreciate the protection you soldiers gave us. There will be more soldiers here in the morning with wagons. They will help you until we depart for Joppa to take possession of my ships. Just so you know, Centurion Baroni and Principale Bardo have assigned ten soldiers in uniform to watch this neighborhood for our safety. Tribune Cerrone is using us as bait to attract Hadar."

"I'm sorry you had to help us," Neta said. "They crept up on us in surprise. That's how they killed my men. I hate them. They're cowards. Thomas, could you go with us to bless my men's graves?"

"Let me know when you are ready," Thomas said. "Stephen and I will go with you."

Tuesday April 9, 125 A.D.

Thomas and the others were up early for breakfast. They went out in the courtyard, when three wagons came up to the gate at the estate. Neta and his men had installed gates and fencing made from wood poles and rope during the night. He opened the new gates. Baroni and Pardi were on horseback. The wagons were pulled by three teams of horses. Peter told the drivers where to tie the horses. Neta talked to one soldier, directing him to put up his tent where they could share the fire-pit with him and the other soldiers. Paz, Mark and David walked in through the new gates. Mark led the missionaries and soldiers to show them what was to be loaded onto each wagon.

"I'll stay here to help supervise the loading," Peter said.

"Thanks Peter."

Thomas invited Stephen, Baroni and Pardi to the terrace. Elizabeth brought out dates and cheeses on a tray. Leah brought four goblets and small amphoras of juice. The four of them sat in the shade of a tree next to the terrace. Pardi complimented them on the gates and the organization.

"I thought you should know that Cerrone has invited Rebecca and some friends a couple of times to the palace to dinner parties," Baroni said. "They seem to make a great couple, but Rebecca has now gotten a little nervous about the relationship. You know how Jewish women apparently get nervous, but Cerrone thinks she just needs a little more time. She would be marrying a future Roman Senator. I think many people in Jerusalem will be very pleased if their relationship blossoms into marriage. It'll be like a pact between the Romans and Jews."

"Nasi Judah also mentioned that Cerrone invited him and his wife to bring Rebecca to the first dinner party," Thomas said. "The Nasi is pleased with their relationship and hopes to continue the friendship."

Wednesday, April 10, 125 A.D.

Two days later, they were up before sunrise in the dark, eating. At sunrise, Paz, Mark and David arrived. Thomas talked to Neta and Bardo's soldiers about maintaining the watch of the estate and his family. As the horses pulled the wagons through the gates, Neta came out to shut the gates and drove stakes into the road. They waved to Cleophas and Neta.

As they approached the palace, horses stomping and the chatter of the soldiers could be heard. When Pardi saw them coming, he stepped out to direct the drivers. Another twenty wagons were loaded in line. They stepped down to the ground. Baroni led the seven missionaries to a location where they could hear Cerrone hasty instructing the other officers.

Fort Sebaste and Fort Caesarea had each sent fifty soldiers to accompany them. The total contingent would include two hundred foot-soldiers and one hundred horse mounted soldiers. Bataglia from Sebaste and Bagli from Jerusalem would march with the foot soldiers. Horses were held for Cerrone, Baroni Pardi and the missionaries. Everyone mounted and cantered up to the front of the wagons behind the foot soldiers. Crowds of people had come out to watch their departure.

"Who will be in charge of the palace and garrison here in Jerusalem?" Thomas asked.

"Centurion Felone rode in from Caesarea with the fifty soldiers, and was assigned to take charge of the palace and garrison," Pardi said. "He has the command of two hundred sixty soldiers while we are gone."

As they got close to the Jaffa Gate, the whole contingent stopped. Baroni rode up front to see what the problem was. He returned before long.

"Ten men were lying on the road to stop us," Baroni said. "I asked them to get out of the way. One refused, so I rode up and hacked his arm off. The others got up and dragged the injured man away."

The procession resumed and then the whole movement stopped again. Baroni went up again to see what caused the delay. He came back to tell Cerrone that men were dead in the street and were being dragged off the side of the road. Bagli told me that when the gates were opened, he saw armed men coming at them and yelled charge and to kill them. The rebel men were yelling death to Thomas, and they never knew what hit them. He pulled the dead men off the road and ordered the guards at the gate to send for help from Centurion Felone.'"

Thomas was astounded that they had not left the city before several men were killed. He turned to Pardi and said, "I can't believe this Hadar has his men making repeated attempts to come after me. I hope there isn't a group going to my estate."

Baroni said, "One of the men told Bagli before he died, 'Hadar will govern Jerusalem when the Romans are dead."

They were blessed with large well-trained horses. Thomas was enjoying the weather and the view over the top of the foot-soldiers. They were close to where the stream runs over the road. There was a shout and the soldiers stopped. Baroni went forward. He came back in a short time.

"The foot-soldiers were about to descend a hill," Baroni said. "They have spotted what may be the rebel Jewish Army coming our way, but probably they can't see many of our soldiers because of the hill."

Cerrone invited Thomas to ride forward with Baroni, Pardi and him. They stopped to stare down on a large number of men coming towards them. Bagli and Bataglia marched up to them.

"Principale Bagli, lead a hundred men along the top of the hill to our left and get into position," Cerrone ordered. "Principale Bataglia, march a hundred men forward down the hill. Principale Pardi, lead fifty men on horseback over to our right."

When Bataglia came to within about three hundred paces of the rebel army, both groups came to a stop. "Where are you going," Bataglia shouted.

"We want to kill all you Romans," the leader shouted back.

"Go up the hill," Bataglia shouted to his men.

At the same time, he gave a hand signal to Bagli for his soldiers to start down towards the rebels from the left. While his men were retreating, the rebel army started forward

Cerrone gave a signal to send the fifty soldiers on horseback down and around the right side of our retreating soldiers. By the time the rebel army of about one hundred men caught up with Bataglia, Cerrone gave a signal for Bataglia to turn his men around, forming a wedge with shields facing out and then ordered them to move forward and fight. At the same time, the soldiers coming down the hill from the left attacked. The mounted soldiers had taken off down the hill from the right and circled to the back of the rebels. The screaming of the men, the noise of the horses, the clang of swords and shields and the thumping of horses and bodies slamming each other was horrendous.

It was obvious that the commander of the rebel soldiers had not expected over one hundred soldiers to come at them from each of two sides, let alone soldiers cutting off retreat. Within a short period of time most of the rebels were dead or dying.

Thomas waved for Stephen to ride down to watch. Three rebel soldiers survived. The remaining dying men were dispatched with swords by the soldiers. The circumcised penises were cut from the dead Jewish soldiers and dropped into a bag. All of the dead were then dragged off the road and stacked. Soldiers went off in several directions and came back with wood. The firewood was laid out and the bodies were thrown on top as more wood was piled around and over the bodies. The wood was set on fire in several places. Soon the fire was roaring.

Baroni came forward and ordered mounted soldiers, the foot soldiers and wagons to go down the road to where the stream went over the road and set up camp. He ordered Pardi and Bataglia to take some men out on patrol to see if others were around. Thomas sent his fellow missionaries ahead, but he and Stephen stayed to see what would be done next.

The acrid smell of blood was heavy in the air. The ground was wet with pools of blood.

"You three surviving Jews come over here to me," Baroni ordered. "One of them recognized Thomas. "You are a deserting blasphemer," he shouted. "You have denigrated the cause of the Jews."

Baroni swung his sword and the Jew's head fell to the ground. Baroni picked the head up by the hair and ordered the other two Jews to pick up the body and deliver it to the fire. They did as they were told and the head was tossed into the fire after the body. Baroni came back with the two Jews.

"Principale Pardi, give the bag of penises to these two Jews," Cerrone said. "You Jews take this bag to your rebel commander and tell him of the events here today. Tell him we will not attack his army unless we are attacked by them. He'll have little doubt about the death of his Jewish soldiers."

Thomas watched the Jews scramble away carrying the bag. "Let's pray for the dead Jews." he said.

"Let me pray with you," Cerrone said.

The three knelt and Thomas prayed, "Please, Father forgive those who were killed here and at the Jaffa gate today. Father, please bless the Jewish people that they will see the folly of fighting the Roman army. We pray they may soon see the light and some form of unity may prevail. Jesus, please continue to bless us on this journey to Joppa. Amen."

They got to their feet and rode down the hill to the camp that was now almost set up.

Thomas and Stephen looked for their missionary companions and found them working on their assigned tent. Thomas told them about the mutilations and the order given to the two survivors.

"What we saw is a clear picture of the great danger that is here in Judea," he said.

"Why were the penises cut off and bagged?" Ben asked.

"For a demeaning message to the leaders of the Jewish army," Thomas said. "The circumcised penises will prove without question the deaths of the Jewish soldiers. They need to know that their actions will lead to laying waste to their people, their religion and their nation."

They heard a horn blow and stepped out of their tent. "What does the horn mean?" Thomas asked a soldier.

"That horn means it's time to eat," laughed the soldier.

The food was set out on serving ledges on three wagons. The soldiers were lined up.

A soldier came to Thomas and said, "Please follow me to where you will eat."

They followed him to a large tent. Inside were two tables set up with food.

Cerrone walked around from behind a screen that divided the tent into two rooms. "Thomas, please bless the food."

"Jesus, we thank you for our safety today. Please bless our food, the soldiers and us. Bless us that we might have a safe trip. Please, Jesus, bless the Jewish people that they might choose to live in peace under Roman rule. Amen."

"Thomas," Cerrone said. "Your prayers for Jews are puzzling. Why do you care?"

"I'm a Christian, but I have a Jewish heritage," Thomas replied. "Jesus loves everyone so I should pray for everyone."

"God, I wish they could get a reasonable leader," Cerrone replied. "I don't like to kill the Jewish people. We only fight with them when they attack us. I regret the battle and the mutilations you witnessed. I know those people could have been friends and compatriots of yours in other times."

"Thank you for your consideration," Thomas said.

They heard horses coming into camp. Pardi came into the tent and saluted.

"What did you see on patrol," Baroni asked.

"There were no persons to be concerned about in the areas of my patrol," Pardi said.

"I am concerned about Bataglia," Baroni said, standing. "He should have been back by now."

Everyone walked outside and looked to the east and to the north. The soldiers were relaxing around the camp. The sun was getting lower in the west. Just then they saw Bataglia and his men coming back on the road rather than from the north.

"There is a Jewish army of two hundred men just north of us now, so we turned around and returned the way we had gone," Bataglia said.

"Are the rebels coming our way?" Baroni demanded.

"No they are camped and the two men we sent with the bag full of penises were there."

"Do they know we are camped here?"

"I doubt it."

"Do you think they will come our way?"

"I think they'll evaluate what they hear from the two men. The Jews will either be furious enough to look for us or frightened enough to run away for now."

"What would you recommend?"

"First, I'd like to lead some soldiers northeast to a bluff where I can watch for any movement. If they start our way, I can come back to help with the defense."

After taking a nap, Thomas and his companions headed over to the large tent for the evening meal.

Bataglia entered the tent. "The rebel army left and marched north. We followed them for a while and decided they would not be here tonight."

"Where do you think they are going?" Baroni asked.

"If I were to guess, it appeared they are going to Apollonia on the coast."

Pardi appeared with four sleepy soldiers.

"The rebel army may be on their way to attack Apollonia," Baroni told them. "You are now messengers. Ride to Fort Sebaste to warn Tribune Pasquali. You other men ride to Joppa, Apollonia and Caesarea to inform them."

Baroni gave each messenger team a metal medallion from Cerrone. "This medallion will tell the receiver that the message comes directly from Tribune Cerrone."

After the two messenger teams rode off, Baroni invited the officers and missionaries back into the large tent and said, "Thomas, tomorrow we'll split up the mounted soldiers, half of them following us and the other half leading the foot soldiers. It's likely we'll meet another unit of the rebel army. They apparently are recruiting and training heavily here."

"Thomas, you and your missionaries have ridden well," Cerrone said. "Can you or will you fight if you need to save yourselves? If you will, we'll give each of you uniforms and weapons."

"We have fought before," Thomas looked at each missionary. "Do any of you have a problem carrying weapons and putting on armor?"

"I think we all fear walking into a life or death confrontation," Ben said. "Wearing armor makes us a target, but I will fight."

"We'll fight to protect each other," said each missionary in turn.

Baroni called one of the aides. "Pull seven soldier tunics, armor and weapons from the wagons and take them to the missionaries' tent. You missionaries continue to amaze me. I appreciate associating with each of you."

"I knew we could count on you to act like a Roman when we need you," Cerrone said, grinning. "You never know when that could be important to you or me."

"Thank you, but I've had enough excitement for one day," Thomas said. "We'll go to our tent."

As they got to their tent, two aides were delivering uniforms. Everyone tried on tunics, heavy leather chest and skirt to the knees and helmets.

"We look like Romans which makes us Christian soldiers," Thomas said, laughing. "Jesus commands us to "turn your other cheek. Does that apply here?"

Thursday, April 11, 125 A.D.

The next morning, it seemed awkward to walk around with the new uniforms on, but they needed to get used to it. They wore an undershirt with a tunic-like shirt over it that came to their knees. Over the tunic they wore a heavy double thick leather slipover protecting their chest and back to their knees. They wore a thick leather wraparound shin guards over their calves and shins with leather sandals. Their helmets were shinny and covered their ears. The top of the helmet had a metal center to hold the short brush. They used their own swords and short knives.

The camp came alive and the tents were taken down and packed. The breakfast bell was rung and the soldiers lined up at their food wagons. The missionaries sat at the tables with the officers. The cooks brought them eggs and fried chicken. After breakfast, it was more difficult to mount their horses wearing the new uniforms than they had expected. Some of the soldiers smiled and snickered. Everything was packed and the caravan set off.

"You look as good as the soldiers," Cerrone yelled. "Please stay centered on your horse, falling off is not pleasant."

That comment got laughs from the soldiers bringing up the rear. After some time, the missionaries began to appreciate the excellent physical condition of the Roman soldiers.

They stopped for lunch. After some time, everything was packed up, in position and on the road again. Pardi, Cerrone, Baroni and the missionaries rode up front to lead the mounted soldiers. They continued steadily until early afternoon and came into the outskirts of Joppa.

✝ Chapter 16 ✝

The Free Spirit and the Islander
Friday, April 12, 125 A.D.

The mayor, the magistrate and Principale Benito came out on horseback to welcome them. The magistrate welcomed Cerrone and Baroni.

Baroni asked, "Mayor, do you remember Thomas, Stephen and Peter from their last trip to order the ships?"

"What are you doing in Roman uniforms?" the mayor shouted.

"We were honored to wear the uniforms for protection," Thomas said.

The mayor and magistrate turned around and were followed by the officers and the missionaries. When they were all in the fort area; Centurion Markus welcomed Cerrone and Baroni to Joppa. Baroni introduced the missionaries.

"But you are in Roman uniforms," Markus said.

"The last part of this trip the missionaries wore the Roman uniforms for their own protection," Baroni said. "We will tell you about our trip later."

"We have had arrangements for a feast to be served the day after your arrival," the mayor said. "Thomas and Stephen, we would be honored if you would give us some words on Christianity. The feast will be tomorrow afternoon in the town plaza. The sunken theatre will be prepared for your lectures for tomorrow night."

"We will be ready for the presentation," Thomas said smiling. "Are our two ships here?"

"When would you like to see them?" the mayor said.

"We would like to change into our personal clothing and return these uniforms."

"It's early," the mayor said. "Take as long as you need. I'll return in a while to lead you to your new ships. Tribune Cerrone, we invite you to see new ships. I'll arrange for dinner for all of the officers, missionaries and city guests at the inn after they've seen them."

The missionaries changed. The mayor and the representative returned and led them and the officers toward the ships.

"Both of the ships are moored in a secure area at the pier not far from the inn," the mayor said.

"There are your ships," the representative said.

As they walked over to the first one, Thomas noticed a plaque on the side of the ship.

Stephen read it out loud. "DANGER--THIS SHIP IS PROTECTED BY ROME"

"There are three signs like that: one for each side and one on the stern high on the pupas," the representative said.

He moved everyone to the prow and pointed to the carved swan. On the sides of the swan were the words "FREE SPIRIT."

They walked to the next ship and noticed it also had the danger signs. Thomas walked to the front to look at its swan and saw the words "THE ISLANDER."

"I'm very pleased," he said, grinning. "But, how did you get all this done so quickly?"

"Rome buys many ships from this ship builder," Cerrone said, laughing. "I sent word to have the names of the ships carved with the names FREE SPIRIT and ISLANDER the way you see it. I also ordered the DANGER signs. I thought you might need them in your travels to find the island. "

"Cerrone, I thank you," Thomas said. "You continue to surprise me."

"Please, go aboard each ship," the representative said. "I had the boarding planks set out for you."

Thomas was the first to go up the gangplank and set foot on Free Spirit. When everyone was on deck, the representative showed the location of the oars and how they fit into each position. He reviewed the unique design of the full deck.

Peter asked, "Could I go below to check out the lower decks?"

He returned and said, "The decks are as I designed them. The ship is very functional. The three cabins on the second level have five double bunk beds in each. This gives us thirty beds. They will be a little crowded, but comfortable enough, especially in stormy weather. The galley is small but there are two cabinet areas with one area to store personal items and another area to store food, utensils, goblets and amphoras."

Thomas led everyone to the deck of the Islander. The design seemed to be the same. Peter went below and came back to say, "The floor material on every deck is made from heavier planking. It is a very sturdy ship for hauling heavy loads."

"Very good," the representative said. "I'll meet you later for dinner. I can review other features of the Islander and Free Spirit then."

The mayor then led the missionaries and Romans down the street to the Joppa Inn. The Joppa magistrate and the innkeeper welcomed everyone as they came through the door. The small tables were against one wall. A large table dominated the center of the room. Three servers appeared with medium amphoras of juice and Chiam.

"May Jesus smile on Joppa and its Roman protectors," the mayor proposed.

Everyone raised a goblet and took a sip.

The innkeeper invited them to find a bench seat at the table. Stephen looked out the door and saw a crowd had gathered. A number of Roman soldiers were lined up across the front of the inn. They learned later that the Roman soldiers were volunteers from the foot soldiers. Thomas wondered how the Romans found such loyal men for their army.

Dinner was a delight. First they were served fillet of fish, white bread and light olive oil. Next roast chicken with roasted turnips and mushrooms, then Lamb chops were served with a sweet conserve of berries. A final serving of baked cake was served with a choice of juice or Chiam.

"What a wonderful meal," Thomas observed, sighing. "All of you look very tired."

"Bataglia and I must get back to the Fort," Cerrone said standing up.

"Cerrone cannot handle very much of that Chiam," Baroni said after Cerrone was gone.

"He is a wise man to recognize his abilities and not to exceed them," Thomas said.

"That's an unusual comment," Baroni replied.

"None of us will be considered very wise if we do not know our limits," Thomas said.

"I want to talk about a subject that Pardi and I discussed in Jerusalem," Baroni said as he settled back in his chair. "I've heard that Valentinus believes that spirits come from a pure god. When our spirits become a part of a mortal or material body they become corrupted and lose their knowledge. He believes that the supreme god created thirty pairs of god couples. The last couple created had the female name of Sophia. She broke with her male consort in an effort to learn more about the big picture of her unknowable Father. She was supposed to have conceived a malformed child whom she called Ialdabaoth. Sophia's passions produced elements of the material dark world of mankind. Ialdabaoth thought he was the only god and urged mankind to worship him. From Sophia, her divine spark was trapped within the heart of man. Salvation comes from a redeemer such as Jesus. It is this special knowledge and the spark of Sophia that allows our spirits to be saved."

"I don't know anything about this Valentinus," Thomas said, sitting up. "His concepts are pagan and unnecessary. Jesus taught there is no special knowledge needed to be saved. '*He who believes and is baptized will be saved; but he who does not believe will be condemned.*'[74] '*In him we have redemption through his blood, the forgiveness of sins, according to the riches of his Grace...*'[75] I understand Valentinus also did not believe Jesus lived in a mortal material body. Stephen and I know through our families that Jesus led a material life. He was here more than just as a spirit. Valentinus has no appreciation of why Jesus came to save us. It's important that we teach others through telling the story of Jesus' life, death and resurrection."

"I am grateful to have met you," Baroni said, smiling. "You have the true essence of the real Jesus. I am learning so much. Thank you. From time to time some people begin to boast about their superior knowledge. It may be an attempt to prove their importance and glorified sense of self."

Everyone walked to the new ships to find twenty soldiers standing there. Baroni said, "Thomas I have selected these men to be our guards while traveling on the ships. He then divided the soldiers assigning ten to stay on each ship. Each group had a senior enlisted soldier. He said, "Men you will

---

[74] Ibid, Mark 16:17.
[75] Ibid, Ephesians 1:7.

be guards for the two ships. I want two guards from each ship out here all the time. The two of you senior men divide the times up for your men."

Baroni and the missionaries looked at Thomas who said, "Let's divide our group for the night. Mark, Peter and Paz, you can make yourselves comfortable on the Islander. Mark, you can choose the cabin you want to use and get agreement on the cabin for the soldiers to use. Baroni, Peter, Stephen and I will do the same on the Free Spirit. We need to decide in the morning how we are going to present the story of Jesus tomorrow night. Think about it and let's get some sleep."

✝ Chapter 17 ✝

Feast and Plays in Joppa
Saturday, April 13, 125 A.D.

Thomas awoke in the sleeping quarters of one of his new ships, the Free Spirit, at dawn to the smell of the sea water and the new oil finish. He went up to the top deck to see five soldiers from each ship standing on the pier in the fog. Baroni and the four missionaries walked down the gangplank just as the three from the Islander came down their gangplank. They then went to the dining room in the Inn and joined Principale Pardi. The ship builder's representative came in with the mayor, as they were finishing breakfast.

"Thomas," the mayor said. "Could you and Stephen walk with me to review the events for today and look at the amphitheater?" The mayor led them to the town plaza. The fog cleared but the day was overcast.

People were setting up fire pits, tables, benches and decorations to celebrate the feast and their overnight stay. Workmen were hauling in food while others had set up a location for the dispensing of watered wine and juice.

Bataglia arrived with fifty soldiers. "I will have the soldiers here until dark," he said. "Those who would like to view the presentation in the theater can stay. The rest of them will be free to return to the fort. Pardi will bring in another fifty soldiers before dark."

The mayor led them to the theater that had been built so long ago. It was much like an amphitheatre but had smaller seating areas and a smaller stage. They looked down to see several workmen sweeping the seating areas. Other workmen were scrubbing the stage or performance platform.

"Is there a possibility of trouble from the local Jewish population, or any other religious groups?" Thomas inquired.

"Your group is being sponsored by the Romans," the mayor said. "The message being delivered and posted this morning is described as a Christian play by former Jewish actors from Jerusalem."

"Tribune Cerrone will be here for the play tonight and will participate with Thomas and Stephen," Bataglia said. "He'd like both of you to meet him at the fort a little before dark."

Thomas thanked the mayor and Bataglia. They walked back to the pier. Much to their surprise, wagons arrived with food and their tools and supplies. They went up the gangplank. Peter and the others were busy directing where the food and supplies were to be stored.

"Thomas and Stephen get out of the way," Peter said. "Go sit up on the helmsman's seat over there at the stern while we get all this put away. I want to get to the tools and equipment we brought from Jerusalem. I want the heavier equipment stored on the Islander. The lighter tools I will store on the second lower deck on the Free Spirit."

"Did you check out the sails?" Thomas asked. "Did they get the big red star of David[76] on each of the main sails for both ships?"

Mark nodded, "Peter had the rest of us take all the sails out on the pier. For each ship, we have two main sails each with the big red star. We have four smaller side sails. There are extra parts for the yardarms. There's plenty of line for the sails. There are additional ropes for tying up the ship as well as large extension ropes. We even have extra rudders and control arms. There are brass replacement parts for the side paddles."

"When we get everything put away, we can relax and enjoy this afternoon and evening," Peter said. "We are very prepared to leave tomorrow. Let's hope the fog clears early."

"Let's go on over to the plaza," Stephen suggested.

---

[76] Authors' note: The Jewish star did not start to be used until it was documented in the twelfth century. Christians were known to use the six sided star. The star of two triangles superimposed over each other literally means shield or G-d. Many say it means the Star of David was from God protecting him in his fight with armies much larger than his own. The Star of David is often blue but in this story Thomas chose red.

"Peter and Ben, we'll have food for your lunch brought to the ships," Thomas said.

"Better still, find a couple of maids to bring our lunch," Peter said, smiling.

"We'll see what the mayor suggests," Thomas said.

"Maybe I'll stay here," David joked, as everyone laughed.

As they were going down the gangplank, two men introduced themselves as assistants to the mayor. "The mayor is very busy talking to various citizens, including the Jewish rabbi. He's not happy with the play being held on the Sabbath, so the mayor asked us to lead you to the plaza. He wants to make a speech and introduce you as the leader for the evening entertainment."

They followed the mayor's assistants to the plaza. Much to their surprise, several hundred people were milling around, watching the food preparation.

They were led to an elevated stand. The mayor turned around and smiled. "Come over here and meet our rabbi," he said, and introduced Thomas to an angry looking man.

"I know who you are," the man said. "You should avoid giving blasphemous statements. I say this knowing you will. You should know what could happen."

"First of all, I have been a Christian in the Nazarene Ecclesia all of my life," Thomas said. "Rabbi, you must warn your members. I have seen almost one hundred Jews killed in the past two days. I do not want to see more. And yes, I do know what a blasphemous statement is and the reaction."

"What happened that you saw that many killed?' the rabbi asked. "What happened to them?"

"The rebel army is recruiting men in this area," Thomas said. "One poorly trained unit of one-hundred attacked us the day before yesterday. The Roman army killed all but two of them and burned their bodies."

The Rabbi stood staring, speechless.

"A warning isn't the issue," Thomas said. "Get them under control."

"I will inform my people and warn them as you suggest," the rabbi said, backing away.

"Thomas, please step up on the stand with me," the mayor requested.

They looked out on the milling crowd. The mayor pointed to one of his assistants who picked up a horn and blew three short blasts. The crowd filled in around the stand.

Stephen Thomas White

"Welcome citizens of Joppa," the mayor called out. "The feast will begin soon. There is watered wine available for the adults and juice for the children. Please do not drink more Posca than two goblets this afternoon. It is important to stay out of trouble and do not start any fights. Please be aware that there are Roman soldiers here to keep the peace. They will not hesitate to use lethal force."

The mayor let the crowd absorb what he had told them. "We are fortunate to have the leader of the actors here. He is a special guest of Tribune Cerrone and also the owner of the two ships, the Islander and the Free Spirit, at the pier. We announced them as Jews, but they are not of the Jewish faith. They are Christians in the Nazarene Ecclesia from Jerusalem. This is Thomas, who converted the Tribune to Christianity and baptized him into the Nazarene congregation."

The crowd erupted into discussion. Thomas raised his arms in the air until the crowd was quiet again. "My name is Thomas. We have been asked to be your entertainment tonight at the amphitheater. It is our privilege to be the guests of your city and Tribune Cerrone. We will be presenting a Christian play tonight, which should be both informational and entertaining. We may offend some of you tonight, but we will try to be respectful of those who are not Christians."

Some shouting and talking erupted again. The mayor pointed to the assistant who picked up his horn and blew the short blasts again, quieting the crowd. The mayor threw his arms in the air. "Lunch is served!"

After stepping down from the stand, Thomas asked the mayor, "Could you arrange for some maids to take food for themselves, Peter and Ben to the ships. They will want some Mulsum as well."

"Well at least two in your group are human," the mayor said, smiling. "I'll see to their lunch."

The magistrate came up to say, "We have a table set up for you and the officers, please follow me."

People were in lines for various cooked meats. Other lines were for fresh bread. And still other lines were for the fish being roasted in large green leaves.

Thomas and the others arrived at an area with tables under canopies. Baroni and Markus were there. Standing behind them was the tall, handsome blue-eyed Cerrone. He smiled and said, "We have everything you may want for lunch. Please join us."

They sat down at a large table with benches. The officers' aides brought small courses of the meats, fish, bread and fresh fruits.

"How is your relationship with the people here?" Thomas asked Markus.

"You have changed everything here," he said. "Your relationship with us has enhanced our standing. I do not understand it."

"I don't either," Thomas said.

"Markus," Baroni said. "Thomas and Stephen don't know the power they possess."

"It's our goal to leave a warm-improved knowledge of Christianity among the population," Thomas said. "Even we forget at times that we are missionaries."

After eating, they toured the area, disappointed that many people still had not eaten.

"Why are people still going without food?" Thomas asked the mayor.

"Many of these people are from the country or other towns," he said, looking forlorn.

"But I understood this feast was for anyone who showed up," Cerrone said.

"This is a city expense," the mayor said.

"I want the rest of the people to perceive this to be a Roman feast as well," Cerrone said. "I will pay for the balance. Get those people fed."

The mayor ran out to talk to his assistants. Thomas climbed up on the stand and invited Cerrone to speak.

"No," Cerrone said. "Markus will speak for me. "This is his city."

After a brief moment the aide with the horn came running. Thomas pointed to him. He blew his horn in bursts of three. Everyone came to the stand again.

"I have an announcement," Thomas yelled. "The mayor has provided a great feast, but planned for only city residents. Tribune Cerrone has arranged to enlarge this feast to include guests from outside the city and from other towns."

"More meat is on its way along with more bread and fish," Markus said. "Please be patient. While you wait, more Posca and watered wine is now available. Please, enjoy and thank Rome, Caesar Hadrian and Tribune Cerrone who is here with us." A great cheer went up.

"You're unbelievable Thomas," Markus said. "This could have turned into a riot."

"I thank Jesus for inspiration and Tribune Cerrone for his wisdom."

"This could be a great day for Joppa and for my area of command," Markus said.

"The positive side of this is this is interesting; it is good for Christianity," Cerrone said. "There is another interesting side to this; many of these people are unknown to most people in Joppa and maybe new friendships will occur."

"This could be an opportunity to reduce the recruiting here for the rebel army," Thomas said.

The mayor returned to say, "As I was talking to my messengers, I asked them to spread out and get a feel for the number of people wanting to see the play tonight. Our crowd is about twice what I had expected. There are too many to fit in the amphitheatre if they all want to attend."

The mayor took a big breath and said, "Thomas, what do you think we should do?"

"We will just have to do it twice," Thomas said, laughing. "Do you have any musicians in town?"

"We do, but why?"

"Music is entertaining and calms a crowd," Thomas said. "Could we plan a musical program on the plaza while the plays are performed?"

"That's a wonderful idea. It's short notice, but I think we can do that."

"Are there enough torches to light the plaza and the theater?" Stephen asked.

"There are plenty of torches at the fort," Markus said. "I'll have a group of soldiers bring them over."

"Paz, David and Ben, let's go back to the ships and see how Peter's doing," Mark said. "We shouldn't miss out on meeting the maids."

"Thomas and Stephen, would you be guests of Baroni and me at the fort?" Cerrone requested.

"We have some time before the first play," Thomas said. "We'd be delighted to be your guests."

They headed back to the fort. The other missionaries went to the ships. When Cerrone, Stephen and Thomas got to the fort, Markus met them, saying, "Could I join you?"

"I believe you'd be welcome if you could serve us some of that drink you called Passum," Thomas said, grinning.

"I'm beginning to think you are in charge around here," Cerrone said, laughing with him.

"I'm intrigued with how the plays go," Cerrone said. "I'll be with you in both plays."

Markus poured Passum for everyone.

"Why do the Jews try to fight, when they are so easily overwhelmed?" Baroni asked.

"They would not listen to Jesus when he said, '*What (name) is on the denarius?* 'They said to him, "Caesar's." And he said to them, '*Render therefore to Caesar the things that are Caesar's and to God the things that are God's.*'[77] They believe that the messiah will come, help throw you Romans out and become king," Thomas said. "They don't understand the might of Rome."

"Thomas, why aren't there more Jews like you?" Cerrone asked.

"For starters, the Jews you are talking about follow the faith of Judaism and I am a Nazarene believing the message of Jesus," Thomas said. "It's a clash of belief systems you're talking about. You know that we believe in the salvation that Jesus brought to us. The Jewish religion has rejected that Good News. Many of us have tried to convince them to become followers of Jesus. Many of them have become even more radical, I'm sorry to say."

****

Thomas and Stephen hurried to the Free Spirit to find their men watching the maids dancing in a style strange to them.

"What is this dance?" Stephen asked.

"They call it a dance from the belly," Mark said, smiling.

"Have these maids been here all afternoon?" Thomas asked.

"They came after noon with food and Mulsum," Peter said. "Ben and I ate with them and drank their honey-sweet Mulsum. They danced and told stories that made us laugh. Mark, Paz and David came later and they have continued to entertain us."

"You've had a good time, but the actors are due at the theater," Thomas said.

The missionaries left, but Peter stayed to send off the maids and guard the ships with the soldiers. The missionaries hurried past the plaza and

---

[77] Ibid, Mathew 22:21.

watched briefly as torches were lit. The musicians were setting up on the stand that had been used earlier for announcements.

The theater was full of people in the open air seated in a half circle around the stage. Cerrone and his officers were sitting in the front row. Soldiers were standing around the top of the theater and down both sides. There was a murmur going on until the missionaries began to walk down the steps. By the time they walked onto the stage it was quiet. They positioned themselves to have a good view of each other.

Thomas waved to the mayor who looked up, smiled and came down the steps and threw his arms in the air. They could hear the music start over at the plaza. Thomas gave a sharp whistle. The crowd quieted.

"We are grateful that the actors from Jerusalem agreed to two performances tonight," the mayor shouted. "The gentlemen are in fact Nazarene Christian missionaries who bought the ships, called the Islander and the Free Spirit. They plan to leave here tomorrow or the day after to cruise on their maiden voyage to Caesarea. The play tonight is designed to tell the story of Jesus. May I introduce a new Christian, Tribune Cerrone?"

The mayor went back to his seat. Cerrone walked onto the stage and looked around at the quiet faces in the audience and said, "Centurion Markus and Magistrate Gamaliel and I welcome all of you here tonight. I have enjoyed meeting you fine people from Joppa and surrounding towns and villages. Not long ago I met Thomas and Stephen who prayed for me. I soon became a Christian and have enjoyed their friendships. Thomas and his missionary companions are dedicated to their work. I now introduce you to Thomas."

The audience cheered as Thomas walked to the front of the stage and held up his arms. The crowd became quiet again and he said, "How did you like that feast today?" The crowd cheered. "How did you like that watered wine that was made available for all of you?" This time the cheering and clapping was like thunder.

"The food and the wine were made available by this great city, your own Centurion Markus and Tribune Cerrone. We should give special thanks to Caesar Hadrian. Isn't it wonderful what we can do together?" With some cheering, the crowd started chanting, "Thomas-Thomas-Thomas-Thomas."

"Let the play begin," Thomas shouted.

The audience quieted. Thomas pointed to each missionary as he introduced them, and then they proceeded as they had practiced.

"Who was Jesus?" Thomas said and pointed to David.

"Jesus was born Jeshua Ben Joseph and his name means Jehovah is salvation," David said.

"What was his genealogy?" Thomas asked, pointing to Paz.

"He was of the house of David. He could have been king of Israel, but that honor was given to Herod by our friends the Romans."

Thomas kept asking questions and pointing to one after the other of them for the answers. The transfers went on smoothly until it came back to Thomas who stepped to the front of the stage. "Let me tell you about something Jesus said to a woman in Samaria at Jacob's well, *"Whoever drinks of this water will thirst again, but whoever drinks of the water that I shall give will never thirst. But the water that I shall give him will become in him a fountain of water springing up into everlasting life."*[78]

"Jesus went on to tell her, 'But the hour is coming and now is when the true worshipers will worship the Father in spirit and truth; for the Father is seeking such to worship Him. God is Spirit, and those who worship Him must worship in spirit and truth.'"[79]

"The woman said to Him, 'I know that the Messiah is coming. When He comes, He will tell us all things.'

Jesus said to her, 'I who speak to you am He.'"[80]

Thomas looked at Cerrone who stood up and stepped back onto the stage. "Here is Tribune Cerrone, again," Thomas shouted. "He has the faith and experienced the baptism."

Cerrone smiled and turned to look at each of the missionaries and then to look slowly across the faces in the audience, as they became quiet and sat down. "Please explain the meaning of Jesus' death," Cerrone asked, pointing at Ben.

"Jesus died to atone for our sins," Ben said, walking forward on the stage. "His death was in trade for our forgiveness. His death was for our redemption. He paid the price so animal sacrifice is now meaningless. Paul wrote to the Ephesians saying: *'In him we have redemption through his blood, the forgiveness of sins, according to the riches of his grace which He made to abound toward us in all wisdom and prudence.'*"[81]

---

[78] Ibid, John 4: 13-14.

[79] Ibid, John 4: 23-24.

[80] Ibid, John 4: 25-26.

[81] Ibid, Ephesians 1:7-8.

There was no sound except for the music in the plaza.

"BECAUSE OF JESUS WE'RE SAVED," Cerrone shouted.

The audience jumped to their feet clapping, then sat and quieted, Cerrone pointed to Thomas who said, "Peter was one of Jesus' apostles who came to him and asked, *'Lord, how often shall my brother sin against me, and I forgive him? Up to seven times? Jesus said to him, 'I do not say to you up to seven times, but up to seventy times seven.'"*[82]

Thomas looked at the quiet crowd, waiting for him to continue. "But Jesus cautioned, 'If you are forgiven but do not forgive others who owe you then you will have punishment worse than others.'"[83]

"Luke, who knew Jesus, quoted him, 'Therefore be merciful, just as your Father also is merciful. Judge not, and you shall not be judged. Condemn not, and you shall not be condemned. Forgive, and you will be forgiven. Give and it will be given to you: good measure, pressed down, shaken together, and running over will be put into your bosom. For with the same measure that you use, it will be measured back to you.'"[84]

"Harkin to what Jesus said." Thomas said, throwing his arms in the air and shouting, "WE'RE SAVED!"

Thomas pointed to Cerrone as he went back to his seat. He was clapping and so was everyone. The missionaries then walked up the steps and stood in a line outside of the theater wall. Many of the people shook their hands as they left. Almost everyone headed to the plaza. The last to come up to them were the Roman officers.

"Well, you made that look fun," Cerrone said.

Thomas congratulated him on his participation.

"Thomas, you were different because of the Holy Spirit," Stephen said. "People were moved peacefully. You were on fire."

"I know it was the Holy Spirit," Thomas said. "I'm surprised at times, as to how strongly the Holy Spirit moves me. I feel very animated at times. I think it is going on with all of us."

"I agree that all of you get animated," Cerrone said. "But Thomas, you were really on fire on stage with enthusiasm and animation. You're fun to watch. Your whole group gives off the love of Jesus."

---

[82] Ibid, Mathew 18: 21-22.

[83] Ibid, Mathew 18: 22-35.

[84] Ibid, Luke 7: 36-38.

"I felt the Holy Spirit as never before tonight," Thomas said. "It's good to know that it was not my imagination. I wonder if we will receive the Holy Spirit in this next performance."

"I know you will be filled with the spirit; but we are going to our patio area by the plaza for a glass of juice or watered wine while the theater fills again," Cerrone said. "Please join us?"

"It is an honor to join a fellow actor," Thomas said.

It was only a very short walk to the Roman patio. When they got there, the aides brought grape juice and watered wine in goblets to choose from for everyone. Baroni and Markus sat asking questions about the play. They were really interested in the information.

Pardi, Bagli and Bataglia came in and sat down. "How have the crowds behaved?" Markus asked.

"So far there has been no trouble," Bataglia said. "The additional food, Posca and watered wine were well received. I did send twenty soldiers over to the ships. Many of the people from the first play went on over to look at them. I thought some additional protection would be appropriate."

"All of this morning's fifty soldiers stayed for the play," he said, looking at Cerrone. "Many of them came up to me and offered to stand guard-duty at the plaza so the second group could go to the second play. We have great soldiers with us here."

"I'm please with the second performance," Thomas said. "It allows everybody to experience the power of the Good News."

"The theater is full again," the mayor said, walking up to them. "We have saved seats for the officers and me."

They walked down the side of the amphitheatre, with the mayor in lead. He introduced Cerrone who introduced Thomas who then pointed to each missionary, stating their names. He started with the first few questions which were answered by whomever he pointed to and then asked Stephen a question, "Is Jesus able to forgive our sins?"

Stephen smiled and said, "When Jesus was in Capernaum and a paralytic man demonstrated his faith, Jesus said to the paralytic, 'Son, your sins are forgiven you.' A scribe sitting there said, 'Who can forgive sins but God alone?' Jesus said, 'But that you may know that the Son of Man has power on earth to forgive sins. He said to the paralytic, 'I say to you arise, take up your bed, and go your way to your house.' And immediately, he *arose, took up his bed and went out…'* Clearly, Jesus does have the power to forgive. "[85]

Stephen pointed to Thomas and asked, "Tell us what your great-grandfather did after Jesus' resurrection."

Thomas turned to face the audience, smiled and said, "My great-grandfather was Apostle Thomas who needed proof and appeared to be a doubting man. The first time Jesus appeared to the apostles, Apostle Thomas was not there. *'The other disciples later said to him, 'We have seen the Lord.' But he (Thomas) said to them, 'Unless I see in His hands the print of the nails, and put my finger into the print of the nails, and put my hand into His side, I will not believe.'*"[86]

Thomas looked to the audience turning his head to see as many as he could, then said, "Eight days later, Jesus appeared to His disciples again. *Then He said to Thomas, 'Reach your finger here and look at My hands; and reach your hand here, and put it into My side. Do not be unbelieving, but believing.'*"[87]

Thomas backed up, throwing his arms in the air and said, "What do think my great grandfather said?"

The audience answered saying, "WHAT'D HE SAY?

Thomas smiled and said, "And Thomas answered and said to Him, 'My Lord and my God.' Jesus said to him, 'Thomas, because you have seen Me, you have believed. Blessed are those who have not seen me and yet believed.'"[88]

Stephen continued pointing to other missionaries and asking questions and getting good answers. He then pointed to Thomas and said, "Tell us more,"

Thomas shouted pointing to Cerrone. "Here is Tribune Cerrone again, a new Christian, who I had the honor of recently baptizing."

Cerrone strode onto the stage and pointed to Ben and said, "Tell us the meaning of Jesus' death."

"Jesus died to set us free," Ben said, walking forward. "As Paul wrote to the Ephesians saying, *'In him we have redemption through his blood, the*

---

[85] Ibid, Mark 2: 5, 7, 10, 11 and 12.
[86] Ibid, John 20: 25.
[87] Ibid, John 20: 27.
[88] Ibid, John 20: 28-29.

forgiveness of sins, according to the riches of his grace which He made to abound toward us in all wisdom and prudence.[89] His death was our redemption."

The crowd became very hushed with expectation.

Cerrone walked around the stage with his arms in the air with a firm look on his face. He turned and he looked at Thomas, who pointed at Cerrone. "It's for you Tribune Cerrone."

Cerrone started to smile and turned to look at each of the missionaries and slowly looked at all of the audience. He then repeated himself and shouted, "THANKS TO JESUS, WE'RE SAVED."

The crowd jumped to their feet cheering and clapping. As the crowd quieted, he pointed at Thomas.

"WE ARE SAVED," Thomas shouted.

Cerrone waved and walked back to his seat. Thomas led the missionaries up the stairs and stood in line again. The crowd was mostly from farms and small villages. They kept saying, "I have never experienced anything like the feast and the play."

Everyone wanted to thank them and shake Thomas' hand. They had never seen anyone get animated the way Thomas had. Most of these people had come to stay the night. They slowly made their way to the area cleared for them. Residents gradually went to their homes.

"We will stay one more day," Thomas announced to the Roman officers.

The officers were pleased. The mayor thanked them profusely then left. Baroni and Pardi accompanied the missionaries back to the Free Spirit. They found Peter sitting on the pier talking to a number of soldiers.

"We had most of the people from both plays come by to look at the two ships," Peter said. "There was no trouble, but I was glad to have these Roman soldiers here to watch over the audience and the ships. Ben and I met a man earlier today that could be a good captain for the Islander. He stopped by to introduce himself and said he can find us good seamen. I asked him to come by at dawn."

The soldiers and missionaries resumed their positions on the two ships and slept with the Roman guards on duty on the pier.

---

[89] Ibid, Ephesians 1:7-8.

✝ Chapter 18 ✝

New Christian Ecclesia of Joppa
Sunday, April 14, 125 A.D.

Thomas and his companions slept soundly. They were awakened by a conversation on the pier between the guards and a few men. Peter recognized one of them. He and Thomas walked down the gangplank to talk to the man Peter knew. "Thomas, this is Tamir, the ship captain, I told you about last night," Peter said. "He was the captain of a ship owned by Hadar. He docked it here a week ago and quit when he found out what Hadar was doing for Simeon ben Kosiba. His second mate took over the ship and sailed away. Several of his men quit with him. They are looking for a new assignment."

"Tamir, I'm happy to meet you," Thomas said. "Where did you sail from to get here?"

"I was contacted in Tyre and asked to transport some goods to Gaza," Tamir said. "On the way here, the second-in-command told me the goods were for the rebels to fight the Romans. If I had known that in Tyre, I wouldn't have taken the assignment. Five of the men on the ship worked for me before and wanted off the ship. I docked it here and I told the second-in-command we were quitting. He told me Hadar would track me down and kill me. He sailed the ship out of here with a reduced crew and I guess went on to Gaza."

"Peter is a Christian and a missionary," Thomas said. "I would like the captain and crew of the Islander to also be Christians. Are you firm in the Jewish faith?"

"No, I have never been firm in my Jewish beliefs," Tamir said. "I learned a lot about Christianity in Damascus before coming here. We talked with Ben and Peter about your plans and the fact that Hadar is also after you. Peter recommended I take my men and watch the play last night. We did and after the play, we discussed what we had heard. We decided to become Christians and would be happy to go with you on the Islander."

"I'm pleased to hear you want to become a Christian," Thomas said. "Do you want to be baptized today?"

Tamir looked at the other men around him and then said, "We'd like to be baptized today."

"My last question," Thomas said. "How do I know I can trust you? Could you be a plant by Hadar?"

"You are here with Centurion Baroni," Tamir said. "I've worked for him in the past. I believe we are still friends and that he can vouch for me. Peter says Principale Pardi is here. He knows me as well."

"That is good news," Thomas said. "I want to talk to them. Tribune Cerrone will want to talk to you about the ship you commanded for Hadar."

"Peter, I want you to talk to each of the seamen separately," Thomas said. "Give me your evaluation of each man's capabilities and experience. Decide whether you can work with them. Go give Tamir and his men a tour of the Islander."

****

Thomas and his missionaries met in the dining room a little after sunrise with Baroni and Pardi.

"We interviewed a man who might be our new captain for the Islander," Thomas said. "He says he knows both of you. He says he was the captain of one of Hadar's ships and he quit in Joppa when he found out the goods on his ship were for the rebel army. He says he is from Damascus and his name is Tamir. He said his second in command on the Hadar ship told him Hadar would kill him for quitting."

"Pardi and I know him from work he did for us in Cyprus," Baroni said. "I'm surprised he got mixed up with Hadar, but he can be trusted. Pardi and I will talk to him further. Cerrone will insist on interviewing him. Is Tamir a Christian?"

"No, but he and five seamen with him want to be baptized today," Thomas said. "They attended one of our plays last night. How long will it take to get to Caesarea from Joppa?"

"I've been told it is less than a day's cruise," Baroni said.

"Not to change the subject, but what will we be doing today?" Paz asked.

"There is a need for a Christian congregation and house of worship to be established here," Thomas answered. "We'll get the mayor's and Cerrone's thoughts on this. I would like to go over to the fort to see if any new developments from last night need to be addressed. We need to talk to Cerrone about Tamir."

"Let's go there now," Stephen said.

"Pardi and I will go to the ships and meet with Tamir," Baroni said. "Your companions can come with us. We'll see you at the fort."

When they arrived at the fort, the mayor had already been there for a while and said, "I've been up for a while checking on our guests in the park by the plaza. There is so much excitement. Your play stirred up a hornet's reaction. Some of the Jewish citizens were angry and confused. The other people were eager to become Christians. Others asked if it was another Jewish trick."

"What do you think of establishing a Christian congregation here again?" Thomas asked. "Vespian wiped out the Christian ecclesia here years ago, before the destruction of Jerusalem by Titus."

The mayor closed his eyes. After some time he opened them and smiled. "Thomas, we have Christians here, but it has been over sixty years since we had a bishop. But who would you choose to be that man?"

"Do you have anyone qualified and willing to take the job?" Thomas asked.

"Other than you or one of your missionaries, I do not know," the mayor said.

"Let's talk to Cerrone."

They walked into the reception area. Markus stood talking to Benito, Bataglia and Bagli. Markus looked at Thomas and said, "Now you've done it. We have people from out of the city that will not go home until they can become Christians. We have local citizens at the pier and coming to the fort to find out how they can become Christians. This could be explosive. I hope it doesn't get out of hand."

"Everything will be fine," Thomas said with a grin. "That is what we do. We are Christian missionaries you know."

"Thomas, I think of you as being a politician," Markus said, laughing. "What do you suggest we do?"

"The best way to handle this would be to send soldiers out to the camp area and down to the pier," Thomas said. "Have the soldiers announce at each location that the missionaries will meet with anyone wanting to become a Christian in the plaza at mid-morning."

"You heard what I need done," Markus said to Benito. "Go select three soldiers to make announcements and arrange for thirty soldiers to be there early. Be there with them to make sure they know what to do."

"I'll have another thirty soldiers stationed around the plaza as well," Principale Bagli said. "They could be needed there more than sitting here."

"Do you have a suggestion as to whom we should designate as the initial head of the Joppa Christian congregation?" Thomas asked the mayor.

"This is a strange question for me," the mayor said. "I am not even a Christian. However, there are those who would be good for this, but I do not know their desires. We should see who shows up."

Cerrone came out of his room and said, "I heard your question, Thomas, and I have a suggestion. The magistrate told me he wants to become a Christian. We normally would rotate him as magistrate. But he wants to do something different. He's from Iconium, but does not want to go back there. Should I send for him?"

"I like him and yes, please send for him," Thomas said.

"Please follow me onto the terrace," Cerrone said.

They followed him out through the door to the terrace where a table was set up with benches and two jars of flowers. They all sat. An aide came out with water and juice.

"I enjoy flowers," Markus said. "I have them planted around the terrace here and the fort. These in the jar came from the flower garden at the fort."

"I'd like to complement you on your taste," Thomas said. "These are different from those you had last fall."

"Cerrone, thank you for coming here to Joppa," Markus said. "The rebel Jewish army has recruited many young men from around here. Did you see any other rebel army units besides the one you fought?"

"I can see the value of my visit," Cerrone said. "I thought it was time to check out some of what I had been hearing. To answer your last question, yes, we did see about two hundred rebel soldiers moving toward Caesarea,

Sebaste or more likely Apollonia. I sent riders to warn the Roman garrisons in those towns."

The magistrate came out on the terrace.

"Magistrate Gamaliel," Cerrone said. "You told me you wanted to find something new to do and that you wanted to stay here. You also told me that you would like to become a Christian. Thomas wanted to know if there was anyone who could head up a new Christian congregation and possibly build a house of worship here in Joppa. I think you might be that person."

Gamaliel sat silent, thinking. Finally, he smiled and said, "I never thought about becoming a religious person, but I like the idea. It would be an honor to accept this new leadership position. First, I need to know how to become a Christian."

"We'll baptize you today and any others who have experienced conversion," Thomas said. "We're meeting those interested in baptism at the plaza at mid-morning. You should be there with us."

"I'll see you there," Gamaliel said, leaving.

Baroni, Pardi and Tamir walked onto the terrace.

"Tribune Cerrone," Baroni said. "Do you remember Tamir?"

"Why, yes I do," Cerrone said, standing. "We did business with you in Cyprus, Tyre and Damascus. It's good to see you."

"Thomas interviewed Tamir this morning to possibly be his captain for the Islander," Baroni said. "Pardi and I just met with him and learned about his aborted captain's job with Hadar."

"Tamir, what were you hauling for Hadar?" Cerrone asked.

"Steel swords, knives and clothing were already loaded on the ship before I was asked to captain the ship," Tamir said. "During the voyage, I checked the cargo and asked the first mate what this type of cargo was going to be used for in Gaza. When he told me it was for the rebel army, I pulled the ship into the port here at Joppa and quit. I also took five of my men with me."

"You were smart to do so," Cerrone said. "Thomas, you would have a good man in Tamir. You can trust him."

"Good," Thomas said. "I'll baptize him and his men today. Tamir welcome to the team. Go with us to the plaza."

****

Thomas, Stephen, Baroni and Tamir excused themselves to walk to the ships before going to the plaza. The fog was gone and the weather was clear. When they arrived, there were about sixty people standing around watching Peter swab the deck of the Free Spirit. The twenty soldiers assigned to the ships were positioned around the pier.

As the missionaries walked up the gangplank, the crowd recognized them and began to cheer. When they got on the ship, they turned and waved to their group of admirers. Mark and David came up from below deck.

"Peter, Tamir is highly recommended by Cerrone," Thomas said. "Tamir, inform your men and follow me to the plaza. After the baptisms, bring your personal belongings on the Islander. Inspect the ship for anything you will need. There is food on board now."

The missionaries went down the gangplank and headed for the plaza with Tamir and his men following. The crowd around the ship also headed toward the plaza. As they approached, there were many more people milling around. The mayor was standing next to the platform and smiled as they came up to him.

"Thomas, you have more converts than you may be able to handle," he said.

"Jesus can handle them all," Thomas said, laughing. ""Remember Jesus fed four thousand with seven loaves of bread.[90] Don't worry my friend. We will get started soon and the baptisms will be done rapidly."

He stepped up on the platform, looked over the crowd, the missionaries and then to the mayor. The magistrate came through the crowd to stand by the mayor.

"Thomas-Thomas-Thomas," the crowd chanted.

Thomas raised his arms in the air. Gradually the crowd quieted. "I'm happy to see so many people here who are interested in Jesus, his Good News and are considering conversion to Christianity."

"We came to be baptized," one shouted.

"Thanks for the reminder," Thomas shouted. "Yes, we are here to determine who has converted to Christianity and wants to be baptized today."

"We are forming a new Christian congregation here in Joppa today, "Thomas said, looking around. "To head the new congregation, we have selected a new leader that many of you know. I'm introducing you to the first

---

[90] Ibid, Mark 8: 5.

person who will be baptized. Magistrate Gamaliel, please come up here on the stand. Tribune Cerrone released him so I can appoint him as your bishop. A new magistrate, who is Gamaliel's cousin, will be on the way from Iconium."

The crowd was stunned, looking at each other in surprise.

"I knew about and believed in Christianity," Gamaliel said. "But Thomas and his missionaries convinced me it's time to become a Christian. I hope you experienced the joy that I did. If you did, I welcome you."

"Who wants to be baptized today," Stephen asked, climbing up on the platform. "Those of you, who do, please form seven lines. The lines will be headed up by Peter, Mark, Ben, Paz, David, Thomas and me. We will line up over there. Those of you, who are here to watch, please stay back. When the lines are formed we will proceed to the end of the pier and go into the bay for the baptisms. When we get to the beach, Thomas will take Gamaliel out for the first baptism. The baptisms will be conducted one at a time by each of us, with a prayer and by submersion in the water. The baptism will wash away your sins and your spirit will be reborn again."

The missionaries climbed down off the platform and walked to the edge of the crowd nearest the pier. The seven lines formed up quickly. "Please follow us out to the beach," Thomas shouted.

They started walking; Stephen looked back and saw that about a third of the crowd did not get in a line. The mayor led the group that was not in the lines. The walk was brief. When they arrived, all of the missionaries kneeled and Thomas prayed.

"Thank you, Jesus, for this wonderful place called Joppa and its fine residents. Please bless these new members and accept them into your congregation with the baptisms we will perform today. Please Jesus; bless this new Congregational Ecclesia in Joppa."

Thomas and Gamaliel walked out into the bay until they were waist deep in the water. Thomas held his arms in the air. The water seemed to become still. He looked up to see a flock of ducks flying over the beach and a group of pelicans flying in from the bay.

"God is with us," he shouted, then started the baptism prayer with his hand on Gamaliel's head. He had him submerge himself, then completed the prayer and pulled Gamaliel back up. Both walked to the beach. When they were out of the water, Thomas threw his hands in the air again. "Now meet the official new bishop of Joppa."

There was cheering and clapping.

"Let the baptisms begin with the help of Bishop Gamaliel," Thomas shouted. "The missionary that is at the head of your line will perform your baptism. When your baptism is done, go over to Bishop Gamaliel and the mayor to be registered as a new member of the congregational ecclesia of Joppa. We will start now."

Each missionary took their first in line and walked to a separate part of the beach. The baptisms went on until late morning. The crowd and the new members stayed to watch. During the baptisms the ducks flocked on the beach. The pelicans were clustered in the water by the pier. Hundreds of seagulls flew in and stayed on the water's edge. They seemed fascinated by the crowd.

When the baptisms finished, Bishop Gamaliel came out to say, "Two hundred and thirty-five new members have been baptized. One hundred and twenty were citizens of Joppa and one hundred and fifteen were farmers or from nearby beach villages."

"We're pleased for you to accept these new members into the new Joppa congregation," Thomas announced.

"Let's give thanks to Thomas," Stephen said.

Thomas stepped away and raised his hands. The cheering and yelling started. His hands must have given the pelicans, ducks and seagulls a signal. They all flew into the air and departed in several directions. Thomas lowered his arms when the birds were gone and the crowd quieted. "The spirit of God attracted those birds," he shouted. "They are attracted by the Holy Spirit. We are living in a very explosive time with such exposure to the Holy Spirit. I believe this is a very nascent time of a whole new beginning. The growth of Christianity represents a zeal we have never experienced before; who knows what will happen next."

****

The missionaries walked to the Free Spirit. Tamir and his five men came by and they congratulated them on becoming new Christians. On the deck of the Islander, the mayor and the new bishop of Joppa caught up with the missionaries.

"We would like to invite you to lunch at the inn," the mayor said. "What you just said about this being a nascent time intrigues me. I want to hear more. Most of these new members were not Jews. It's too early to tell what's coming. It's unclear, very nebulous, but it's surely filling a strong need in everybody."

"Well, we are hungry and this will be a good time to talk further with Bishop Gamaliel," Thomas said happily.

They walked into the Inn. Cerrone and Baroni were standing with the innkeeper. A large table had been prepared and the mayor directed them to that table. The Roman officers congratulated everyone, and then chose seats on each side of the table. The innkeeper, his wife and waiters brought Mulsum and juice for everyone.

"We are pleased with the establishment of the congregational ecclesia in Joppa," Baroni said. "Bishop Gamaliel, you are charged with locating or building a meeting place for your new congregation. We suspect your new flock will grow and you will need to select at least two more members to assist you."

Markus came into the inn and selected a vacant chair at the end of the table. "I heard about the large number of new Christian baptisms," he said. "I'm pleased that you, Gamaliel, have become Bishop Gamaliel. Your new flock will give our city some balance. I will provide you with whatever assistance and protection I can. Cerrone is going to request additional soldiers for my command. The rebel Jewish army is becoming a serious threat here. Hopefully, the unity of a Christian ecclesia will help stop some of the recruiting by the rebels."

The waiters served roast lamb, fish, bread and fruit. Watered wine was brought. As they ate and enjoyed the moment, everyone talked about the baptism ceremony, the attraction of the large number of birds and the diversity of the new converts.

Cerrone stood. "Baroni is accompanying Thomas and his missionaries aboard one of the ships going to Caesarea," he announced. "Peter will stay with the Free Spirit and Tamir will stay with the Islander in Caesarea. Baroni and the six missionaries will ride by horseback to Jerusalem. Markus and I must get back to the fort to prepare for my departure in the morning. Thomas, good luck and we will see you again in a few days back at the palace in Jerusalem."

The two Roman officers left the inn. The innkeeper came to the table to offer a sweet drink and special bread. Baroni nodded. The waiters brought out the sweet drink in special goblets and sweet bread.

Thomas pulled from his robe some Roman coins and handed them to the innkeeper who was delighted. "Those coins are to pay for our meals," he said to Bishop Gamaliel, "The Nasi of the Nazarene ecclesia in Jerusalem gave Cerrone and me papyrus rolls with words of Mark, Mathew, Luke, John, Paul, Barnabas and others. He has several scribes working on more. I am sure Nasi Judah can send you copies. The Nazi can also get you a copy of the Talmud or Torah, which has the Jewish literature and the prophecies concerning Christ."

When their drinks were gone, the mayor and Bishop Gamaliel stood and wished the missionaries a safe voyage and a good trip back to Jerusalem.

When they were gone, Baroni and the missionaries walked out of the inn.

Upon the arrival at the Free Spirit, Peter and Tamir stood staring at them.

"Dinner will be brought to us after dark," Thomas said. "And yes, I am sure the maids will be here."

"In the meantime, let's bring up the three sails and lines from below," Peter said. "Tamir, go do the same on the Islander."

Mark, Ben and David hauled the mainsail up to the others and laid the mainsail down on the deck. The other sails were handed up one at a time and finally, the necessary lines. Thomas looked over to the Islander to see they had their sails on the deck.

"Thinking about today's events, we seem to be at the forefront of explosive growth in Christianity." Stephen said. "I've never seen anything like the excitement at the play and the large number of baptisms we experienced today. It's turning out to be a very different journey than we planned."

Thomas said, "Let me remind you, Jesus gave me five missions. The first is to find the Island-of-Dreams. The second is to move the documents and relics. The third is to perform missionary work. And the fourth is to move the Nazarenes and fifth to develop the Christian religion. My guess is the missionary effort will be much more productive and demanding than anything I ever dreamed. Never the less, I'm tired."

Everyone but Peter found a spot on one of the decks to take a nap. Thomas awoke later to the sound of wheels rolling along the wooden pier. He looked out to see six maids walking behind a large cart. He jumped up. Peter had quietly lit torches on the pier and in several locations on the Free Spirit. Peter walked down the gangplank and welcomed the very attractive young maids.

"Can you stay while we eat," he asked.

"We have come from the inn with your dinners and would like to serve you now," the first maid said, smiling coyly. "We can stay until you finish dinner, then we must take the dishes and cart back to the inn."

"We'll eat on the deck of the Free Spirit," Thomas said, leaning over the railing. "Tamir bring your men over here for dinner."

When everyone finished eating, the plates, utensils and the table were returned to the carts. "You have enough juice and Chalybonium for one last goblet each," one of the maids said. "We can't stay. Your goblets and amphoras are gifts from the innkeeper. Good night."

Relaxing, they enjoyed finishing their drinks.

"I would like to assign who will be on each ship for the voyages tomorrow," Thomas said. "Since we will leave early in the morning, you should sleep on your assigned ship. I want ten soldiers on each ship. Tamir, I want three of your men to join us on the Free Spirit. You decide who should come over here. Mark, David and Paz, you have already been assigned to the Islander."

Those changing ships moved their personal belongings and Peter and Tamir confirmed cabin and bunk bed sleeping location assignments. Everyone on both ships bedded down for the night.

✝ **Chapter 19** ✝

Sailing to Caesarea
Monday, April 15, 125 A.D.

They were awakened during the night by a storm. The ships rocked around on their mooring lines. Lightning and thunder flashed and crashed. Then it started to rain hard. Two new ships had rowed in close, crashed against the pier and then slid back out. Men cried out. Peter, Tamir, Thomas and Baroni jumped out of their bunks to see what the problem was. The wind was about to shove the ships onto the pier.

They ran over to help the men on the newly arrived ships tie down. They nabbed their lines and tied them tight, pulling the ships snug against the pier. Thomas was not sure who they were. The weather was so bad they couldn't take time to talk to them, but they appeared to be a tough looking crew.

They ran back to the ships to their bunks. When they awoke later, the rain had stopped. They could hear shouting and got up again to find a number of Roman soldiers by the two ships. It was starting to get light, but it was hard to see through the light fog. They could barely make out three ships behind the ships they had tied down.

"Everyone, stay here and I'll see what this is all about," Mark said.

He was gone for a while and then came running back and said, "I talked to one of the sailors. He was rude, pushy and used foul language. Those ships are being taken over by the Romans."

Baroni was standing looking over the rail. "I think they're pirate ships," he said. "The Romans want the crews to come out unarmed, but they are refusing. A battle will probably take place soon."

Pardi came running down the pier with about twenty soldiers. He had his men surround the two ships to support the soldiers that had come from the three Roman ships.

"Centurion Baroni, you and the missionaries should move your ships out before we attack those ships," Pardi said, coming over to the Free Spirit. "Let me help untie the lines."

Thomas and Mark pushed the Free Spirit away from the pier with the oars. Peter stood on the transom with the rudder bar in both hands. The missionaries and seamen stepped down into the rowing seats and engaged their oars. They pulled the Free Spirit around the three Roman ships and out of the bay where they caught a light wind. Thomas looked back to the Islander to see it come around the ships at the pier. Both ships pulled further out into the sea with their oars. The mainsails on both ships were tied to the yardarms and pulled up. They caught the wind and skimmed away from Joppa. They looked back to the pier. Fighting was going on, arrows and spears flying. Smoke rose from one of the two pirate ships.

"That was close," Peter said. "It's good to be gone. What a wild morning."

He guided the Free Spirit far enough away from the coast to avoid hitting any sand bars or rocks. The Islander was along their port side, further out to sea. With the wind to their backs, they put the oars away. The side sails were raised which gave more speed.

About mid-morning, they encountered two Roman ships leaving the small pier at Apollonia. The first ship hailed them to stop. All sails on both ships were pulled down. The first Roman ship came quickly along side. "Where did you depart from?" a soldier called.

"We departed the Joppa pier after sunrise," Baroni yelled.

"Have you seen any pirate ships?"

"Your ships and the army in Joppa surrounded them and were fighting at the pier when we left," Thomas shouted.

The soldier saluted to them and they began to row off into the wind. The sails were pulled up again and they continued towards Caesarea with a steady wind.

Ben went below to get bread, dates and a water bag. The water bag was passed around a few times until it was dry. They enjoyed watching a flock of pelicans flying in formation between The Free Spirit and the beach.

The weather became glorious, both ships handling very well. Peter was in his glory. Ben took over the bar to the side paddles during lunch and he was pleased with how responsive the Free Spirit was to changing the rudder paddles and how the sails responded to the attached lines. Peter ordered Ben to change the pitch on the side sails. The mainsail moved easily with one line. They practiced slowing the ship and speeding up by changing the pitch of the three sails. The practice helped them to learn the feel and personality of the new ship. Thomas and Peter commented on how well Tamir and his crew were managing the Islander further out to sea, but staying with the Free Spirit. Just then the main sail swung towards the port side and knocked Stephen over into the water.

Peter screamed at Ben for lack of a warning. He had the sails pulled down. Stephen was a distance behind the ship swimming towards them. Thomas threw a line which dragged slowly along the water as he kept letting more out. Finally, Stephen caught the rope and was then pulled to the back of the ship. He climbed up the ship and around the tender tied to the back.

"I'm disappointed, Peter," Thomas said. "You should have warned us about that problem."

"Ben, that should be a lesson to everyone," Peter said. "I'm at fault for not training everyone to shout a warning when changing the main sail. Never the less, Ben, we all must use our head with changes to the mainsail."

Peter stopped to study the map. "Caesarea should be right ahead," he said.

Soon the land with Herod's Caesarea Palace jutting out on the promontory at Caesarea was visible. They took down the small sails and manned the oars. Peter took over the bar from Ben. The mainsail was kept up as they sailed towards the man-made marina and the narrow opening to the pier.

The main sail was pulled down. The missionaries and seamen had their oars ready to pull the Free Spirit to the pier. A small boat came out towards them with three soldiers standing, two others rowing. They came along side of the Free Spirit and one soldier threw a boarding ladder over the starboard rail. He climbed on deck and stood up. Baroni was there to meet him.

"I am Principale Guido," said the soldier. "I will guide you into the pier where both ships can be moored for as long as you need."

"Principale Guido, did you expect us?" Thomas asked.

"Yes, we knew you were coming. The Free Spirit and the Islander both stopped here on their way from Cyprus to Joppa. Both ships were the talk of the town. Tribune Cerrone sent word with a soldier to warn us about the two hundred Jewish rebel army units headed our way. He confirmed you would soon be here. Tribune Mascaro has your assigned patrol unit for tomorrow ready and invites some of you to dinner tonight in his quarters at the Caesarea Fort. I will take the rest of the missionaries to the non-commissioned officers' quarters. Row the ships to where those soldiers are pointing."

The Free Spirit and the Islander bumped the pier with a side platform between them. Two soldiers tied the lines to the cleats. Peter knew both of them and they each hugged him.

Baroni and the soldiers on both ships met on the pier and he said, "Your assignment is to stay here with the ships and provide additional security until the missionaries return.

Thomas said to Tamir and Peter, "We'll be back in two weeks, maybe less. I want both of you to stay here with the ships and recruit five more seamen and six more men to be used as seamen and provide security when we stop in other ports. Tamir you can keep your five seamen with you on the Islander. The new recruits should be Christians or be willing to become Christians, but I will leave it up to your judgment. "

"Peter and Tamir you will have your own security with these twenty soldiers," Guido said. "However, there are full time guards here day and night."

Guido turned to Thomas and Baroni and said, "I will lead you to Sebaste in the morning. On our trip we are on horses because we will need to ride fast with all the rebel units seen between here and there."

He led Baroni and the six missionaries down the street to the fort. Walking through the gates and into the officer's quarters, they were met by Centurion Taccone who saluted to Baroni and said, "We have dinner set up in the non-commissioned officers' quarters. Tribune Mascaro would like Thomas, Stephen, Centurion Baroni and me to join him for dinner with his Lady. David, Mark, Ben and Paz please follow Principale Guido."

Thomas and Stephen followed the officers. They came into the dining room where a beautiful lady held the arm of a man in a familiar uniform with purple strips who said, "Centurion Baroni, it is good to see you again. Welcome. Please join us for dinner."

"May I introduce missionaries Thomas and Stephen to you," Taccone said. "Thomas and Stephen may I introduce you to Tribune Mascaro and Lady Lydia?"

Mascaro was tall like Cerrone, a young officer and looked very regal. His black hair and brown eyes sparkled in the candlelight. Meeting Lady Lydia was a pleasant surprise for she was quite lovely and gracious. She wore a beautiful conservative gown. Her light brown hair was combed to a luster falling down her back. Her slender hand lay on Mascaro's arm. Two aides brought goblets of water and juice. Others went about lighting candles.

"Thomas and Stephen, Lady Lydia and I welcome you to Caesarea," Mascaro said. "Taccone has arranged for Principale Guido to accompany you to Fort Sebaste tomorrow. Tonight, we hope you will enjoy dinner with us. If we are at dinner and we are not in front of our soldiers or the public, you can drop our titles when addressing us."

"Lady Lydia, my great grandmother was named Lydia," Stephen said. "I have always loved that name. She was a sister of Jesus. Apostle Thomas was a brother of Jesus and is Thomas' great grandfather."

"It is an honor for us to dine here with you," Thomas said to Lady Lydia. "Please forgive us, if we speak a little rough. It seems that we spend most of our time with our missionary companions and soldiers."

"I do not know very many Christians, although I understand there are a large number in Caesarea," Lady Lydia said. "I met many Christians in Cyprus. Stephen, thank you. I didn't know Jesus had a sister named Lydia. It's sweet that she was your great grandmother."

"Dinner has been prepared for us," Mascaro said. "Shall we find a place at the dining table?"

He sat at the end of the table and suggested Thomas sit on his right and Stephen on his left. Baroni sat next to Thomas. Taccone seated Lady Lydia at the other end of the table and then took a seat next to Stephen. The two aides took their water goblets away in exchange for wine goblets. They returned with amphoras and poured white wine.

"This is called Mareoticum, grown in Egypt and is one-third wine and two-thirds water. Adding water makes it very smooth."

The aides brought out a salad of watercress, cucumbers and green onions with a vinegar and olive oil dressing. Radishes and olives were served on the side.

"Cerrone told me about the Roman custom of client and Patron," Thomas said. "I would be pleased to be your client in the future."

Stephen Thomas White

"Yes, Thomas that custom is appropriate for us," Mascaro said. "I believe you and I will have reason to look out for each other. It sounds like you understand the relationship, so I accept that obligation. These relationships become more important to us as time goes by. Enough said."

"I'm pleased with this future relationship in the future," Lady Lydia said.

"Thomas, I am not a Christian, but I was educated about Christianity when I lived in Rome," Mascaro said. "I learned much more in Cyprus. Apostle Paul was an important bearer of the Good News of Jesus. I understand he wrote several letters that have been preserved. From a Roman's viewpoint, he was well respected, even though our crazy Caesar Nero had him killed. Apostle Paul's adopted father was an important Roman Senator by the name of Pudens whose son was Rufus Pudens Pudentianna, the aide-de-camp of the Roman general, Aulus Plautonius. Rufus was Paul's half-brother who married Gladys, the daughter of the British Pendragon Caractacus who was living in exile in Rome. The Pudens lived in the British palace; a large estate on one of the four hills overlooking Rome called Palladium Britannica. They were neighbors with Caesar Claudius. This British home later became the Nazarene ecclesia. Rufus Pudens and his wife, Claudia, claimed Apostle Paul's martyred body and buried him in the family cemetery on the Via Ostensia. Did you know that?"[91]

"I knew that Paul was a Roman citizen, but I didn't know how important his adopted father and half brother were," Thomas said. "Peter stayed with Paul's relatives whenever he was in Rome. He stayed there when he ordained Clements as the second Bishop of Rome. Clements was converted by Barnabas and Joseph of Arimathea when they were in Britain. He came to Caesarea to meet Apostle Peter.[92] Saulus, before he became Apostle Paul, incited a group who forced Joseph of Arimathea, Clements,

---

[91] The relationship of the Roman family of Pudens and the British Silurian family is documented in Usher, *British Ecclesiastic Antiquities 19,* Archdeacon William's, *Claudia and Pudens*; *St Paul in Britain* by Rev. R.W. Morgan, Conybeare and Howson's *Life and Epistles of St. Paul*, Vol II, p. 581,582,584,585, Baronius' *Annales Ecclesiastic*, Vol. 1, p. 228, re Vol 2, Sec. 56, p. 56, 64; Sec IV and V, pp. 111-112; Sec I and II, Ibid, George F. Jowett, pages 148 and 150; and Ibid, Lionel Smithet Lewis, pages 23-26.
[92] Ibid, Lionel Smithet Lewis, page 93.

Lazarus, Martha, Mary Magdalene and several others onto a boat without oars or sail in Caesarea. They landed in Marseilles and went on to Glastonbury Britain. While all of them were in Glastonbury, they developed the School of Avalon. After a few years, Clements went on to Rome and Lazarus, his sisters and several others moved to Gaul."[93]

Stephen said, "I can add to the story of Paul. Not long after Saul sent everyone off to Marseilles, he was sent by Jonathon ben Ananas, the Sadducean High Priest, to Damascus to look for and bring back some of the Apostles. But Jesus visited him on the road. Saul, after being blind for three days, changed his name to Paul.[94] Years later he visited Rome and ordained Linus, a Silurian Prince from Britain, as the first bishop of Rome. Linus was the son of the captured and British Pendragon, Caractacus. Sometime later Linus was martyred and Apostle Peter ordained Clements."

Baroni looked back and forth and said, "General Aulus Plautonius captured the Silurian family in Britain after sixty battles. Caractacus was betrayed by his cousin. They were brought to Rome in chains and paraded before the population. Caractacus was allowed to testify before the Roman senate. Caractacus' daughter, Gladys, refused to leave her father, and became the first female or child to stand in the Roman Senate. The Roman senate gave Caractacus a standing ovation after his speech. They granted him and his family freedom conditioned that he remain in Rome for seven years and swear to never take up a sword against Rome again."

"In Britain, General Aulus Plautonius married Gladys, Caractacus's sister, who changed her name to Pomponia Graecinia," Mascaro said. "This Gladys was converted to Christianity in Britain by Joseph of Arimathea before the Silurian family was captured. Caractacus' daughter Gladys was adopted into the family of Claudius Caesar and renamed Claudia. A year after the senate trial, she married Rufus Pudens, Paul's half brother."

"We have a copy of Apostle Paul's letters," Thomas said. "They are wonderful and we try to read them as often as we can. Paul mentions, *'Eubulus greets you, as well as Pudens, Linus and Claudia.'*[95] Eubulus is Aristobolus. I guess Pudens is Rufus Pudens, Claudia is his wife and Linus is Claudia's brother. He also says, *'Greet those who are of the household of*

---

[93] Ibid, Lionel Smithet Lewis, pages 93-95.
[94] Ibid, Acts 8: 1-19.
[95] Ibid, II Timothy 4: 20.

Aristobolus.[96] He says, '*Likewise greet the church that is in their house.*'[97] Their house was the British Royal Palace, the Palladium Britannia in Rome."

"This history is going to be important to Stephen and me after we find the Island-of-Dreams," Thomas said. "I expect we will be visiting both Britain and the Marseilles area where descendents of converts by Joseph of Arimathea, Lazarus, his sisters and others settled and brought the Good News of Jesus."

"I love this history," Baroni said, "But to change the subject, Mascaro, did you receive the warning we sent to you of the two hundred Jewish rebel soldiers headed your way?"

"The warning of the rebel unit was appreciated," Taccone said. "We have not heard of an attack by them here or at Sebaste."

Mascaro said. "On another subject, we have now heard Hadar is importing horses and other tools of war into Israel for the Bar Kokba movement."

"Thomas, what is this Jewish army?" Lady Lydia asked. "You said they are rebels."

"Most Jews have never consented to any outside power ruling them. There are many radical elements within the Jewish faith which are led by a man named Simeon ben Kosiba, who is known by his messianic title of Bar Kokba.[98] He believes he is the Messiah who has come to remove the Romans. They do not believe the Messiah could be Jesus. That is why so many Jews reject Jesus."

"We should be giving this Christian faith our support," Lady Lydia said to Mascaro.

"We are starting to do just that," Mascaro said. "Rome doesn't kill as many Christians as we used to. I was telling you just yesterday about Governor Pliny's[99] suggestion to Caesar Trajan about fifteen years ago. He

---

[96] Ibid, Romans 16: 10.

[97] Ibid, Romans 16: 5.

[98] www.ancientwarfare.com: Simon bar Kokba.

[99] Trajan's letter back to Pliny--You observed proper procedure, my dear Pliny, in sifting the cases of those who had been denounced to you as Christians. For it is not possible to lay down any general rule to serve as a kind of fixed standard. They are not to be sought out; if they are denounced and proved guilty, they are to be punished, with this reservation, that whoever denies that he is a Christian and really

said it may be illegal under Roman law to kill Christians just because of their religious beliefs. Trajan agreed and ordered that only Christians who are committing documented crimes would be punished."

"There have been many Christian martyrs," Thomas said. "Some were killed by Romans and some were killed by the Jews. I hope Governor Pliny's advice is followed."

"Maybe we should talk of more pleasant matters," Lady Lydia said. "I have been finding the views of Christians and Jews to be so different from what I grew up being taught. We Romans have our various gods which allow people to worship a favorite god. I never knew anyone to argue with such passion over just one god like the Jews and now the Christians do. What is even more interesting is the belief in an afterlife and resurrection by the Christians. This is so different from what we learned. I am curious and want to learn more."

"It was interesting the way you described the differences you have observed with gentiles, Jews and Christians," Thomas said. "You did not show any animosity. I grew up with quite a different view of religion than you and am convinced that we, as Christians, are acting through the will of Jesus. I hope this doesn't make you angry."

"No, you don't make me angry," Lady Lydia said. "Your words are respectful. I know you will do very well as a Christian missionary."

They fell quiet as the aides started clearing the salad plates and the goblets. They brought in the new Taenioticum wine with water and goblets. Then the aides returned with the main entrée of roast lamb and fish with fresh wild berry slaw. They ate quietly for a while.

"My husband and I have heard Christian conversions are occurring all over the Roman Empire. Do you think you will be involved in this explosive growth in the non-Jewish population? Tell me, Thomas, what are your future plans?"

Thomas smiled, "To answer your question Lady Lydia, we will return to Jerusalem to get our supplies and tools. We will be coming back through

---

proves it--that is, by worshiping our gods--even though he was under suspicion in the past, shall obtain pardon through repentance. But anonymously posted accusations ought to have no place in any prosecution. For this is both a dangerous kind of precedent and out of keeping with the spirit of our age.

here to load everything onto the Free Spirit and the Islander. We have been astounded by the acceptance of the story of Jesus, the conversions and the baptisms in Joppa. It has made us wonder how much of our future will be tied up in the conversion of what we call the gentile population. I hope calling you gentiles does not offend you."

"Being called a gentile is funny and does not offend me," She said, laughing. "I've heard about both of your ships. I am sure you will be astounded by your future missionary success. My guess is you will be very busy. I understand the Islander will be the construction ship and the Free Spirit will used to bring you back to Israel and make other voyages. I'm sure the gentiles are anxious to hear the Good News of Jesus. I know I am. These are very unsettled times and you men are the only ones giving us good news and real hope for the future."

Thomas said. "Lady Lydia, once we return here and load the ships, we plan to sail into the Mediterranean to find a small island I saw in a dream. Once we find this island, we plan to build a house of worship and houses there. We will plant some gardens and a vineyard. When we have the house of worship under construction, we will visit Gaul, Britain and Espania. Some of us will return here and travel onto Jerusalem. Cerrone is using us as bait to try to capture Hadar and expects us to do some other work in exchange for the security he has given us and expects to provide us after we leave here. Eventually, we will transport our family records, artifacts, family and friends to the Island-of-Dreams. Many of our family and friends will likely move to Gaul, Britain or Espania."

"Cerrone sent me notice of the security he is providing you," Mascaro said. "Pasquali in Sebaste and I will participate in your security. I don't know what else he wants you to do."

"Lady Lydia and Mascaro, thank you for your gracious hospitality and lively conversation," Thomas said. "We must excuse ourselves and get some sleep for the trek in the morning."

"Thomas and Stephen, thank you for joining us and sharing your future plans," Mascaro said. "I know Cerrone was converted to Christianity and respects both of you a great deal. We look forward to your return. Lydia and I hope we can have dinner and talk more about Christian history."

"Thank you for sharing your knowledge of Apostle Paul," Thomas said. "I hope we can do this again."

"Thomas and Stephen, we hope you will join us in the officers' quarters," Taccone said. "Your fellow missionaries are being taken care of by Principale Guido."

Thomas and Stephen thanked their hosts and departed with Taccone and Baroni.

"I had Guido send two soldiers back to the ships to retrieve the Roman uniforms for the six of you to use on your trip back to Jerusalem," Taccone said, as they walked to the officers' quarters. "You may have to ride hard and may even need to defend yourselves. You will need to pack your personal clothing and sandals in saddlebags."

When they arrived at their quarters, the Roman uniforms, weapons and saddle bags were on their beds. Taccone came to each of them to say, "We will awaken you in time for some breakfast before you leave," he said. "Have a good night's rest. You will need it."

"I'm afraid I'm enjoying these Romans more than I expected," Thomas whispered, before he drifted off to sleep.

† Chapter 20 †

Riding Horseback to Sebaste
Tuesday, April 16, 125 A.D.

Stephen and Thomas did not awaken until Baroni pounded on their door. They got up, dressed in their Roman uniforms and packed their clothing in their saddle bags. They walked down to the corral and found their companions and Guido eating breakfast. They ate quickly and then found their horses ready for their departure. The thirty soldier patrol unit was already mounted up. Guido and the six missionaries mounted their horses. Thomas struggled with some fear in his heart, remembering the killing on the way to Joppa and then comforted himself, knowing Jesus would protect him and the other missionaries.

After Guido led them out of the fort, Thomas looked back towards Caesarea and the pier. Both had some cloud cover, but it was clear at the fort. When everyone cleared the gate, they set a fairly fast trot. Guido told them it would take half a day to get to Sebaste. After a short period letting the horses gallop, they slowed to a walk. The lead soldier held his arm in the air, the signal to halt and be quiet. He turned his horse around and rode back to Guido.

"There are people walking ahead of us," he said.

"Could it be a rebel army unit?" Thomas asked.

"It sounds like men marching towards us," he said. "It could be the rebel army."

Guido ordered the unit and the missionaries to ride into some trees for cover and quietly wait. They went about three hundred paces from the road. The men marching on the road numbered about one hundred.

Guido sent one soldier back to the fort at Caesarea to warn them. The marching rebels stopped when they saw the soldier on horseback ride towards Caesarea. Their leader looked around, but did not see the group in the trees. He turned his men around and marched back the way they came. Guido watched them march off on a side road and then waited for a while before returning to the main road. They reached the top of a hill and stopped to rest the horses. After a short time, the soldier who had gone back to the fort returned to report to Guido.

"I warned Centurion Taccone," he said. "He sent me back here."

"They took a road going south," Guido said. "We need to keep moving."

After an hour or more, they stopped at a stream, took a break and let their horses have a drink. All of them refilled their water bags. They mounted up and walked their horses in formation for a while.

"This is a flat area so let's allow the horses to gallop again," Guido said. "We'll be at Fort Sebaste soon."

Galloping and then walking the horses a little farther, Thomas could see the road with the rows of Roman pillars lining the road in Sebaste. They entered the gates to the fort, walked their horses to the corral and gave the reins to the groomers.

Bataglia came out to greet them. "Bagli and I just arrived with our men this morning," he said. "We had a nice trip back to Jerusalem from Joppa. Cerrone showed us around and treated us to a great dinner. Centurion Felone is staying until you return, Centurion Baroni. We left at sunrise this morning and rode hard without seeing any Jewish rebels. I'll go with you tomorrow with my patrol unit. I'm looking forward to seeing Jerusalem again. Who doesn't like visiting the palace?"

"It was an honor to lead you and your missionary companions to Sebaste," Guido said. "I'll leave you now. I must take my patrol unit back to Caesarea in the morning. You wore your Roman army uniforms well and no one fell off their horse. I am sure I will see you on your return trip to Caesarea when you set sail on your new ships."

"Bataglia, please take these four missionaries to the junior officers' quarters and set them up for tonight's stay," Baroni said. "Thomas and Stephen, we must find out why we have not been met by an officer."

They walked towards the officers' quarters and were greeted by an officer in a familiar purple stripped uniform. He walked up to Baroni, saluted and said, "I am Tribune Pasquali. I have been expecting you. Come in and we can talk."

They walked into the reception area and out onto the terrace. They found benches and relaxed.

"Sir, why wasn't a Centurion officer here to greet us?" Baroni asked. "Is something wrong?"

"When the soldier you sent to warn us that the rebel army might be heading our way, I decided we could not just sit here," Pasquali said. "I sent one hundred and twenty men out under the command of Centurion Natali to look for them. He had Principales Rizzo and Tyrus under his command. They encountered the two hundred rebels on the road to Caesarea and they were headed this way. Eighty of our soldiers were on foot. The rebels were warned to turn back, but they came on anyway. Centurion Natali sent twenty soldiers on horseback to hit one side of the advancing Jews. Centurion Natali was on his horse and took a spear through his chest. He and twelve of the soldiers on horseback were also killed, including Principale Tyrus. Forty-five foot soldiers were killed and Principale Rizzo brought back twenty wounded soldiers. Two have had legs amputated and four lost arms. It was a tragic loss.

Pasquali caught his breath and said, "The rebels are learning more about war. They were stubborn and fought well. In the end over a hundred rebels were killed. The rest hauled and dragged off a number of wounded men. The others ran back the way they came. While I am still very angry at our losses, the death of over a hundred Jews also gives me great pain. We are not here to kill them, but what can we do when they attack us? It will be a never ending conflict, since they believe their God is on their side."

It was quiet as everyone took in what he had said, and then Pasquali continued, "I have sent a soldier with a message for Mascaro in Caesarea. Governor Rufus is in Rome to request more soldiers to be transferred to Judea. Hopefully, Mascaro can get word to Governor Rufus. Now do you know why you were not greeted as you should have been?"

"I am sorry," Baroni said. "I was too quick to suggest lack of protocol. We are indebted to you and your soldiers. We encountered about a hundred rebels in a formation on the way here from Caesarea. They saw the messenger that was sent by Principale Guido. They turned around and went back on a road that goes south."

"I hope that Governor Rufus is successful in Rome with his request for more soldiers," Pasquali said, as he stood. "My chef is sick, so our food service tonight will be less than it should be. However, his assistants have prepared a good meal. We plan to dine a little early so you can get a good night's rest. Please, let's go into the dining room."

The aide brought them their choice of juice or watered wine in new goblets. Two assistants served salads.

"Did you have dinner in Caesarea with Mascaro?" Pasquali inquired.

"Yes, and we were privileged to meet Lady Lydia at dinner," Thomas responded. "That was very enjoyable for us."

"You were fortunate to meet her. She is a delight and a highlight when meeting Mascaro," Pasquali said. "How did you like the Free Spirit and the Islander?"

"They are fantastic and easy to sail," Thomas said. "Learning to sail was exciting. The wind has a mind of its own. May I ask how you know about the ships?"

"Several of us were transferred here from Cyprus," Pasquali said, smiling. "All of us know that shipbuilder. We even know about your conversion of Cerrone and his baptism into Christianity. It's common knowledge that you plan to find a special island and build a house of worship there. As you know, we are very supportive of your efforts and your safety. It will be a grand and rewarding venture. Did you find it strange that you arrived in Roman uniforms and we still knew who you were?"

"Yes, I was surprised," Stephen said.

Baroni leaned forward and said, "Thomas and Stephen have discussed with Cerrone and Mascaro the agreement to establish the Roman custom of client and Patron. I would advise you, Thomas and Stephen establish that kind of relationship with Pasquali as well."

"I was assuming we were, Pasquali said. "Thank you for the clarification, Baroni. I'm pleased to be your Patron, Thomas and Stephen. With this Bar Kokba movement and this Hadar supplying them, I need you and you need me. We have a common problem as client and Patron."

"Stephen and I are in your debt as your clients. I'm pleased and thank you."

The assistant came back and served the steaming dish of meat and vegetables with hot bread.

"We are so grateful to all of your fellow officers," Thomas said. "We pray that Jesus helps us as much as you and others have helped us. We are establishing these workable relationships and we will not treat our obligations lightly."

"While we've been traveling, we have had several occasions to discuss non-Christian concepts," Baroni said, smiling. "I know you have encountered these types of concepts in your travels as well. Thomas and his companions cover the basic truth in Christianity in the plays they have conducted."

"Yes, we have discussed these concepts among ourselves," Thomas noted. "Yet there are these questions, like where do our spirits go when we die? We just keep them to ourselves. Jesus was silent on these subjects."

"I have had discussions many times about where your spirit or soul goes when you die," Pasquali said, looking perplexed. "I only want to know if I will live beyond this life. I think your Jesus says we can. We can't know what God's plan could be for eternity; but we can appreciate he has a plan."

"Jesus says we will all be resurrected when he returns," Stephen explained. "This is part of the Good News and why we say you will be saved if you believe in Jesus and are baptized. We are clearly central to God's plan."

"Did you talk to Mascaro about his knowledge of Christianity?" Pasquali asked. "He prides himself in what he knows."

"We had an interesting discussion about Apostle Paul and his adopted father, an important Roman Senator by the name of Pudens and his half-brother Rufus Pudens," Thomas said.

"I'm surprised he didn't talk about Apostle Peter," Pasquali said. "Mascaro knows quite a bit about Apostle Peter's wife and in-laws."

"What do you know about them?" Baroni asked.

"Apostle Peter married Perpetua[100]," Pasquali said. "She was the daughter of Aristobolus who was the son of Herod of Chalcis.[101] Aristobolus had a brother named Barnabas, a sister named Mary and a nephew, John Mark, who was Mary's son. Since they were grandchildren of Herod the Great, they and their father were very wealthy. Herod of Chalcis had his own

---

[100] Ibid, Mark 1-29-31. (Peter's mother-in law was Aristobolus' wife).
[101] Ibid, Lionel Smithett Lewis, M.A., pages 119- 120.

area of northern Judea to rule. Aristobolus helped Apostle Peter and Perpetua acquire a very nice Roman villa in Capernaum. Jesus must have chosen Apostle Peter to be in charge of missionary work throughout the world, partly because Apostle Peter had the wealth to travel as he wished."

"That's interesting," Stephen said. "Aristobolus' sister Mary owned the home in Jerusalem that is now the Nazarene synagogue. The second floor was used for the last dinner before the Passover that Jesus had with his Apostles before he was crucified the next day. Mary's son, John Mark, gave the house to James the Just to be used by the Nazarene Ecclesia. Nasi Judah and the Nazarene Ecclesia use it regularly today. All of us have been to regular worship meetings conducted there by Nasi Judah. John Mark wrote 'The first Gospel According to Mark."

"We now have a copy of 'The Gospel According to Mark,' Thomas said. "We also have copies of the gospels by other apostles and disciples."

"I understand Apostle Paul sent Aristobolus to Glastonbury Britain with Bran the Druid, the father of Caractacus, to become the second bishop of Britain,"[102] Baroni said. "Before that, Apostle Phillip sent Joseph of Arimathea with twelve companions to Britain to be its first bishop."[103]

"You had a lot of success in Joppa with all the conversions and baptisms," Pasquali said. "Is this the start of something big for Christianity? Could it be the nascent of new Christian conversions? It's truly a new birth."

"We were surprised and talked about this possibility," Thomas said, grinning. "This may be the birth of substantial growth of Christianity for the gentile population. It's beyond our understanding and I feel certain it's not accidental."

"I keep learning more about Jesus' friends and family," Pasquali said. "Let's talk about this some more when you come back to take your building equipment to your ships."

"Yes, it's getting late. You have given us a great meal, and conversation," Thomas said. "I pray your trouble with the rebels ends soon. Because of a man named Simeon ben Kosiba, now known as Bar Kokba, it will not end soon and for that reason we are sorry. There is no clear way to tell what the future will bring."

---

[102] Ibid, Lionel Smithett Lewis, M.A., pages 118-119.
[103] Ibid, Lionel Smithett Lewis, M.A., pages 100-101.

"Baroni, please show Thomas and Stephen to the Officers' quarters," Pasquali said. "Have a good night."

They stood, said good night and went directly to the officers' quarters and to bed.

✝ **Chapter 21** ✝

A Detour to Jerusalem
Wednesday, April 17, 125 A.D.

During the night, Thomas woke up thinking about the plans to find the Island-of-Dreams. He found his plans continuing to be more complicated, but had enjoyed himself with Mascaro and Pasquali. They were such quality people. Will Jesus approve of his relations as a client to these Romans?

They were awakened before daylight by Baroni. They dressed in their Roman uniforms and were served some bread, honey and raisins. The thirty soldiers in the patrol unit had eaten, were getting their horses saddled and filling their water bags. Their horses were brought to them with saddles on. They checked their water bags and made sure their personal items in the saddle bags were tied securely.

"You missionaries look good in your Roman uniforms," Bataglia said. "If you're ready, we can leave."

"We are more than ready," Thomas said. "We are excited."

"Principale Bataglia, let's go," Baroni said.

They were led out of the corral, through the fort grounds and out the gates. In a while they came to a road that led up an incline. Bataglia had them stop to rest the horses just below the top of the ridge. He sent one of the soldiers ahead to scout the area on top. The soldier galloped his horse back over the incline leaning forward. "There are at least a hundred Jews in formation marching our way," he shouted. "They have a scout ahead of them. He'll be coming over the rise anytime."

Bataglia conversed briefly with Baroni and agreed it would be wise to retreat and go through the demolished town of Shechem. He sent the scout ahead of them, and they left at full gallop. The road to Shechem was halfway back to Fort Sebaste. When they arrived at the Shechem road, they stopped to rest the horses again. Then Bataglia led them along the road at a steady walk. Wild flowers were blooming. They talked about how nice it would be if they didn't have to worry about the rebel army coming at them.

After traveling for a short while, they saw about twenty rebel soldiers and five women carrying bows and arrows. Bataglia whispered, "Let's walk our horse into the trees and let them pass."

Bataglia had them wait quietly until the rebel men and women walked on by, and then came back to the road and walked a short distance.

"We'll stop here and have lunch," Bataglia said.

After a short break and lunch, they rode around Shechem, which had been a small walled community, but lay in ruins since it was destroyed by Alexander the Great and captured by the Seleucid Governor John Hyrcanus.[104] There were a few houses that had been rebuilt by some Samaritans but no one watched them.

Thomas said as they walked their horses, "Akiva's daughter Sahar lived here for a while but she has since moved to the big house next to mine in Jerusalem. Her great grandfather was Apostle James the Just, my great grandfather's brother. I don't see how she lived over here. But she didn't get crucified either."

In the late afternoon, they came to a stream.

"Centurion Baroni, I think we will spend the night here," Bataglia said.

They went about five hundred paces off the road near the stream. The area had trees and brush.

"It will be necessary to mount up and run in case a larger group of rebels come by," Bataglia said. "I want soldiers to patrol and others to guard the camp. We will set up three areas for the horses to avoid congestion in

---

[104] Biblical Archaeology Review, November/December 2010 – Volume 36, Number 6. The Samaritan Temple on Mt. Gerizim (Bells, Pendants, Snakes & Stones) by Yitzhak Magen, Page 26. (Author's note; Caesar Hadrian rebuilt Shechem after the Bar Kokba war after 136 A. D. as a reward for helping fight the Jews in the Bar Kokba war.)

case we need to leave in a hurry. Keep the saddles on but loosen the cinch straps."

A fire-pit was constructed and all vegetation around it removed. Several soldiers searched for fire-wood and built a large blaze. The sun went down and it was getting dark.

"We could roast some birds for dinner, if we had any," Bataglia said, with a wry laugh.

Thomas stepped forward to say, "Let us missionaries go hunt for some birds."

Several soldiers thought it was pretty funny, but the missionaries set off on foot into the trees. Thomas had them split up in three pairs. They looked for birds sleeping in lower branches then sneaked up and grabbed them by the neck. When they had killed about twenty wild hens, they walked back to camp.

The soldiers muttered among themselves, sure the missionaries either used magic or were holier than they thought. Thomas supervised the cleaning and skinning of the birds. Baroni had six spits made from cut limbs to slide the birds on for roasting.

After the birds were roasted and everyone had eaten some, a conversation started around the fire. Several soldiers wanted to know more about Christianity. They also wanted to hear how God helped them hunt the birds. Thomas asked Stephen to tell a brief version of Jesus' life and history. Stephen finished the story with an explanation of how they are saved through grace, if they believe in Jesus and receive a baptism. The soldiers were intently listening. Thomas thought they needed to hear more and explained how they caught the sleeping birds.

Another soldier wanted to know how the missionaries' lives were changed as Christians and what their plans included. Thomas assigned Ben the job of explaining the groups' role as missionaries. He got up and walked around the fire gesturing and talking. Thomas assigned David to tell them about their mission to find the Island-of-Dreams, build a house of worship and return to take some records back to the island for storage. Several of the soldiers wanted to go with them.

"Thomas, would you tell us why you have the support of the Roman army," Bataglia requested.

"The Governor of Cyprus was converted to Christianity by Apostle Paul and Barnabas about eighty years ago," Thomas said. "The Roman officers in command in Israel now served time in Cyprus and met many Christians there. Stephen and I converted Tribune Cerrone in Jerusalem to Christianity with a miracle that healed his wounded leg and convinced him to become a Christian. Cerrone has arranged for our security in exchange for our assistance in helping catch Hadar."

Bataglia thanked them and ordered everyone to get some sleep.

✝ Chapter 22 ✝

Packing Records and Relics
Thursday, April 18, 125 A.D.

Before sunrise, they mounted their horses. Bread was handed out and they left for Jerusalem as the sun was rising. A scout was sent ahead as they walked their horses on a steady pace and soon came to the Damascus gate at mid-day. When they arrived at the palace, everyone dismounted and retrieved their personal items from the saddlebags. Thomas thanked Bataglia.

Baroni invited Thomas and Stephen to join him in seeing Cerrone. The other four missionaries excused themselves and left. The three walked into the reception area. Cerrone came out from the terrace with three Jews, who left in a huff. He came over to salute Baroni and welcome Thomas and Stephen. H led them back out onto the terrace.

"Those Jews say they represent the High Priests," he said. "I told them they are imposters since their leader is Simeon ben Kosiba. They came to make demands I would not grant. One request was to search Jerusalem for old temple records and relics on behalf of Hadar, who is now going after everyone. How was your trip?"

Baroni told about leaving Joppa and visits in Caesarea and Sebaste. Thomas described the conversations with Mascaro and Pasquali, including the client and Patron discussions with both. They described Pasquali's battle and loses and the encounters on the way from Sebaste. Baroni described the rebels they saw going to Sebaste, the one that caused them to detour through Shechem and the small group close to old Shechem.

"Mascaro and Pasquali are fine important men," Cerrone said. "I'm pleased you talked about the Patron subject with each of them."

"How was your trip back from Joppa? Baroni asked. "Did you see any more rebel units?"

"Our trip back was uneventful," Cerrone noted. "We saw many more citizens going both ways, compared to our trip when you were with us. We also made it back in a day and a half. It sounds like the rebels were over in the Samaria area. Governor Rufus is in Rome, but should return soon. He listened to us complain about the rebel Jewish army and is trying to get at least five-thousand soldiers transferred here to deal with our problems. We have seen how moving about the country is very dangerous now."

"We have seen more rebels than I thought we'd see," Thomas said. "Have you seen Rebecca since you're back?"

"Yes, I invited her over to have dinner with me two nights ago," Cerrone said. "She's such a charming lady. We talked and talked. She told me about growing up and her short marriage to Nasi Joseph. His death was such a tragedy for her. I told her about my life growing up. She wanted to know about my wife who died giving birth to our first child. Rebecca was so sympathetic. I'm falling in love with her and I think she would be a wonderful hostess to help me in my career."

Thomas nodded. "My aunt told me that Rebecca was an organized person when she was the Nasi's wife. I've always admired her. If you married her, you'd improve your position in this city. Believe it or not she is friends with many Jewish women in Jerusalem. If you marry a local woman like Rebecca, she could help you while you live in Jerusalem and help you enter the local community wherever you are sent."

"Thank you for your kind advice," Cerrone said. "I assume you had dinner with Mascaro and Lady Lydia. Did you talk about anything interesting with him?"

"Yes, Mascaro is very knowledgeable about Christian history," Baroni said. "He talked about Apostle Paul and his family."

"I was fascinated by the information about the British Silurian family," Thomas said.

"Did you talk about anything interesting with Pasquali," Cerrone asked. "He is, also, pretty knowledgeable about what's happened in the Christian world."

"Yes, we talked about Apostle Peter's family," Thomas said. "The relationship of Apostles Paul, Peter and others in their involvement in Rome and Britain is fascinating."

"It sounds like you had fun and learned some information from my fellow officers," Cerrone said. "I know you're anxious to get on with your search for the Island-of-Dreams. Thomas, when do you expect to leave for Caesarea?"

"We would like to leave tomorrow, if we can be ready," Thomas said.

"Be ready in the morning," Baroni said. "We'll have Pardi go there at daybreak with wagons, drivers and guards."

"Are you coming with us?" Thomas asked Baroni.

Baroni turned to look at Cerrone then back to Thomas. "I need to talk to my superior," he said. "We'll let you know after we have talked privately."

Thomas and Stephen excused themselves and left for the Thomas estate. As they walked, there were many Jews milling around in groups. They listened to one group whose spokesman was telling about the Romans killing men in the Jewish army. He was demanding justice. "They kill our men and burn them like they are waste lumber."

This inflamed the crowd because of the Jewish belief that the entire body must be buried before dark. Thomas and Stephen decided to quietly leave. They walked faster, realizing they were still wearing their Roman army uniforms.

"It keeps getting worse and the ultimate clash is coming," Stephen said. "Something will occur to set off an all-out war."

"If Rome sends only five-thousand troops, it could be disastrous," Thomas said. "I'm afraid fifty thousand will not be enough. It's bad wherever we go. Rome will have to fight all fronts at the same time."

"These people must have thought we were Romans, yet they kept on talking," Stephen said. "They're becoming brazen and that scares me."

When they arrived at the Thomas estate and Neta came in from a different direction. "They know you are here," Neta said. "Your Roman uniforms don't fool Hadar's men, but they seem to be holding back. Bardo has six more men coming to give us more coverage at night. They'll be here shortly to put up another tent. If you go to the tomb, wait until my men surround the house and the neighborhood to keep Hadar's men from seeing what you do. We may never have enough men, Thomas, you must leave soon."

They met with Ben on the way to the house. "Paz, Mark, and David went home for the night," he said. "They checked the remaining tools and supplies and are a little concerned about leaving tomorrow, but agreed it had to be. Your family is waiting for you."

Thomas went in the house to hug Ada and Cleophas. Leah and Elizabeth were gracious, but conservative. "Ben tells me you took possession of the ships and are happy with them," Cleophas said. "Let's go into the great room."

Thomas, Stephen and Ben took turns telling them about everything that happened on their trip.

"We need to go out to the tomb and bring some gold and silver bars into the house," Thomas said. "Neta has six more men coming and wants me to wait until he and his enlarged group have surrounded the area. He'll let me know."

"I made two wooden boxes for the gold and silver you wanted," Cleophas said. "I also acquired four clay jars like we discussed with wood stoppers and a jar of wax. We should pack the wood boxes Adam built and brought over here last fall. You need them packed and put in the second room."

When they sat down to eat, Thomas said, "Cleophas, we saw Jewish rebels wherever we traveled. The battles with the Romans are becoming more frequent. I believe there is going to be an all-out rebellion and war within a few years. You should talk to your children about leaving Israel and coming with us when we leave with the records and relics. Talk to Neta, his men and their families about coming with us. Inform Jacob and Amira. Also inform Sahar. All of us will be in great danger."

"What if Nasi Judah and others want to go," Cleophas said. "If the Jews rebel again, we could see destruction and death as bad as or worse than when Vespian and Titus came here sixty years ago."

"When we find the Island-of-Dreams, we will get construction started on the homes and the house of worship," Thomas said. "Stephen and I will travel to Gaul to locate descendents of Lazarus and others to choose a place for our friends and relatives to relocate. I don't want to take the records and relics until the vault and house of worship are close to completion which likely will be the year after next. I will see if the Romans can help transport whoever wants to relocate. I think it will be a good time for Nazarenes to safely leave. If it gets really bad, get word to Cerrone. He will get your message to me. I hope the war doesn't explode before then."

Someone knocked on the door. Thomas answered and Neta said, "I have my men in place and the area is secured. I suggest you come out and do your work now."

Thomas got up. "Let's get busy. Bring what we need to the tomb. I'll take the torches and open the first door."

Two torches were set in the first room. Thomas unlocked the door to the second room, and Stephen set two torches in there. They took the writings of Apostle Thomas and the records from the temple and put them in three clay jars and sealed with stoppers and wax. The gold and silver bars were packed in the wood boxes brought by Cleophas and moved to the house.

Thomas and Cleophas sealed the jars from the cave with wax and packed them and the jars with the writings and temple records in three wood boxes with padding. The mercy seat was lifted from the Ark of the Covenant. He pulled the Ephod and Breastplate out. Inside the Ark were two flat stones with writing. "These must be the second set of tablets with the Ten Commandments God made and gave to Moses."[105] Thomas said. "We must wrap them separately before we put them back in the Ark.[106] It makes me nervous to hold such ancient and holy stone tablets.[107]"

He wrapped the tablets and placed both back into the Ark with one on top of the other. Thomas put the pure gold crown in a small pad and packed it on top of the wrapped tablets. He repacked the Ephod and Breastplate with the Urim and Thummim then replaced them back the bag. He placed the bag into the Ark and replaced the mercy seat. The Ark of the Covenant was set down in the big wood box and packed tight.

"Cleophas, the records of Moses, King David and King Solomon were saved by some Jews when Babylon destroyed the temple more than seven hundred years ago," Thomas said. "Some other Jews saved the relics we found in the two rooms in the cave at that same time. Now because of the Sadducean priests, Dan and Guy, we have the records and the relics here to be transported to the Island-of-Dreams. The Ark of the Covenant, Ephod and

---

[105] Ibid, Exodus 34: 1-4 and d 29.

[106] Ibid, I Kings 8: 9 (There was nothing in the ark except the two tablets of stone which Moses put there at Horeb, when the Lord made a covenant with the children of Israel, when they came out of the land of Egypt). This excerpt describes the condition of the Ark and the tablets in 986 B.C. at the dedication of Solomon's Temple.

[107] Authors note. The tablets were the second set and were created in 1314 B.C. by God at the time when Moses saw the burning bush. See Jewish Virtual Library, A Division of American-Israeli Cooperative Enterprise.

Breastplate with the Urim and Thummim and stone tablets were made by Moses and God. I believe this is what Jesus instructed me to save.[108] I hope we can find the Island-of-Dreams without any incident. I pray that we can move this without the ship sinking. Jesus told me he will instruct me on how to build the vault and pack it."

When they left the tomb, locking both doors behind them, Neta said, "The men saw several Jews milling around who could be Hadar's men. I'm glad Bardo's men are staying the night."

Thomas and the others were sitting in the great room when Cleophas said, "We were in a service at the Nazarene ecclesia. Cerrone said he can't understand why the Jewish community doesn't seek peace, strive for unity and be cooperative with the Roman effort to help Jerusalem be more like the city was during King David's reign. He said Jewish beliefs demand they can't be obligated to another country or group like Rome. They believe their calling is to be a dominating world leader like King David was."

"I'm not surprised to hear he said that," Stephen said. "But I believe the whole nation of Israel may turn into a war zone. I think something will happen soon to set it in motion."

"Cerrone thought more missionary work should be done in Jerusalem," Cleophas said.

"Jesus told me in my dream to follow the lead of Apostle Paul," Thomas said. "Even he could not convert people in Jerusalem without getting into trouble. Paul was connected to the Greek and Roman world so he went there. He found that people of the world outside of Jerusalem were eager for some good news. They knew little of forgiveness or hope. We have learned that can be the heart of our message, as we meet people and tell the Jesus story and his Good News. We found that to be true in Joppa but not here in Jerusalem." He sighed deeply. "What will the future bring?"

They ate and got to bed early.

---

[108] Authors note. The reader can decide how reasonable this story is for priests to have saved almost all of the items in or used in the Holy of Hollies room before the Babylonians came in to destroy the temple in 586 B.C. But it appears that if the priests were to save and hide the Arch of the Covenant they would have saved all of the other relics used in the Holy of Hollies room, as well.

† Chapter 23 †

To Sebaste, the Play and Baptisms
Friday, April 19, 125 A.D.

After breakfast, Paz, Mark and David came carrying their personal items and wearing their Roman uniforms. Thomas, Stephen and Ben walked out, also dressed in their Roman uniforms and talked to Neta. About that time twenty Roman soldiers on horseback came to the Thomas estate, with six extra horses on halters. They were followed by ten wagons pulled by teams of horses. The Roman in charge was their friend, Pardi. The soldiers on horseback dismounted and held the reins to the twenty-six horses.

Neta opened the gates and let the Romans pull the wagons into the compound. Neta and several men loaded the equipment while the drivers kept the loads balanced. They loaded the boxes with gold and silver bars with the clothing, sleeping mats and personal items onto the tenth wagon. The items on each wagon were covered with rough linen covers and tied down. The wagons moved up the lane, were loaded and moved around the olive tree and tents back down to the road. When the ten wagons were on the street, the missionaries mounted the extra horses and waved to Cleophas, Ada, Neta and his men.

Riding along, Thomas said to Stephen, "I hope Hadar's men think we have taken the temple records with us. That's why I wanted everything covered. I hope this plan will protect my family."

They arrived at the palace to be greeted by Bardo and sixty soldiers on horseback. With eighty mounted soldiers, they proceeded out of Jerusalem in the early morning, enjoying the beautiful weather and birds singing. Many people came out and watched them as they rode along. As they approached the Damascus Gate, they were joined by another twenty mounted soldiers, led by Baroni. They had six wagons with food, water and wine for their trip to the coast.

Baroni put Pardi in charge of the soldiers leading the wagons. Bardo was in charge of the soldiers following the wagons. The procession continued down the hill away from the city.

They traveled until midday when Pardi, selected a wooded site with a stream of water to stop. It was a very private place to have lunch, rest and let the horses eat and have water. The drivers of the food handed out prepared meats and fruits for lunch.

Baroni and Pardi discussed the problems they had encountered on their return from Caesarea to Jerusalem. Even though they had run across rebels a few times, the rebels they'd seen had marched away. Word must have gotten out about how many of them had been killed in clashes with the Romans.

After lunch, the drivers climbed back on their wagons. The missionaries and soldiers mounted the horses and were ready to leave, but just then thirty Roman soldiers rode up on horseback led by Bataglia.

"We'll follow you to the fort," he said. "We have rebel trouble-makers to track down over the next few days. What my soldiers and I want to do tonight is hear your Christian lectures at Fort Sebaste."

As they traveled at a good pace, Baroni told a little about the history of Sebaste. "Herod the Great started his first project after becoming king here," Baroni told Thomas. "He renamed the city Augustus which is Sebaste in Greek. He built this roadway with over six hundred columns leading to a public forum and a basilica. There was considerable destruction when Titus and his army came through, before attacking Jerusalem. Herod's stadium was built into a hillside which we will use tonight. The temple is further up the hill overlooking the whole area."

They entered the fort's gates and left their horses, walking out of the parade-ground and up the path to the officers' quarters. As they entered the command headquarters, they were met by Pasquali. He was almost like an old friend now, taller than Thomas remembered. His hair and neatly trimmed beard were quite gray.

"I still have not received replacements for the soldiers and officers killed last week," he said.

"We'll check in Caesarea on your request," Baroni said. "You certainly need them. After we left to travel to Jerusalem, we met over a hundred Jewish rebel soldiers who caused us to backtrack and go through Shechem. We went around twenty rebel soldiers and four women rebel archers."

"I hate all these rebels marching around," Pasquali said. "Thomas, let's go out to the parade ground. I want to check on dinner and make announcements for your Christian lecture or play for tonight."

****

As the sun started to set, torches were lit around the food lines and the trail to the stadium area. The serving was done at five locations. Everyone went to their area and lined up. Pasquali announced that the soldiers and cooks were free after dinner to return to their barracks or to go to the stadium for the lectures on Christianity. Much to the missionaries' surprise most elected to attend the lectures.

"What kind of reaction do you think these soldiers will have to our play," Thomas asked. "Will it be just entertainment to them, or are they truly interested in the Good News of Jesus?"

"I believe you will be surprised by their reaction," Pasquali said. "I've heard there will be great curiosity. Do not be surprised if many of them want to convert to Christianity and be baptized."

Pasquali climbed onto the stage. He looked at the soldiers in the audience. "It's my pleasure to let you hear what our guests will have to say about Christianity. Most of you are aware that these missionaries converted our commander in Jerusalem, Tribune Cerrone, into Christianity. I will start the program tonight by introducing the leader of the missionaries. They are in Roman uniforms for their own protection. Now, I give you Thomas."

As Thomas stepped in front to begin, everyone stood and applauded. He waited until they were seated again.

"Tribune Pasquali is right, do not be confused by our uniforms," he said. "We are not Roman soldiers, although my missionary companions and I are very impressed with all of you. I thank both Tribunes Cerrone and Pasquali for their support and hospitality. We have been fortunate to have Centurion Baroni and Principales Pardi and Bardo traveling with us. Principale Bataglia has also been helpful to us."

When the shouting and cheering died down, Thomas told of his mission to find an island and build a house of worship.

"Tonight we will discuss Jesus Christ," he said. "We will be presenting the information in what some have called a play. It should be fun and informative. It's fun for us because it is good news. How long has it been since you heard good news?"

Thomas started by explaining there were several prophesies predicting Jesus. They spent a while asking and answering questions about events in the ministry of Jesus. Then he pointed to one after the other of his missionaries to answer questions about friends and family of Jesus. He then pointed at Stephen to continue. Stephen started with a review of Jesus' differences with the Jewish priesthood and how it led to his arrest and trial leading to his death on the cross.

"Jesus was identified to the temple guards with a kiss by one on his own apostles, Judas Iscariot," Stephen said. "When the guards laid hands on Jesus, Apostle Peter cut of the ear of the guard with his sword. Jesus said to him, '…*do you think that I cannot now pray to My Father, and He will provide Me with more than twelve legions of angels? How then could the Scriptures be fulfilled, that it must happen thus? In that hour Jesus said to the multitudes, Have you come out, as against a robber, with swords and clubs to take Me? I sat daily with you, teaching in the temple, and you did not seize Me. But all this was done that the Scriptures of the prophets might be fulfilled.*'[109]

Jesus went through with these events even though he had the power to stop it. The traitor, false trial and crucifixion were predicted in the scriptures. The death of Jesus was an act of Pontius Pilate, completing Jesus' mission of being tried and killed for all men's sins."

For some reason these troops and drivers were captivated by this concept and liked it. Stephen then pointed to Mark. Mark continued explaining the death of Jesus and interment in the garden tomb. He also explained that the tomb was actually Jesus' great uncle Joseph of Arimathea's burial tomb. Mark then pointed to David.

David reviewed the Jewish Sabbath concept which includes Saturday and special Jewish holidays. He explained how Joseph of Arimathea negotiated to have Jesus taken down from the cross and interred before dark on that Wednesday. Joseph of Arimathea, a Roman Decurio, was helped by a friend of Jesus, Nicodemus. He explained that the Jewish Sabbath of Passover was on Thursday and was measured from sunset on Wednesday and ended at sunset on the Passover Sabbath on Thursday. He went on to explain how Mary Magdalene went to the burial cave early on Sunday morning the day after the second Sabbath of that week. She found the round stone had

---

[109] Ibid, Mathew 26: 49-56.

been blown away, lying flat on the ground several cubits away. The centurion was standing back in awe and the temple guards had run away.

David then pointed to Ben who explained how they found that Jesus' body was gone, even though there was a centurion and temple guards watching the entrance.

Ben pointed to Paz who said, "Jesus met Mary Magdalene outside of the tomb and told her, 'Do not cling to Me, for I have not yet ascended to My Father; but go to My brethren and say to them, 'I am ascending to My Father and your Father, and to My God and your God.' Mary Magdalene ran and told the disciples that she had seen the Lord, and that He had spoken these things to her. Then, the same day at evening, when the doors were shut where the disciples were assembled for fear of the Jews, Jesus came and stood in their midst, and said to them, 'Peace be with you. Now when He had said this, He showed them His hands and side. Then the disciples were glad when they saw the Lord. Then Jesus said to them again, Peace to you! As the Father has sent Me, I also send you. And when He had said this, He breathed on them, and said to them, Receive the Holy Spirit. If you forgive the sins of any, they are forgiven them; if you retain the sins of any, they are retained."[110]

At this point, Paz pointed back to Thomas, who looked into the eyes of many in the audience and asked, "Do you feel guilty for what you must do for the army?"

The audience murmured and shuffled their sandals. Thomas threw his arms in the air. "YOU ARE FORGIVEN," he shouted.

Some in the audience leaped to their feet, clapping and shouting. Thomas calmed them down. "If Tribune Pasquali would grant permission, we will be available all day tomorrow for those who wish for baptism at a nearby stream."

Thomas ended with a prayer, and then Pasquali came onto the stage.

"I hereby grant permission to any of you who want baptism tomorrow," he announced. "You must, however, notify your superiors by sunrise."

The soldiers started leaving in a mass of confusion, but eventually the stadium cleared out. The officers and missionaries went directly to their rooms.

---

[110] Ibid, John 20:26-29.

"Once we leave Judea and the Roman support, I'll miss having a separate room and bed," Thomas whispered as he knelt to pray. "Jesus, thank you for the influence you have exercised with our Roman friends. Thank you for blessing us on this trip. Help us deal with the explosion the zeal and joy of the gentiles who hear your story and Good News. Your blessing is a powerful rousing of love and hope that is being shared with us. Please bless the men in the rebel army that they may soon see the folly of their fight."

Saturday, April 20, 125 A.D.

Thomas came out of his room as the sun was rising and was greeted by Stephen and Baroni. They went to the terrace, where Pasquali was seated, talking to one of the cooks about breakfast.

"Pasquali, do you have a feel for the number of soldiers who want to be baptized?" Baroni asked.

"I don't have an exact count, but I believe there will be more than two-hundred-fifty soldiers, plus Principales Bataglia, Pardi, Bardo and me. I sent one hundred men to the stream for security, with all these rebels lurking about. None of them had wanted to be baptized."

"We are pleased that you have chosen to become a Christian," Thomas said. "May we be honored to do your baptism first?"

After everyone finished breakfast, they went with the guards to the stream. There were several lines of soldiers in their tunics only. Thomas lined them up into six lines.

"Your Commander, Tribune Pasquali, will be the first to be baptized," Thomas announced. "Will you honor him by watching him become the first new Christian this morning? Tribune Pasquali, please remove your armor and leathers."

Just then there came a sound of wings flapping and a flock of seagulls landed on the opposite side of the lake. Wild hens and pheasants flew in from the trees to land by the seagulls. Everyone was surprised and a hush came over the men. Thomas said, "The birds are attracted to the Holy Spirit. Do not fear."

Pasquali took off his leathers, armor, sword and short knife, handing them to Pardi and Bataglia. Thomas and Pasquali then walked into the stream where it widened into a large pond. Thomas had Pasquali kneel down, and then put his hand on top of his head. He started the prayer, lowered Pasquali under the water briefly and then finished the baptism prayer. Thomas pulled him out of the water and they waded to the shore to clapping and cheering. Two aides handed him a large towel, helped him change his tunic and put on his leathers and armor.

After Bataglia, Pardi and Bardo were baptized, Thomas and his companions began baptizing the soldiers. By mid-day they were done. When Thomas lifted his arms in the air and started to thank Jesus, the seagulls flew away. The wild hens ran through the trees and the pheasants flew off in a burst of air and flapping wings. Thomas announced, "The Holy Spirit has departed."

Everyone walked back to the fort. Soldiers were talking about the birds and the wonder of the baptisms they had experienced.

"I feel greatly blessed that we have baptized over two-hundred-ninety soldiers and twenty drivers, as new Christians," Thomas said to Stephen.

Their cooks came over to the missionaries. They had talked amongst themselves and had decided they wanted to be baptized. "Great, we will meet you at the stream in the morning after breakfast," Thomas said.

During dinner, Pasquali said, "I lost my wife in a shipwreck when she was traveling to meet me in an earlier duty in Egypt. I'm pleased to be a Christian, but I wish she could have been baptized before her death."

"That makes her death even more of a tragedy," Thomas said. "I'm sorry we never met her."

✝ Chapter 24 ✝

Camping for Baroni
Sunday, April 21, 125 A.D.

They were up again before sunrise for breakfast and then went with their guards, cooks and soldiers from Fort Sebaste to the stream. When they arrived at the stream fifty soldiers were standing guard. There were a large flock of seagulls nestled around the pond. Thomas and Stephen baptized the cooks while some of the wild hens walked in to watch. When they finished the wild birds were gone and the seagulls flew through the trees. They returned to the fort and learned Baroni had organized the wagons with their drivers sitting on board. The hundred mounted soldiers were ready. The missionaries walked to the front of the line to thank Pasquali. They wished him great happiness.

"I have never met anyone like you," Pasquali said. "I will designate one of our soldiers to be our fort Christian leader. We will work towards starting Christian services at the fort for the new Christians and any others who wish to join. I am sorry we could not talk further about Christian history."

"You have a good plan," Thomas replied. "I recommend you send your Christian designate to Nasi Judah in Jerusalem and request his assistance. Have him request Judah to supply copies of the apostle and disciple writings, as well as a copy of the Torah."

"You give good advice and I will," Pasquali said, with a smile. "I wish all of you great success in your future journeys."

The hundred mounted soldiers, six missionaries, three officers and wagon drivers traveled on for most of the morning until Baroni found the perfect place to stop. The officers, missionaries and soldiers ate a lunch of meats and fruits with juice. By early afternoon, they were loaded and on their way again.

Just before sunset, they camped near a small village. Baroni organized latrine duty and set guard duty schedules. Most of the horses were in temporary roped off corrals with their tack removed for the night. The cooks prepared more meat and fruits for dinner.

"We'll stay at this camp until noon tomorrow," Baroni announced. "I'll assign soldiers to scout ahead. They should talk to villagers to make sure we won't be attacked while we are here or when we leave. I want a party to patrol ahead of us and another to patrol to travel back the way we came."

After dinner, they showed Baroni a map Peter had obtained while on a Roman ship. Baroni had been on several ships and thought he was an experienced sailor and knew maps very well. He studied a map of the Mediterranean, discussing each island to the extent of his knowledge. "The "Island-of-Dreams" doesn't appear to be on the map, but then I can't be sure," he mused, "But, I do know you'll enjoy most of the islands you visit."

The scouts returned to report that no signs of trouble were seen either by skirting the village or in conversations with village residents. A large fire was burning with most of the soldiers and drivers sitting around eating. Pardi selected a dozen guards to relieve the other guards he had stationed before dinner. Ben started to sing a song with which no one was familiar. Everyone clapped when he finished either because they liked it or were glad he finished.

Monday, April 22, 125 A.D.

The next morning, after the sun came up, Thomas, Stephen and Baroni had just left their tents and were on their way to meet the other missionaries, Bardo and Pardi for breakfast. The guards shouted a warning, "Rebels are attacking a patrol from Fort Sebaste led by Principale Bataglia."

Baroni ordered Pardi to send fifty soldiers to support Bataglia. Within minutes the clang of swords, shields, shouting and screaming escalated. After a short time, Pardi came marching back with his men behind him. He ordered the soldiers to return to their breakfast and then walked over to Baroni and saluted.

"What happened out there?" Baroni asked.

"Sir, the Jewish rebels started to run away when we marched up," Pardi said, standing at attention. "Bataglia had been handling the attack quite well. Several of his men took arrows, but most were protected by their armor and shields. I also saw more mounted Roman soldiers arriving. Bataglia's men chased the rebels, so we turned around and came back. "

Just then Centurion Felone with Pasquali rode in from the battle area on horseback ahead of another fifty mounted soldiers. They stopped and helped two soldiers with arrows in their arms. Then Pasquali and Felone rode into camp.

"The Jews are creating a very bad situation for you," Thomas observed. "That could have been us they attacked."

"Now you see why Cerrone chose to send the sizable detachment with you?" Pasquali said.

"We're grateful for his leadership and foresight," Thomas said. "And are thankful your men were nearby. I'm surprised you and Felone are out here."

"I was on my way from Jerusalem to Sebaste before dawn when I saw about fifty rebels," Felone said. "I rode hard into the fort and told Pasquali what I had seen. He ordered Bataglia to take fifty men to follow the rebels. The rebels marched fast and went on by Sebaste. Pasquali and I came with fifty more soldiers. When the rebels reached you, they turned and attacked Bataglia's men. When the rebel leader saw soldiers coming from every direction, he ordered a retreat leaving his dead and wounded."

"We Romans realized you are more important than you will ever understand," Pasquali said to Thomas and Stephen. "Felone, let's go see how our wounded soldiers are doing. We need to return to the fort."

****

After lunch, they left, traveling for a good distance, and met Guido and another thirty Romans on horseback from Caesarea. Baroni invited them to spend the night at a camp. "We just left a great site to camp," Guido suggested. "It's near another village with two protective hills and a small lake surrounded by palms and other trees."

The horses, soldiers and wagons rumbled into the secluded and beautiful site with the lake and the trees surrounded by the grassy hills. The palm trees had dead fronds all the way to the ground and green palm fronds at the top were swaying in the breeze.

The hundred and seventy horses were allowed to drink water at the lake, and then let loose in three corrals made from trees, poles and ropes. They had one hundred and thirty soldiers scattered around. After dinner, the missionaries walked over to a large fire-pit. As they relaxed in the light of the fire, a few torches were set up.

Baroni looked around the fire and said, "I wanted to take some extra time on this trip to talk about a few concepts I need clarified to resolve my questions. There are some so called Christian theories that differ from what you missionaries teach in your plays. We have talked about some of this but I need more information. The first is the young Marcion[111] who has adopted the Cerdo line of Christianity. Marcion[112] is a ship-owner living in Sinope and wants to become a Christian bishop like his father. Cerdo lives in Syria. One of their concepts is the idea that all matter is evil and was created by the Jewish God. They teach that God adopted Jesus to be his son. They maintain that it was the moment of baptism when the mortal man, Jesus, had the spiritual Christ come into him. This is what empowered Jesus to do his healing and teaching ministry. Immediately before his death the Christ departed and went back to heaven. This is backed up by noting that Jesus cried out in such anguish on the cross, *My God, my God, why have you forsaken me?*" [113]

"The other teaching I have listened to comes from Egypt by a young Christian by the name of Valentinus. [114] He has written 'The Gospel of Truth.' [115] From what I understand Valentinus believes that people coming into this world are not alike. He says there are three definite classes of human beings. There are the 'Choics' or the earthly carnal ones only concerned with the material world. The next are 'psychics' who become Christians and live by faith and good works. The third group are the 'pneumatics' whom he calls the Gnostics like himself, and who received the divine spark of the seed of Sophia—Sophia, the desire for wisdom."[116]

---

[111] After Jesus, The Triumph of Christianity by Readers Digest, Page 83.

[112] The New Testament, A Historical Introduction to Early Christian Writings by Bart D. Ehrman, page 5.

[113] Ibid, Mark 15:34.

[114] The Gnostic Scriptures by Bentley Layton, page 217.

[115] Ibid, Bentley Layton, page 250.

[116] Early Christian Heresies by Joan O'Grady, pages 35-36.

Pardi was on the other side of the fire. "Yes, I've heard both of those concepts discussed, but I rejected them as unacceptable to me," he said. "I think Marcion is grappling with his hatred of the Jews. Valentinus is a very smart and educated Jew who thinks he's smarter than everyone else. It has been educational to learn about their concepts, but my questions have been answered by Thomas and the missionaries. That is another reason why I became a Christian with my baptism in Sebaste."

Thomas was sitting by Baroni where the fire was the brightest and said, "Please tell us more about Valentinus and his beliefs."

Baroni stood up and threw more wood on the fire. "Valentinus believed that most of the humans are born as 'Choics' and there is no hope for them to be saved. He believes that Jesus Christ came as the Redeemer to allow the psychics and pneumatics to repent. He said the psychics can never reach the height of the pneumatics. His system classifies all humans into these three spiritual levels. We could all be psychics, but some of us may be pneumatics. For example, what are Thomas or Stephen? Are they pneumatics or psychics? I have never believed in the concept of Sophia or her desire for knowledge or a spiritual seed. I personally think we are all on the same plane with different levels of education and background."

Stephen sat quietly listening and staring into the fire. He looked up and said, "I've been reading some of Thomas' scrolls he received from Nasi Judah. It is pretty clear to me how we are saved. When I was reading Apostle Paul's letter to the Ephesians, he said: *'Praise be to the God and Father of our Lord Jesus Christ, who has blessed us in the heavenly realms with every spiritual blessing in Christ. For he chose us through Him before the creation of the world to be holy and blameless in his sight. In love he predestined us to be adopted as his sons through Jesus Christ, in accordance with his pleasure and will---to the praise of his glorious grace, which he has freely given us in the One He loves. In him we have redemption through his blood, the forgiveness of sins, in accordance with the riches of God's grace that he lavished on us with all wisdom and understanding.'"* [117]

"I read something similar in Acts written by Luke," Thomas said. "It says: *'But none of these things move me; nor do I count my life dear to*

---

[117] The New International Bible, Ephesians 2:3-9.

myself, so that I may finish my race with joy, and the ministry which I received from the Lord Jesus, to testify to the gospel of the grace of God.'[118]

Stephen said, "I like the words spoken by Jesus to comfort his disciples. In the book of John, he said: *'Let not your heart be troubled; you believe in God, believe also in Me. In My Father's house are many mansions; if it were not so, I would have told you. I go to prepare a place for you. And if I go and prepare a place for you, I will come again and receive you to Myself; that where I am, there you may be also. And where I go you know, and the way you know.'*"[119]

"We continue to hear these teachings that are not consistent with what we know to be the message that Jesus brought," Thomas said. "I found that Paul wrote: *'But even if we, or an angel from heaven, preach any other gospel to you than what we have preached to you, let him be accursed. As we said before, so say I now again, if any man preaches any other gospel unto you than what you have received, let him be accursed.'*"[120]

"Thanks for your words," Baroni said. "I need to think about everything we've talked about tonight."

As the fire went out, everyone went to bed.

Tuesday, April 23, 125 A.D.

The next morning, Thomas awoke and could hear the cooks and soldiers chattering and talking in low voices about the conversations last night around the fire.

"I have received the conversion," Baroni confessed to them. "Last night did it for me. I want to receive a baptism today. If I do, then at that point our entire group will be Christians. One day I may become a missionary myself. I don't understand what's happening to me."

Thomas walked over to sit with them and eat breakfast.

Guido said to him, "I was very impressed with what I heard last night from Baroni and Pardi, but when you return, could you and your missionary companions give me and my men a more complete, but abbreviated version of the presentation you gave at Fort Sebaste?"

---

[118] Ibid, Acts 20:24.
[119] Ibid, John 14:1-4.
[120] Ibid, Galatians 1:8-9.

"We would be delighted to give you a quick overview when we return," Thomas said.

Thomas and Stephen left with a few cooks, Baroni and more soldiers to be baptized. When they returned, they went ahead to do a shortened version of the play. Ben ended with, "Jesus died to atone for our sins. His death was in trade for our forgiveness."

"WE ARE SAVED," Thomas shouted.

This startled Guido and his men and they cheered with the rest of the group watching.

"Many Jews believe that animal sacrifice is necessary," one of soldiers said. "Do you still believe that?"

"Animal sacrifice is no longer necessary after Jesus' death, He is the sacrifice and our redemption," Thomas said. "However, I do not know the current status of animal sacrifice in the Jewish religion. Animal sacrifices were only done in the temple and it is gone. I know the Jews who left and went to other countries don't sacrifice animals anymore in their religious practices."

"How do you know Jesus died for our sins?" another soldier asked.

"Isaiah foretold many, many years ago that the Messiah would die for us," Stephen said. *"But he was wounded for our transgressions; he was bruised for our iniquities, the chastisement for our peace was upon him, and by His stripes we are healed. We all, like sheep, have gone astray; we have turned, every one to his own way; and the Lord has laid on him the iniquity of us all."*[121]

The soldier looked mystified and asked, "How did Isaiah know what would happen to Jesus Christ?"

"This is called Jewish prophecy," Stephen said.

Baroni spoke up to say, "I told Cerrone I wanted to take some extra time on this trip, so I have his authority to stay at this site a while longer. Anyone wanting to be baptized tomorrow should meet at the lake at midmorning."

"When you leave, I will accompany you to Caesarea," Guido said. "My time is flexible."

The cooks rang a bell to line up for lunch. They had prepared roast chicken, a berry slaw and baked bread. More wood was gathered after lunch to keep the fire burning.

---

[121] Ibid, Isaiah 53:5, 6

"The Jewish army rebels are very persistent," Guido said. "What do they expect to gain? If they were able to make all of us Romans leave, don't they understand how vulnerable they would be? Any power could come in here and take them over again. What we do is protect them from themselves and from outsiders."

Stephen replied, "You're exactly right. I think this Bar Kokba is a madman. It's crazy when religious extremists try to run the world. They feel it's necessary to kill all people who oppose them. Will this extremism go on forever?"

"The possibility of an attack or all-out rebellion is off in the future," Baroni said. "Rome is starting to beef-up the forces here. Governor Rufus is in Rome asking for more soldiers. I only hope this messiah, Bar Kokba, disappears, because he is asking for dire consequences to the Jewish people."

After dinner the conversations continued around the fire until late at night. Baroni, Bardo, Guido and Pardi assigned soldiers guard duties at four locations for the night. Guards came and went all night long relieving each other. Luckily no more rebels came around. During the night, Thomas and Stephen were awakened by the guards. They got up and talked to one group of Romans soldiers about acceptance of Christianity. After they left Thomas said. "What they seem to want is our personal view of Christianity. I guess it's because we are related to Jesus."

"We are being treated like very important people," Stephen mused. "The soldiers want to be with us as though it is an honor. The soldiers treat the time with us like a holiday. I guess we enjoy it the same way. I had no idea that missionary work would be so much fun and challenging with so many accepting our teachings. But in these terrible times everyone desires something near and good to overcome the doom and gloom. Cerrone's conversion, baptism and support have been a great help."

Wednesday, April 24, 125 A.D.

Everyone was up at daybreak. Several of the soldiers were swimming in the lake. Others were washing at the edge. With one hundred-thirty soldiers, six missionaries, three officers and twenty drivers to feed, the cooks were doing a remarkable job. The food wagons had been restocked at Fort Sebaste before they left. After breakfast four guards who had not slept were now sound asleep and four fresh guards had taken their place. Baroni sent four soldiers out on horseback to scout out the surrounding area.

Baroni talked to the thirty soldiers who had joined them the night before. He pointed at the missionaries and said, "All who want to be baptized meet at the lake."

Thomas and Stephen headed for the lake followed by all thirty men. When they got near, ten broke off to stand to watch. Everyone stood watching several wild hens walking towards them. The rustle of wings could be heard and dozens of seagulls fluttered in and landed on the side of the lake, near them.

Thomas smiled and said, "The Holy Spirit has attracted the birds. We'll let them watch."

They walked to the edge of the lake. After the soldiers removed their battle armor and leathers, Thomas and Stephen baptized them one at a time. When they finished, five more soldiers had dropped their leathers and armor. They waded into the water. After they performed their baptisms, Thomas congratulated them. He then went over to the five men who had declined to be baptized and thanked them for their consideration to the others.

"You are converting many; have there ever before been such large numbers converted to Christianity at one time?" one soldier asked.

"Yes, forty days after Christ was crucified, the Holy Spirit came upon Jerusalem during Pentecost and over three thousand were converted," Thomas said. "Christianity must be accepted by choice. Join when you believe in Jesus. Consider it carefully, for you need to be saved."

When everyone was dry and fully outfitted, Thomas turned towards the birds and lifted his arms. The seagulls flew away. The wild hens were already gone. They walked to the wagon serving shelves for a hearty lunch. The missionaries talked of their efforts to get permission to find the island and build the house of worship. The building was a serious topic of conversation. Would it be like a pagan temple or would it be very different? They talked about the tools and equipment they were taking with them.

"You have the tools, but what will be your source of the building materials," one soldier asked.

"We expect to quarry our stone and cut our own supply of timber from sources on the Island-of-Dreams," Thomas said. "We may need to bring in some of the materials from Sicily, Gaul or Iberia,"

The conversation switched to the harbor where they were headed. They discussed the grandeur of Caesarea that Herod had built. Baroni discussed the amphitheater, harbor and Herod's Caesarea Palace, all of which were built over a hundred years ago. He said, "The palace is on the hill that protrudes into the Mediterranean. Most of the water consumed in Caesarea is brought in from the north in the aqueduct Herod built."

"There were riots in Caesarea sixty years ago before the Jewish war," Baroni said. "The Jews were later defeated with the destruction of Jerusalem. Twenty thousand Jews were massacred in Caesarea by the Romans. It is safe for Jews and Christians again but continues to be a little tense at times. I don't expect trouble once we arrive in Caesarea. The Free Spirit and the Islander will be ready to load the construction tools when we get there."

"I wonder how Peter and Tamir are doing," Thomas questioned. "I hope they have been able to recruit more acceptable seamen and guards."

"Peter has probably let Tamir do the recruiting while he made converts, including some of the young women in town," Baroni said laughing.

The afternoon was spent peacefully, napping or resting. They were awakened by the four guards on horseback riding hard into the camp.

"We encountered a large group of Jewish rebels on foot marching towards Fort Sebaste," one soldier said. "We rode hard to warn the fort and then circled back another way to camp."

"Are we in danger?" Baroni asked.

"We would be if they came our way," the spokesman said. "But I'm pretty sure the rebels were going straight for the fort."

"How many rebels were on the move?" Pardi asked.

The spokesman looked at his fellow riders. "We estimated about three hundred."

Baroni dismissed the soldier and ordered Pardi to send four new men to watch for any change in the rebel's march. They all agreed that they would leave early the next morning.

† Chapter 25 †

Leaving Camp for Caesarea
Thursday, April 25, 125 A.D.

The short night was uneventful. Everyone was up long before daylight, ready to leave. The drivers had been up before most of the soldiers, hitching the teams to the wagons with their tack and equipment. Food was handed out to everyone. Bataglia and his men went out first. Pardi led with half of the mounted soldiers followed by Baroni and the missionaries on horseback leading the wagons. Bardo followed the wagons with fifty mounted soldiers.

The morning was warm, with a partly cloudy sky. The trail back to the road was clear and bumpy, but on the road they moved at a faster pace. They stopped when a wheel on the lead wagon started to wobble. While the wheels and axles were repaired, the cooks handed out dried meat to everyone. After they left, they soon came into the fort at Caesarea and went to the parade ground again.

Taccone came out to welcome them. "Baroni, you are invited to dinner with the fort commander, Mascaro, and his Lady Lydia," Taccone said. "Thomas and Stephen, you are also invited to dinner. Please accompany me to the officer's area to freshen up."

Thomas and Stephen changed out of their Roman uniforms. They went with Baroni, entering the dining room led by Taccone. He showed them around again and discussed some of the artifacts Mascaro had collected. They were served a sweet drink and sat at a side table discussing the Jewish rebel situation. Mascaro entered with his charming wife, Lady Lydia, her hand on his arm. After they were reacquainted, a uniformed soldier appeared to say, "Dinner will be available after everyone has finished their drinks."

After Mascaro, Lady Lydia and the others seated themselves, he said, "Baroni, tell me about your visit to Fort Sebaste and the Jewish rebels you encountered."

"Our visit to Fort Sebaste was very interesting and fun," Baroni said. "Pasquali put on a nice dinner and then most of the soldiers went to the stadium. Thomas and his missionaries put on a special play that had the soldiers standing, shouting and clapping. The next day they baptized over two hundred and ninety, including Pasquali, Pardi, Bardo and Bataglia. The cooks with us were baptized the next morning. We camped at a lake and twenty-five of your soldiers and several of mine were baptized, including me. On the negative side, a couple of days ago Bataglia engaged about fifty rebels and our guards observed three hundred rebels yesterday marching to Fort Sebaste and rode hard there to warn the fort."

"I want to reward the lead soldier who spotted the rebels and warned the fort at Sebaste," Mascaro said. "A promotion should be in order."

"With the number of baptisms at Fort Sebaste and camping at the lake, you have baptized almost three hundred soldiers and officers," Lady Lydia remarked. "Baptizing Pasquali is a bit of a surprise."

"I was surprised as well and they baptized me at the lake," Baroni said. "I found the faith, belief in Jesus Christ and his message of hope and love."

"I'm not surprised at Pasquali," Mascaro said." He has been looking favorably at joining a Christian congregation for some time. Baroni, you really surprise me. Thomas and Stephen, you must have put on a convincing play. I'm sure your private conversations with Pasquali were important. Let's go into the dining room."

Mascaro led them to the dining table. Taccone directed each to assigned seats. Two aides served their dinner of roast fish, a cooked grain dish, and hot bread and butter with fresh fruits.

"I heard about the conversion and baptism of Cerrone in Jerusalem," Mascaro said. "We talked last time about this evolving gentile acceptance of the Good News of Jesus. I'm absolutely amazed at the number of conversions and baptisms of our soldiers in Sebaste and at the lake. Each of your visits and presentations are very successful. The teaching seems to be well accepted. I wouldn't be surprised for you to experience this zeal and acceptance where ever you go."

"It could be the soldiers liked the idea of being forgiven for what they do in the army," Thomas said.

"Our soldiers, citizens and slaves are anxious to hear the Good News you bring," Lady Lydia said. "I believe we are living in a special time with the Holy Spirit coming down."

"Lady Lydia, you may be right," Thomas said. "I know we always feel the Holy Spirit's presence when we gather people together and they are truly touched. I see it in their eyes. All kinds of birds are attracted and show up at the plays and baptisms to watch."

"You, Baroni, Guido Bardo, Pardi and Bataglia are now Christians," Mascaro said. "With all of the trouble the Jews are causing, how is it we have Jewish Christians who are so loved by our men?"

"These missionaries do not act or think like those of the Jewish faith," Baroni responded. "They are followers of Jesus. The men and I believe Jesus came here on earth to save us."

Lady Lydia said, "The last time you were here we talked about your religion, but I still do not know much about it. The discussion about the family of Apostle Paul was very interesting."

"Knowing the history of Apostles Paul and Peter is important to me right now," Thomas said. "I am concerned about the developing problem in Israel with Simeon ben Kosiba and his rebel army. I know more Roman soldiers will come here, but I fear they will not be enough. In my dream with Jesus, he warned me to help Nazarenes leave Israel. He said Nazarene and Christian members in Israel are at risk if this gets worse and I believe it will. I have a problem with Hadar coming here from Syria with his wealth and his plan to restore the Jewish Temple. Hadar believes I have some old temple records and wants them from me. He's wants to kill me to get them."

"We have had several battles with Hadar's men on the way from Joppa and in Jerusalem," Stephen said. "This man is a real danger to us and anyone around us."

"We plan to sail to find the Island-of-Dreams and get the construction started on new houses and the house of worship," Thomas said. "It will take at least two years to get the vault we need to build and the house of worship in the final construction phase. If we relocate as many from Israel as I think we will, we must take the time to get organized to find other locations where we can relocate them. Stephen and I will visit Gaul, Espania and Britain after construction is started this year. We hope to find the descendents of Joseph of Arimathea in the British Isles to see if they can help us with the relocations."

"Then Joseph is important to you," Mascaro continued. "He was a member of the Sanhedrin, as well as a legislative member of the provincial Roman senate here in Jerusalem. He was a Roman Nobolis Decurio in charge of metal mines.[122] He and many others moved to Caesarea. They were persecuted by the Sadducees in Bethany and Jerusalem after the death and resurrection of Jesus. They moved here and stayed with Deacon Phillip. Arrangements were made for their protection with Centurion Cornelius here in Caesarea."[123]

"It is interesting to me because Jesus knew Centurion Cornelius in Capernaum.[124] While living in Capernaum, he met Jesus in Galilee. Cornelius' servant was suffering from paralysis. He asked Jesus to just say the word to heal his servant and it would be done. Jesus was astounded at his level of faith and healed his servant.[125] Before leaving Capernaum, Apostle Peter baptized Cornelius and his family."

"Joseph of Arimathea had one of his ships in the Caesarea marina. Apostle Peter had sent Apostle Phillip to Gaul to scout out the region for future missions. Cornelius was not in Caesarea when several Jews forced Joseph of Arimathea and his friends onto Joseph's ship.[126] The Jews took the sails and oars off the ship and pushed the ship out into the Mediterranean. Lucky for them, the ship apparently sailed with the prevailing winds, which took the ship to Cyrene in North Africa where they obtained sails and oars. They sailed on from Cyrene to Marseilles, landing on a nearby sandy beach at first.[127] Cornelius never forgave himself for failing to protect them."

"That's an amazing story," Thomas said. "The other people who were with Joseph of Arimathea on that ship were his sister Mary Salome and Sarah her handmaiden, Mary Cleophas, Lazarus, Martha and Marcella her

---

[122] Ibid, George F. Jowett, Page 17 and Ibid, Lionel Smithett Lewis, M.A. Pages 31-32.
[123] Ibid, John W. Taylor, page 69.
[124] Ibid, Acts 10: 1-48.
[125] Ibid, Mathew 8: 5-13.
[126] Ibid, John W. Taylor, page 105.
[127] Ibid, John W. Taylor, page 70.

handmaiden, Mary Magdalene, Maximinus, Sidonius called Restitute, and Zaccheus the Bishop of Caesarea.[128] Who have I missed?"

"You missed Clements[129] from Britain who later became the second Bishop of Rome," Stephen said. "Eutropius, Martian, Saturinus and Trophimus were all on that ship.[130]" As I recall, Maximinus was very wealthy and looked after Mary Magdalene."

"Lazarus was quite a man having been raised from the dead by Jesus," Mascaro said. "He was a member of the Jewish Sanhedrin and the regional Roman senate in Jerusalem. Later, he became the bishop of Bethany and then gave the Bethany palace to the Nazarene Ecclesia for the House of Prayer. He was a bishop in Cyprus for a couple of years. He later was a teacher in the Avalon school in Britain. Then he became the bishop of Marseilles and built the cathedral there.[131]"

This conversation has been wonderful but it's late," Thomas said. "To repeat, our plans are to leave here to find the Island-of-Dreams."

"What is special about your Island-of-Dreams?" Mascaro asked.

"I had a dream with Jesus. I was there with him as he showed me the island. It's a small island with no one living on it. It has the forest and rock cliffs in the middle, which can provide a stone quarry and the lumber for construction material. He told me he and Joseph of Arimathea stopped there once on a trip from Britain to Israel."

"I don't know of such an island," Mascaro said. "I should warn you, however, that an island with the cities of Pompeii and Herculaneum was destroyed about forty years ago with the eruption and explosion of Mt. Vesuvius. I hope that wasn't your island."

"Your description most likely suggests a small island," Lady Lydia said. "I, therefore, do not think it was the island with Mt. Vesuvius since that island had quite a large population."

"There are a large number of small islands," Mascaro said. "Your search efforts could take time. I wish we could help you."

---

[128] Ibid, John W. Taylor, page 105.

[129] Ibid, Lionel Smithett Lewis, M.A., page 116.

[130] Ibid, John W. Taylor, page 105.

[131] Ibid, George F. Jowett, Page 164 and Ibid, John W. Taylor, page 105.

"You can help by giving us special documents to present to other Romans for their help in other locations," Thomas said.

"That's a good idea," Mascaro said. "I'll have those documents prepared for you and your companions before the ships set sail. If Governor Rufus returns before you leave, I'll get him to sign the documents or give you special medals."

They stood and thanked Mascaro and Lady Lydia. Taccone led them back to the wagons. They found a lively discussion going on about the Jewish rebels. Ben was finishing a discussion of the rebels' beliefs.

"We don't agree with them and want to leave to get away from them," he said.

The soldiers hooted and applauded.

"What has gone on while we were with Mascaro?" Baroni inquired.

"We had the best dinner I ever experienced," David said. "We discussed the fact that there are requests from many of the men stationed here in Fort Caesarea who want to hear about Christianity and Jesus. We gave them short lessons. Many will want to be baptized before we leave."

Baroni, Thomas and Stephen said good night and went to the officers' quarters with Taccone.

† **Chapter 26** †

What, a Feast and a Play?
Friday, April 26, 125 A.D.

After breakfast, thirty soldiers rode hard into the fort. Thomas watched them dismount. One was Bataglia. He went directly to the officer's quarters where he was met by Taccone. They saluted and came back to where the other riders were still holding their horses.

Thomas, Stephen and Baroni walked up to inquire what had happened.

"Centurion Taccone, please inform Tribune Mascaro that a battle has occurred with the rebels before they reached Fort Sebaste," Bataglia said. "Over a hundred and fifty rebels were killed. The others we estimated to be about another hundred scattered in several directions. Forty of our Roman soldiers were killed and twenty-four were wounded."

"Those rebels are crazy," Taccone said, looking angry. "I will inform Mascaro about this battle."

After Taccone left, the missionaries and officers talked to Bataglia. "Twenty of the dead soldiers were Christians," he said. "I am glad they had been baptized before their deaths. With their baptism, they are saved."

Taccone returned with Mascaro who looked furious.

"Centurion Taccone, have Principle Bagli take fifty mounted soldiers and scour the area on the way to Sebaste for any rebels getting back together," Mascaro said. "Principale Bataglia, tell your commander I am sorry for his losses. Take your thirty men and go with Principle Bagli and help him scout for rebels on the way to Fort Sebaste. Baroni, have Bardo take his soldiers back to Jerusalem. Have him help Bataglia if he needs assistance on the way to Sebaste. Have Bardo inform Cerrone what has gone on with the battles out of Fort Sebaste, as well as the Christian conversions and baptisms in Sebaste and at the lake. Let Cerrone know we will send his wagons back with the supplies he ordered."

"I'll order Bardo to leave right away," Baroni said.

"I'm concerned about the Senatorial Governor Rufus, who lives here in the palace at Caesarea," Mascaro said. "The governor is of proconsul standing and has been gone for about a month. He went to Rome to discuss the rebel disturbances. As important as the governor is in Roman status, he felt he still needed to go to Rome to personally explain the situation to Caesar Hadrian and request more soldiers. He is due back any day by ship. I'm concerned because Aelius Hadrian does not spend much time in Rome. Baroni, please have Pardi and his men go with you and the missionaries to the Free Spirit and the Islander."

"Go to the stable and bring your teams of horses out to the wagons," Baroni said to the drivers.

Pardi's group of thirty soldiers and twenty-four drivers and cooks were organized by Baroni and Pardi. They prepared the wagons and the others mounted their horses. The missionaries left Fort Caesarea and traveled to the pier. The drivers pulled the first two wagons onto the pier in front of the Free Spirit and Islander. The other eight wagons could be pulled up to replace the wagons as they were emptied. Peter and Tamir appeared and waved from the upper deck of the Islander. They came down the gangplank smiling.

"Tamir and I have recruited the five seamen and the six guards you requested," Peter said.

"Good work," Thomas said. "Mascaro's instructions are to get the tools and supplies off the wagons and loaded onto the ships. These wagons need to be loaded with supplies Cerrone has ordered. Mascaro wants us to be ready to depart as soon as we can. Call your ten seamen and six guards to help load the equipment and tools. I can meet the new ones now."

Men poured off both ships and lined up along the pier. As Peter introduced the new seamen and guards to the missionaries, Baroni was telling the twenty soldiers to guard the wagons and help remove the covers. The first wagon held the two boxes of gold and silver bars which Stephen and Mark carried onto the Free Spirit and stored in storage bens behind one of the cabins on the first lower deck where they could be locked.

Peter and Tamir stood by the gangplanks of their ships to direct which tools and equipment went to each ship. Everything was taken below decks for storage. The missionaries stood with the soldiers watching.

Several citizens from Caesarea came up to the soldiers and asked why they were in such a hurry.

"We're concerned about the Jewish rebels," Baroni said.

"The rebels wouldn't dare come near Caesarea," the spokesman said. "The Jews that live here are under watch by those of us who dislike them. Any advance by this rebel army will be met by the citizens here. We are armed and have men out to watch for them."

Baroni thanked them and came over to Thomas and said, "Take your time. The local citizens seem to think the rebels are afraid to come into Caesarea. I don't know why the rebels are more afraid of the citizens here than the Roman army, but apparently they are".

"I guess we can calm down," Thomas said, looking at the other missionaries. "We really should leave early in the morning, but we'll plan for relaxation and fun tonight."

After all of the tools and equipment were loaded, Peter said, "Divide the dried meat, grain, other food items and wine between the two ships and store everything in the galley of each ship in back of the cabins on the first lower deck."

When it was late afternoon, Baroni said to the head cook, "Have the drivers take the wagons to the fort. Use one or two wagons to bring food and drink back to the ships for thirty-eight men, including twenty soldiers, two officers, seven missionaries, ten seamen and eight guards. Pardi, send your men back to the fort for tonight."

The wagons and Pardi's soldiers left. The missionaries went with Peter and Tamir to inspect the food, tools and equipment now stored on the two ships. When they came out on the deck of the Islander, two wagons pulled in between the two ships. The cooks climbed down and set out food, drinks, plates, utensils and goblets on the pull-up serving shelves.

They were just finishing their meals when several local citizens came up to the guards. Everyone looked at them and one of the guards came over to Baroni, "This new group is headed by the mayor of Caesarea," the guard said.

"What do they want?"

"They want to say a few words to whoever is in charge," the guard said.

Baroni walked over with the guard. After a brief conversation, the group of locals left and Baroni came back. "The mayor invited the missionaries to a feast to be held tomorrow," he announced. "He explained that people knew about Peter and Tamir. Many locals have now heard about the rest of the missionaries arriving, and the large number of conversions and baptisms on their trip from Jerusalem. The invitation for the feast tomorrow includes a request for the missionaries to make a presentation to the citizens similar to ones made at Fort Sebaste and Joppa. Caesarea has a large amphitheater. The mayor has already made arrangements with Mascaro."

"How'd they learn about the presentation at Fort Sebaste?" Thomas asked.

"It came about at a lunch the mayor had with Mascaro and Taccone today," Baroni replied.

"You mean they had lunch today while we were loading the ships?" Stephen asked, groaning.

"Yes, that's what happened," Baroni said. "Will you have the same enthusiasm this time?"

"Should we stay for the feast and the play," Stephen asked. "This could be the best yet."

"Yes, we'll stay, but let's eat and have a good time tonight," Thomas said. "As you said, the passionate fervor we feel may explode again. It seems we are clearly being called by Jesus. The people want to hear the Good News of Jesus. When they hear the Good News they feel the same intense zeal we feel. We must be ready again."

"I like the extension of your time here in Caesarea," Baroni said with delight. "I love this work. Watching all of you perform is exciting. The people enjoy what you do."

"Did the mayor tell you who would attend the feast," Thomas asked. "The Jewish religion is a minority in Caesarea, and what about the other religions? Could they create a problem meeting together tomorrow?"

"The mayor will provide the feast for any citizen who wants to attend," Baroni said. "I'm sure he will arrange for two presentations at the amphitheater. The second presentation will be for the Jewish citizens. The first presentation will be for gentiles."

Thomas breathed a sigh of relief. He looked at Stephen, relieved about the arrangement.

"Why'd I have a feeling this would happen?" Thomas said. "Jesus must be with us."

"Mascaro suggested these arrangements to the mayor," Baroni said. "The mayor said Mascaro would provide two-hundred soldiers for security. But interestingly, he said the soldiers were as anxious to see these presentations as the soldiers were at Fort Sebaste. You have become very popular wherever you go."

"We seem to find ourselves preaching wherever we stop," Mark said. "I had no idea converting people to Christianity would be this easy, yet so demanding. They seem to be coming to us. We don't even get a chance to go out and visit anyone."

"This missionary work is exhausting, but it's always exciting," Stephen said. "The need for this work will go on forever."

"This is what we do as missionaries," Thomas said. "We are to take every opportunity to make conversions."

"How many citizens might attend our play tomorrow?" Ben asked.

"He said several thousand will attend the feast. A large number of soldiers will attend the plays and the mayor estimated several hundred citizens will also attend the plays," Baroni said. "The mayor told me he would send messengers throughout the city in the morning to announce the feast and the plays in the amphitheater. The soldiers will be charged with keeping the crowds in line during the feast and the plays."

"As I mentioned, we will stay here with you tonight," Baroni said. "Mascaro is expecting more soldiers and officers to arrive tomorrow. I'm anxious to use the beds in the cabins again."

Peter and Tamir made suggestions to the new people where they should sleep on each ship.

"Thomas, there are thirty beds on each of your ships," Baroni said. "This provides beds for all of us and the soldiers. Pardi and I will stay here tonight with the twenty soldiers as guards. Men you have been guards for Peter and Tamir since they picked up the ships in Joppa. You will continue that duty until the missionaries leave. I want ten of you to take the watch from now until midnight and the other ten to stand guard from midnight until sunrise in the morning."

"I'm glad we have excess beds," Thomas said. "But there are only two extra if all of us were in bed at the same time. We have two floating hotels."

† Chapter 27 †

The Arrival of Governor Rufus
Saturday, April 27, 125 A.D.

It was a bright and glorious morning when the missionaries awoke. The water lapping and rocking the ships had been conducive for sleeping. They were greeted by one mounted soldier and two wagons. "Missionaries and officers are invited to breakfast at the fort," the mounted soldier said. "We have breakfast in this wagon for the soldiers and guards."

"Men, breakfast has arrived, but continue your guard duties," Baroni said.

"Guards, go ahead and have breakfast with the soldiers," Tamir said.

The missionaries, plus Tamir, Baroni and Pardi climbed into the wagon. They rode into the parade ground at the fort to find food wagons with breakfast being served to the rest of the soldiers.

Taccone came over to the wagon and said, "Baroni, Thomas and Stephen please accompany me to Mascaro's quarters. Guido and Pardi take care of the other missionaries and Tamir."

Taccone led the way to Mascaro's quarters and said, "Mascaro and his Lady are waiting for us."

They entered Mascaro's quarters and went to the breakfast table where Lady Lydia was seated.

"I'm so happy to see you again," she said. "I had been saddened to see you leave so quickly. It is more reasonable for you to stay for a few days. One day is not enough."

"Thank you for your kind words," Thomas said.

Baroni said to Lydia, "I forgot last night that Cerrone told me to tell both of you about a beautiful and wonderful woman he has met in Jerusalem. She's the widow of Nasi Joseph who was killed by Governor Luscious Quietus. She was the Nasi's second wife and was only seventeen when she married him eight years ago."

"She is very young even now," Lady Lydia said. "I hope they can make a successful marriage. He needs a good wife. It was sad when Cerrone lost his wife and child in childbirth. He was full of joy looking forward to the birth of their first child, and was so shocked and saddened by their deaths. It's time for him to marry again."

Mascaro seemed pleased and ordered the waiters to serve everyone breakfast.

"Mascaro, I understand you had lunch with the mayor yesterday," Thomas said.

"Taccone thought it would be good to see the mayor's reaction to the Jewish rebels and the possible danger to residents of Caesarea. The mayor reassured us that the rebels posed no danger at all. He pointed out that they could be easily trapped in Caesarea and not able to get out."

"How'd the feast idea come up," Stephen inquired. "It is sudden and will cost a lot."

"The mayor pointed out that a feast had been planned for an Aphrodite holiday some time ago," Taccone said. "That religious holiday was resented by the Jewish residents, but then the weather had turned out very bad, so the feast was canceled. The non-Jewish residents were disappointed and the Jews were happy. The opportunity to have a feast where all residents might want to attend was an opportunity the mayor hoped to exploit even though Jews will object to a Christian play."

"It sounds good, but I'm concerned about a possible riot," Thomas said. "Feelings run wild here. On the other hand, we've seen so many people want to become Christians after our plays. They have been peaceful and calm and people become full of fervor and joy. Could that happen here?"

"I'm confident that two-hundred of my soldiers can keep everyone calm," Mascaro said. "I'm intrigued to see what happens. What you have described in Joppa and Sebaste is hard to believe."

As they finished their breakfast, Thomas thanked Mascaro and Lady Lydia. Taccone led them back to the parade ground. Their companions were just finishing their breakfast along with Pardi and his soldiers. The soldiers at the fort were now coming out to the parade ground and forming lines.

"Let's go into the town square," Baroni said. "We should go now before the soldiers leave. Pardi lead your thirty men and follow us to the town center and keep a circle around us when we get off the wagon."

They crowded onto the wagon and the driver circled around to go out through the gates. Many local citizens were on foot, walking toward the town center. Thomas gasped as he viewed the size of the crowd and wondered what this experience would bring.

"Will we convert large numbers of people or be stoned for calling Jesus the Son of God?" Stephen asked.

Thomas said, "I remind you, only the Jews will stone us. The soldiers will not let that happen."

"We don't have time to baptize several thousand local citizens," Ben said with a big smile.

"This is crazy," Stephen said. "Who would have thought our quiet little exit from Judea would be this public? We are learning the old saying, 'when the fruit is ripe, you pick it.'"

As they came close to the pier, they noticed that two Roman ships and one Egyptian ship were pulling into the harbor. They wondered if that could be a problem. As their drivers drove past the pier towards the town square, they looked back to see citizens gazing at the Free Spirit, the Islander and the three ships coming through the opening in the artificial bay towards the pier. The drivers slowed the teams to avoid hitting people who were crowding everywhere. When the driver stopped, they climbed down and met the mayor, a Rabbi and two high priests. The only one smiling was the mayor. Thomas walked over and greeted everyone. They were welcomed cordially by the mayor.

"Who do the Rabbi and the high priests think we are?" Thomas whispered to the mayor.

"Don't be alarmed," he answered. "You are our guests and our religious leaders welcome your presence. They look forward to learning more about your perspective on the Christian religion. We thought we knew, but they want to know how you have converted extensively where ever you go."

"The conversions have been heartwarming, but we are just excited young Christian priests on our way to build a house of worship," Thomas said. "We teach where we can. Even we have been amazed at the acceptance and conversions. The need seems great."

The Rabbi and the high priests seemed reluctant to say anything. Other local leaders came by to welcome them, and to view the fire-pits, where several whole sheep and lambs were cooking at a number of fires. Other fires had pots of stew cooking.

They learned each stew was different. Some had vegetables and wheat. Others had barley and bones from the slaughtered animals. Still other fires had rabbits and chickens cooking. Several drying racks were around the fires where filets of fish were being smoked. Several tables had been brought in for the preparation of vegetables. The fires and the cooking food gave off a wonderful aroma mixed with smoke and heat.

The people seemed to know who the missionaries were. Children came up to touch them. Others waved from further away. Being treated like royalty seemed a bit strange. With all this euphoria, there was an undertone of contempt from some they encountered. Thomas became more and more concerned. He sensed danger.

"Thomas what's wrong?" Stephen asked as they stopped.

"I'm anxious and bothered by this event. These missionary events and conversations are important, but so is our job to find the Island-of-Dreams and move the records and relics there."

Thomas went to Baroni and expressed his concern and said, "I feel the presence of evil and believe Hadar's men are here watching us. I may be over reacting, but I want to be cautious."

Baroni understood and ordered the Pardi's soldiers to stay close to the missionaries wherever they went during the day. Thomas looked up to see two hundred Roman soldiers from Fort Caesarea marching down the road. Behind them came fifty solders on horseback. This was an impressive show of power. The local residents were startled and apprehensive.

The mayor climbed up on a stand and announced, "The soldiers are here to celebrate with us and keep the peace."

The soldiers spread out in groups to surround the feast area. Many soldiers began to mix with the crowd. A new group of more than a hundred soldiers marched closer. Leading them were two officers on horseback. Taccone and an officer they had not met dismounted and walked over to where the missionaries were standing. The new officer was introduced as Centurion Angelo Heleni. He was the officer in charge of the new soldiers, who had been delivered to the pier by one of the three ships they had seen coming into the harbor.

"Each ship has delivered seventy-five soldiers transferred here from Syria and Egypt," Centurion Heleni said. "These soldiers are part of an increase in manpower requested by Governor Rufus because of the rising trouble with Jewish rebels. One hundred-fifty soldiers are on their way to Fort Sebaste to give Tribune Pasquali support. Seventy-five will stay here today for the feast and presentations. They will march over to Fort Sebaste tomorrow."

"You may have noticed that one of the ships was larger than the other two," Heleni continued. "The larger ship had the senatorial Governor Rufus and his entourage, who have gone directly to his palace. He wanted to have Tribunus Laticlavius Mascaro go to the palace to brief him on the events since he left and why a celebration is going on in Caesarea. After the briefing, the governor will be concerned about the Christians. He will attend the play for the non-Jewish locals."

"I requested Centurion Heleni to order his soldiers to take up positions around the city as backup to the soldiers from Fort Caesarea," Taccone said. "Food for the soldiers is being prepared at the fort and will be brought throughout the day."

"I noticed that and it is fine with me," Heleni said.

"Heleni, where are the ships going in the morning?" Peter asked.

"All three ships will go up the coast to Syria to pick up another two-hundred-twenty-five soldiers to bring back to Caesarea," he said. "The Governor went to Rome and this will lead to a buildup of another five thousand soldiers throughout Israel. Many are marching in from Syria. Others are marching in from Egypt.[132]"

Heleni left to give orders to his soldiers. The missionaries followed the mayor to a special area set up with a shade from the sun. Everyone in their party found a seat for a short rest.

The mayor came to Thomas and said, "I told my messengers to announce a presentation to be given by seven Nazarene missionaries. What the messengers announced was seven Christians from Jerusalem will present

[132] Jewish Virtual Library, The Bar-Kokba Revolt (132-135 C.E.) by Shira Schoenberg, "The Jews organized guerilla forces and, in 123 C.E., began launching surprise attacks against the Romans. From that point on, life only got worse for the Jews. Hadrian brought an extra army legion, the "Sixth Ferrata," into Judea to deal with the terrorism. Hadrian hated "foreign" religions and (later) forbade the Jews to perform circumcisions. He appointed Tineius Rufus governor of Judea (in 118 A.D.)".

the Jerusalem Area Commander Cerrone's favorite play. It appears that most people will expect a play and all of you to be famous actors."

Thomas turned to the other missionaries and grimaced. "This could be good since there is less risk of being accused of proselyting," Thomas said. "Usually, they don't kill actors, do they?"

Everyone laughed nervously. They decided to go over their parts again.

"The governor and his entourage are coming down the street," Baroni said, and stepped out to greet them.

A man dressed in special Roman purple attire came up to Baroni and saluted. This person turned out to be a new Legatus Legionis officer who had returned with the governor. He introduced himself as Dominic Mercelli and explained, "My Greek first name was given to me by my Greek mother."

Mercelli led Baroni over to introduce him to the governor. They were soon laughing, but Thomas and Stephen were very nervous when the governor came over to the tented area. Baroni introduced each missionary to Mercelli and Governor Quintus tenius Rufus.[133]

Governor Rufus[134] said to Thomas, "Centurion Baroni tells me you are missionaries on your way to a special island."

"Yes, a very special island," Thomas said. "But we must find it first."

"I was impressed with your new ships at the pier," the governor said. "My officers and I are intrigued by the names the Free Spirit and the Islander. Baroni said the Islander will be your construction boat when you find your uninhabited island and the Free Spirit will be your travelling ship. Tribunes Mascaro, Pasquali and Cerrone have some work for you to do. I do as well, but I'll talk to you further tomorrow."

"Thank you for your interest," Thomas said. "Your officers helped me with the purchase of the two ships and the signage."

---

[133] Jewishencyclopedia.com Tineius Rufus. Many sources, including rabbinical ones, have made him familiar as governor during the Bar Kokba uprising. He was replaced by Sextus Julius Serverus from Britain in 133 A.D. Julius Severus, Celebrated general, who suppressed the Bar Kokba uprising (135). He is designated in an inscription "C. I. L." iii. No. 2830) as "legatus pro prætore provinciæ Judææ."

[134] Yahoo Answers.com (Governor Rufus' official title was Praetor which carried an annual pay of 200,000 Denarii at the time of Pontius Pilot. Rufus had one Legion reporting to him which carried a pay scale of 500,000 Denarii and when he was given a second Legion his pay would have risen to 900,000 Denarii.)

"I'm told your group has converted and baptized many Roman soldiers and officers," said the governor. "While it is no concern of mine, Caesar Aeolus Hadrian has had many Christians killed. You are well-respected and liked by my officers; try to keep it that way. I'm told you were asked by the mayor to present your religion to the city, including to my soldiers at the fort and the soldiers arriving today. I will allow this, but religious discussions can end in violence. How do you plan to present your religion tonight?"

"I respect your worry and hope our approach will meet with your approval," Thomas responded, smiling. "The mayor has had us announced as Christian actors from Jerusalem who will be putting on a religious play tonight. We hope to keep it light and entertaining. We used this approach in Joppa and had no problems. We baptized over two-hundred people the next day."

"Yes, I heard about Joppa," the governor said. "I also heard about your success with our soldiers in Sebaste. You are very cleaver to keep your activities under the control of my officers. You're not afraid of me are you?"

"We're terrified of you, but I respect the way you have treated us," Thomas said, smiling. "Thank you."

"I will see what you missionaries do tonight," the governor said. "I'll see how productive you are in Caesarea."

The governor turned to Mercelli and Baroni. "Please reserve forty seats in the center close enough for us to hear properly. I want at least one-hundred fifty soldiers stationed around the amphitheater. I'll give you a list of who will be in the forty reserved seats."

"There will be two plays tonight, one for the Jews and one for the rest of the population," Baroni said. "It's the mayor's idea. The Jewish presentation will be last."

"I agree," the governor said. "We'll attend the first play."

He walked away with his entourage and resumed his tour around town.

"You're one lucky Christian," Baroni said. "The Governor was responsible for the death of many Christians before his tour in Cyprus."

At this point, some of the town officials came to the tented area. Several women carried food of all kinds so they could make their choices. Other women offered wine or juice to drink. Everyone sat down and enjoyed their food. The local people were getting their food and going off to various locations to enjoy their feast. It was a warm delightful afternoon. After eating, they wandered to the ships.

✝ Chapter 28 ✝

The Plays in Caesarea
Saturday, April 27, 125 A.D.

The missionaries were nervous as the time for the play came closer. "What we'll be doing tonight is similar to what we did in Joppa and Sebaste," Thomas said. "It should be alright."

They stood in front of the Free Spirit and were met by Baroni who said, "I had Pardi and his soldiers go over to the amphitheater early. The governor, the mayor and their entourages were seated first. The rest of the seats are taken by local people, but there are twice as many waiting outside."

"Tamir, you, the soldiers, your seamen and guards should attend the second play," Thomas said.

"I'll have Pardi and his thirty soldiers guard the ships while you attend the second play," Baroni said.

They followed Baroni to the amphitheater. They were met at the entrance by the mayor and Mascaro. "You need to schedule a third play and modify the Jewish seating," Mascaro said to the mayor."

Thomas nodded his agreement.

The mayor was delighted and went off to find his announcers. Mascaro went into the audience to inform Governor Rufus and take his seat. By the time they stepped onto the stage, the mayor returned. They looked out at the audience to see there were no vacant spaces left at all. The mayor went to the center of the stage to announce, "The play will be in the form of questions and answers."

The audience seemed to accept this with a nervous, quiet manner, possibly just anticipation.

"I would like to introduce Thomas," the mayor said. "He's the leader of the missionaries and is the owner of the Free Spirit and the Islander at the pier. I will now turn the play over to him."

As he returned to his seat, Thomas walked to the middle of the stage. The rest of the missionaries assumed their positions with three sitting on the sides of the stage, where they could easily jump up. Thomas introduced each missionary.

"Why are you here?" Thomas shouted.

"We're here for the play," they shouted.

"Yes, but what kind of a play?"

"You're here to show us the Christian play," the audience shouted back.

"We're Christians and we will tell you the story of Christ in a series of acts in which all of us will participate."

Thomas started with the first question for Peter asking, "Who predicted that the Christ would come to earth?"

"He was foretold by many Jewish prophets over the past several hundred years," Peter shouted.

The play went on as they had rehearsed it. Many of the questions asked by various speakers were answered by the audience. The breaks between speakers were met with clapping and some cheering. The audience jumped to their feet several times during the play.

Mark asked Paz, "Can disbelief be a problem?"

Paz replied, "Yes, Jesus and his apostles were preaching one day. And when he came to his disciples, He saw a great multitude around them. Immediately, when they saw Him, all the people were greatly amazed, and running to Him. And He asked the scribes, *'What are you discussing with them?'* One of the multitudes answered, *'Teacher, I brought You my son who has a mute spirit. He (Jesus) answered him and said, O faithless generation, how long shall I be with you? How long shall I bear with you?'*"

"If you can believe, all things are possible to him who believes. Immediately, the father of the child cried out and said, with tears, 'Lord, I believe, help my child.' He (Jesus) rebuked the unclean spirit, saying to him, 'You deaf and dumb spirit, I command you, come out of him, and enter him no more.' Then the spirit cried out, convulsed him greatly, and came out of him. His disbelief had allowed the bad spirit in. His new belief forced the spirit to be thrown out."[135]

Paz asked David, "What did Jesus say about judging others?"

David jumped up to say, "Judge not, that you be not judged. For with what judgment you judge, you will be judged; and with the same measure you use, it will be measured back to you."[136]

David asked Stephen, "What did Jesus say about asking?"

Stephen threw his arms in the air and said, "Ask, and it will be given to you; seek and you will find; knock and it will be opened to you. For everyone who asks receives, and he who seeks finds, and to him who knocks it will be opened."[137]

Stephen asked Ben, "What does Jesus' death mean to us?"

Ben explained, "Jesus' death was an exchange for all of our sins."

Ben asked, pointing to Thomas, "What does this exchange mean?"

"This exchange is in return for our redemption," Thomas said. "When Paul was in Rome he wrote to the Ephesians saying about Jesus: *'For he himself is our peace, who has made both one and has broken down the middle wall of division between us, having abolished in Him the enmity, that is the law of commandments contained in ordinances, so as to create in Himself one new man from the two, thus making peace, and that He might reconcile them both to God in one body through the cross, thereby putting to death the enmity.'"[138]

Thomas asked Ben, "What did Jesus say was the best rule you should follow?"

Ben walked around in a circle and when he faced the audience he said, "Therefore, whatever you want men to do to you, do also to them, for this is the Law...."[139]

Ben pointed to Thomas and said, "Thomas take it."

"We sometimes feel guilty; well, now we do not need to – WE ARE FORGIVEN," Thomas shouted. "THROUGH JESUS WE ARE SAVED."

---

[135] Ibid, Mark 9: 14-26.
[136] Ibid, Mathew 7: 1-2.
[137] Ibid, Mathew 7: 7-8.
[138] Ibid, Ephesians 2:14-15.
[139] Ibid, Mathew 7: 12.

The audience stood clapping with some cheering from the soldiers. They went out the back of the amphitheater stage. It was dark by this time, with a cool breeze coming in from the Mediterranean. The missionaries were met by Baroni and Pardi with his men right behind him. They strode back to the ship to wait for the audience to leave and allow the reseating of the Jewish population and other waiting citizens.

"Tamir take everyone over to the amphitheater to get seated," Thomas said. "Pardi, you and your men are in charge of security here at the ships while we put on the next play."

They evaluated their performance and discussed some weak moments in their presentations. Everyone agreed the weakest moments were the transition from one speaker to the next. This seemed to be caused by the answering speaker jumping in too fast and being unsure the previous speaker had completed his part.

"Point and say the next speakers name to insure clarity to the answering speaker," Stephen said.

"The seating for the next session is almost complete," Taccone said when he arrived. "As it turned out, the Jewish audience was very small. The balance of the seating and standing room has been filled by non-Jewish residents. A crowd is still waiting for session three, which is pretty large. Many people from the first session have gone around encouraging people to stay for the last session. I guess no one has ever seen anything like your play."

They laughed. "We've hit on a success with this format," Ben said. "I never thought being a missionary could be so exciting and demanding, and also so rewarding. But then, who would have thought we would be asked to put on these plays? We have talked about this before, but maybe we are in the nascent of significant growth in Christianity. Who would have thought all these people here in Caesarea would want to see our play? It's a new beginning far beyond what we'd first planned."

"I think the town's reception of this play is especially funny," Taccone said. "Governor Rufus' reaction was a bit strange. The governor, Mercelli and Mascaro enjoyed the play. They think all of you have missed your calling and all of you should be great actors. The governor said if you believe in Christ the way you presented the play, Christianity could become a substantial force in the Roman Empire. He said that giving good speeches and acting is a sought after skill by most Caesars in the past. Hadrian is especially proud to see good speakers and plays. This is one of the reasons he is considered to be like a Greek. The governor told me to tell you he will do his best to look out for you while you are here. He also requested that you leave them a good Christian who can administer to the people who want to become Christians after you are gone."

"This request will require us to stay another couple of days," Thomas said to Taccone.

"I'm pleased," Taccone said. "I'll tell Governor Rufus and the mayor your decision. They will be pleased that you are willing to do this. Right now you need to get back to the amphitheater."

Baroni and the twenty soldiers acting as guards on the ships led them back to the amphitheater. The missionaries went into the back of the stage. This session was just as crowded and included more soldiers than the first session. The mayor greeted them as they walked onto the stage. They scattered around again and Thomas walked up to the mayor who had a big smile on his face. He welcomed Thomas and waved his arm around the stage. The mayor was clearly having a great time. The breeze from the sea was cooler, but it was still pleasant.

"The first play was received with high excitement," the mayor announced. "Governor Rufus, Legatus Mercelli and Tribune Mascaro attended the first session and all three declared the first play to be outstanding. You have probably heard about the play and reactions from those who attended. This presentation will be even better. I would like to turn the play over to Thomas."

Thomas waved his arm around the stage, introducing each missionary and telling the audience of the order to their play.

"Why are we here?" Thomas shouted.

"Tell us," the audience yelled back.

The Jewish audience was seated together, very quiet and being ignored by the rest of the audience. "I'm surprised there are any Jews here at all," Thomas whispered to the other missionaries. "It's the Jewish Sabbath today. They shouldn't be here at all. Curiosity may have gotten the better of them."

The soldiers were the loudest in their response. Many residents looked at them and seemed amused. Most people did not usually mingle with soldiers and this experience was amazing for some. The Jews did not seem amused.

"How would we have reacted if we had the Jewish faith?" Stephen whispered to the others. "Christianity has somehow released us and we have become very different people. It's the joy of Christ's love. They don't seem to feel it."

Starting the play, and pointing at Stephen, Thomas asked, "How do people change when they become new Christians?"

Stephen walked to the center of the stage and said, "We love our neighbors as we love ourselves. I feel the forgiveness and that starts my heart singing for joy. Joy abounds in all I say and do. It's so opposite the fear felt everywhere."

The questions and answers were even more animated than the first session. The transition from one speaker to the next was smoother and the audience followed it as well as the speakers. During this play, a breeze picked up in intensity.

David pointed to Mark and said, "What did Jesus say about forgiving the most and loving the most?"

Mark stood up smiling and said, "Jesus was invited to eat at the home of Simon a Pharisee. 'And behold, a woman in the city who was a sinner, when she knew that Jesus sat at a table in the Pharisee's house , brought an alabaster flask and fragrant oil, and knelt at His feet behind Him with her tears, and wiped them with the hair of her head; and she kissed His feet and anointed them with the fragrant oil. Now when the Pharisee who had invited Him saw this, he spoke to himself, saying, This man, if He were a prophet, would know who and what manner of woman this is who is touching Him, for she is a sinner. And Jesus answered and said to him, Simon, I have something to say to you.'"

Mark walked around and asked what did he say? He said, "Jesus asked Simon, '-if two debtors owed 500 dinarii, and the other 50 dinarii and he forgave both, who will love the creditor more? Simon answered, 'the debtor owing the 500.' Jesus said, 'You're right. So think of how she gave me water for my feet and you didn't. She washed my feet with her tears and you didn't. She kisses my feet and you haven't. And she anointed my feet with fragrant oil and you haven't. Her sins are forgiven and that's why she loves so much. He who forgives little loves little; but he who forgives the most loves the most.' We need to tell this story over and over because everybody sins."[140]

---

[140] Ibid, Luke 7: 36-50.

Stephen knelt and asked Thomas, "Did God create us and have a plan for us before we were born?"

Thomas turned back to the audience and said, "*It is God himself who has made us what we are and given us new lives from Christ Jesus; and long ages ago he planned that we should spend these lives in helping others.*"[141]

Thomas smiled and said, "The Apostle Paul said to Timothy his friend, who he called his beloved son, when he was in a Roman prison, '*Therefore I remind you to stir up the gift of God which is in you through the laying of my hands. For God has not given us a spirit of fear, but of power and of love and of a sound mind. Therefore do not be ashamed of the testimony of the Lord, nor of me His prisoner, but share with me in the sufferings for the gospel according to the power of God, who has saved us and called us with holy calling, not to our own works, but according to His own purpose and grace which was given to us in Christ Jesus BEFORE TIME BEGAN, but has now been revealed by the appearing of our Savior Jesus Christ, who has abolished death and brought life and immortality to light through the gospel ...*'"[142]

Thomas walked to the side of the stage and pointed to Ben on the other side and said, "What did Apostle Paul tell us to do as teachers in Christianity?"

Ben walked to the center of the stage and said, "*...we should no longer be children, tossed to and fro and carried about in every wind of doctrine, by the trickery of men, in the cunning craftiness by which they lie in wait to deceive, but speaking the truth in love ...*"[143]

When they finished, they ran out the back of the stage. The audience leaped to their feet clapping and with some cheering. Thomas then ran back to the front of the stage and shouted, "THROUGH JESUS, WE ARE SAVED."

This resulted in more shouting and applause. The rest of the missionaries ran forward on the stage, bowed and then ran out the back of the stage again. There couldn't help but be an explosion of love and joy to everyone who sees and hears. It was clear they wanted to be like Jesus in their hearts.

---

[141] Living Bible, Wheaton, IL: Tyndale House Publishers (1979). Ephesians 2: 10.

[142] Ibid, 2 Timothy 1: 6-10.

[143] Ibid, Ephesians 4: 14-15.

The missionaries watched the Jewish residents leave quietly with a look of surprise at all the laughing and shouting. "They are mystified at what they witnessed us do and the reaction of most of the audience," Thomas said. "I thought they would be angry, but they look kind of sad."

Baroni, Tamir and the others caught up with them on the way back to the ships. They were feeling some fatigue. "We should have some juice and take care of our personal needs before the last session," Thomas said. "Let's go over to the tented area."

When they were finished, they came back and Pardi dismissed his soldiers to return to the fort and said, "The rest of us will sit around until you return. Good luck with this last play. You men are on fire."

Taccone came to lead them back to the amphitheatre. As they went in through the back of the stage, the audience started to cheer. They walked onto the stage behind the mayor who was smiling and clapping. Everyone settled into to their spaces around the stage.

"This is Thomas, the leader," the mayor said. "Governor Rufus, Legatus Legionis Mercelli and Tribunus Laticlavius Mascaro attended the first session and declared it be outstanding. I want to thank all of you in the audience, including the soldiers for your patience in waiting for this third session. This has been such a public response in this amphitheater. We all agree we see the love and joy of Jesus in these missionaries' hearts. They will be loved by all they meet on their journey and our joy will be full when they return."

Thomas turned to the audience and was about to ask his question about why were they there. Before he could speak, the audience stood as one. "We are here to see the play if that is what you want to know," they shouted.

Obviously, word had gotten around to everyone about Thomas' question. Thomas smiled and clapped. Without a hitch, he went on with his questions. They responded and the play went on even better this time. The temperature continued to drop and clouds rolled over the city as the play continued. As Ben finished, it started to rain.

"WE ARE SAVED," Thomas shouted.

The audience cheered and clapped in the rain.

"Thank you; now let's go find shelter," he shouted.

Running out the back of the stage, Baroni and Pardi joined them as they jogged back to the pier. When they reached the ships, Tamir stuck his head over the railing on the Islander and said, "All of us are in bed." The missionaries, Baroni and Pardi went to their assigned ship and got into bed.

The rain lasted quite a while, but eventually the clouds moved on past the city. Before dawn, Thomas, Baroni and Peter went to the upper decks to look out at the open sea. They spotted several ships in the moonlight sitting far out in the Mediterranean, beyond the artificial bay. They were waiting for daybreak to come into the marina. Tamir came over to the Free Spirit.

"Taccone talked to me last night," Baroni said. "Thomas and Stephen, you, are invited to visit the palace in the morning to meet with Governor Rufus. We'll first meet at the mayor's house for breakfast. Second, we'll have a brief meeting with Mascaro at the fort. He will then take the two of you to the palace. Taccone said he had never seen Mascaro or Governor Rufus mingle with the residents like they did, let alone sit in a crowded amphitheater. Governor Rufus asked Taccone to report to the palace after the second play. He wanted to know how many Jews attended and how they behaved themselves. Taccone did not tell me what he told Governor Rufus, but he was not gone very long."

"I agreed to stay two more days to set up an organization to take care of the converts," Thomas said. "I wonder how many converts there will be, and whether we will need to baptize them. I expect the new congregation leadership to baptize all who show their desire to be saved."

"Look at the ships waiting to come into the harbor and to the marina," Peter said. "I can't be sure how many ships are out there. I think there are about a dozen. I heard this is part of the Roman Legion, Legio XXII Deiotariana[144] and is coming in from Egypt. It was formed about a hundred and seventy five-years ago in Galacia. It originally had 22,000 men and 2,000 horses."

"The officers' quarters are crowded with all these new officers coming in here," Baroni said. "It will be an interesting treat to stay out here on the Free Spirit."

---

[144]Allexperts.com, Encyclopedia Beta. The Roman Empire integrated the Galatian kingdom and this legion. It had been trained by the Romans and had fought under Roman commanders when it became part of the Roman army. The last record of XXII *Deiotariana* is from 119 A.D. In 145 A.D., when a list of all existing legions was made, XXII *Deiotariana* was not listed. Probably, XXII *Deiotariana* was destroyed during the Jewish rebellion of Simon bar Kokba (132–136 A.D.).

The soldiers on the two ships were now up looking at the ships in the bay. After giving up on the ship count, Thomas, Baroni and Pardi went back to bed. Tamir returned to his bed on the Islander.

† Chapter 29 †

The Meeting with Governor Rufus
Sunday, April 28, 125 A.D.

As the sun came up, they heard ships easing their way into the marina. There were ten ships coming in, three at a time. The first three tied up around them. Baroni saluted the ship's officers, while the soldiers helped tie up the ships.

"Do you think this is part of the five thousand soldiers requested by Governor Rufus?" Stephen asked Thomas.

"I am sure it is. Governor Rufus said many of the soldiers would arrive by ship."

As soon as a ship was tied up and the gangplank lowered to the pier deck, soldiers started walking out to the road where they lined up. After a while Thomas had counted seven-hundred and fifty soldiers lined up in the street. Twenty Principale officers were distinctive with medallions hanging from their necks. They had bright feather hedges rising from the center of their flashing helmets. They stood waiting together in front of the soldiers.

Taccone and Mascaro came down the road on horseback. They had twenty mounted soldiers following them. As they approached the lineup, the twenty soldiers stopped. Mascaro and Taccone walked their horses up to the twenty Principale officers. Two stepped forward to hold the reins while they dismounted. Mascaro stepped back and saluted.

"Welcome to Caesarea Israel," he said. "March your men to Fort Caesarea where they will camp outside the fort. Two officers are to organize the transporting of the soldiers' supplies. A number of dock-workers are on their way here with horse-drawn wagons."

"We should get out of the way," Baroni said to the missionaries. "We need to walk to the mayor's house to have breakfast."

They followed Baroni, with the soldiers from the ships behind them. The mayor's home was not far. As they approached the house, they could see several dozen people already in line for breakfast. The people stepped away from the food tables and allowed them to be first in line. The mayor came out to welcome them.

"We are eating food left over from yesterday," the mayor said apologizing.

"Please do not apologize," Thomas said. "This is great,"

"The food was heated and spiced for breakfast," one cook said. "You'll enjoy it."

When they had their food and were seated, the rest of the people got back in line. The mayor sat by Thomas. As they ate their breakfast, he said, "Governor Rufus told me last night that a house of worship would need to be built for the new congregation and a leader picked by you. The governor will want to interview and approve whoever you choose for his appointment. He thinks an acceptance of the Christians is starting to occur in Rome. They used to kill them as fast as they could locate them. He hopes that has stopped. Think what this new hope can mean for our community and the whole Roman world."

"Word of Governor Pliney's recommendation to Trajan over fifteen years ago led Trajan's declaration that prohibition of killing a person just because he is a Druid or Christian, has helped. Trajan gave orders to stop accepting unfounded complaints against Christians.[145] It was shown that the Christians could become very good citizens because of their love for each other and non-violent beliefs. However, I must tell you that Aelius Hadrian has not been convinced."

---

[145] Ibid, Trajan's letter back to Pliny

"Caesar Hadrian and those who ruled before him always worried about new philosophies and religions that could cause the Romans to lose control," Baroni said. "This large growth in Christianity could be a nascent, a new beginning that might scare Caesar Hadrian. We need to be careful how it is perceived."

"We will need your advice on this," Thomas said. "This acceptance worries me because it will be perceived as frightening to Roman leaders. We need to show how it can be beneficial to the Romans. Do you know of anyone I should consider for the head of the congregational ecclesia of Caesarea?"

"I was approached last night by a good candidate," the mayor said. "This candidate is a prominent citizen by the name of Ibrahim. He is a Jew, but is not well liked by his Rabbi or other Jews who know him."

"Does this Jew want to convert to Christianity and be baptized?" Stephen asked.

"He is eager to be baptized."

"How long has this Jew lived in Caesarea?"

"His family has lived here for many generations."

"He sounds like a possible good choice," Thomas said. "Please send him to the Free Spirit as soon as you can."

Thomas, Stephen and Baroni walked to the fort to see Mascaro. The other five missionaries, Tamir and the guards walked back to the ships. The unloading of the newly arrived ships was progressing smoothly. As Thomas and Stephen walked up the path to the officers' quarters, Taccone came out.

"Good morning," he said. "Have you encountered any problems this morning?"

"No and we had a great breakfast at the mayor's home," Thomas said.

"I talked to Pardi earlier. He informed me the rest of his men are doing well this morning," Taccone said to Baroni. "He sent ten of his men to your ships. Thomas, Stephen and Baroni, may I take you in to see Mascaro?"

They walked into the building and on into the dining room. Mascaro was seated talking to Legatus Legionis Mercelli. Both men stood to greet Thomas, Stephen and Baroni.

"I was just telling Mercelli what an overall success the feast and the three plays were last night," Mascaro said. "Thomas, have you any ideas for a leader for the Christians here in Caesarea? You are going to have many converts to baptize."

"The mayor is sending a Jew by the name of Ibrahim over to the Free Spirit for me to interview later this morning," Thomas said, smiling. "He wants to be baptized and be the leader of the Nazarene Congregation here in Caesarea. He's an ideal candidate because he is well known."

"I have met Ibrahim," Mascaro said. "I think he's a good choice. There needs to be a good strong leader here. As you know the new leader must have my approval before I will take him to see Governor Rufus. You and Stephen need to go now with Mercelli to see Governor Rufus. He is waiting to talk to both of you."

"Baroni, will you accompany us as we walk over to the palace?" Mercelli said. "Follow me. "

"Where did you transfer from?" Baroni asked.

"I came from Rome with the governor," he said. "I'm part of the troop transfer he requested. I oversee all of the soldiers in Israel and report directly to Governor Rufus."

They walked past guards outside the palace and into the entrance. The governor came into the reception area and greeted Mercelli. He turned to Thomas. "Good morning. I had no idea you and your missionaries were so talented. Everyone I talked to last night and this morning said each play was performed better than the play that preceded it. I have never circulated among the population like I did at the feast and the play. There was no anger or negative emotion anywhere, which is unusual here. Thank you for the way you and your missionaries participated in the feast and the plays. Your Christian love was felt by all."

"I feel that Jesus watched over us yesterday and last night," Thomas said.

"If he is helping you, I hope he continues," the governor said and smiled for the first time. "The reason I invited you here to the palace this morning is to fulfill the request you presented to Mascaro. I will present ten identification coins for each of you to carry one wherever you travel in the Roman Empire. With these special coins, you should receive all the co-operation you will need."

"Thank you Governor Rufus, Thomas said.

"I have a second reason I wanted to talk to you. I have a message from Cerrone telling me there is a Jew by the name of Hadar after you because he thinks you have some old temple records. Cerrone has learned that Hadar is shipping in swords, knives, shields, horses and supplies to this Simeon ben Kosiba and his rebel army. Cerrone says Hadar's men have attempted to kidnap you a couple of times, attacked you and our men on the road from Joppa and at your home in Jerusalem. I was sorry to learn that your aunt and her handmaiden were raped repeatedly and the handmaiden brutalized and murdered. I applaud your hiring security men and Cerrone says some of his men are assigned to assist them. Mascaro says you hired a ship-captain in Joppa who had quit a job as ship-captain for Hadar. This is all good news because we need to capture and kill this Hadar and his men."

"Cerrone and I talked about me being used as bait to attract Hadar," Thomas said. "Cerrone told me I'll need to do other things as well, in exchange for security to be provided in Israel and when we leave to find the Island-of Dreams."

"There is a third reason I wanted to talk to you," Rufus said. "Principale Pardi has asked for his retirement and we have granted it. He wants to help you with your Island-of-Dreams and can be released from duty when you leave. He needs to go home to Sicily he says and then join you. Baroni, you have been a very loyal Roman Centurion, but I understand you want to retire in a couple of years. I'm releasing you from duty in Jerusalem. I understand you have been in charge of security for Thomas and his missionaries. I want you to continue this protection. I'm assigning to you three ships now stationed in Crete. The ships have a crew of sixty soldiers and three Principale officers. When you leave with Thomas, I will have two transport ships follow you to Crete for security. I will get you a packet with the orders and the names of the ships and Principale officers you will command."

"Thank you," Baroni said. "This assignment pleases me."

"Back to you, Thomas," the governor said. "Baroni's job is two-fold. He'll provide protection for you and your ships and try to capture or kill Hadar if they come after you, which we hope he does. Tell me what your plan is."

"We'll set sail to find the Island-of-Dreams," Thomas said. "We'll stop in Crete to let Baroni take over the three ships and then proceed to Sicily to let Pardi visit his home and obtain grapevine starts. After that I hope to find the Island-of-Dreams using the maps we have and my memory of it in my dream with Jesus. I'll leave Mark and a few men with the tools and equipment, now on the ships. I want to start construction on the homes and the house of worship on the island. Tamir and the Islander will be used to bring in workmen and supplies. After that I want to travel to Gaul, Espania and Britain to look for locations to relocate some friends and family. I will then return to Jerusalem for the fall and winter."

"I understand you want to transport your records and artifacts from Jerusalem to the Island-of-Dreams," Rufus said. "When will you do that?"

"It'll take a couple of years to build the homes and house of worship," Thomas said. "I need a vault built in the house of worship to hold the records and artifacts. I want to return to the Island-of-Dreams with the plans for the vault early next year. The year after next I want to transport the records, artifacts and people from Israel. We will take the records and artifacts to the island and the people to Gaul, Espania or Britain."

"Your plans seem well thought out," Rufus said. "Next year after you return to your island with plans for the vault and check on construction, I want you and Baroni with his ships to sail to Cyprus. It has been very unsettled since the Kitos war and the removal of all of its Jews eight years ago. Cyprus's Governor Valerian and I believe we need to do something to reduce the mistrust the followers of Apollo and Aphrodite have for Christians. They still think Christians are Jews and are afraid of them."

"What do you want us to do in Cyprus?" Thomas asked.

Governor Rufus smiled and said, "My officers and I have seen what you and your missionaries can do here in Israel to convert gentiles to Christianity and leave the leadership under the command of our local officers. We believe Christians become peace loving citizens. There are many Christians on Cyprus. It is important for Greek and Roman gentiles to be more informed about Christianity to reduce the distrust and violence. There are amphitheaters all over Cyprus which can be used for you to put on your plays and interact with the local population and Roman officers. Several of the officers are new and need to tour parts of Cyprus under their responsibility. I believe you will improve the peace and understanding in Cyprus wherever you go."

"This'll be a great opportunity for us to do our missionary work there," Thomas said. "Will we be asked to do this in other places besides Cyprus and Israel?"

"I would like to see you perform your plays in Crete, Sicily, Malta and any islands near your Island-of-Dreams this year," Rufus said. "I have already sent messages to my friends, the Governors of Crete, Malta and Sicily. They should expect you and I hope assist you. I have asked them to help you put on a play in an amphitheater of their choice. By the way Baroni, when you get to Thomas' island, I want you to line up two or three Roman ships to protect the Island-of-Dreams and the Islander. I will get you written orders for local commanders."

"On another subject, I understand you have become, in the Roman custom, clients of Cerrone, Pasquali and Mascaro. I'm told you understand and support this kind of relationship. I'm pleased to also be a Patron to you. Do you agree to be my client?

"Yes, I do understand this relationship and its obligations," Thomas said. "I'm pleased to be your client. I'll endeavor to do as you ask."

"Good, I was sure you would. Thomas, I want you to see me when you return from your island."

✝ Chapter 30 ✝

Christian Ecclesia of Caesarea
Sunday, April 28, 125 A.D.

Thomas, Stephen and Baroni followed the path back over the hill and down past the fort. They watched the newly arrived soldiers setting up tents and getting organized. As they walked towards the pier and their ship, they were confronted by five men in front of the pier. One of the men stepped forward and introduced himself.

"I am Ibrahim," he said.

"Yes, the mayor told me about you," Thomas said. "You are of the Jewish faith, but want to become a Christian."

"It has been my desire for a long time to become a Nazarene Christian." Ibrahim smiled, then laughed and said, "I made this final decision last night during your play. I've thought about it for a few years. Your group was so convincing and entertaining. You gave me the answer I was seeking. I think I can enjoy the faith and deal with any person who wants to become a Christian. I have heard much about Jesus, but you made him real. If only I could present the story the way you do. God bless you and your fellow missionaries."

"Ibrahim, we are staying two extra days to help set up the congregational ecclesia of Caesarea at the request of the governor," Thomas said. "I have authority from Nasi Judah in Jerusalem and also an order from Governor Rufus to set up a congregation here in Caesarea for citizens who want to become Christians. If I decide you are the one to become the head of the congregation in Caesarea, I will need to take you to Tribune Mascaro at the fort. If he approves of you, then we must go to the palace to meet with Governor Rufus to obtain his approval. He is having considerable trouble with Jews throughout Judea and the rest of Israel at this time. Because of this Jewish trouble, you can see the soldiers and their supplies are arriving to deal with it. As a Jew, you will feel much anxiety, fear and conflict. But you will understand Jews better than many. Show the people here how to love and find joy in their life."

"I know your name is Thomas," Ibrahim said. "You are related to Apostle Thomas, Jesus' brother and one of his twelve apostles. You are downplaying your importance as a power in the Christian world. I would say you have the authority to appoint me."

"Ibrahim, if I appoint you and obtain Governor Rufus' approval, I do so as an interim step which you will need to have ratified in Jerusalem," Thomas said. "If you have Governor Rufus' backing, I am sure you will get that approval from Nasi Judah."

"I agree to the interim appointment; I will work for the later approval by Nasi Judah," Ibrahim said. "I have heard good words about Nasi Judah, and I am anxious to meet him."

"That is good. Ibrahim, you will need to contact Nasi Judah in Jerusalem for scrolls that can assist you," Thomas said. "He gave me a copy of the words of Mark, Mathew, Luke, John, Paul, Barnabus and other disciples written on papyrus scrolls. He has several scribes working on more copies for leaders like you. You'll also need a copy of the Torah or Talmud. You will find yourself reading and rereading constantly."

"Ibrahim, will you have any assistants?" Stephen asked.

"These four men with me want to be baptized and assist me with the organizing of the congregation," Ibrahim said. "They want to help build a house of worship where we can hold services and baptize new converts. With all the people now interested, I'll need all the help I can get."

He then introduced the men with him to Thomas and Stephen. They had been at the second play.

"Are all of you of the Jewish faith?" Thomas asked.

"Two are of Jewish faith and two are not," Ibrahim said. "None are Christians now but they want to be baptized with me."

"Good, this congregation is for converted Jews and gentiles alike," Thomas said. "The baptisms should be done immediately. Follow me to the site where Peter has conducted some earlier baptisms. We will take a trail off to the right and down a slope to a small pond in a stream that drains into the sea."

Thomas walked down the pier and then down the trail. As they were walking, two flocks of seagulls flew in and over their heads. They circled back and landed on the hill above them. Upon arriving at the pond's edge, some of the birds flew down close to the pond. A flock of pelicans flew overhead, landed and walked as a group over to the pond. Thomas exclaimed, "The Holy Spirit is attracting the birds and is here ahead of us."

Thomas waded into the pond and asked Stephen to assist him. Ibrahim was first and then the other four were baptized. They all stepped out of the water.

"YOU ARE SAVED," Thomas shouted, throwing his arms in the air causing the seagulls to fly into the sky, some flying past Herod's Caesarea palace and some flying up the coast along the water aqueduct. The pelicans ran down the beach and burst into flight up the coast over the marina.

"Congratulations on your baptism," Thomas said. "All of you go home and freshen up. Ibrahim be back at the pier as soon as you can."

Ibrahim and his team walked towards town. Baroni and the missionaries joined them and all looked at each other and laughed. "Is this moving too fast?" Thomas asked.

"We had better speed up then, and get to the ships," Stephen said.

As they walked to the pier, the last three ships were leaving the marina. Wagons full of supplies were being pulled away from the pier. Thomas and Stephen freshened up with a change of their robes. They combed their beards and hair.

In a short while Ibrahim came back. Thomas went out to meet him. Ibrahim was so happy that he was giddy. Thomas laughed with him and calmed him down. Taccone with a driver pulled up to the pier and motioned to them to get into the wagon. Baroni went with Thomas and Stephen to talk to Taccone.

"I am entrusting the safety of Thomas and Stephen over to you," Baroni said.

"Thank you, but you should come with us," Taccone said.

With that Thomas, Ibrahim and Stephen climbed into the back seat of the wagon. Baroni sat with the driver and Taccone. The driver turned the wagon around and rolled along the road to Fort Caesarea and to the palace.

They watched camp after camp being set up by the soldiers. It looked like total chaos, soldiers everywhere, tents going up, latrines being dug and

Stephen Thomas White

supplies piled everywhere. As they got closer, it began to look more organized. The officers' and soldiers' mess tents were now going up. They pulled into Fort Caesarea and stopped in front of the path to the fort commander's entrance.

They walked over to where Mascaro was standing. "Tribune Mascaro, this is Ibrahim, a new Christian," Taccone said.

Mascaro seemed pleased with Ibrahim. "Ibrahim you need to know that Thomas is well respected by Governor Rufus. You will be taking Thomas' temporary place here in Caesarea. Don't get into trouble with Governor Rufus or me, and we'll give you freedom and our protection. But we must work together. You will have your hands full with the high degree of interest in Christianity that Thomas and his companions have generated."

"Baroni, let me know how Ibrahim is accepted at the palace," Taccone said, then saluted and left.

Mascaro, Baroni, Ibrahim, Thomas and Stephen walked over and got into the wagon. The driver drove out the gate. Thomas liked how the palace was south of the fort up on a hill above Caesarea, overlooking the Mediterranean. It was a marvelous sight. The driver stopped the wagon in front of the entrance. They stepped down and were met by four soldiers who saluted Mascaro. They came through the grand entrance and walked into the meeting area. Mercelli and the Governor were sitting, talking to one of the food servers.

"Welcome. Thomas, would you introduce us to Ibrahim?" Governor Rufus said standing up.

"Governor may I introduce Ibrahim, the newest Christian in Caesarea," Thomas said. "Ibrahim, please meet Governor Rufus and Legatus Legionis Mercelli."

"Ibrahim, I heard about your baptism this morning," Governor Rufus said. "Are you willing to be loyal to me? Will you keep me and my officers informed of all your plans and all the people with whom you have conversions?"

"I will keep you informed and keep my records of conversions available for your representative to review at any time," Ibrahim said.

"Thomas, why do I like you?" the Governor asked.

"Because I can help you," Thomas said.

"You already have," the Governor said. "You are the smartest Christian I have ever met. It is encouraging because you have a Jewish heritage. We need more like you right here."

- 242 -

"Governor Rufus, my companions and I know we are different from those with Jewish faith,"

Thomas said. "The reason we are different is because we are free from the Jewish law. Part of it is the openness we feel because we can convert gentiles like Apostle Paul did. His mother was a Jew and his father was a Roman."

"Am I a gentile?" The Governor asked laughing.

"Yes, you are and I hope I have not offended you?" Thomas replied.

"You have not offended me because I know the term," he said. "You have such honesty. I think you will be affecting me long after you have left."

"May I quote from Apostle Paul, who was a Christian missionary as you know?" Thomas asked.

"If you keep this up you will make a Christian out of me," Governor Rufus said, smiling.

"I would be delighted. Apostle Paul wrote a letter to the Colossians saying: *'Walk in wisdom toward those who are outside. Let your speech always be with grace, seasoned with salt, that you may know how you ought to answer each one.'* [146] We try to follow these words.'"

"Those are remarkable words," Governor Rufus said looking firm again. "They will continue to assist you as you leave here for your Island-of-Dreams. My advice is for you to keep every bishop you appoint under the direction and control of the local Roman officer in charge as you have done here and in Joppa. I look forward to your return. Stephen, please take good care and keep Thomas safe."

Mercelli turned to Thomas and handed over a case with several medals and said, "Tribunus Laticlavius Mascaro promised you a document to identify you after you leave. Governor Rufus said he would issue to you these medals to be used instead of the documents. These special medals[147] will assist you and your companions in your travels. Each medal has a hole for a chain to put around your neck so they don't get lost. Each will identify

---

[146] Ibid, Colossians 4:5-6.

[147] The Countermarks found on ancient Roman Coins, By Richard Baker. (X, XF and LXF were on coins issued by Legion X, Fretensis. Found primarily upon the local coinage of Judaea and Samaria.)

you dead or alive to our people as being part of the Tenth Legio here in Judea and to treat you and your companions as if all of you are citizens of Rome."

"I thank you," Thomas said. "I am honored and delighted. Legatus Legionis Mercelli and Governor Rufus, I would like to express my deep appreciation."

"Baroni, when Thomas finds that special island send me a message where it is located," Governor Rufus said. "Thomas, use the medals I have given you to obtain aid in getting your house of worship built. Be bold and ask for help. When it is completed, I want to journey there and see it. When you find the island, return to Caesarea and see me. We will help you with whatever you need."

The governor turned and walked into another room.

"Thomas," Mercelli said. "I'm amazed at what I saw last night in the play. I'm even more amazed at the level of support that Governor Rufus has given you. My advice to you is, use his support wisely. Do what he asks. Are you that good? Maybe you are."

Now on another subject Mercelli continued, "The governor has become a Patron to you and Stephen and both of you are his clients. Both of you will have continuing client involvements with Cerrone, Pasquali and Mascaro, I would appreciate having both of you as my clients and I would like to be your Patrons. Do both of you accept?"

"I'm pleased to become your client," Thomas said. "I accept the obligations we have created between us."

Mascaro said, "Stephen, please consider being my client and I will be your Patron."

"I'm pleased both of you have asked me," Stephen Said. "I have watched these relationships develop with Thomas. I understand the obligations as your client and I accept the responsibilities."

"Thomas, you should know that Governor Rufus was baptized in Cyprus," Mercelli said. "He usually keeps that information private. You are his client now and you should know."

"Mercelli turned to Ibrahim, "Ibrahim keep that knowledge private unless the governor authorizes you to talk about it. You may become one of the most powerful members of this community. Keep us informed and we will help you make your new congregation lively, challenging and expanding. We will do this for the sake of our soldiers and the citizens."

The governor returned smiling.

Ibrahim bowed to Mercelli and pledged his loyalty. Thomas and Stephen bowed. Mercelli and the governor smiled.

"WE ARE SAVED," The Governor and Mercelli shouted, smiling and laughing as they walked away.

*****************************.

They went outside and got in the wagon, smiling at each other. "Thomas, you are truly unbelievable," Mascaro said. "I don't know how, but you have the support and friendship of Mercelli, Governor Rufus and me. You are friends with and have converted Cerrone and Pasquali, all in a short time. This is an unusual set of events for you and Christianity. Both of you should be pleased with this web of personal friendships with your new Patrons."

"Stephen and I feel extremely lucky to have found such good friends who can support my efforts," Thomas said. "Jesus has asked me to do the tasks we have planned and he told me he would be with me and help. He said to find good Romans to help me and I have. I'm very pleased to be doing what Jesus requested."

"Thomas, you will be a hard act to follow," Ibrahim said. "You set an exemplary example, but I look forward to the work."

When they arrived at the ships, the other missionaries came out to see what happened in the visit to the palace. Thomas, Stephen and Ibrahim took turns telling them about the visit. Thomas then showed them the medals in the case. They were delighted with this level of support.

"It makes us feel venerated and maybe we'll be treated with deference among Romans," Thomas said. "And that will be unbelievable."

"Thomas, I continue to be impressed with you," Baroni said. "Ibrahim, have you any idea how many in Caesarea want to be baptized?"

"No, but my guess is several hundred," Ibrahim said. "This could lead to several thousand. I will have a good start with what you have done. I'm very thankful you attended the feast and performed the three plays. Everybody is astonished. The place is turned around in ways no one expected."

They sat down to watch the red glow of the sunset in the sky and across the Mediterranean. Pelicans and seagulls were flying overhead to land somewhere for the night.

The food wagons arrived from the fort, and the cooks set up a table on the pier between the ships. They started to line up to take some meat and fruits. Before long the missionaries, their guards, seamen, Tamir, Baroni, Pardi and the new congregation staff who just arrived were enjoying a sumptuous meal.

Baroni began to sing in his tenor. Everyone joined in with his own version. After more singing, Ibrahim and his group bid a good night and left for home. Pardi sent his ten soldiers back to the fort.

"We should get a good night's rest," Thomas suggested.

Even though their ship was a good distance from the new camp and Fort Caesarea, they could hear the talking and some occasional singing.

"We can hear them because of the gentle breeze that flows down the hill into the sea after the sun goes down," Peter said. "Tamir and I have noticed that for as long as we have been here."

It was a warm and pleasant evening. The water lapping on the ship and the pier made a comforting sound that put them right to sleep.

✝ Chapter 31 ✝

Services of the Caesarea Ecclesia
Monday, April 29, 125 A.D.

Thomas went up to the top-deck early in the morning. It was chilly with heavy fog, so he returned to bed in the cabin. As the sun raised higher the fog cleared, clouds moved in, and it rained for a while. Not long after the rain stopped, Ibrahim and his four assistants arrived at the ship.

"Let's go down to the baptism pond where there is room for all of us to sit down," Peter said.

The missionaries, Baroni, Pardi, the guards, Ibrahim's group and four soldiers made their way off the ship and the pier. Baroni assigned the soldiers to watch the trail. The twenty of them sat around on the grass, Thomas and Stephen began to review the Jewish prophesies of the coming of Christ. They clarified and repeated the prophecies. Even their Jewish converts were not fully aware of these words.

"I need to get a written copy of the Torah," Ibrahim said.

Stephen reminded Ibrahim that anything he needed, he should formally request from Governor Rufus. Thomas reminded him of the resources that Nasi Judah had in Jerusalem. Cerrone knows him very well and can help you."

"How can the governor get a written history or Torah?" Ibrahim asked.

"The Torah is the Jewish history," Thomas said. "The governor can find one here in Caesarea. Just ask the governor for them."

"I will do as you suggest," Ibrahim said.

For the rest of the morning, all of the missionaries told the story of Jesus and his life. They went over his death, resurrection and return visits after his death when he met with the apostles, Cleopas, Joseph of Arimathea on the road to Emanus and Mary Magdalene to help anchor Ibrahim's faith.

"Ibrahim, more than five hundred people saw Christ after his resurrection," Thomas said. "He was here in person for forty days before his ascension into heaven."

Here again, there were many questions and a lot of clarification.

"You need to continually be in contact with the Nasi in Jerusalem. There are bishops in Rome, Damascus, Joppa and Alexandria," Thomas said. "You also need to request Governor Rufus to assist you in these communications. Remember, he is sending communications to those cities frequently."

"I am beginning to understand you," Ibrahim said. "You take what is offered to you."

It was now mid-day. "We missed breakfast," Baroni said. "Why don't we stop for lunch?"

"I almost forgot," Ibrahim said. "The mayor asked us to invite all of you to another lunch."

"Where will the lunch be served?" Thomas asked.

"It will be in the amphitheater," Ibrahim said. "Many people in town, including many women, wanted to celebrate our re-establishment of the congregation at Caesarea. They wanted to do this before the actors from Jerusalem left for their island."

"I wonder if we would be known as anything other than actors," Stephen said.

"Must we care about our reputation?" Thomas said.

"None of you need to worry," Ibrahim said smiling. "We will make sure you are known as the missionaries. When you come back, several young women would like to know you better."

"If you would, sir, let's go to the amphitheater," Thomas said to Baroni.

"I believe we all have seen history in the making and I'm glad I was here to participate in it," Baroni said.

Everyone was quiet for a few moments. "WE ARE SAVED," Thomas shouted. That surprised everyone and brought them out of their thoughts. Uniformly, every one responded, "WE ARE SAVED."

They were happy as they marched back up the trail. When they met the soldiers, Thomas said. "Tamir, go back to the ships and bring the guards and seamen to the amphitheater."

The missionaries and Ibrahim's group were followed by the soldiers. Governor Rufus, Mercelli and Mascaro were coming along the road behind them with about fifty soldiers all on horseback.

"Where are they going?" Thomas asked Baroni.

"They may be going where we're going," Baroni guessed.

"May the party continue," Thomas said smiling. "If this becomes widespread, it could change Israel forever."

As they came near the amphitheater, there were at least another hundred soldiers along the paths leading into it. Several hundred citizens were already seated. More people had lined up with food on platters.

"Thomas, does anyone ever work here?" Stephen remarked.

"Not while we are here, my friend," Thomas said laughing. "Let's relax and enjoy it. It is our last day here."

"Should we let Governor Rufus go into the amphitheater first," Peter asked Baroni.

"Ask him yourself," he said.

They turned around to see Governor Rufus and his entourage coming up to Thomas.

"Thomas, I hope you are not too surprised by all of this," Governor Rufus said. "You have handled everything expertly up until now."

"Governor, we are humble servants of God," Thomas said. "We are not used to this kind of attention."

"I'm sure you could get used to it, but this afternoon, we wanted you to see what you leave behind here," Governor Rufus said laughing. "Ibrahim, we will enjoy some lunch. Then we will expect you and your assistants to go to the stage and teach us more about Christianity."

Ibrahim was astonished. "How can I compete with the Jerusalem actors?"

"That will be hard, but I believe you can do it," the governor said.

"Thomas, where should we sit?" the governor asked.

"If you will follow me," Thomas said.

Thomas led the governor and his entourage to the middle of the seating and requested some of the residents to honor the governor by giving him their seats."

People were happy to move. The mayor waved and led the missionaries and the Caesarea ecclesia leadership to the stage, where tables and chairs were set up. Ibrahim and his group had a table at the front of the stage. They looked up to see soldiers taking up the last three rows and standing along the back. Baroni went to the front of the stage and gave several Roman salutes to soldiers in the back, and then saluted the senior officers with Governor Rufus.

The servers started with the first food going to Governor Rufus and his entourage and the second to those on stage. When the dishes were being gathered, the mayor came down the steps to the stage in the front and center. He waited while the audience saw him and stopped talking.

"The first service of the Nazarene congregation of Caesarea will begin now," the mayor said.

Governor Rufus stood up quietly for a few moments. "Ibrahim, we are here to be saved. Give us the word of God."

Ibrahim looked afraid as he rose to his feet. Then he seemed to become a new man and stood proudly. He began with a prayer.

"We thank you God for sending your only begotten son to save us. Thank you for the missionaries from Jerusalem. God bless the missionaries wherever they go. Help them with their mission to find the Island-of-Dreams and build your house of worship. Please bless the new Nazarene congregation here in Caesarea. Please God, help us, and bless the new building we will build to worship you. Amen."

Ibrahim and his assistants began the lecture with questions and answers about the Jewish Torah and the life and deeds of Christ Jesus. Each of his assistants and sometimes the audience answered questions. The discussion, questions and answers went on for a while. Ibrahim invited questions. Some were directed to the missionaries, but Ibrahim or his assistants were able to answer them. After some time went by, the questions stopped. Ibrahim then asked the missionaries to come out for a last view by the audience. For this they took a bow. The mayor stood up and walked onto the stage.

"Welcome to the new Nazarene congregation at Caesarea," he said. "It's been a heart-warming and thrilling beginning."

They remained on the stage as the audience left the amphitheater. Governor Rufus came forward to the stage. "Thank you, Ibrahim," he said.

"And Thomas, I wish you a safe hunt for your island. Remember what I said about keeping me informed about finding the island and your success with building the house of worship. When you return, I want to hear about your adventures and what you find. One day I will see your house of worship for myself."

With that the governor walked down and out the back of the stage with the Roman officers following him.

Thomas and Stephen went over to Ibrahim and his people. "Thank you for your spontaneous performance," Thomas said. "We wish you good luck and God speed in growing your community of believers."

They went out the back of the stage and sauntered back towards the ship with Baroni and the guards following. Thomas could see Tamir, the seamen and guards were almost back to the ships. On the way to the ship, they met Pardi and eight soldiers and Thomas said, "Your involvement has been deeply appreciated."

Pardi bowed to Thomas. "I knew you and your companions were very important when I took this assignment," he said. "I have learned just how important your group really is. I appreciate your helping me to become a Christian. I wish to talk to you."

"Let's go to the Free Spirit to talk privately," Thomas said. "I also need to talk to you."

When everyone was back at the ship, Pardi said, "Are you aware that I have retired and plan to leave with you tomorrow?"

Thomas smiled and said, "Yes, I want to apologize to you. Governor Rufus told me you were retiring and going with us tomorrow. I just haven't taken the time to tell you this. I told the Governor we would drop you off at your Palermo port in Sicily to go home to your family. I hope you can get us some premium grape starts. We'll return to pick you up and take you to the Island-of-Dreams. I will want you to manage the vineyard, the gardens and help Mark supervise the construction of the homes and the house of worship."

"Thank you," Pardi said. "I was worried, but I am glad the Governor told you. I'm excited about the island, the vineyard and the building projects. I can help you find workers and help manage them. I have had some rock quarry experience, including cutting granite slabs. I also supervised one project that required some concrete mixing[148] and pouring. Baroni has some changes in his duties. Have you talked to him?"

"No, I haven't." Thomas looked over the deck to see Baroni staring at him. "Baroni, could you come over here? Have you received your orders and information as to the ships and their captains you will meet in Crete? Have you met with the two ship captains that will follow us to Crete?"

"I have my orders and the information I need," Baroni said. "The two transport ships are in the pier now and the captains are expecting me to meet with them today. I would like to introduce you, Stephen, Peter and Tamir to them."

"Good," Thomas said. "The Governor said you plan to retire in a couple of years. I know what your duties include until then. What are your plans after you retire?"

"I could return to my home town, find a wife and settle down," Baroni said. "The trouble is that's not enough. I like traveling with you and your missionaries. I would like to settle wherever you settle. I'm sure you'll keep your missionary work up for a long time. I don't want to see you killed. I think you'll need me."

"I'm flattered," Thomas said. "I would be delighted to have you continue to travel with us and be our friend and neighbor when we are home, wherever that may be."

"We can leave as soon as it starts to get light in the morning," Peter said, walking over to them. "Tacone's men have helped me stock both ships."

Ben, with a smile on his face, came forward. "I applaud Thomas' great comment," he said.

They all looked puzzled. Ben then raised a hand and shouted, "WE ARE ALL SAVED."

They broke out laughing. Baroni began to sing. By now everyone knew his songs.

"We are getting pretty good," Thomas said, as they were singing.

"We are ready and everything is tied down," Peter said. "But are we really finally going to leave in the morning?"

---

[148] Authors' note: See Israelimages, Israel's Picture Library, for an example of using concrete. "The (Caesarea) harbor was built using materials that would allow the concrete to harden underwater."

"Yes," Thomas said. "Yes we are. Baroni, what about the twenty soldiers we have had on the two ships."

"They are assigned to us and will continue with guard duty for your two ships. They will be returned to active duty once we return to your home in Jerusalem. Pardi is turning responsibility for his thirty soldiers over to Guido as we speak. Pardi will be back here before long."

"Now, can we get some sleep?" Stephen said to break the silence.

Everyone went to their cabins in the two ships and found their beds. Five of the soldiers stayed awake for guard duty and greeted Pardi when he returned.

✝ Part VI ✝

✝ Chapter 32 ✝

Sailing to the Island of Crete
Tuesday, April 30, 125 A.D.

Everyone on the five ships was up and preparing to leave. Those on the Free Spirit were Baroni, Pardi, Thomas, Stephen, Peter and Ben. On the Islander were Tamir, Mark, David and Paz. Both ships had on board five seamen, three guards and ten soldiers. Some bread, cheese and dates were handed out on the Free Spirit. As the sun came up over the horizon, Thomas saw Mascaro and Taccone riding in on horseback, then stop and dismount. The mayor walked up to them. The three of them walked onto the pier between the two ships.

"We are privileged to be honored with your presence," Thomas called out.

Baroni and Pardi saluted, and then Baroni shouted, "We'll see you in a few months."

"My lady thought I should say goodbye again from both of us," Mascaro shouted. "We wanted to wish all of you safety and success in your voyages."

"I wanted to say goodbye," the mayor shouted. "Thomas, I plan to have Ibrahim baptize me."

"We are delighted with your decision," Thomas called out.

"Lady Lydia and I want to attend a few congregation meetings," Mascaro said. "There are many people who feel the same. You've brought us new life and hope for very unhappy and scared people. Our history will be different now. We had Christian residents before you came, but now we will have many more. The new people will be full of joy. We wanted to let you know we will be baptized soon. Good luck to you, Jerusalem actors. Could you come down to the pier?"

When Thomas came down to the pier, Mascaro said, "I have gold to present to you from Governor Rufus and me. We want to help you with the cost of building the house of worship."

"Thomas, I also have some gold for the house of worship from the City of Caesarea," the mayor said.

Thomas thanked Mascaro and the mayor. He ran up to the deck of the Free Spirit carrying the two sacks of gold. He shouted his delight and thanked them again.

Everyone on the decks of the ships laughed. The soldiers at the dock untied the Free Spirit and the Islander and pushed them hard. Both ships floated away from the dock. They used their oars to move out of the artificial marina. Once they floated out of the entrance, they were carried by the current. They stood and waved back at their friends on the dock.

Peter had them pull the mainsail up. They unfurled and pulled the small sails up one at a time. When they had all three sails properly set, the Free Spirit picked up speed. Thomas looked over to see the Islander off the starboard side with its three sails full of wind. Everybody was excited and exhilarated with high expectations.

"The two Roman transport ships are way over to our port side," Stephen yelled.

Peter showed them how the wind could be channeled to send them on their northern route even though it was blowing mostly west. It seemed like magic. Peter's crew was learning quickly.

"We'll sail north for a while and then turn to sail west for Crete.

It was a bright morning and their sailing ship seemed to feel smaller, yet very responsive as they got further out in the Mediterranean. The sun was bright in the blue sky. The water was green and glimmering. They could smell the salt and feel the humidity on their skin even through their robes. They were stunned by the beauty. The city of Caesarea gradually disappeared from view. Peter tried to keep the shore in view, but the wind and tide took them out until no land was visible. Thomas and Stephen walked over to Peter. He had turned the paddle bar over to one of the seamen and was studying his map and looking back and forth. He had been a sailor on Roman ships and knew the sea. He was glad to be sailing the sea again.

Clouds moved in bringing rain squalls with heavy wind. Stephen and Ben were not sailors and had hoped to keep land within view all the time. The wind and squalls made some of them a little sea sick. They were thankful Peter was a top sailor and the ship was steady. Their plan was to sail across the Mediterranean to Crete where Baroni would take command of the three Roman ships and say goodbye to the two Roman transport ships.

They passed other ships on their way and worried one might be Hadar's ship. Thomas had put the Roman metal emblem box from Governor Rufus in one of the cabinets by his cabin. Everyone wore their own emblem hung around their neck on new leather strips

During the storm most of the men had gone to the cabins. The four missionaries sat in their cabin talking about the house of worship they planned to build. Thomas said, "The bishop in Rome encouraged me in his letter to build the house of worship to become a meeting place for the creation of a new Order of The Red Robe.[149] The island's community should produce all of its own food, wine, clothing and material needs. What the bishop did not know was we will have the Islander during construction and the Free Spirit when we are there."

Stephen nodded and said, "The unrest all over Israel with the Jewish rebels can only lead to war, sooner than later. Our current plan is to remove Apostle Thomas' records, the ancient temple records and the artifacts in about two years. I hope we have enough time before Simeon ben Kosiba and his messiah bar Kokba elements turn the country into a crisis. When we get back to Jerusalem, I wonder how many people Cleophas will have contacted about leaving and how many will want to go."

"The wind has died down outside," Peter said. "Let's go up to the top-deck."

Coming out on the top-deck, Peter quickly spotted the Islander off the starboard side. He could barely see the two Roman transport ships way off the port side. They talked to the seaman holding the rudder bar, who said the ship performed well during the storm. Peter consulted his map and

---

[149] Author's note. Many of the early isolated houses of worship gave their priests a group order name.

determined that it was time to change directions and go west. "We will encounter Cyprus going north." he said.

They turned around and accepted slices of meat and a goblet of watered wine from one of the guards. Ben joined them with his lunch and said, "We are finally on our way and I love this ship."

Baroni and Pardi had been sitting on the stern talking about the future. They walked up to the bow to talk to Peter and Thomas, and then Baroni said, "I have looked at my orders further. We are going to the port in Crete called Iraklion which is sometimes called Candia. It is in the middle of Crete on the north side in what is called the Cretan Sea. My three ships are docked there. We are to dock the Free Spirit and the Islander for a few days. The Roman garrison will have horses for us to ride through a large agricultural area over to Gortyn, the Roman capital of Crete. There is an amphitheater, a smaller theater and an Odeon for small performances. Gortyn is about the size of Joppa. Governor Rufus sent word ahead of us to have the Governor and mayor of Gortyn informed of our arrival."

"How far is it to Gortyn from Iraklion or Candia?" Thomas asked.

"I understand it is a morning's ride of about twenty-three miles," Baroni said. "We'll have to cross a stream, but it's quite small. The amphitheater is very nice. We can expect considerable interest in a play and may find a feast set up for us. They produce some excellent wines in that region."

"I have been to the Candia port," Peter said. "Will the Roman transport ships pull into the port?"

"No, they'll follow us there, but will set sail for Sicily to pick up more soldiers," Baroni said.

"How large is the island of Crete," Ben asked. "Is it a small island?"

"I have been told it is about one-hundred-seventy-five miles long," Baroni said. "The widest part of the island is about thirty-five miles west of where we are going to at Gortyn. It has some mountains that are several thousand feet high with some large canyons. It originally had three kingdoms. It now has about six marinas."

They enjoyed their lunch. Peter said, "Tamir seems to be handling his ship expertly, but he does have more experience than me. Tamir has been to Candia on one of his voyages. I talked to him about the port. He says there is a small town called Amnissos at the port, and the route to Gortyn goes by some old ancient ruins that he says are rumored to be the Minoan city of Knossos.[150]"

One of the two soldiers on deck walked over to Peter and said, "The two of us were on guard duty last night and would like to get some sleep."

Peter smiled and said, "Right now is a good time for a nap. Go join the three other soldiers who are asleep in the cabin. We should arrive in Crete in the morning."

"I think we should follow their lead and have a nap," Thomas said.

Most of the men went to their cabins and crawled into bed for a nap. Peter and another guard stayed on deck to spell the guard who had been handling the rudder paddle bar.

Thomas, Baroni and Pardi awoke to a loud thump and turbulent movement of the ship. They scrambled up the stairs. "What happened," Thomas asked

"I think we hit a log floating in the water," Peter said. I felt it hit the port side of the ship and the paddle on that side. We were lucky, sometimes floating logs sink ships."

It was sunset and men were coming up to stand and watch it. "This is the first time for me to see a sunset while sailing," Thomas said. "I'm delighted with the ship, the wind and the humid salty feel of my skin."

Everyone enjoyed dinner of bread, cheese and some fruit. Thomas shared some very good wine with all the men. Peter made three assignments for tending the paddle bar for the night saying, "I want at least three men up here all night at each watch. We have a bright moon, so one man should sit in the bow to watch for floating logs or wreckage. Two should sit together and take turns holding the rudder bar and be sure no one falls asleep.

Wednesday May 1, 125 A.D.

Thomas went up at dawn to check on their progress. Peter was talking to one of the soldiers, who held the paddle bar. Baroni, Pardi and Stephen came

---

[150] Authors' note: Crete's ancient Palace of Knossos is a super-sophisticated Bronze Age civilization of the Minoans. Knossos has been partially reconstructed as it may have been several thousands of years ago. No one knows what happened to them but they may have been destroyed in eruptions in nearby islands.

up and sat on the stern. Another soldier was at the bow watching the water. Pardi walked up front and ordered the soldier to go get some sleep. Pardi took over watching for logs. They were sailing fast and some logs are below the surface. The sun came up with most of the men on the ship watching it. They were looking for the Roman transport ships and the Islander. Stephen saw the Islander off the starboard side, but trailing them by about a mile but coming towards the Free Spirit. "Tamir must have spotted the island of Kassos east of Crete," Peter said, "We need to slow down for Tamir to catch up with us. Lower the small sails and pull the main sail half way down."

Baroni was the first to see the Roman ships which were still off to the port side, but were ahead and sailing towards them. He shouted, "We must be getting close to Crete for the Roman transport ships are too far south of us. They are turned sailing north towards where we will be before long."

The speed of the Free Spirit slowed as they waited for the Islander to catch up and the Roman transport ships to get closer to them on the port side. As the sun rose higher in the sky, the Islander caught up and sailed along the starboard side, but behind the Free Spirit. "I can see the island of Kassos off to our starboard bow," Peter said. "We will now watch for Gramvousa island and stay west of it. Thomas, keep an eye on each of these islands in case they are your Island-of-Dreams."

Baroni stood watching intently as the Roman ships came closer to the Free Spirit and then drop back behind the Islander, but still on the port side.

Stephen and Ben stood on the stern and waved to the Islander and could see several men in its bow waving to them.

Pardi shouted, "There's an island with high cliffs off our starboard bow. It must be Gramvousa island because we passed Kassos island.

"So far, none of these islands are my island," Thomas shouted.

"We will pass the very small Dionysadis islands on our port side now," "Peter said. "Look past Dionysadis. You can see the island of Crete, near Sitia."

At mid-day, they sailed into the port at Amnissos and docked at the pier. The Islander sailed in and docked next to them with a strip of pier between them.. The Roman transport ships continued on west. Roman soldiers on the dock took the lines and tied both ships up to the pier. Gangplanks were lowered on both ships. Most of the men on both ships came down the gangplanks greeting each other.

Baroni announced from the bow of the Free Spirit, "Men, we'll be docked here for a few days. I will lead the missionaries across part of the island to Gortyn to put on a performance in the amphitheater. Tamir, Pardi, the guards, seamen and soldiers will stay here to take care of the ships. Tamir will be in charge while we are gone."

Thomas turned to Tamir and said, "You'll need to buy food in the market in Amnissos for everyone. If you want any cooked meals you'll need to ask around where you can have a fire. I gave you Roman coins to use when we were in Caesarea."

"Thomas, don't worry, I'll take care of everything, including the ships until you return," Tamir said.

Thomas then turned to Pardi and said softly, "Assign two soldiers to watch out for the gold and silver bars and the coins stored on the Free Spirit, but don't let them know what is in those wood boxes."

"I'll take care of the security and work with Tamir," Pardi said. "I think Tamir and I are going to be working together for a long time."

"I'll go see where our horses are," Baroni said. "If the captains of the three ships come by, introduce yourself and ask them to wait here."

Tamir took five of the seamen and five soldiers with him to Amnissos. Three Principale officers came down the pier and walked up to Pardi who introduced himself to them. They introduced themselves and asked for Centurion Baroni. Thomas came over and told them Baroni had just left to find their horses, but asked that they wait for him. Peter came over and introduced himself and found that he already knew two of them.

"Thomas, may I introduce you to Principales Alonso, Bernardus and Drago," Peter said. "I met Alonso and Drago one time when we were in port in Caesarea."

"Centurion Baroni has orders from Governor Rufus," Drago said. "Can you tell us what we are going to do?"

Thomas smiled and said, "I can give you some idea. You have been assigned to Centurion Baroni to provide protection for us. While we are here in Crete we are going to ride by horseback over to Gortyn to an amphitheater to perform a Christian play there tomorrow. When we return, you will follow us to Palermo, Sicily, to drop off Principale Pardi to go to where his home is. Next we'll sail to Syracuse, Sicily, and we may put on a play there. Most of the men on these ships are Christians. When we leave here, you will follow us for a brief stop in Malta and then on to Sicily. After that we'll sail to one of the Balearic Islands where I believe my Island is located. I call it the Island-of-Dreams because Jesus showed it to me in a dream. We will get construction started on the island and then possibly visit Gaul, Espania and Britain. There is more to tell, but that should give you some idea."

"We will be with you for a few months by the sound of it," Drago said. "Alonso and some of his men are Christians. Bernardus and I are not Christians, so we have a lot to learn."

"Part of the reason the missionaries need protection is because of a man named Hadar," Pardi said. "Hadar is a rich Jew who is supplying the rebel army in Israel with arms and supplies. He is after Thomas because he believes he has old records from the temple that was destroyed fifty years ago by Titus. We Romans want this Hadar eliminated for arming the rebels. Thomas is acting as bait to attract Hadar. If he attacks Thomas's ships, your job will be to defend and kill those who attack. Maybe you'll be lucky and kill Hadar."

Baroni and twenty soldiers rode in on horseback, leading seven spare horses. He dismounted, came over to introduce himself to Alonso, Bernardus and Drago and pulled out his orders. He handed the orders to Drago, who read them and passed them to Alonso and then to Bernardus.

"Principale Pardi and I told them what they are going to do for us," Thomas said.

"Excellent," Baroni said. "Men, do you have any questions?"

Drago said. "We know enough for now. You can tell us more when you return. I gather you are in a hurry to ride over to Gortyn."

Baroni introduced the missionaries to Principale Amedo who was leading the mounted twenty soldiers. They mounted their horses and rode away, following Baroni, Amedo and the soldiers. The road was an incline and the horses were tired when they reached the stream. Baroni was in the lead and turned right to go up another hill. When they reached another plateau, there were old ruins every where they looked. "These are the fabulous ruins of Knossos, built by an ancient civilization," Baroni said. They were the Minoans who lived here and on several other islands. No one knows what happened to them, but something destroyed this huge building. There's quite a bit of it left below the rubble. As you can see, they used many solid carved stone pillars. This was a very large building made from stone."

Later in the afternoon, they rode into Gortyn and were met by a man holding the reins of a horse. Baroni and Thomas dismounted and introduced themselves. "I'm Mayor Carsten," he said. "Your messenger arrived yesterday. This morning Governor Stefano and his officers rode over to Matala. They did not expect you for a couple of days. I was asked to meet you if you arrived before they returned. I will show you our Odeon for your play and provide you with dinner to share with our bishop and our high priest."

"What is an Odeon," Thomas asked.

"It's like an amphitheater, but smaller," the mayor said. ""We have a larger amphitheater, but it needs repairs and I don't think we will need its size. We are scheduling your play for the day after tomorrow. Your messenger mentioned a feast, but most of the people are working on the farms. They will come over here tomorrow evening to see your Christian play. It will be after dark, but we have plenty of torches to light the Odeon and the stage. Follow me to the stables."

"When everyone came out of the stables, the mayor was talking to a man, who turned and said, "I'm Bishop Philip[151] of Gortyn. We have only a small Christian membership here, so most of the audience tomorrow night will be followers of Apollo. High Priest Hector will be here and has expressed concern about this play. I'm delighted and he isn't. We can walk over to the Odeon if you want to see it."

"We'll follow you," Baroni said. "Principale Amedo, take the blankets and sleeping mats over to the fort by that big tree.

"Yes sir," Amedo said. "You can take ten soldiers with you. Men, you already know who is to go with Centurion Baroni and with me."

Baroni and Thomas walked along with the missionaries and soldiers following them. There was a high hill off to their right about thirty paces high. They came to the Odeon which had a stone building at the back. They walked around it. "Is this for box seats for important spectators?" Baroni asked.

No," the mayor said. "This building houses the Greek city rules of government. It is engraved in Dorian Greek on stone work inside the building. It has been there for several hundred years. We built the building to

---

[151] Bishop Philip of Grotyna, an Early Christian Apologist, wrote in the time of Marcus Aurelius against Marcion. He was mentioned with great praise by Dionysius of Corinth in one of his letters to the Christian Community in Gortyna. He is celebrated by the Catholic Church noting his death in 180 A.D.(Author's note, at the time of meeting Thomas and the missionaries he would have been age twenty-five.)

protect it. It is a fabulous artifact. I will walk over to the fort to see about dinner."

Thomas turned around and realized the Odeon was on a plateau with a drop-off behind the stage and garden area. The seating appeared to be able to hold about one-hundred-fifty people.

Stephen walked over to Thomas and said, "This is a beautiful theater, but it is the smallest we've seen. I wonder what is on top of that hill behind the box building."

"I wondered that too," Thomas said. "Let's look at the writing on the stonework before it gets dark."

"That is an amazing engraving," Baroni said. "Let's go out and sit to watch the sunset."

Everyone sat around in the Odeon to watch the sun go down.

"We don't have any plans for tomorrow." Baroni said. "Let's ride over to Matala. It's just a few miles from here. We can see some caves and the beaches. I've seen it from the Mediterranean in a ship, but I would like to see it up close. We might be able to ride back with Governor Stefano and his men."

"I like that idea," Thomas said. "We can also get more views of the farmlands and that mountain to the west of us. Let's leave early."

"Before it gets dark, let's walk over to the fort," Mark said.

When they got to the fort they found a glowing fire in a large fire-pit with ample seating. Sitting there was Bishop Philip and Mayor Carsten. Next to them was a man in a priest robe with silver threads and precious stones sewn onto his chest. He had a large necklace and wore a tall hat. All three of them stood.

"Centurion Baroni and Thomas please meet Bishop Philip and High Priest Hector," Carsten said. "Hector administers the Temple of Pythean Apollo."

"I know you wish to get acquainted with Bishop Philip, so I will listen," Hector said. "We will have time to talk tomorrow."

The high priest made a small bow and Thomas, Baroni and the missionaries did the same.

"We have dinner prepared," Philip said. "It will be served to us here at the fire with some of our local wine. Please come and sit with us."

"Apostle Paul had a companion named Titus[152] who lived here in Crete in Fair Haven,"[153] Philip said. "Titus converted many Greeks in Crete and set up an organization in all of the cities which I now oversee. We are grateful to Titus and Apostle Paul."

"His converts here were uncircumcised gentiles as I recall," Thomas said. "We are finding gentiles to be easier to convert than men of Jewish faith."

"In Israel, we have been hearing about Marcion and his views on Christianity," Stephen said. "Do you know about him?"

"Yes, I know what Marcion teaches and I believe his views are Gnostic, and that must be stopped," Philip said. "I am studying them further, but I will be writing to other bishops to try to stop his teachings."

"I support your efforts," Thomas said. "We keep running into people who have heard his opinions."

"Yes, I was confused by Marcion's teachings," Baroni said. "Thomas and Stephen set me straight. When I rejected Marcion, I converted to Christianity."

They talked about the rebel events in the Roman Provence of Judaea which Thomas knew as Israel. When Baroni talked about the conversions and baptisms in Joppa and Caesarea, the three hosts were surprised to learn almost all were not Jews. When Thomas talked about the conversions and baptisms in the Sebaste fort, the bishop exclaimed, "You're baptizing mostly gentiles and a lot of them. We have Jews here in Gortyn, but they probably won't come tomorrow night."

"We are finding what Apostle Paul found more than seventy five-years ago," Thomas said. "Gentles are more receptive to Christianity than people of Jewish faith. I believe they will blossom and be the salvation of Christianity. We will try to avoid any problems for you, High Priest Hector.

---

[152] Ibid, Titus 1:4 and 5 (To Titus, my true son in our common faith. For this reason I left you in Crete, that you should set in order the things that are lacking, and appoint elders in every city as I command you--)

[153] Ibid, Acts 27-7-8 (--we sailed under the shelter of Crete off Salmone. Passing it with difficulty, we came to a place called Fair Havens, near the city of Lasea)

Our goal is to help your people better understand Jesus and his Good News in these troubled times."

Dinner was served on large plates and the goblets contained a lush local wine. As they were finishing their meal, Thomas asked, "Where do we sleep?"

Each of you had a sleeping mat and blanket on your horses," Baroni said. "I had Principale Amedo bring them over here."

Everyone stood and said good night to their three hosts. Amedo came over with the soldiers and set the sleeping mats down next to a pile of blankets. Everyone grabbed a sleeping mat and blanket and found a place to sleep for the night. Baroni and Amedo found space together on one side of the fire and the missionaries were on the other side. The soldiers had their own sleeping area.

Stephen whispered to Thomas, "This makes me appreciate the Free Spirit."

Thomas smiled, sat up and said, "Father in heaven, we thank thee for the blessings of safety you bestowed on us during this trip. Thank you for the success of our trip and the beautiful trail ride to Gortyn. Please bless us that we may conduct a successful play tomorrow. Please Jesus, be with us to inspire us as you have in the prior plays. We do this in your name. Amen."

The sky was clear and stars were bright, but sleep came quickly to everyone around the dwindling fire.

During the night, Thomas was dreaming. He was on the stage of the Odeon facing Jesus. As he opened his eyes he could not see at first. He blinked several times and then he could see Jesus. *"I have been following your progress, Thomas. You have made great strides befriending important Romans. You are now aware that in the Roman world, you become a client of each Roman and each of them becomes your Patron. Your ability to relate to them has gotten you the protection I advised you to get. I am reminding you of the resources available to you on the island. You need to use it wisely to help many others to accelerate and foster the growth of Christianity. I will tell you more about this later. The need for you to remove Nazarenes from Israel is more important than ever. Find a place to relocate them. I will help you with this. Continue to meet and enjoy important Romans and they will help and protect you. You have become a client of each of them and they are now your Patron. Continue to learn more about this custom and use them wisely."*

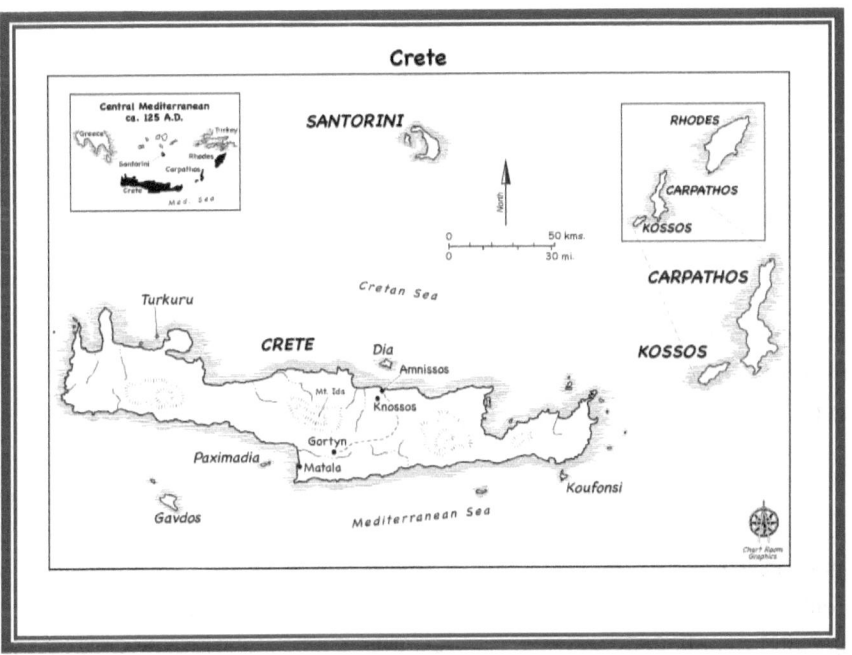

<table><tr><td>✝</td><td># Chapter 33</td><td>✝</td></tr></table>

Visiting the Island of Crete
Thursday May 2, 125 A.D.

Before dawn, Thomas woke Stephen and Baroni. "I had another dream with Jesus," Thomas whispered. "He talked about me about becoming a client of each important Roman and they become my Patron. He knows how the system works."

"This is how the empire works," Baroni said. "As we have talked about this, these relationships form a colossal pyramid of mutual aid. A powerful Roman is a *ptronus*, or protector, of many hundreds or even thousands of "clients," not just in Rome or Italy, but across the Mediterranean. A patron looks after his clients' interests. For example, Governor Rufus is your current patron and you are his client. Each of Tribunes, Cerrone, Pasquali and Mascaro as well as Legatus Mercelli are also your patrons and you are their client. You have entered this web of relationships as understood by Jesus. It can expand as you become friends with future important Romans.[154] You are good at becoming friends with your patrons as you have seen. You do what they request and they will be obligated to help you. "

At dawn, the roosters crowed one after another bringing everyone awake.

---

[154] Hadrian, and the Triumph of Rome by Anthony Everitt, page 27. ("A powerful Roman was a *ptronus*, or protector, of many hundreds or even thousands of "clients," not just in Rome or Italy but across the Mediterranean. A patron looked after his clients' interests.")

Baroni announced, "We are going to ride over to Matala. Fold your sleeping mats and blankets. Each of you has food in your saddlebags. Let's go on over to the stables."

As the sun came up, the missionaries and the soldiers rode back the way they came into Gortyn. When they passed the hills to the west, Amedo took a left. The road went on a southwest direction with farm fields on both sides. "This is called the Messara plain which has been farmed for thousands of years," he said.

The road began to go downhill and by early morning they could see the ocean down off to their left. Baroni stopped to gaze at a giant white rock that looked like a huge pancake poured onto the beach stretching out into the Mediterranean. Its top was on the same slope as the ground that went down to the beach. Where the white rock ended several hundred feet up from the beach, the face was vertical and about one-hundred feet high.

"That white rock formation is where the caves are located," Baroni said. "Amedo lead us down there to the beach and over by the white rock formation. We want to explore the caves."

They carefully rode down the steep hill and then out on a slope that ended at the beach. They spent a short time exploring some caves while the soldiers waited and held their horse's reins.

When they returned, Baroni said, "Amedo, lead us over to the town of Matala. The governor is probably at the pier."

Amedo led everyone around the base of the white rock formation and then followed the beach for some distance before arriving at the Port of Gortyna. "Stay here," Baroni said as he dismounted, giving his reins to Thomas. Let me find the governor."

Before long he returned to say, "I found the governor and his officers. Thomas and Stephen come with me. Amedo, there is a stable over there. When you have the horses in the stables, take the other missionaries and the soldiers to the camp at the end of the pier where the Governor's soldiers are camped. They will provide everyone with lunch."

Baroni led Thomas and Stephen down the pier to a building facing the port. They went inside to find several Roman men seated at a table. As they walked up to them, they all stood. "This is Thomas the leader of the missionaries, and his cousin, Stephen," Baroni said. "This is Governor Stefano, Tribune Flavio and Centurion Enrico."

"It's nice to meet you Thomas and Stephen," Stefano said. "Sit down everyone."

"We came over here to enjoy some fresh fish for dinner and a couple of lunches," Flavio said. "We just sat down when Baroni came in. I've ordered for everyone."

A waiter arrived and Flavio said, "Serve us now."

"We are delighted to meet all of you and be here on this wonderful island," Thomas said.

"We weren't sure when you would get to Gortyna," Centurion Enrico said. "We knew Baroni would find us if we left and here you are."

"Yes, it was a nice ride over here. Last night we were treated to a nice dinner around the fire at the fort," Thomas said. "We met Bishop Philip, Mayor Carsten and High Priest Hector."

"Good, but I'm intrigued," Stefano said. "How did you get Governor Rufus to let you put on Christian plays in the country he governs? Has he become your patron? I know Christianity began in what we call Judaea. Now Rufus is sending you out of the country to do the same. You are performing the plays under Roman control."

"We are clients of Governor Rufus and let me explain about the plays," Thomas said, smiling. "I ordered two ships in Joppa and had them built in Cyprus. I had my missionary companions with me when we took delivery of the ships. The mayor of Joppa asked us to tell the citizens about Christianity. We agreed to do that, but the mayor had us announced as actors from Jerusalem. The citizens were expecting a play. So we gave them a play that was a bit unusual, but they liked it. We simply told the story about Jesus and his Good News. We were asked to put on the play again in Sebaste for the Roman army based there and again in Caesarea. We converted hundreds of people in Joppa, Sebaste and Caesarea. Luckily, there was no violence."

"I'm impressed and I'll permit this here," Stefano said. "But now you're my client, as well. Why have you brought two ships and are traveling outside of Judaea? I understand you are going to Sicily next. Why are you doing all of this?"

"I had a dream and Jesus appeared to me on an island and gave me orders," Thomas said. "Luckily, I inherited some wealth that came down to me from my great-grandfather, Apostle Thomas. My orders are to find that island, build a house of worship there, eventually take some records from Jerusalem and store them in a vault. I've been calling this the Island-of-Dreams."

Thomas adjusted his seat and said, "The visit here in Crete was for two reasons. One, Baroni has orders to take command of three ships. Two,

Governor Rufus would like us put on a Christian play. The visit to Sicily is in part to deliver a retiring Principale officer by the name of Pardi to his home in Palermo. Pardi is joining our group and arranging for grape starts to be gathered to plant on the island when we find it. Governor Rufus is friends with Governor Salvatore and wants him to allow us to perform a Christian play there."

"You're lucky that you have received no complaints," Enrico said. "Christians have been killed quite regularly. As a matter of fact, it is against the Caesars' continued decree to be a Christian, which requires the death penalty. But Governor Pliny has slowed that down with his letter to Caesar Trajan."

When everyone finished their lunch, Stefano asked, "Did you enjoy our wine grown here?"

"It was excellent," Thomas said. "The fresh fish was a delicious treat. Thank you."

"It is strange, but I feel comfortable with you and Stephen," Stefano said. "Of course, Baroni is always a treat. Baroni, Thomas and Stephen, I have a new Preatorium palace which has bedrooms for guests. I invite the three of you to stay in the palace while you are here. Men, let's return to Gortyn."

"Baroni, take the missionaries and the soldiers under the command of Principale Amedo and go ahead of us," Enrico said. "We need more time."

"Governor, we'll see you at the palace," Baroni said.

They walked out onto the pier and turned right to find the Romans' camp. Amedo saw them coming and ordered his men to take up position. Baroni saluted and Amedo led his men towards the stables.

"Are there any problems," Paz asked. "Are there any change of plans."

"All is well," Stephen said. "We had the privilege of dining with three fine Romans, who already knew Baroni. Baroni, Thomas and I are invited to stay in the palace tonight. Amedo will make arrangements for the five of you."

The soldiers first brought out the horses for Baroni and the missionaries. They soon were riding back to Gortyn. It was late afternoon when they rode into the stables. When everyone came out, Baroni said, "Amedo, take care of missionaries David, Mark, Paz, Peter and Ben for dinner and get them sleeping quarters at the fort. I need ten soldiers to accompany us over to the palace. The other soldiers will be here soon with the Governor."

As they were walking to the palace, they saw High Priest Hector and several men coming towards them. When they met, Hector smiled and said, "I never considered you Christians to be a problem. Now I think you are. I normally have the Romans under my spell and they protect me. Now you have them and they are protecting you. It's very ominous to have you come in here riding with Roman soldiers."

"I have men trying to kill me and they are men the Romans want dead," Thomas said. "So we have a mutual need. The Romans will protect you just like me. Please don't worry. We want a relationship with you that is respectful. As I told you last night, we are here to provide information and then leave. Bishop Philip was here before we came, and he will be here when we are gone. I hope you and Bishop Philip can continue to respect each other as you have in the past."

"I guess you're staying at the palace tonight?" Hector said.

"Yes, we are guests of the Governor," Baroni said. "We'll look forward to seeing you tomorrow at the Odeon."

"Thomas, please take no offense," Hector said. "If you have time tomorrow before the play, come over to the temple and I will show you and your companions around. It is a wonderful building."

"Thank you for the invitation," Thomas said. "We'll enjoy seeing you tomorrow. Good day."

As Hector turned around to leave, Governor Stefano and his officers rode to the palace. The rest of the soldiers rode to the stables. Soldiers came out of the palace and rode the officers' horses to the stables. The governor and the officers stood watching them.

"I see you were talking to High Priest Hector," Stefano said. "Is he jealous?"

"Yes, but I would call it more of a question of concern," Baroni said. "But Thomas turned it around and has a meeting to tour the Temple of Pythean Apollo tomorrow before sunset."

"That's pretty good," Flavio said. "Even Bishop Philip has never seen the Temple of Pythean Apollo."

"Hector is a good man," Stefano said. "But he needs to be concerned about doing his best. I feel he is going to lose some membership with Thomas and your companions being here. I'm excited to see what you do in your plays. Centurion Enrico, would you show Baroni, Thomas and Stephen to their rooms. We will meet for drinks on the veranda at sunset."

They went into the palace and Enrico provided an educational tour of the palace and then showed them to their rooms. "I enjoyed showing you around," Enrico said. "The palace was completed less than a year ago, so enjoy. I'll see you on the veranda at sunset."

Thomas walked around his room studying the art work and the furniture. Hearing a knock on his door he opened it to find Baroni and Stephen standing there. "Let's go out to the veranda for a drink," Baroni said. "We can't do much in our rooms. We have no change of clothing. We should have gotten our personal saddlebags. Maybe Enrico has someone that can go fetch them for us."

As they walked out on the veranda, aides came out with goblets of local wine. Centurion Enrico came out, carrying a goblet. "How are your rooms?" he asked.

"The rooms are very nice," Thomas said. "But Baroni has a question for you."

"We need to have one of your men go to the stables and fetch our saddlebags," Baroni said. "Whoever you send should check with Principale Amedo first. He can identify our saddlebags."

"I'll take care of that for you," Enrico said.

The three of them sat down and Flavio came out and sat with them. He greeted everyone then said, "Governor Stefano is still wondering what Governor Rufus was thinking in Caesarea sending you here and to Sicily. None of us are Christians, but I thought about it on the ride back from Matala. I told the governor that it is a good idea. It will give me a greater access to the people here, no matter whether they are converted to Christianity or not. If a lot of people convert to Christianity, the community will be better balanced."

Enrico came back carrying two goblets, set both down and said, "Your personal items will be taken to your rooms. The Governor and his wife will be right out."

Governor Stefano and his wife came out and everyone stood. "My dear, this is Centurion Baroni, Thomas and Stephen," he said. "This is my wife, Gina. Please, let's sit and watch the sunset."

Enrico stood up and handed the two goblets to Stefano and his wife. He raised his hand for a signal and returned to his seat. An aide came out with a goblet and a tray of small cakes.

"I enjoy something sweet before dinner," Stefano said. "Now, we can talk about your play tomorrow, if you would like. Flavio thinks it is a great idea for good reasons. I'm still curious about what is going on in Judaea. Baroni tell me about the rebel situation there. How bad is it?"

Baroni reviewed the rebel army groups he had seen all over Israel. He talked about the battles with the Roman army with the deaths on each side. He noted the five-thousand men Rufus was transferring in to bolster his forces and the ships full of men arriving as they left Caesarea.

"Thomas, what do you think of the rebel situation?" Stefano asked.

"The rebels are led by a man named Simeon ben Kosiba," Thomas said. "He believes he is the messiah Bar Kokba and is sent by God to free Israel from Roman occupation. His movement has been developing a rebel army for about three years. He is getting supplied with horses, swords, knives, shields and other supplies by a Jew named Hadar who ultimately wants to be the ruler of Jerusalem and build a new temple. I don't believe five-thousand additional Roman soldiers will be enough to stop him. The Bar Kokba movement is preparing to raise an army of over one-hundred thousand men. I think he will raise even more."

"I hope you're wrong," Stefano said. "Governor Rufus had a hard time justifying five-thousand."

Gina sat up straight and said, "Thomas, tell us about the play. I'm anxious to see it."

"I told your husband over in Matala how we got started doing the plays," Thomas said. "The plays are really a series of acts telling the story of Jesus and the Good News he brought. We do this by asking each other questions and pointing to the person that is to answer it. The answer is given and then that person asks a new question and points to another person. There are seven of us in the play and we mix it up by sitting, standing, walking and answering in different tones of voice. We try to have fun with it and keep the story moving."

"Thomas and his missionaries are converting almost exclusively people who are not Jews," Stefano said. "These non-Jews, like us, are called gentiles. Baroni says Jesus had an apostle by the name of Paul who had a Jewish mother and a Roman father. Jesus' other apostles converted many Jews to Christianity. Paul visited them, but had more success with the gentiles. Thomas believes the gentiles are where his missionary work will be done."

"The sun has set," Flavio said. "Our dinner should be ready. I recommend we move to the dining hall. Leave your goblets here and follow me."

Everyone stood and followed Flavio. When they were seated, the servants served dinner and a choice of wine or juice. Thomas appreciated the ornate dining table and artwork of statures and paintings.

"Baroni, you are serving to protect Thomas, his missionaries and ships," Stefano said. "While this is not new, it is for you. What are your plans?"

"I've had an enjoyable and successful career serving as a Centurion in several countries and visiting many more. I'm close to retiring, but I never thought much about it until I met and traveled with Thomas and his companions. I've been baptized as a Christian. I served with Principale Pardi who is also a Christian. Pardi has now retired and will join Thomas and his efforts with the Island-of-Dreams. He wants to plant and tend a new vineyard which his family has done for generations in Palermo Sicily. His decision influenced me to retire in two years. Governor Rufus has been kind enough to keep me in the role of defender for Thomas and his ships during this period. I'm also helping Thomas lure the Jew, Hadar, to come after him. We want to capture and kill this man."

"It sounds like Baroni will also join you when he retires," Gina said. "What would Baroni do for you or with you?"

"Baroni and I have not discussed this." Thomas said. "I know he enjoys the plays and the traveling. It's my desire to let him do what he does best which is to introduce and promote us to new missionary opportunities. Of course, if he wants to continue with security, as well, I would be very pleased."

"Thomas, do any of you have plans to marry?" Gina asked.

"None of us do at this time. After we bring our records back and store them on the Island-of-Dreams, I believe all of us will want to get married. When we take the records the year after next, we will also be relocating some friends and relatives out of Judaea. Some of those may be wives by then."

After dinner they walked out to the veranda to finish their wine. Before long everyone left for bed. When Baroni, Thomas and Stephen reached their bedrooms, they found their own saddlebags on their beds.

Friday, May 3, 125 A.D.

At dawn, Baroni knocked on Thomas' and Stephen's doors. They went downstairs and were greeted by Gina. "I have hot bread, cheese and honey for you in the kitchen," she said. "Follow me. My handmaiden has some for the three of you and Flavio."

They were eating and talking to Gina when Flavio came in to eat his breakfast and said, "I can take you on a tour of the fort when we are done."

When they were finished with the tour, Baroni said. "I would like to spend some time in the hot baths. This would allow all of us to be presentable tonight."

As they arrived at the palace, Thomas said, "Will we have lunch before the baths?"

"The men and women at the Nymphaeum will provide us with lunch," Flavio said. "The Nymphaeum is the name of our hot baths. Local people are infatuated with the myth of the Nymph. I am infatuated with the baths because water is not plentiful here in Crete."

Flavio led Baroni, Amedo and the missionaries walking down the road. There were many more people out today. Flavio stopped in front of a large temple and said, "This is the Egyptian temple dedicated to Isis and Serapis. The Greeks and Cretans became enthralled with Isis, Serapis, Hermes and Anubis for about three hundred years before we took over. The temple was built here before Rome arrived.

"When did Rome take control of Crete?" Stephen asked.

"A successful siege was led by Metellus who had been assigned by the Roman senate to take over Crete to eliminate pirates based here," Flavio said. "Metellus had the support of the Jewish people here in Gortyn and that is why we are headquartered here. We have been in control of Crete for over a hundred-fifty years. The population here in Gortyn has grown and grown."

They arrived at the Nymphaeum and were given towels. They went into the change room leaving their clothing and sandals. Wrapped in large towels, they found a seat in the heated steam room. Stefano, Enrico and Bishop Phillip were talking to High Priest Hector. "Pull your seats over here," Stefano said. "Hector was telling us about some of the mythological stories leading to Apollo. Have you had lunch?"

"No, we just finished our tour." Flavio said.

Stefano waved at a male servant. He came over and Stefano ordered lunch for everyone.

"Crete is the home of the Zeus family history and religion," he said. "I would like to have you and Phillip listen to the real story. Hector, could you start your story over?"

"I'll be brief, but I'll start way back in history," Hector said. "Zeus was born in the cave called Odeon on Mount Ida here on Crete. Later he fought with his father Coronus and defeated him taking power. On one of his voyages he kidnapped Europa, a daughter of a Phoenician king. They returned to Crete and were married in Gortyn under a Plane[155] tree. That marriage changed the Plane tree so that it is always green, never losing its leaves. Zeus fathered twelve children gods. Minos, one of his children, was the legendary king of Phaestos. His brother, Radamathys, had a son named Gortys, who founded the city of Gortyna. Zeus, Minos and other Olympian gods visited regularly the cave of Odeon. To this day there is an ivory throne in the cave for them to use when they visit there."

Three maids came in carrying trays of food and goblets. They handed out the food and the goblets and left the room.

"How does Apollo fit into this history or mythology?" Thomas asked.

"I'm glad you asked," Hector said. "Zeus had another wife named Hera. Zeus got a nymph by the name of Leto pregnant and Hera refused to allow her to give birth. Leto left Crete and two stories follow. Either she went to the island of Delos or Lato. Lato is a small island now called Paximadea, a short distance south of here in the Mediterranean. At any rate, the goddess Themis was there and allowed Leto to give birth to Apollo and a twin sister named Artemis. Themis raised Apollo feeding him ambrosia, the nectar of the gods. Artemis became the god of hunt and wild things."

Hector took a deep breath and continued, "Apollo never married, but he was a young, manly, blond god. He enjoyed the charms of dozens of nymphs. He went on to have flings with Cassandra giving her the gift of prophecy. Another fling was with Daphne who fled his embrace and turned into a laurel tree. He then had a romance with Calliope and she bore a child named Orpheus, the goddess of singing. Apollo had another child named Asklepios. She became the god of healing. We worship him for his handsomeness, his powers, his support of the arts of civilization and his freedom to do as he wished. He is represented by driving his chariot across the sky."

"That helped us understand the history of Crete and your religion," Thomas said. "I respect your willingness to share this religious history with us. We talk about Jewish and Christian religious history and I think it is important that we know your religious history."

"Hector, I appreciate your letting me share in this religious history," Phillip said. "We have been friends and sharing our histories is a respect we

---

[155] The Plane tree is only found on the Island of Crete and never loses its leaves.

both can share. Neither of us should be ignorant of your or our beliefs. We both share our revenue with Provence of Crete. You have more than I do, but I hope we never have to fight about it."

"Now that everyone has finished their lunch, let's start in the caldarium with its hot baths," Stefano said. "We will then move to the tepidarium with its warm waters and then finish in the frigidarium with its cold water. Just follow me when I move from one room to the next. Leave your robes in a pile when you enter the caldarium. When we get out of the frigidarium, aides will hand each of us a towel. We will end up in the changing room to get dressed."

They had a hard time getting into the caldarium, but enjoyed it as they got used to it. The tepidarium was a very pleasant time. The frigidarium was a shock, but they came out refreshed. In the changing room, Hector said, "Baroni, Amedo and you Christian missionaries can follow me to the Temple of Pythean Apollo."

"We will be at the Odeon to make sure all is in order for your play," Stefano said.

They came out of the Nymphaeum, following Hector. He led Phillip and the missionaries to the Temple and into its sanctuary. The tour was interesting with its statues of Apollo, Aphrodite, Artemis and others. Its' pyramid altar for animal sacrifices was very large. When they came back out of the entrance, Thomas turned to Hector and said, "You have been a courteous host giving us this tour. Your discussions in the Nymphaeum about the history of Zeus, his family, including Apollo was fascinating. Come now and be our guest at the Odeon for our Christian play."

"Thank you for the tour of the temple," Phillip said. "You are always welcome for a tour at my house of worship. Let's go see what Thomas and his companions present to us tonight."

✝ Chapter 34 ✝

Plays in Gortyn Crete
Friday, May 3, 125 A.D.

As they walked down the road, they were following many people on foot, but many more were going the other way. They encountered a ring of soldiers on the road to the Odeon. They were letting only certain people through, but Baroni, Amedo, Hector, Phillip and the missionaries were let through by the soldiers.

When they reached the Odeon, Enrico came over to them to say, "To our surprise, we have more citizens wanting to see the play than we can accommodate here in the Odeon. The governor suggested this morning that we have you and the missionaries perform two plays, one here and one in the large amphitheater. We have a strong Jewish community here and they want a private showing in the Odeon. Stefano complied with their wishes, so I had the large amphitheater swept and prepared for your play to start after you finish here. High Priest Hector and Bishop Philip you need to go there to conduct some lectures on their respective religions while Thomas and his companions perform here. Can you do this?"

"This is short notice," Hector said. "But if Bishop Phillip is willing, I am as well."

"I'm willing," Phillip said. "Let's go see what we can do."

"Enrico, we can do as you described," Thomas said. "But, I want at least fifty soldiers standing around the Odeon behind the seating and behind the stage. People of the Jewish faith can get pretty violent. Their leaders can use vituperative language which means they can be abusive and berate anyone who questions them."

They stood behind the stone building housing the City laws while Enrico made the arrangements with the soldiers. The mayor explained the reasons for the soldiers to the Jewish audience. Stefano came over to Thomas to say, "I'll enter the stage with you and introduce Flavio."

At the completion of Carsten's comments, the Jewish audience clapped. Stefano led the missionaries and Flavio around the seating area and out onto the stage. Stefano walked up to Carsten and the missionaries scattered around the stage.

Mayor Carsten smiled at the audience and said, "We have very special actors here from Jerusalem. They were sent here by the Roman Governor Rufus for the Provence of Judaea. Before they are introduced, I would like to introduce Governor Stefano."

After some clapping, Stefano said, "Your ancestors were supportive of Rome when the Cretans and pirates ruled the island. Their invitation to Rome and the desire to rid the island of pirates brought General Metellus here in a successful siege, freeing the island. We have just completed recently the Governor's Preatorium where I now live. We have a growing city here in Gortyna and you are part of our community. At your leader's request this morning, we have reserved this Odeon for the first Christian play. Now, I would like to introduce Tribune Flavio, my representative to this portion of the island of Crete."

Stefano walked to the center seating and sat by his wife, Gina. Flavio walked to the center and looked around the faces in the audience. "Most of you do not know me. My job is to handle many of the problems that occur between the area's residents and Roman governance. Most of the people in the Gortyna area are of Jewish, Christian or Pythean Apollo. Tonight we have a Christian play which I am told tells the story of Jesus and his Good News. This play will help everyone better understand Christianity. I now present you to the great-grand-son of Jesus' brother, Apostle Thomas."

Flavio was startled by ducks flying in from the West. The audience watched in awe as several dozen ducks landed to the left of the crowd and the rest circled overhead and landed at the top of the hill behind the crowd. Pelicans, seagulls other sea birds came flying in and then flew around landing wherever there was room to set down.

"I have never seen this many ducks and sea birds fly in around a crowd before," Flavio said.

Flavio went to the middle seating and sat down by Stefano.

Thomas walked around the stage looking into the audience and said,

"You may be wondering about the birds. We have found they are attracted to the Holy Ghost, who has a habit of showing up at our plays. Don't be alarmed; enjoy them."

He then began by introducing each of the missionaries, who were around the stage kneeling or standing. Each waved as he was introduced. Thomas started with a question to Stephen who answered and asked a question of David.

David pointed back to Peter and said, "What mattered most to Jesus in his teachings," Peter asked pointing to Ben.

'Love means living the way God commanded us to live. As you have heard from the beginning, his command is this; *Live a life of love,*"[156] Ben said. "Apostle Paul said, '*No matter what I say, what I believe, and what I do, I'm bankrupt without love.*'"[157]

"Did Jesus have more to say about love?" Ben asked, pointing to Stephen.

"*Because God is love, the most important lesson he wants you to learn on earth is how to love. It is in loving that we are most like him, so love is the foundation of every command he has given us,*"[158] Stephen said. "*The whole law can be summed up in this one command: Love others as you love yourself.*"[159]

"What do the ten commandments have to say about relationships with people?" Stephen said pointing to Thomas.

"*Four of the Ten Commandments deal with our relationship to God and six deals with our relationship with people,*"[160] Thomas said. "This means two things: love God and love people. Jesus said, '*You must love the Lord your God with all your heart...*' This is the first and greatest commandment. A second is equally important: 'Love your neighbor as yourself.' All the

---

[156] New Century Version Bible, Dallas: Word Bibles (1991), 2 John 1: 6.

[157] The Message Bible, Colorado Springs: Navpress (1993), 1 Corinthians 13: 3b.

[158] The Purpose Driven Life by Rick Warren, page 123.

[159] Living Bible, Wheaton Il: Tyndale House Publishers (1979), Galatians 6: 14.

[160] Ibid, Rick Warren, page 125.

Stephen Thomas White

other commandments and all the demands of the prophets are based on these two commandments."[161]

Stephen talked for some time of Jesus' words and messages and then pointed to Mark and asked a question. The questions and answers went on for a while.

Stephen pointed to Thomas and asked, "Did Jesus feed thousands of people with five loaves and two fish?"

"Yes, he and his disciples had crossed the Sea of Galilee after hearing of the beheading and burial of his cousin, John the Baptist, who had baptized Jesus. Thousands of people from the cities had heard of John the Baptist's beheading and followed Jesus and his disciples around the lake on foot. Jesus was pleased when he saw the multitude. He felt compassion for them and healed the sick. When it was evening, His disciples thought they should just send everyone home to eat.

"But Jesus said to them, 'They do not need to go away. You give them something to eat. And they said to Him, We have here only five loaves and two fish. He said, 'Bring them here to me." [162] *"And He took the five loaves and the two fish, and looking up to heaven He blessed and broke and gave the loaves to his disciples and the disciples gave to the multitudes. Now those who had eaten were about five thousand men, besides women and children."* [163]

Thomas asked Stephen, *"Did Jesus walk on water?"*

"Yes, after feeding the multitude, *'... Jesus made His disciples get into the boat and go before Him to the other side, while He sent the multitude away.* [164] *Jesus then went up into the mountain to pray. But his disciples were in the middle of the sea, tossed by the waves, for the wind was contrary. ...Jesus went to them, walking on the sea. And when the disciples saw Him walking on the sea, they were troubled saying, 'It is a ghost.' And they cried out in fear. But*

New Living Translation Bible, Wheaton Il: Tyndale House Publishers (1996), Mathew 22: 37-40.
[162] Ibid, Mathew 14:17, 18.
[163] Ibid, Mathew 14:19-21.
[164] Ibid, Mathew 14:22, 23.

- 282 -

*immediately Jesus spoke to them saying, 'Be of good cheer! It is I; do not be afraid.'"*165

Stephen asked David, "Did Jesus ask his apostles to walk on water?"

David replied, *"Yes, '---Peter answered Him and said, "Lord if it is You, command me to come to you on the water. So he said, 'Come.' And when Peter came down out of the boat, he walked on the water to go to Jesus. But when he saw that the wind was boisterous, he was afraid; and beginning to sink, he cried out saying, 'Lord save me!' And immediately Jesus stretched out His hand and caught him, and said to him, "O you of little faith, why did you doubt?"*166

"Did Jesus create an organization," David asked Paz.

"Yes, Jesus appointed twelve Apostles to travel with him," Paz said. "He organized the Nazarene Ecclesia with Jesus as Nasi or leader, Apostle Levi Mathew as Sagan and Apostle Peter as the religious officer. He appointed seven deacons to work with the poor. He formed his own Sanhedrin with seventy disciples and sent them into the cities of Israel to spread the Good News. When they returned, Jesus sent the seventy disciples out to the world to preach and set up new congregations whose members are now called Christians. He told the apostles to wait and preach in Israel for twelve years, before going out into the world."

David pointed to Thomas who finished an answer and pointed to Ben. "Who was Lazarus?"

Ben jumped up and ran to the front of the stage. "Lazarus was the very wealthy brother of Martha and Mary Magdalene. Mary Magdalene went to the tomb to administer to the body of Jesus, but she saw it was empty. When Mary Magdalene later told Lazarus about the empty tomb, he knew Jesus had been raised from the dead because he, himself, was the first to be raised from the dead by Jesus. Many in Israel in those days believed in Jesus before his crucifixion because Jesus raised Lazarus after he died. The Lazarus story was one of the reasons the Sadducean priest Caiaphas wanted Jesus dead. Later, after Jesus' resurrection, Lazarus spent a couple of years as Bishop in Larnaka Cyprus. He went back to his palace in Bethany to become the bishop

---

165 Ibid, Mathew 14:26,27.
166 Ibid, Mathew 14:28-31.

of Bethany. After more persecution, Lazarus took his sisters, Joseph of Arimathea and others to Deacon Phillip's house in Caesarea. After they were forced onto a ship in Caesarea, he spent time in Glastonbury Britain helping Joseph of Arimathea start the missionary school of Avalon. Lazarus took his sisters and moved to Marseilles, Gaul, to become its first bishop."

The play went on with more questions and answers.

Thomas pointed to Stephen and said, "Explain the last supper. "

"Jesus entered Jerusalem on the back of an ass," Stephen said.

This got some chuckles from the audience.

"Jesus knew he would be betrayed and killed in Jerusalem," Stephen said. "The last supper was for his closest associates. After that supper Judas Iscariot, one of the twelve apostles, slipped out and told the Caiaphas where Jesus would be and promised to kiss Jesus so the temple guards would know who to arrest. The Jewish leaders did not believe Jesus was the messiah and wanted him dead for declaring animal sacrifice was no longer needed, and his popularity was rising. When Judas Iscariot kissed Jesus, the temple guards arrested him."

Stephen pointed to Mark. "What happened to Jesus?"

Mark smiled standing up and walking he said, "Jesus was tried by Ananas the Elder, Caiaphas and the Jewish Sanhedrin. They brought Jesus before Herod who mocked Him then turned Him over to the Roman governor Pontius Pilate. They demanded the death of Jesus, but the governor asked, *What has this man done?* Caiaphas claimed Jesus would be king and should be no friend of the Caesar. They demanded Jesus be put to death. Jesus' great uncle, Joseph of Arimathea and his friend Nicodemus testified to defend Jesus, but they were ignored. They were both members of the Sanhedrin and the local Roman senate. Joseph was a Nobilis Decurio in the Roman army and Nicodemus was his wealthy banker friend. The governor eventually washed his hands of Jesus' blood and consented."

Mark pointed to Thomas. "Was Jesus killed?"

"Jesus was beaten and scourged. He was sentenced to death on the cross," Thomas said. "Jesus had a crown of thorns placed on his head as he dragged the cross up the hill. Jesus was nailed through his wrists and one large nail through both of his feet to the cross. He was in great agony as the cross was dropped in the hole in the ground. A sign was placed on Jesus, reading *Here is the King of the Jews*. What a mockery. YES, JESUS WAS KILLED."

The questions and answers continued as they had practiced the plays in Israel. They had taken no break and after Ben finished, Thomas ran forward and shouted WE ARE SAVED."

The audience was courteous and clapped during the bows taken twice by the missionaries. Thomas led them out the back and around the soldiers. They stood as the audience left the Odeon. Soon, Stefano, his wife Gina, Flavio, Enrico, Baroni and Amedo joined them for congratulations. "Your play was marvelous," Gina said. "I'm looking forward to seeing it again. All of you were on fire with enthusiasm."

"Your concern for violence with these Jewish people was not a problem," Stefano said. "Maybe your requirement for soldiers in back and in front of them kept them calm."

"I'm glad they stayed calm," Thomas said. "Maybe I overreacted, but my experience tells me to be careful with Jewish audiences. Thanks for the compliment on the play. It was fun to do."

"Enrico, lead us to the amphitheater," Stefano said.

They walked up the road behind soldiers from the Odeon, who noticed them and stood back to let the governor, his wife, the officers and missionaries to go on past. When they reached the amphitheater, they could hear the people talking in a low rumble. The soldiers at the entrance let them through. They walked to the stage to find the mayor, Bishop Philip and High Priest Hector. The crowd stood and clapped. Philip and Hector bowed and found a seat next to their wives on the opposite sides of the amphitheater.

Mayor Carsten put his arms in the air and the audience quieted and sat down. He said, "Thank you for waiting and enjoying the information provided by Bishop Philip and High Priest Hector. The first play has just completed for our Jewish neighbors. Now I would like to introduce Governor Stefano."

The mayor found a seat. Stefano described the history of Roman rule in Crete, introduced Flavio and sat down. Flavio gave his welcoming message and then introduced Thomas, who was startled by the ducks flying in from the Odeon landing across the road behind the stage. Seagulls flew in to land in flocks near the ducks. He was about to speak when several pelicans flew in and landed on the road. "The birds are attracted by the Holy Ghost descending on us," Thomas shouted. "This is a common occurrence when we start a new play. Enjoy their presence."

Thomas started the play with the first question to Paz. "Was Jesus a surprise or did the Jews know he was coming?"

"The prophet Isaiah gave various prophecies of his coming in the Jewish history,' Paz said. "For example, the Jewish prophet Isaiah said: *"The people who walked in darkness have seen a great light."*[167] *For unto us a Child is born, unto us a Son is given; and the government will be upon his shoulder. And His name will be called Wonderful, Counselor, Mighty God, Everlasting Father, and Prince of Peace."*[168]

Paz looked around taking his time and then said, *"I will also give you as a light to the Gentiles that you would be My salvation to the ends of the earth. Thus says the Lord, the Redeemer of Israel, their Holy one. To him whom man despises. To Him whom the nation abhors, to the servant of rulers: Kings shall see and arise."*[169]

Paz pointed to Mark, "The Son of man paid a price for us all."

Mark said. *"With his suffering and death as predicted by a Jewish prophet, Isaiah who said: 'But he was wounded for our transgressions, he was bruised for our iniquities; the chastisement for our peace was upon him. And with his stripes we are healed. We all, like sheep, have gone astray; we have turned everyone to his own way; and the Lord has laid on him the iniquities of us all.'"*[170]

Mark pointed to Thomas who walked back across the stage and pointed to David and said, "Does Jesus meet the requirements of those prophecies?"

David answered discussing the house of David and how Jesus fit those predictions.

David pointed to Ben. "Did Jesus have a problem when he was born?"

Ben walked to the center of the stage and said, "Herod, the ruler of Israel, at that time tried to have Jesus killed because he was warned of Jesus, the messiah, who could be king and had been born in a manger. Joseph, his adopted father, heard from God of Herod's plan and took Mary and Jesus into Egypt."

Ben pointed to Stephen. "Who was John the Baptist?"

Stephen discussed the mission of John the Baptist and who he was. He talked about the baptizing of Jesus by John the Baptist. He pointed out how the white dove descended on Jesus after the Baptism and its relevance to the

---

[167] Ibid, Isaiah 9:2.
[168] Ibid, Isaiah 9:6.
[169] Ibid, Isaiah 49:6-7.
[170] Ibid, Isaiah 53:5, 6.

birds clustered around the amphitheatre now. He talked about how the heavens opened and God spoke. *"You are my beloved son; in you I am well pleased."* [171]

The questions and answers continued and then Thomas pointed to Ben. "What happened to Jesus?"

Ben walked forward on the stage again and said, "Joseph of Arimathea, Jesus' great uncle negotiated with the Roman governor to obtain Herod's permission to take Jesus' body from the cross before the sun went down. A soldier was instructed to pierce Jesus' side through his heart to be sure He was dead and then His body was pulled down and taken by Joseph of Arimathea to his private garden tomb. Joseph of Arimathea and Nicodemus washed Jesus' body and treated it with aloes and myrrh. They dressed him in a new linen shroud. A large heavy round stone about four cubits in circumference was then rolled in a track to seal off the cave entrance. A Roman centurion and temple guards were stationed outside the tomb to stop anyone from entering the tomb without their knowledge. Caiaphas wanted to squelch Jesus' prediction that he would arise again."

Ben then stepped back a few steps and pointed to Stephen. "Is that the end of Jesus?"

Stephen looked around and breathed slowly. The audience was very quiet waiting for him to continue. Finally, he walked forward. "On the morning after the second Sabbath[172], Mary Magdalene, the most significant woman in Jesus' life, came to the cave. She found the stone blown out of its track lying flat on the ground several cubits away and Jesus' body was gone.

---

[171] Ibid, Luke 3:22.

[172] A Koinonia House Publication from Chuck Missler, Focus on Jerusalem, The Day Jesus Died (The Friday view is based on the wording of Mark 15:42, which says that Christ's crucifixion occurred on the day of preparation, "the day before the Sabbath". Since the Hebrew Sabbath is on Saturday, the Church traditionally held that Jesus was crucified on Friday. However, Jesus prophesied that he would be dead for three days and three nights before his resurrection. The problem appears easily resolved by a clarification of what Mark meant by "Sabbath". Along with the weekly Sabbath day, the Jews had other "Sabbaths" throughout the year, marking high holy days. In Matthew 28:1, the Greek should be translated, "at the end of the Sabbaths" - a plural word - noting that there had been the Passover Sabbath the previous week.)

The Roman centurion was standing back in fear and the temple guards had run away."[173]

Many oohs and ahs came from the audience.

Stephen pointed to Ben. "Why did Jesus come to us?"

"Jesus came to die for our sins," Ben said. "He died for our atonement. His death was a trade for our forgiveness and our redemption. After his resurrection, He later in the day met with Mary Magdalene to ask her to arrange for the apostles to be together at sunset. He then left and returned to see his apostles. They each felt His healed side and holes in His hands." [174]

"Blood from the cross forgives all sin," Ben shouted.

Thomas ran to the middle of the stage, threw his arms in the air shouting, "BECAUSE OF JESUS, WE'RE SAVED!"

The audience jumped to their feet and applauded and shouted praises. The missionaries linked arms in the middle of the stage and bowed several times. Thomas threw his arms in the air and shouted, as you leave be careful of the birds. It is dark and they will stay here tonight."

The standing audience poured out of the amphitheater. The mayor, bishop, high priest, the governor, his wife, the officers and missionaries met in the middle of the stage. They congratulated each other and waited for the audience to depart. Some of the audience lived nearby, but many came in by horseback and wagon. The soldiers showed the audience from the countryside where they could use their sleeping mats to stay the night. Principale Amedo left to join his men.

Centurion Enrico led the group from the stage to the palace. At the entrance, Flavio announced, "Governor Stefano and his wife, Gina, invite you to stay for dinner. Please follow me to the terrace. They walked through the palace and out to find it was lit up with torches surrounding the stone terrace. Thomas noticed a few dozen soldiers stationed around the entrance where they came in, inside the palace and discreetly around the terrace. Servers came out carrying trays of goblets. They stood around talking to one another until a uniformed servant came out and announced, "Dinner is ready to be served in the dining hall. Your names are on your plate"

They followed Gina and Stefano into the dining hall to a table which was longer than the night before. Everyone walked around the table to find

---

[173] Ibid, Mathew 28:4.
[174] Ibid, John 20:28-29.

their name. When everyone had found their seat, Governor Stefano said, "Please be seated."

Thomas found himself next to Gina. She looked at Thomas and asked, "How did you think the non-Jewish audience reacted in the big amphitheater?"

Thomas looked at her and then at Bishop Philip. He smiled and said, "They seemed to follow the questions and answers very well, and clapped and cheered more than I expected. Bishop, what did you think of the audience's reception to our message?"

"I watched many people I did not know," he said. "I believe I am going to find many people coming to my services and wanting to be baptized. Some behind me were saying that during the play."

Flavio from across the table said, "Your message of being saved and becoming eligible for life after death was very meaningful. One of you said that baptism forgives you of your sins and your soul is reborn. I haven't heard anything like that in worshiping Apollo or from the Jewish meetings I've attended. I'm going to seriously consider converting."

Dinner and wine was served to everyone. Mayor Carsten said, "One of our best vineyards donated the wine we are consuming tonight. I had them bring it over to the palace today."

Governor Stefano sat looking at Flavio and then turned to stare at Thomas and Bishop Philip. Finally, he said, "Thomas, did you convert any officers in Judaea?"

"Stephen and I met Tribune Cerrone in Jerusalem and he asked us to pray to heal his injured knee," Thomas said. "We did pray for the healing and within a few minutes heat hit his leg and his leg was healed. He converted and I baptized him in the River Jordan where John the Baptist baptized Jesus. Tribune Pasquali in Sebaste converted after our play there and I baptized him the next day with several other officers. When we were leaving Caesarea, Tribune Mascaro and his wife Lydia told me they were planning to be baptized. Of course, Centurion Baroni over there converted and was baptized. Why do you ask?"

"I did not expect that many," Stefano said. Then he asked, "What about Governor Rufus."

"Governor Rufus was baptized in Cyprus," Thomas said. "Governor Valerian in Cyprus is also a Christian. We have been invited to go to Cyprus next year and perform plays in a number of cities there."

"I have been leaning towards converting to Christianity," Stefano said. "But, I've been afraid of what I have seen in Rome with the Christian executions performed there. Gina and I have talked about Christianity, but fear has kept us away."

"Death can occur at any time from many directions," Thomas said. "It is prudent to respect actions that can result in death. The way I look at it, I believe in Jesus Christ and his Good News. I want to be saved and live after this life. You should want that as well as me."

"I like your thoughts on life after death," Gina said. "I don't fully understand the rebirth of my spirit or being forgiven for my sins, but I like the sound of both. Could you explain either of those?"

Thomas smiled at her and said, "I'll try. We call the first man, Adam, and the first woman, Eve. They were created by God and placed in the Garden of Eden. God commanded them to not eat the fruit from the tree of life. They became tempted and ate the fruit. God punished them by casting them from the Garden of Eden. This sin caused all of the generations of Adam and Eve's descendents to lose eternal life. That sin is one of the sins you are forgiven in baptism, which restores your right to eternal life. Jesus' death paid the price for that forgiveness. The rebirth of your spirit is the bringing back to life your spirit's right to eternal life."

"That is the best explanation I have ever heard," Bishop Philip said. "I must remember that explanation for future talks to my members."

"Thomas, Gina and I will take the risk and seek our baptisms from Bishop Philip," Stefano said.

"Bishop Philip, would you come and visit with Flavio, Gina and me tomorrow?"

Thomas finished his meal and drank the last of his wine. He looked around the table watching most finish, as well. He said, "Gina, Governor and Flavio, I'm pleased for your decisions. Bishop Philip, I leave them in your capable hands."

The talking around the table stopped, as more wine was poured into everyone's goblets. The Governor stood and then everyone around the table stood. "I would like to toast the plays that Thomas and his companions performed tonight," he said. "After you take a sip to my toast, let's move to the terrace again."

They walked out to the terrace and stood talking to one another. High Priest Hector and his wife walked up to Thomas, introduced his wife and said, "Your presentation was so convincing, I fear I will lose many of my members. I heard what the governor said about being baptized. I congratulated the governor, his wife Gina, and Tribune Flavio. I'm a good loser. I don't need to wish you good luck in the future, because you already have good luck. Have a safe trip and I hope for your success with your Island-of-Dreams."

"High Priest Hector, you are very noble to accept what the governor and his wife have decided," Thomas said. "Your status here will be very sound. Thank you."

Stefano and Gina were at the front door saying good night to their guests. Baroni, Enrico, Flavio, Thomas and Stephen stood staring at each other. Baroni said, "I'll take a few of your men out front to walk over and give instructions to Principale Amedo. I want him to meet us here with his men, the missionaries and our horses after breakfast in the morning."

After everyone said good night, Thomas and Stephen made their way to their bedrooms and fell into bed.

Saturday, May 4, 125 A.D.

Baroni knocked on the bedroom doors for Thomas and Stephen. They came out carrying their saddlebags and went downstairs. A servant took the saddlebags and said, "Breakfast will be served shortly in the dining hall."

"They went in and found the Governor, Gina and Tribune Flavio seated and smiling. "Good morning." Stefano said. "Please join us."

They sat and Thomas asked, "Are you comfortable with your decision this morning."

"Yes, Gina and I are happy with our decision," Stefano said. "You helped convince me and took some of my fear away. You gave me the balance in the decision I needed. It's funny because I have never been afraid of anything else. Must I fear my own people? I won't do it."

"I have always been curious about an afterlife and spirits," Gina said. "You really cleared it up for me."

"I was half way ready to convert before you came here," Flavio said. "Spending time with you and your companions' yesterday morning and watching the plays almost convinced me. But your comments at dinner cinched it for me. I'm happy about becoming a Christian."

Centurion Enrico came in and sat down as breakfast was served. "I have been out talking to the soldiers and trying to get a feel for what they felt about the plays," he said. "There was discussion about the play that centered on three subjects. The first was how impressed they were with the missionaries. I mean they liked the way you rode your horses and seemed unafraid to be with the Governor and the officers. Several mentioned you, Thomas, how you seem to take command. They liked that about you. The second was how we sponsored the plays. At first they were confused about why you were here and why you were being sponsored by the Governor and the army. The third issue was the play. They had never been allowed to learn that much about Christianity. They did like what they heard."

Stefano looked somewhat concerned and asked, "Do you think very many of them will want to be baptized? I ask this with your knowledge that Flavio, Gina and I will be baptized."

Enrico smiled and said, "Right now many of them will convert to Christianity. When they hear the three of you got baptized, that will convince many more to seek baptism. You know they highly respect the three of you. Bishop Philip will need a larger house of worship."

"If you will excuse us, we need to mount our horses and leave," Baroni said. "Thomas and Stephen, we must move on. There is work to do."

They walked down the entrance path and mounted their horses. As they rode away, they waved to those at the front door. Riding out of Gortyn, they let their horses gallop until they went over the first hill. It was a little after mid-day when they came down the hill into Amnissos. They continued on out to the port and stopped in front of the ships.

Baroni and the missionaries dismounted and took their personal items out of their saddlebags and gave their reins to the soldiers. Baroni and Amedo saluted, and then the soldiers rode back the way they came following Principale Amedo. "I'll miss my horse," Paz said. "I enjoyed the ride and the visit to Gortyn."

Tamir and Pardi came down the pier and said, "I hope your trip to Gortyn was a success. Tamir said. "We survived while you were gone, but we had visitors."

"Our trip to Gortyn was very successful," Thomas said. "But who visited you?"

"After you left, Pardi and I had the names of Free Spirit and Islander on the ships covered," he said. "We figured Hadar may send out ships to find us. We had a big fire the night you left. All of the soldiers on the three ships and all of the men with us had a nice feast around the fire. We told everyone about Hadar and why he is after us. Pardi warned them to say nothing about you, ships with large red stars on the sails, the Free Spirit or the Islander, if anyone asks. I figured if they can't find the ships with those names, maybe they would move on. Well, two ships came in and docked yesterday morning. Men from those ships asked around wanting to know if we had seen a man named Thomas or his ships the Free Spirit and the Islander. They asked if we had seen any ships with a big red star on the sails. They were able to learn nothing and so they left this morning early. Now we know they are looking for us this far west. If we see them again, we can recognize them from the big Jewish menorahs on each of their sails."

"Tamir and Pardi, you do good work," Thomas said. "I'm impressed. Thank you."

† Chapter 35 †

Hadar's Ships Attack
Sunday, May 5, 125 A.D.

At dawn, Thomas got up and went to the top-deck to find Baroni, Pardi and Peter reviewing a map by candlelight. Peter stopped and looked at Thomas to say, "Our plan is for the Free Spirit to leave first.. Everyone knows the plan."

"We haven't forgotten that we are bait for Hadar. Hopefully, we will not see Hadar's ships until we spot Drago, Alonso and Bernardus again south of us. Is the route we discussed last night for getting out of here clear to you?"

"I understand it," Thomas said. "Let's sail."

Peter waved to the dock workers and the lines were untied and thrown to the seamen who rolled and stored them. The soldiers and seamen on board had their oars out and turned the Free Spirit around and rowed out of the marina. Peter ordered the mainsail pulled up and then the small sails. The wind filled the sails and they sailed slowly north. Stephen and Ben came up to join Thomas on the stern. They watched the Islander sail in behind them. Drago's ship was not visible when the Free Spirit turned west. The island of Dia was off the port side and looked like a big lizard in the sea. As they passed Dia, Ben spotted Drago's ship sailing around behind the Islander. Stephen saw Alonso's and Bernardus' ships to the south of them.

Two of the guards came around offering slices of smoked fish, bread and cheese. The sun came up and was very bright as they sailed west. As the sun rose higher, they passed the end of Crete. They passed just north of Turkuru island just north of Chania on west Crete. Peter checked the sun dial to be sure of his heading. Thomas watched Drago's ship sail south to join the other ships. The Islander sailed north and got a little behind.

Peter gave the paddle bar to Pardi and came over to finish his breakfast with Thomas and Baroni, who sat on the stern. Baroni said, "After we drop Pardi off, we sail to Syracuse. Apparently, there is a wonderful amphitheater inland from Syracuse built by the Greeks. There is also a circular stadium built by Romans and is one of the largest ever built. Rufus says we will have to work to get the amphitheater filled. There are many Christians in Syracuse. The Phoenicians, Greeks and Romans have ruled Syracuse in that order over the past millennia."

Pardi asked Mark to take over the paddle bar and came over to talk to Peter, Baroni and Thomas. He sat down on the stern and asked, "Will it be dark when we pass Malta?"

Peter consulted his map and said, "It depends on the wind intensity. We have a fairly brisk wind behind us now, but we will have to determine our speed over the water. Ben I need you to help me."

Peter handed Ben a float with a long line attached to it. "Take this float up to the bow. Pardi hold onto the line attached to the float and hang over the railing on the starboard side to count how long the float takes to get to the end of the stern. Pardi, when you're ready, wave to Ben to drop the float into the water."

Ben took the float to the bow and looked back to Pardi and dropped it as he waved. Pardi counted and then pulled the float back into the ship. He gave Peter the count and then did some mental calculations. He smiled and said, "My guess is we will pass Malta about sunset, unless the wind dies down. We'll check later in the day again. This might be a good time to take a nap. Some of us could be up part of the night tonight."

Most of the men went down to take a nap. Thomas awoke a while later to shouting. He ran up to the top deck. Baroni was standing on the stern waving a flag on a long pole. Several men were in the bow pointing at two ships ahead of them that were turning to come towards them. "They have seen the large red star on our sail. I guess they didn't see the red star on the Islander. Both Hadar ships displayed the Jewish menorahs on their sails," Thomas said to Baroni, "I'm glad Drago told us about those Jewish menorahs. Now, we are sure they are Hadar's ships."

Thomas looked over to the Islander and it was sailing towards them from the starboard side, but behind them a ways. Peter came up from below and asked, "What is going on?"

Baroni looked down from the stern and said, "Look past the bow. I'm afraid we may have Hadar's ships coming our way. The Jewish menorahs are visible on both ship's sails. They were going crossways of our route and turned when they saw us. I'm waving this flag to signal Drago and Tamir to come in to our aid."

"Let's take the sails down," Peter said. "We need to let Tamir and Drago get to us before we meet those ships."

Thomas went to the bow to get a better look. The two ships were trying to get parallel to each other and moving apart. He ducked as the seamen took the sails down. The soldiers came up with swords, pitch, bows and arrows. The seamen, guards and the missionaries went down and brought up their swords and knives. The Free Spirit was stopped in the water, except for the wind blowing the stern. A fire was started in a clay bowl and the pitch was held over it.

Stephen was yelling, "The Islander is coming in fast, but it is still behind us. A number of men are in the bow."

Baroni was still on the stern and took the signal flag down. He yelled, "Drago, Alonso and Bernardus are going around behind those ships. They'll surprise Hadar's men."

As the ships came closer, the sails came down on both of them. The soldiers on the Free Spirit now had pitch on their arrows. Baroni told them to light them. "I want three on the starboard side and two on the port side," Baroni shouted. "Everyone get down and hold your shields over you. They probably have arrows or dart throwers. Ben, you're up there in the bow. Look for archers or dart throws on both ships. Stay down until Ben lets us know."

Thomas took a quick look over the stern and saw the Islander coming up directly behind the Free Spirit. Its mainsail was half down.

Ben yelled, "There are archers on both ships sailing at us. I don't see any fire for their arrows. Drago's ships are coming in fast behind us, but they are still too far away."

As the two ships were about a hundred paces away, the Islander shot around the starboard side and came in on the outside of the Hadar ship. The ship on the port side turned away and the sail came up. It went away picking up speed. Sailors on that ship were standing and pointing back towards the Roman ships coming in behind them.

As the other Hadar ship came along side the Free Spirit, Hadar's men shot arrows, but only hit the railing and stern. Most went on through the ship because no one was standing. The three soldiers on the starboard side shot their flaming arrows at the archers on the Hadar ship then dropped down. Soldiers on the Islander shot their arrows. Now the five soldiers on the Free Spirit loosed another volley of five arrows on fire and ducked down as another volley of arrows came at them. The guards had brought line attached to grappling hooks and they now stood and threw two over the bow of the Hadar ships railing. They dropped back down and pulled on the ropes catching railings and pulling the two ships together.

Drago's ship came up to meet the Islander bow to bow and then threw grappling hooks over the bow's railing of Hadar's ship. Very quickly all four ships were tied together. Soldiers from the Free Spirit, the Islander and Drago's ship were jumping over the railings of Hadar's ship with their swords. The battle was over very quickly as Hadar's men gave up. They thrust their arms in the air. The arrows that had been on fire had hit men in the chest who were now lying dead or dying on the deck. Three of Hadar's men had been stabbed and only one of Drago's soldiers had been stabbed in the chest.

Baroni, Ben and Thomas came over the railing. Ben went around counting the dead and dying and counted fourteen besides Drago's soldier. The soldiers herded the remaining fourteen men from Hadar's ship to the bow. Baroni shouted, "Who is in charge of this ship?"

No one replied. Baroni raised his sword and said, "I will start killing one man at a time until someone talks."

There was still more silence and Baroni ran his sword through one of the men. The man slid to the deck, screaming. Baroni yelled, "Who will be next?"

A man in the middle stepped forward with his arms in the air and said, "I will talk. The captain of this ship is dead over there with a burning arrow in his chest. You just killed the first mate."

"Who sent you here?" Baroni growled.

"This ship is owned by Hadar Shipping," the man said. "Most of us were kidnapped in Israel and forced to serve on this ship. The men dedicated to Hadar are mostly the men dead or dying on the deck. I can show you the others that are dedicated to Hadar."

"What was your goal in coming after this ship," Baroni asked.

The man was afraid, but said, "We were told that a man named Thomas had Jewish records he had stolen from some priests that had saved them from the temple before it was destroyed by Titus. Hadar was sure this would be

Thomas' ship and the records would be here. To be honest, I do not care. As a matter of fact, I hate Hadar."

"Who are the men that were holding you?" Baroni demanded. "What is your name?"

"My name is Joziah," he said. "Let me look."

"Joziah turned around and looked at the faces. He then pointed to two men and said, "These two commanded us, but they are cowards. The others were brave, but are dead. These other ten men are kidnap victims like me. We refused to fight. We would like to join Thomas, whoever he is. If we are forced to go back to Israel, we will either be killed or forced to work for Hadar or Simeon ben Kosiba. They are both tyrants as far as I am concerned."

Thomas was standing next to Baroni and said, "How can we trust you or these others?"

"I really don't know," Joziah said. "We have no proof. You can try talking to each man."

"If I offer you a job, would you work for me," Thomas asked.

"Gladly," Joziah said. "What would I do?"

"You would build houses and work on a Christian house of worship," Thomas said.

"I would love working on those building projects," Joziah said. "I understand you are a Christian missionary. Do you have a problem with Jews? Would you want us to convert to Christianity?"

"I have no problem with you being a Jew," Thomas said. "But, I do have a problem with radical Jews like Hadar, Simeon ben Kosiba and those who support them. I would only want you to convert to Christianity if you become a believer in Jesus Christ and his Good News."

"I hope you will talk to the other ten men I pointed out," Joziah said. "I am sure they feel the same way I do. None of us want to go back to Israel. I think there is going to be war there with the Romans and that's suicide."

"How old are most of you," Thomas asked.

"I'm the oldest at twenty-three," Joziah said. "The others are between seventeen and nineteen."

"Baroni, have the two Hadar men tied up," Thomas said.

While two rebel soldiers were tied up, Tamir climbed over the railing from the Islander and said, "You have acquired another work boat. My first mate can captain this ship and he has a man that can be his first mate."

"Great, we'll get to that shortly," Thomas said.

"Let's get these bodies piled in the bow," Drago said. "All of them are dead now, including one of my soldiers. We will place him in one of our body bags."

"We have enough body bags for all of these others," Baroni said. "We'll dump them right here after we bag them."

"There are plenty of rocks in the bottom of this ship for ballast," Joziah said. "They can be brought up to weight the bodies."

"I'll say a prayer and call out each name as we slide them into the sea," Thomas said.

"Joziah, you and the others stand over by the stern, while we take care of the dead," Drago said. "We'll keep all of you at spear point until we decide what to do with you."

They started herding the men to the stern when both of the bound men dove over the port rail. Both sank, disappearing into the sea. Baroni shrugged and said, "Good. I was going to suggest we kill them anyway. They must have thought we were going to torture them. Problem solved."

Within a short time all of the bodies were ready to be loaded into body bags and Thomas said, "Joziah can you name each of the dead men, if you can stand over here by me?"

"Yes, I can easily name these terrible men," he said. "Can I take my arms down? I'm unarmed."

Joziah stood with Thomas, who had a writing instrument and parchment. "I'm going to write the numbers one to seventeen," Thomas said. "As a body and a rock are placed in a body bag I will write the name you call out and I'll also write the number on the body bag."

The bodies and rocks were loaded as Joziah called out the name and Thomas recorded it and wrote the number on the body bag. When they were finished, Thomas said a prayer for them. Then one at a time the bodies were dumped over the port side as Thomas checked the number and called the name.

Tamir had his first-mate, named Micah, take command as captain of the Hadar ship called the "ben Yaakov." Peter had his first-mate come aboard to be Micah's first mate. New assignments were made for the Free Spirit and the Islander. Micah, Tamir and Peter made an inspection of the ben Yaakov and its cabins, galley and supplies. They came back and announced there was plenty of food and supplies.

Drago came over to Baroni and said, "I had an understanding with Alonso and Bernardus. The agreement was that if we got separated, we would meet in Malta. I suggest I assign ten of my soldiers to man the ben Yaakov for Captain Micah until we get to Malta."

Mark and Paz, I want you to take six of the men from the ben Yaakov aboard the Islander," Thomas said. "Interview them between now and docking at Malta. I want your opinion of them when we get there. We will take Joziah and the other five and do the same. Before we leave Malta, I want everyone's advice on what we will do with these men and the ship itself. I will want a new name for it if we keep it."

The men on the ships were moved around with the soldiers on each ship guarding the survivors from the ben Yaakov. The plan was agreed to sail to Malta together and hope the other two Roman ships would meet them there soon. The grappling hooks and lines were released and the four ships separated and turned to sail west raising their sails as they went. The wind was a little stronger. It was now late afternoon.

The guards on the Free Spirit cut more bread and cheese and served it with watered wine to everyone, including the men from the ben Yaakov. Thomas started interviewing the men, leaving Joziah for last. They found everything Joziah had said was repeated by the five men. The men were young and three of the five were actually Christians. They had never admitted it when they were captured because they had heard they could be killed. One of the Christians said two of the men that went to the Islander were also Christians. Everyone expressed their desire to join Thomas' group and the building projects. The men who still held the Jewish faith expressed the desire to learn more about Christianity and would highly consider being baptized.

When Thomas and Stephen finished the interviews, Peter met with Thomas and Baroni. "Pardi, Ben and I checked our speed," he said. "We will arrive in Malta in the morning after sunrise. I suggest we have the young men from the ben Yaakov sleep on the extra sleeping mats in the bow. We should assign guards to watch them in shifts."

The sun went down by the time the men from the ben Yaakov were on their sleeping mats and guards had been assigned. Thomas, Stephen and Ben retired to their cabin and found others there already asleep. They whispered their surprise over what had happened and went to sleep.

✝ Chapter 36 ✝

A Visit to the Islands of Malta
Monday, May 6, 125 A.D.

Before dawn, Thomas got up to watch for the coast line of Malta. As the sun came up, Peter consulted his map and the sundial. He looked up as Pardi and Baroni appeared. We should see Malta within the next while, let's say by mid-morning. Drago's ship was ahead of them, the ben Yaakov was behind them followed by the Islander. All the men were up and the young men from the ben Yaakov were sitting with their backs to the bow railing. The guards came up with ingredients to prepare hot Calda. They made a fire in the clay bowl to heat the pot of mixed Calda. They served the men from the ben Yaakov watered wine in goblets with smoked fish. The soldiers, seamen, guards and missionaries received goblets of hot Calda, strips of smoked fish, sliced bread and cheese.

The sun was high above their starboard side when Ben shouted, "I see land ahead of us to the south. Drago's ship is turning towards it."

Peter stood to see the land and Drago's ship saying, "Marascala is on the east end of the island. It looks like that's our objective. The pier was built by Sicilians."

Thomas studied the land they were sailing towards and asked Baroni, "Where does the Roman Governor live?"

"Caesar Hadrian granted the island of Malta the status of Municipium eight years ago. The governor of Malta built his castle in Mdina in the middle of the island."

All four ships sailed into the bay that led to the port at Marascala. Dock workers came out and helped them. Drago made arrangements with the pier manager and talked to some Roman officers. The missionaries, Tamir, Baroni and Pardi met on the pier. Thomas talked about the interviews for Joziah and the five younger men. Mark described the interviews he, Paz and David had conducted on the Islander. Thomas smiled and said, "Somehow God has delivered these fine young men to us. We have found no problems with them, but we need to keep them divided between the Free Spirit, the Islander and the ben Yaakov."

They walked around the front of the ben Yaakov, staring at it. The masthead had Hadar Shipping carved in black letters. Thomas said, "Now we need to rename this old freighter and make changes to its appearance. We can't use that sail with the Jewish menorah on it. Tamir, Peter and Micah give me your thoughts on what we can do to change the way this ship looks. I will decide on a name, but if anyone has a good name to recommend, let me know."

Thomas stood listening to the three ship-captains arguing over changes to be made to the ben Yaakov. Pardi came over and said, "I don't think it would be good to give the ship another Hebrew name or symbol. If you are going to use the ship in construction of the house of worship, I would suggest a Sicilian name. I want to have a ship to travel to Palermo for the vineyard. Could we call it the Palermo Vine?"

"That's a good name," Thomas said. "It is a large ship compared to the Free Spirit. It will carry many passengers, and I want to use it for that purpose later. In the meantime, you can use it for the vineyard and hauling construction supplies and workmen. I hope it will last that long and not rot out. Pardi, maintenance of the Palermo Vine will be one of your jobs."

Peter came over and said, "Thomas, we have a list of changes, including new sails with a very different shape, a new head and signs in the prow and a fresh coat of colored oil on the wood surfaces and deck. Have you selected a name yet?"

"Those changes sound good," Thomas said. "Can we do some them here? And yes, Pardi likes a Sicilian name of the Palermo Vine with the grapes below the red star. Pardi, you're technically a Roman soldier until you get home. Could you try to find a sail maker and have our captains go with you to meet with him for the sail design? Have two sails made and don't forget the red star above a large string of grapes for the two new main sails."

Drago came marching down the pier and said, "I talked to those Roman officers over there. They said they can help us with ship repairs. I asked about the Roman governor. They said he has returned to his new palace in Mdina, which was completed two years ago. I asked how you get to Mdina from here. They said you can go by horseback. There are Roman stables nearby."

"Could you introduce Pardi and the captains to those Roman officers?" Thomas asked.

"Yes, I will take them over there right now," Drago said. "They also want to meet you, Centurion Baroni and Principale Pardi."

Thomas, Drago, Baroni, Pardi, Stephen and the three captains walked up the pier and over to the Roman officers who watched them approach. Baroni and Pardi saluted the officers and then Drago introduced everyone. One was a Centurion and the other was a Principale. They were waiting for a ship to take them to Rome. Baroni asked, "When do you expect the arrival of the ship you are to board?"

The centurion said, "My name is Marco. We've been waiting for three days, but it could be another week. I could hear you talking about the governor here. Would you like to have me take you to Mdina to meet Governor Pietro? We could ride over this afternoon and return in the morning."

Thomas looked at Drago and asked, "How long do you think it will take for Alonso and Bernardus to catch us?

"It depends on how far they followed that Hadar ship and whether they caught it," Drago said. "We will need a few days to get two new sails made and complete the other modifications to the new Palermo Vine. You have time to travel to Mdina and back. You said Governor Pietro is a friend of Governor Rufus who said he was sending him a message. He should be expecting you."

"Centurion Marco, there will be just three traveling with you," Thomas said. "Centurion Baroni, Stephen and I will go, after we get some lunch and our personal things."

"Principale Matteo and I need lunch too," Marco said. "Do what you need to do and when you come back, I know a good place nearby that has good fried fish, wine and juice."

Thomas, Stephen and Baroni went to the cabins in the Free Spirit to get spare robes and brushes to take with them. They came out to find the soldiers from all three ships standing around watching Joziah and his ten young associates scrapping and brushing the parts of the hull on the Palermo Vine that was out of the water. Thomas told the missionaries and the three captains he, Baroni and Stephen were going to ride over to Mdina to meet with the Governor. Baroni invited Drago and Pardi to go to lunch.

They walked back to Marco and Matteo who led them down a street and around a corner to a nice set of tables overlooking the beach. Marco went into the building and two servers followed him back out. He sat down and said, "I ordered fried fish for seven. These men have brought juice for the four of us and wine for Drago, Pardi and Matteo."

As they were talking about the Maltese people, the plates of fish and side dishes were bought out to them. Everyone started eating and Marco said, "The Maltese people are very nice. It is amazing when you consider all the marauders that have frequented these islands. They seem to be very happy to have us Romans here to give them some protection. Matteo and I have been here for four years. We are going to Rome to find out where we go next. Where are all of you going? Thomas, you seem to have a varied group of soldiers and people traveling somewhere. Where are you from and where are you going?"

"Those are good questions," Thomas said. "We came from Jerusalem through Caesarea in the Roman province of Judaea. We visited Gortyn in Crete on the way here. We are going from here to Palermo, Sicily, to drop off Pardi. We will then go to Syracuse to meet with Governor Salvatore. After that we pick up Pardi again and go look for my Island-of-Dreams. I hope it is in the Balearic Sea but we will look at other islands as we go."

"Now I have more questions," Marco said. "Why are all you Romans going with Thomas and his people? Why have you got that old freighter with you? Why would you go see Governor Salvatore? What is this Island-of-Dreams?"

Baroni smiled and said, "Thomas has all of us Romans with him, including two ships that have not gotten here yet, because Thomas needs protection from a rich Jew who thinks Thomas stole some ancient Jewish records. We on the other hand are using Thomas and his companions as bait to try to catch this rich Jew by the name of Hadar, who is supplying a rebel army in Judaea with the goods to make war. Yesterday, on the way here, we suckered two of Hadar's ships into making an attack on the Free Spirit. One got away pursued by two of our Roman ships. We overwhelmed the other ship, killed about twenty of their men, kept the survivors and took over the ship bringing it here."

Thomas looked at Marco, who seemed satisfied so far, and said, "We are going to Syracuse to see Governor Salvatore at the request of Governor Rufus in Judaea to put on Christian plays. The Island-of-Dreams was shown to me in a dream when Jesus appeared. He showed it to me and gave me orders."

Marco sat back and rubbed his mustache then said, "This is quite an adventure all of you are on. I wish I could go with you. Maybe you can tell me more on the way over and back from Mdina."

After they finished their lunch and drinks, everyone walked back to the dock. Baroni said to Marco, "I think we should take ten soldiers with us for protection. This Hadar seems to have people everywhere looking for Thomas. Are there enough horses for fourteen?"

"Oh yes, there are plenty of horses," Marco said. "Matteo, you should come with us to take care of the soldiers when we get to Mdina. That way Pardi and Drago can stay here to manage the modifications to the ben Yaakov, soon to be the Palermo Vine."

Back at the ships, Drago selected ten soldiers to go to Mdina. Marco, Baroni, Thomas and Stephen marched ahead of Matteo and the ten soldiers. It was not far to the stables on the edge of the small town. Marco made arrangements with the stable manager. The fifteen men selected their horses, saddles, bridles and saddlebags. When they were ready, Marco and Matteo rode out first and the soldiers followed Baroni, Thomas and Stephen. The afternoon was hot and sunny. The road was dusty and started up an incline. Thomas thought the view down the barren landscape to the Mediterranean was intense. Small villages and ruins were encountered on the way. By late-afternoon they rode by Rabat and continued on to Mdina arriving before sunset.

Marco led everyone to the stables. They left their horses with the stable manager and took their saddlebags with them. They were met by a soldier who introduced himself as Centurion Filippo who knew Marco. Baroni introduced himself, Thomas and Stephen to Filippo. Matteo said, "I will take the soldiers to the barracks."

Filippo looked at Marco and said, "You and Matteo just left here a couple of days ago. You surprised me. What can I do for all of you?"

"We would like to meet with Governor Pietro," Baroni said. "I have papers and orders from Governor Rufus in the Roman province of Judaea."

"Follow me and I will introduce you to Tribune Nicolo," Filippo said.

When they were in the entrance, Thomas could see the Preatorium off to their left. They went into a room off to the right. A man in a familiar uniform with purple stripes stood there. Filippo saluted and said, "Sir, I found these men coming out of the stables. I'm sure you remember Centurion Marco. These other men are Centurion Baroni, Thomas and Stephen."

Nicolo looked very much like Cerrone in Jerusalem. He was clean shaven, tall and probably about thirty. He had a confident, friendly smile and said, "You must have ridden in from Marsascala. Marco, your ship to take you to Rome did not arrive, I gather."

"Yes sir, It will not arrive for a few days yet," Marco said. "I thought you would want to meet Centurion Baroni and these men. They are from the Roman province of Judaea. Centurion Baroni has papers and orders from Governor Rufus in Caesarea."

Baroni showed Nicolo his papers and orders from Rufus. "Part of your orders are to find and kill this Hadar, who is arming the rebels in Judaea. It says Thomas and his companions are to be used as bait to attract this Hadar. Has it been working?"

"Yes, that's one reason why we are here on Malta," Baroni said.

Baroni told about the battle with the men on the ben Yaakov and the departure of the other ship with the other two Roman ships chasing it. He talked about changing its looks and its name. Baroni smiled and said, "We are waiting for the other ships to catch us. So in the meantime, we came over here to meet Governor Pietro. Governor Rufus said he is friends with Governor Pietro. Of course, it is a pleasure to meet you."

"Governor Rufus says Thomas is a Christian," Nicolo said. "Are you a Christian, as well?"

"Yes, I'm a Christian," Baroni said. "I became converted and baptized in Judaea performing guard duty and traveling with Thomas and his companions."

"Thomas, are you a missionary?" Nicolo asked. "If you are, how many missionary companions are traveling with you?"

"Yes, I'm a Christian missionary," Thomas said. "I have six other missionary companions, including Stephen."

"It sounds like you have done some intense work," Nicolo said. "How do you do it?"

"First of all, all seven of us have studied and prepared to do missionary work," Thomas said. "All of us speak and write three or more languages. We have done most of our work so far doing plays. We have performed in Joppa, Sebaste and Caesarea Judaea. More recently we performed two plays in Gortyn Crete. We have had some success."

"Nicolo, they have converted hundreds of people, Roman officers and soldiers," Baroni said. "They converted and baptized Tribunes Cerrone in Jerusalem and Pasquali in Sebaste. Tribune Mascaro in Caesarea and his wife Lydia along with Centurion Taccone were planning to be baptized when we left. We spent two days in Gortyn Crete and Governor Stefano, his wife, Gina, and Tribune Flavio planned to be baptized after we left. Governor Rufus appreciated how Thomas left each new congregation under the control of the local Romans in charge of the area. Thomas is a humble man."

"My, you are humble, Thomas" Nicolo said. "I'm impressed. Let me go see if we can meet with Governor Pietro. He did get a message from Governor Rufus. We can't let you perform a play while you are here because of other commitments the governor has. Maybe you'll want to perform a play at another time."

Nicolo came back before long after a reasonable wait and said, "Governor Pietro and his wife, Caterina, would like to have you join them on the terrace for drinks. Follow me."

They followed Nicolo through the mansion and out a door to the terrace which faced west. The sun was just beginning to go down. Governor Pietro and Caterina stood looking puzzled. "Centurion Marco," he said. "It is a surprise to see you back here. Centurion Baroni, we have met before and it is good to see you again. Now, who is Thomas?"

Thomas stepped forward and said, "I'm Thomas and this is my cousin, Stephen. It is a pleasure to meet you Governor Pietro and Lady Caterina."

"You're a surprise, showing up tonight," Pietro said. "But, all of you are welcome. We knew you were coming but did not know when. Nicolo told us a lot about each of you and your activities. He told you I have a commitment to an appointment, so we do not have time for you to perform a play now. Hopefully, you can return at another time. We have seats here for everyone. Please sit."

Pietro waved to a servant in the doorway. Soon three servants came out carrying trays of goblets, amphoras and small cakes. When everyone had a drink and cake, Pietro leaned back and said, "Nicolo told me some of the Roman officers you have converted to Christianity. Governor Stefano told me he would never become a Christian because he might get beheaded like some have been in Rome. As you know we crucify Christian citizens and behead Romans. You must have told him something to convince him to get over his fears."

Thomas frowned and said, "Governor Stefano had the benefit of spending some time with us and watching two of our plays. After the last play, I was seated by the Governor and his wife at dinner. Both of them expressed interest in the prospect of being baptized which forgives your sins and allows your spirit to be reborn. They both admitted their fear of their own people if they did get baptized. I told them we all face death every day. If you die not baptized, you lose the possibility of eternal life. You have to weigh the risk of being killed with having eternal life."

Caterina squirmed in her seat and said, "I've not heard of eternal life and being forgiven my sins. What kind of sins are you talking about and what is the rebirth of my spirit?"

"You raise the same question as Lady Gina asked," Thomas said. "None of us are perfect, but the big sin is more complicated."

Thomas told the story of the original sin in the Garden of Eden and how that sin was placed on all of their descendents. He smiled and said, "Jesus paid the price for that sin with his death. Now we can be baptized which forgives that sin and any of our other sins. This forgiveness and restoration of eternal life allows your spirit to be born again."

"Pietro, my dear, we have never heard any of this," Caterina said. "No wonder we are hearing about so many new Christians here in Malta, Sicily, Rome, other cities and countries."

"Thomas, you teach a lot more than what you just told us, I assume," Pietro said. "What else goes into your plays?"

"May I answer that question," Baroni said. "Thomas and his companions put on their plays which I guess last about two and one-half hours. The play covers the life of Jesus and the Good News he brought. It is presented in a question and answer format. The audiences seem to grasp the answers and believe. I have never seen anything like it. The beauty is that there has never been any violence. We travel into a new area and the plays and other activities occur with no problems. Thomas believes in leaving the new or old church in the control of our local Roman officers."

"I understand you captured a ship from an enemy of Governor Rufus," Pietro said, smiling. "What do you plan to do with it and its survivors?"

Thomas looked at Baroni wondering how much to say, but then he said, "Our plan is to reconfigure the ship's appearance and let Pardi use it in the vineyard and construction activities. The survivors are a group of eleven young men that had been kidnapped to work on that ship. When the crew attacked us, they refused to fight. All but two of the dedicated men to the owner of the ship were killed, including the captain and first mate. The oldest of the young kidnapped men pointed out the bad men, but only two were still alive. We tied them up, but they dived into the sea and drowned. None of the young kidnapped men want to return to Judaea for fear of death from the rebels. Some of them are secretly Christians and all of them want to work for me. We have interviewed all of them and are quite pleased. Today they have been scraping and applying colored oil to the new Palermo Vine."

Lady Caterina and I want to hear more," Pietro said. "We would like to invite all of you to dinner. We can continue this conversation there. When we finish dinner, we have guest rooms for all of you. I see you each have saddlebags. Leave them here. I'll have them taken and placed in front of doors on the second level. When you go up, identify your saddlebag and that will be your room. Please follow Caterina and me into the dining hall."

When everyone was seated, Pietro smiled and said, "I have some splendid wine to have with dinner. I would like to have you and Stephen engage in some of the questions and answers you perform in your plays. Baroni, if you want to be part of this be our guest. Before you do, let me ask a question. Thomas, are you a client in the Roman custom with Governor Rufus and Governor Stefano?"

"Yes, I'm a client of Governors Rufus and Stefano," Thomas said. "I think I understand the obligations of these relationships and am pleased to be a part of this custom. I'd be delighted to be your client and you become Patron for me. I understand these mazes of relationships are a founding principal of the Roman State. You can always call on me."

"I would be pleased to have you consider me to be your Patron," Pietro said. "You may be a Jewish Christian, but you are becoming like us Romans. I hope to have you return to perform a play. There may be other work I would choose to have you do. In return I will help you with needs you encounter and defend you when you need me."

"I'm honored to be your client," Thomas said. "I like being your friend, but understand the obligation of being your client. You may want to consider being a Patron to Stephen, in case something happens to me."

"Thank you, Thomas. Stephen, I'm offering to be your Patron. Would you also be my client?"

"I would be honored to be your client," Stephen said. "These personal relationships are wonderful and I understand the obligations we are making to each other. Thank you."

The servants brought dinner on large plates and set them down between each person's utensils. Goblets were already on the table and the wine was poured. While everyone ate, Thomas started asking questions to Stephen, then Stephen to Baroni and Baroni back to Thomas. The dinner was interesting, doing a mini-play between bites of food and sips of wine. As everyone finished their food and wine, the servants brought out cheese, fruit and almonds. A heavy red after-dinner wine was served in mini-goblets. Caterina, Pietro, Nicolo, Filippo and Marco asked occasional questions between the play questions and answers.

It was very late in the night when Pietro said, "Our heads are weighed down with your questions and answers. Your information was most enjoyable and informative. I enjoyed the meal, but I can't remember what we ate."

Caterina smiled and said, "I'm a little dizzy with all of this information, but I've enjoyed this time with all of you. I see why you have been successful wherever you go. Please join us for breakfast, because I am sure we will have further questions."

"It has been an entertaining and delicious dinner for us," Thomas said. "We thank you for your hospitality and the wonderful dinner. One last thought for the evening. Stephen, Baroni and I will be coming by Malta on trips to Sicily, Crete and Judaea. It is wonderful to have friends here in Malta. We will always be at your service."

Everyone left the dining hall and departed to find their bedrooms and sleep.

Tuesday, May 7, 125 A.D.

Thomas slept soundly and awoke to sunshine coming through his bedroom window. He got up brushed his hair and beard, and then slipped into a fresh robe. When he came out of his room, the doors to the other rooms stood open. As he stepped off the last stair he saw the saddlebags by the entrance. Thomas went back up to his room, grabbed his saddlebag and stored it at the front door. As he sat it down, Filippo came in the entrance and said, "We are waiting to have breakfast until you can join us. Everyone is out on the terrace. Follow me out there."

When Thomas came out onto the terrace, Stephen was talking about the difference between the Jewish faith and the Christian faith. "Jesus taught that animal sacrifice was no longer needed, "he said. "He felt that the laws of Moses had gotten between the people and God because there were too many rules. Apostles Paul, Peter and James the Just, who took over the religion after Jesus' death and resurrection, deleted the requirement for circumcision for gentiles. "This was done by James the Just, a brother of Jesus and the second Nazi of the Nazarenes, when he ruled as follows: *Therefore, I judge that we should not trouble those from among the Gentiles who are turning to God, but that we write them to abstain from things polluted by idols, from sexual immorality, from things strangled, and from blood.*"[175]

Thomas said, "The Jewish religion still requires circumcision for its male members. This is one of the reasons for the separation of Christianity from the Jewish religion."

Pietro and Marco were listening intently. Marco brightened and said, "The more I know about Christianity, the more I like it. I certainly don't want to be circumcised."

"I agree," said Pietro. "That would drive me away. My thanks go to Apostles Paul and Peter for getting James the Just to settle the issue long ago."

"Caterina has the cooks ready to prepare our breakfasts," Pietro said. "Let's go in the dining hall and get seated."

When they were seated, Nicolo said, "Governor, you should ride to Marsascala with Baroni and Marco. The ship will be waiting to take you to the north island of Gozo. You have your meeting there in two days."

"Yes, I was going to discuss this trip this morning," Pietro said. "Baroni, you have ten soldiers from Drago's ship with you. If I travel with

---

[175] Ibid, Acts 15: 19-20. (See the letter in Acts 15: 22-29 where they wrote saying in part "Since we have heard that some who went out from us have troubled you with words, unsettling your souls, saying 'You must be circumcised and keep the law-to whom we gave no such commandment...'")

you this morning, I can rely on your security to get me to Marsascala. I have soldiers waiting there to go with me to Gozo. Nicolo, you will be responsible here as always until I return."

Lady Caterina came in to greet everyone and then breakfast was served. "I have heard some criticisms of Christianity," Caterina said. "One is that you eat blood in some of your meetings."

Thomas smiled and said, "Yes, I have heard that criticism. The truth is, we do two things in this ceremony. Luke wrote and quoted Jesus in his last supper saying, *"And He took bread and broke it, and gave it to them, saying, 'This is My body which is given for you: do this in remembrance of me.' Then He took the cup, and gave thanks and said, 'This cup is the new covenant in my blood, which is shed for you.'* [176] Therefore we first eat bread in remem-brance of the body of Jesus and then second, we sip wine or water to remember the blood of Jesus that was shed for us. James the Just prohibited the drinking of blood."

"We're relieved to hear that," Pietro said. "I forgot to ask about that last night."

While everyone ate, Caterina and Pietro talked more about this covenant ceremony. Finally, as they finished, Pietro said, "Thomas, my wife and I are seriously considering becoming Christians. We have many Christians in Malta because of Apostle Paul's ship wreck here and the healing and teaching he did at the beach and here in Mdina."[177]

Thomas smiled and looked from Caterina to Pietro and then said, "I am very happy for both of you. I pray that you seek baptism soon. It will be a pleasure to ride with you to Marsascala."

Pietro and Caterina left to go to their private quarters. Nicolo stood and said, "You can go out the entrance. Principale Matteo and the soldiers are mounted and waiting with your horses. I asked them to hold the Governor's saddled horse, as well."

They tied their saddlebags on behind their saddles. The soldiers had waited for a while and seemed anxious to begin the ride to Marsascala. Governor Pietro came out in a new uniform, carrying a large saddlebag he tied on and then mounted his horse. Marco and Baroni took the lead followed

---

[176] Ibid, Luke 22: 19-20.
[177] Ibid, Acts 27: 25-44 and 28:1-10.

by Governor Pietro and Thomas. Stephen and Matteo rode in front of the soldiers who rode in pairs behind them.

Pietro seemed jubilant and said, "Thomas tell me more about the Island-of-Dreams and your dream with Jesus.

"In my dream, the appearance of Jesus was so bright that it blinded me," he said. "He glowed of a brilliant white light, but finally I could see. He showed me the island had a flat area about twenty feet above the Mediterranean. It then sloped up to the top where a large green forest started. The slope was not steep and was covered by swaying grass. There was a much larger island nearby."

"You think the island is in the Balearic Sea?" Pietro asked.

"The note left to me by Joseph of Arimathea said, 'The Island is in the Balearic Sea.' They found it on a trip from Britain, so we're not really sure where it is. They had to sail north to get into the Balearic Sea. We're going to look at other islands along the way."

All I know is there are many small islands and islets in the Balearic Sea," Pietro said. "The good news is there are three main islands. Your island must be one of those small islands near one of the large islands. However, you are right. There are a number of islands south and west of here. There are even more islands around the big island of Sicily."

It was very warm and sunny. They passed flowering bushes with butterflies circling them. Honey bees buzzed around all the bushes and flowers they passed. The citizens they passed smiled and waved. Pietro smiled, waved back then said, "We have warm and friendly people. Most are Maltese, but there are many Sicilians in the area around Marsascala. My meeting in Gozo will help resolve some property ownership disputes regarding defaulted loans from Jewish lenders. The Jews want their money, but have the right by agreement to take the property. I'm going to arbitrate the issues in order to keep the resolution calm."

It was early afternoon when they rode into the stables in Marsascala. Everyone took their saddlebags and turned the horses over to the stable manager. The soldiers marched back to the pier and reported to Drago. The Governor went with Marco and Matteo to a ship at the end of the pier. Baroni, Thomas and Stephen walked to the edge of the pier and saw that the Palermo Vine had changed color, but men were still brushing oil on the bow. Four men were installing a wooden female head.

Two men each held a sign, watching the installation.

Peter and Pardi came from town and stopped next to Thomas. Peter said, "We found the sail maker yesterday and gave him the dimensions and patterns we wanted for the new sail. He is making two sails and each sail will have a red star and a design of a cluster of grapes. We just came back from his shop. He thinks we can pick up the new sails at sunset today. How was your trip to Mdina?"

"Our trip to Mdina was great," Thomas said. "I'll tell you at lunch. Round up Micah while we wait for Marco and Matteo."

Peter came back with Micah, Pardi, Drago, Marco and Matteo

The five officers, seven missionaries, Tamir and Micah walked to beach eatery to have lunch on the tables overlooking the bay. When they got there, Drago went in to order and the others sat down at the tables. Tamir said, "We're proud of the young survivors from the ben Yaakov. They worked hard to scrap it down and brush on the colored oil. They are happy to be with us and rid of the "bad men' in the old ben Yaakov's crew."

Drago came out and sat down to say, "They'll be right out with the food and drinks. When the Governor's ship sailed in from the sea, I was afraid one of my ships had sunk and only one was returning. I was relieved to see it wasn't one of mine."

The waiters came out and delivered plates with fried fish and vegetables. They went in and came back with goblets and amphoras of juice and watered wine. The Governor's ship left the pier and sailed out through the bay while they ate. Baroni, Thomas and Stephen took turns telling about the trip to Mdina. Pardi looked concerned and asked, "What'd you tell the Governor about me?"

Baroni looked puzzled and said, "Thomas told him you were retiring and joining Thomas' group."

Thomas said, "I told the governor you would use the Palermo Vine for the vineyard and construction. He seemed pleased that you had an opportunity with your retirement. But you look concerned."

"I've never been anything other than a soldier," Pardi said. "I'm not used to making big decisions. If I do what you are proposing, it is different than taking orders. I get worried at times and wonder what I would do if confronted by the officers and the governors you have met. We need you to help us do our work. You have developed these client relationships with the governors and other important officers. I fear what will happen when you are gone."

"Pardi, I've been friends with you for several months," Thomas said. "You're a trusted partner of mine. My new Patrons know about all of you. Part of our relationship is that they will help me, including everyone that works with me. What you haven't considered is that you are my client and I am your Patron. I have every confidence in your abilities. We're building a community. I'm glad you have chosen to be part of it. We are all connected. Call on my Patrons if you need them."

Drago had been listening and glancing at the bay. He stood and said, "That looks like my ships coming up the bay. Let's finish and go down to greet them."

Drago led them back to the dock and walked down the pier. They stood watching Alonso and Bernardus sail in to dock their ships. They took the lines thrown to them and tied the ships tightly to the pier. The gangplanks were lowered. Alonso and Bernardus came down from their ships and saluted the Roman officers. Drago looked pleased and asked, "Did you catch the other Hadar ship?"

Bernardus shrugged and said, "No. We got close to them at first, but the wind kept blowing us sideways. We followed them until dark. A storm came through during the night, and when the sun came up, we could not find them. We turned around and sailed back here. Is that ship those men are working on the other ship that attacked the Free Spirit?

Drago smiled and said, "Thomas and Baroni decided to keep the ship which was called the ben Yaakov. We have changed the name to Palermo Vine. It has a new masthead and name signs. It has been scraped and colored oil brushed onto it on the inside and the outside. We will have two new main sails by this evening."

Baroni said, "Alonso and Bernardus, we'll sail in the morning, you need to take care of maintenance on your ships and obtain the food and supplies you need. That goes for everyone else."

As the sun was starting to set, a Roman ship sailed into the pier. The dock workers tied it up. Marco and Matteo came down the pier, waving and saying good bye. They got to the new ship, saluted and boarded.

Thomas and Stephen went down and untied the lines. They waved as the ship sailed away.

Not long after dark, the men on the six ships went to bed for the night.

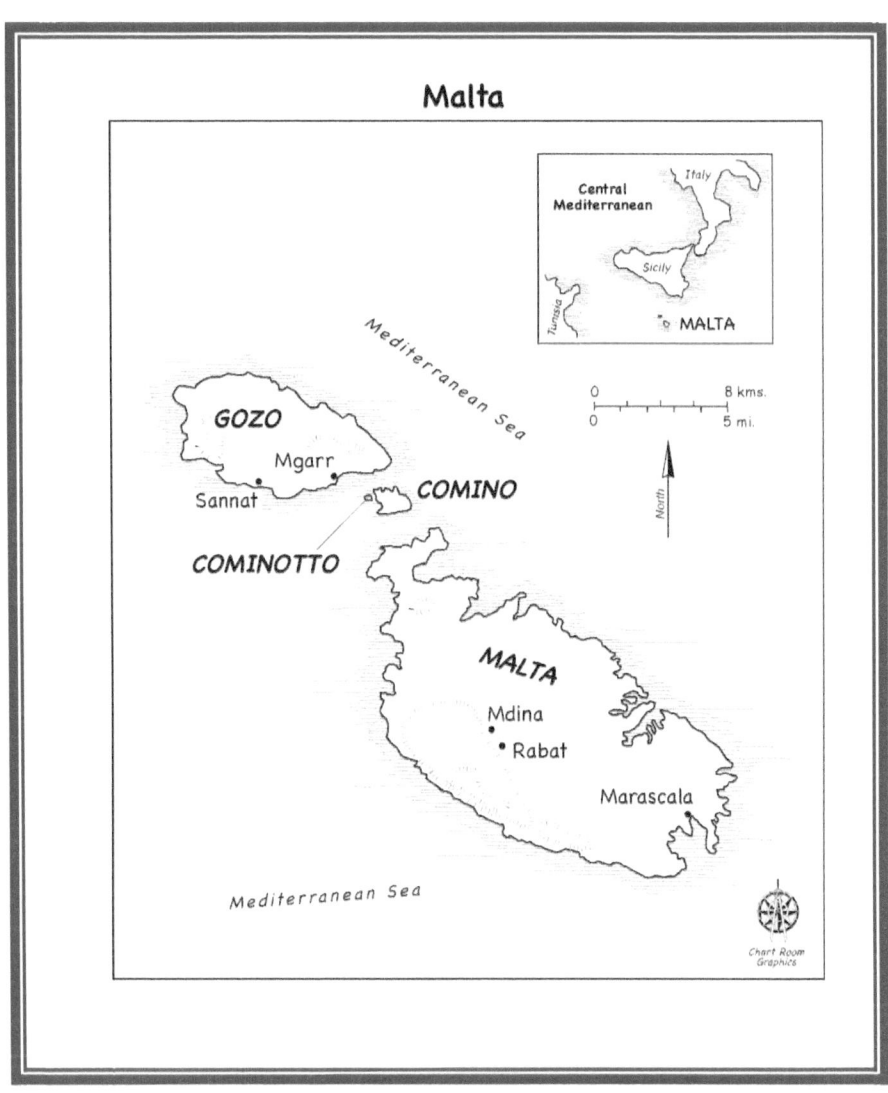

Malta

✝ Chapter 37 ✝

Sailing to Palermo Sicily
Wednesday, May 8, 125 A.D.

Thomas and Stephen awoke before dawn the next morning,. Thomas whispered, "I can't believe we have a new ship and eleven more sailors who want to help with our project. Let's get up and go down to the pier."

They found Peter, Tamir and Micah talking to the Roman captains, Drago, Alonso and Bernardus. Baroni and Pardi came down the gangplank. Baroni said, "We must be prepared to deal with another attack by Hadar. We could resume our original game plan, but we now have the Palermo Vine. It will be a target just like the Free Spirit and Islander. I want everyone to resume their same positions. Micah, I want you to sail the Palermo Vine behind the Free Spirit as close as you feel comfortable. Do not get too far behind."

Drago looked around and said, "I'll take the lead. There are a number of islands we can pass on the way to Palermo. Since it is easy to pass them, Thomas will you look at each of them to see if one of them might be your island."

Everyone returned to their ships. The dock workers came to untie the lines and push the ships back away from the pier. The men on each of the ships used the oars to turn their ships. Rowers pulled one way while rowers on the other side rowed the other way spinning the ship around. Drago got his sail up. The wind caught it and he moved away from the others. The Free Spirit moved out next with its sails full. The Palermo Vine came next with Micah shouting his happiness with its performance. The Islander came along with Alonso and Bernardus following.

Thomas was pleased with his small armada. The bay was beautiful with nice beaches on each side as the bay widened. The seagulls flew overhead and squawked as they streaked down looking for handouts. The sea breezes felt good. Thomas could taste the salt. When Drago cleared the shores of the bay, he turned his ship south. The other ships followed around the east end of Malta to then sail northwest.

Peter studied his maps and had everyone look south. "There are two islands out there. Lampedusa is the largest, but only a few people live there. It has no fresh water, so the residents have to catch rain water and store it. Linosa is small and uninhabited. It is said Linosa was a big stone thrown out of heaven."

"I can see Lampedusa," Baroni said. "It has huge high cliffs on its west shore."

Thomas strained to see it and said, "That can't be it. Those cliffs are too high and it has no water."

When they were nearing mid-day, Drago's ship turned more to north. Thomas spotted an island on their port side. He pointed to it and shouted, "That must be Pantelleria. I can see the mountains. That can't be the island either because of those high mountains."

Drago's ship went southwest and the Free Spirit continued on in a northwest direction. Ben stood on the stern and shouted, "The Palermo Vine is right behind us, but the Islander is going north."

Baroni stood by the port railing and shouted, "The Alonso and Bernardus ships are sailing southwest to catch up with Drago's ship. We are way past Pantelleria now."

The guards came around to serve smoked fish, dates and olives. They poured some wine into a large terracotta bowl and mixed in a whole water-bag of fresh water. The goblets were dipped into the bowl and handed out to everyone.

In the late afternoon, Peter had his maps out looking for islands. He smiled and said, "We are going west of Favignana island while Tamir will go west, but east of the island of Mozia. "

"I'll get Ben and go up in the bow to watch for land," Pardi said. "You can watch the Islander."

Thomas shouted, "Tamir is waving the red flag."

Peter said, "Tamir has seen the island of Mozia."

Most of the crew was now standing in the bow behind Ben and Pardi. Ben shouted, "I see land straight ahead of us. Peter, you need to sail west for a ways."

Thomas watched the island of Favignana, as they went around it. "That island has mountains and is populated, so it is not the island Jesus showed me."

Peter looked up from his map and said, "See that finger of land. It is called San vito lo Capo, which juts north from the main island of Sicily. We'll sail around it."

Josiah was standing on the stern and yelled, "All of our ships are right behind us."

As they sailed around the peninsula, Peter had them change the sails and the side rudder paddles to force the ship to sail due south. As the sun was setting Pardi shouted, "There is land off our starboard side again. We are near Palermo."

The sky was streaks of orange and turning to bright red as the sun was going down.

"What a beautiful sunset," Thomas said.

Peter looked at most of the crew who were looking back at him. He smiled and shouted, "We are almost to Palermo."

The sun had set by the time they sailed into the pier at the port in Palermo. The five ships behind sailed in and docked along the pier, close to the Free Spirit. The dock workers took the lines thrown to them from all six ships and tied them to the pier. The gangplanks were let down. The six ship-captains, Thomas, Stephen, Baroni and Pardi, met to make plans. Pardi said, "I need ten soldiers to travel with me to my family's home and vineyard. We'll find the Roman army stables here and ride out tomorrow."

Thomas said, "Before you select the ten for Pardi, we need twenty soldiers to go with us to have dinner."

While the soldiers were being selected, Pardi and Baroni talked to the port manager about the location of the Roman stables who said, "One of my men lives near the stables and the fort. He will lead your men over there when they are ready."

Baroni and Pardi returned to find a group of twenty soldiers and a group of ten soldiers lined up. Baroni said to Pardi, "You are excused to take command of these soldiers until you return."

Baroni said, "Thomas, I will stay at the fort tonight. I'll be back before sunrise in the morning."

Pardi and Baroni marched off ahead of the ten soldiers, following the man from the Palermo port.

The port manager came over to ask about the arrangements for the six ships. Thomas smiled to the manager and said, "The ship over here is called the Palermo Vine and will remain at the marina for about a week or until we return. The three Roman ships, the Free Spirit and the Islander will leave in the morning. If you have any visitors looking for the Free Spirit or a ben Yaakov, report them to the Roman fort. They are pirates and are wanted by the Romans in the Province of Judaea."

"Who will pay the pier fees?" the manager asked.

"I will pay the fees for my ships," Thomas said.

The port manager smiled and said, "I register the Roman ships and there is no charge for them. I will prepare a billing for your personal ships. The bill will be for one week for the Palermo Vine. Follow me and you can pay the current charges now."

"I would like missionaries and ship captains to go to dinner with me," Thomas said.

The fees were paid and Thomas got instructions to a place to dine. The manager said, "I'll send one of my men to tell the restaurant owner to prepare food for twenty soldiers and expect twelve to eat inside. The soldiers can eat at the tables on the street. The restaurant is not very big."

Thomas whispered to Stephen, "Our group keeps growing and getting more complicated. We must take the time to get to know all of the new men as well as we can. We are depending on each of them."

The twelve of them left, with the twenty soldiers following. The restaurant was around the corner and down two blocks. There were tables in the street fenced off with reserved signs on them. The owner stood at the door and said, "I've been expecting you. We have a large table set up for twelve in the back. We are preparing a meal for your soldiers. I have two waiters and a waitress to take care them. My daughter and I will take care of your party inside."

While the salads and white wine were served, Thomas looked around the long table from where he was seated at one end and said, "We are not ready to search for the Island-of-Dreams yet, but I looked over several islands today and none were it. I don't know what to expect when we get to the Balearic Sea. I wanted this evening to be special to thank all of you for our experiences together so far. Stephen and I have been very fortunate to spend time with the Governors of Crete and Malta. We had a treat with both of those visits to have the Governors' wives dine with us. I have tried to have all of you treated well and I hope you feel you have been. Would you all stand? I drink to our success in finding the Island-of-Dreams.

While they ate the missionaries and Romans argued about Hadar. Drago argued with Peter about how old Hadar is, since they both had heard differences. Tamir ended the argument when he said, "I have enjoyed your arguments, but Hadar is thirty-one. He inherited the shipping business from his father and has acquired several new ships and doubled his business. Some of the goods he buys and resells to Simeon ben Kosiba. In other cases he robs other ships and warehouses. He has numerous customers and sells his stolen goods right along with goods he has bought.

When they were finished, Thomas went to the back to talk to the owner about the meal. The owner whispered, "Who are you? My nephew told me to treat you and your men as important people. Your soldiers were very courteous to our waiters and waitress. They were really happy to have been selected to come with you for your protection. I hope we met your expectations."

Thomas said, "I'm a Christian missionary and I have six missionary companions with me. We have been many places and are on our way to Syracuse to visit Governor Salvatore. We'll put on a Christian play in the amphitheater in Syracuse."

When they got back, all of the men on the ships had gone to bed, except the guards. The soldiers and diners went to their ships and directly to bed.

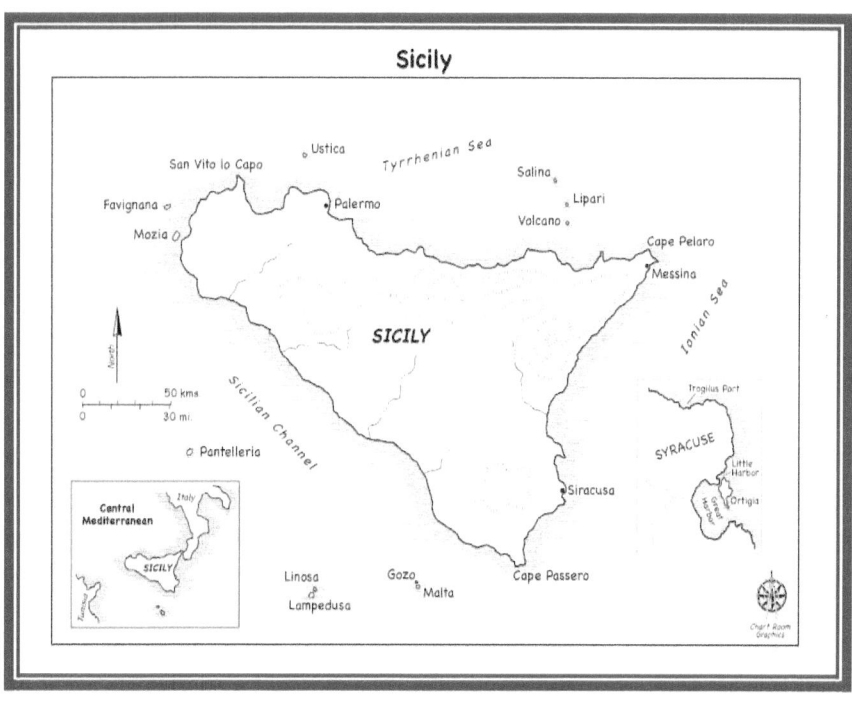

✝ Chapter 38 ✝

Sailing to Syracuse Sicily
Thursday, May 9, 125 A.D.

Thomas and Peter went up to the top-deck just as dawn was breaking. They were soon joined by most of the men on the ship. Baroni, after spending the night at the fort, returned and met with Thomas and the captains. He looked around at each man and said, "Our sailing pattern today will be different because of the Straight of Messina. I think it is very unlikely that any of Hadar's ships will find and attack us today, but we will take precautions anyway. Micah, as captain of the Palermo vine, you will stay here to await Pardi. Peter you sail the Free Spirit into the Tyrrhenian Sea as the lead. Tamir sail the Islander south of Peter in the Free Spirit. Drago, you Alonso and Bernardus will sail north of Peter, but sail south of the island called Volcano."

Everyone returned to their own ships as the sun started to rise above the horizon. The port workers came out and released the lines to the five ships. The Free Spirit was pushed out first and they rowed out of the harbor. The sails were pulled up, but very little air was moving. They continued to row and at last the sails filled and they sailed away. Thomas and Baroni stood on the stern and watched the other ships follow them away from the pier. The Islander began to sail to their starboard side moving parallel with the Free Spirit. Thomas and Ben waved to Mark and David as they moved further way.

The fog was gone and the glare off the water on the port side was blinding for a while. Baroni and Thomas sat down and Ben and Stephen came over to talk to them. Two of the guards were handing out sliced cheese, bread and smoked fish. The third guard brought them goblets of warm Calda. Stephen said to Baroni, "Our visit to Gortyn in Crete was accepted by all of the Romans who seemed to be looking forward to meeting us. In Mdina, Malta, Governor Pietro, Nicolo and Filippo were surprised to see us, but they seemed delighted with our visit. Do you think they will welcome us in Syracuse?"

Baroni frowned and said, "I must say the visits you just mentioned went much better than I expected them to. Governor Stefano knows Governor Rufus very well. He must have briefed his other officers. Governor Pietro wanted to know more about Christianity, because he has many Christians on his island. Governor Salvatore is also well acquainted and friends with Governor Rufus. If he received the message sent to him, we will be welcomed, but he has several officers. My question is, will any of them give us a hard time. You realize that we are at risk every time we visit a new city. I met with the commander of the fort in Palermo. He hardly gave me any notice other than to salute and send me off to eat with a couple of Centurion officers. I don't think we want to try anything in Palermo other than pick up Pardi and the soldiers."

The guards came around to pour more Calda and hand out honey cakes. Peter turned the paddle bar over to Joziah and came over and sat by Thomas. Peter ate his breakfast and seemed pleased with himself saying, "I like Joziah. He is bright and always happy. He told me God must have smiled down on him. He thought his life was over when he was kidnapped in Israel. Now he is with us and says this is exactly what he wanted to do. He also said the other kidnapped fellows are looking forward to finding the Island-of-Dreams, so they can start the construction. They apparently are quite willing to do quarry work, cut trees, split logs to make lumber or any other job we have for them. He thinks most of them can be trained to supervise local workers we recruit to work on the construction."

Thomas walked over to the port railing to see how far away Drago's ships were. At first he could not see them. Then he realized they were a long ways behind the Free Spirit, because they went mostly north while the Free Spirit went northeast. He went back to talk to Peter about slowing down for them. Peter ordered the mainsail to be pulled part way down until the Roman ships caught up.

A little while later, Peter looked at his sundial and said, "We should be getting south of the island volcano."

Ben asked, "Why do they call that island volcano?"

"The island has three volcanoes," Baroni said. "One of the volcanoes is always active and erupts periodically with lava and earthquakes. No one dares to live on it, but many visit it. It made me nervous when I was there years ago."

Ben walked over to the starboard railing and looked south to see the Islander. He went back to the stern and asked Peter, "Why is the Islander sailing towards us?"

Peter pulled out his map, studied it and said, "We must have passed the volcano island to the north. To the south there is a finger of land off Sicily called Miazzo. Tamir has to come our way to go around it. That means we are getting close to the Strait of Messina. Go look for Drago. They should be sailing towards us now."

Stephen was staring at the three Romans ships when Ben walked over to him and said, "Peter says they should start sailing towards us anytime."

Some time went by and Thomas found one of the guards and said, "The sun is overhead. Could you and the others find something to eat? As soon as we sail into the Strait of Messina, I would like you to start handing out lunch."

Peter relieved Josiah from the paddle bar. Thomas noticed the Roman ships were coming in close, with Drago's ship fairly close to the Islander which was right behind them.

Thomas now shouted, "I see land off our starboard side. The water is turning turbulent."

Baroni said, "According to Peter's map, that land is Cape Peloro. The water is turbulent as it flows around the cape."

Peter had the mainsail adjusted to force the ship to go a little north to avoid the turbulence of the cape. They sailed for a ways until the water calmed down some. Stephen shouted, "There's a whirlpool north of us, but it is some distance away."

Peter had Thomas bring the mainsail around and used the bar controlling the side paddles to aid the turning of the ship. Joziah was standing on the stern and shouted, "The other four ships are in line following us around the cape."

The water smoothed out and seemed to move the ship faster. Baroni said, "The current can be strong depending on the stage of the tide. Right now the current and tide is flowing south. We are picking up speed. The strait narrows here and we should be able to see land on both sides of the ship."

Men on each side of the ship were shouting, "I see land." But before long the land on either side could no longer be seen. Baroni shouted, "Welcome to the Ionian Sea."

Everyone finished lunch and were sipping the last of their watered wine when they saw ships sailing in directions, some towards Sicily and some away from there. Peter sailed the Free Spirit close the shore. Soon he could see land ahead and had the ship move away from the shore.

Baroni said, "I believe that land is a promontory called Augusta. It also means we are getting near to Syracuse."

Ben shouted, "I can see an island next to the main land of Sicily."

Peter shouted, "That Island is Ortiga and is part of Syracuse. We will dock at the Porto Grande pier opposite the mainland on the Sicily side of the island of Ortiga. The big port and piers are between the island and Sicily. Ortiga is one of the five cities that make up Syracuse. Syracuse is very large and we will not see very much of it in a short visit."

They sailed south around the tip of the island and took the sails down sailing into the pier. The other ships came in and found spaces. Thomas estimated dozens of ships could dock here at the same time.

After the ships were docked, gangplanks came down. The ship captains, Baroni, Thomas and Stephen met on the pier. They were amazed at the city on the island. There was a large bridge at the closest point connected to the main land mass of Sicily. A heavy man with a full beard came up to them and said, "I'm the manager of Porto Grande. I was told to expect and welcome two ships called the Free Spirit and the Islander. Are the Roman ships accompanying you?"

"Yes, the men on these three ships are our guards," Baroni said. "They report to me. Can you tell us where we are to go?"

"Yes, I sent a runner to let the mayor and the Christian Bishop Luca know of your arrival," he said. "The high priest will come with them. He said he wants to meet Thomas. Is he here?"

Thomas walked closer to the man and said, "I'm Thomas. This is Stephen and Centurion Baroni. What can I do for you?"

"I have orders to register your ships, but there will be no pier charge. I see you have enough soldiers to guard you and the ships. Centurion Sergio told me he would come down. I saw one of the soldiers ride his horse across the bridge before I came over here. I'm sure he is telling Centurion Sergio of your arrival right now. I recommend you have your captains and men move their ships closer to the bridge."

Everyone boarded the ships again and pulled up the gangplanks. The dockworkers released their lines and pushed the ships away from the pier. The men rowed the ships towards the bridge. The Free Spirit pulled in next to the bridge and the other ships were pulled next to it. The dock workers tied them up tight. The same group and all of the missionaries met on the pier. They heard the clatter of horses followed by the rumble of a horse drawn carriage. Several Roman soldiers come over the bridge. Two soldiers dismounted, one saluted and said, "I'm Centurion Sergio and this is Principale Giuseppi. I presume you are Centurion Baroni?"

Baroni saluted and said, "I am. My ship captains are Principales Drago, Alonso and Bernardus."

Sergio and Giuseppi saluted. "Yes, I was told you would be traveling as escorts for seven missionaries with their leader named Thomas," he said. "You are welcome. Governor Salvatore and his officers are expecting all of you. I'm here to see what you need at this time."

"I'm Thomas. We hope to put on a Christian play in the amphitheater, but I understand Syracuse also has a Roman stadium."

"Yes, we have both" Sergio said. "The stadium is better suited for racing, animal acts, and gladiator events. The amphitheater is better suited for plays. We have cleanup work being done on the amphitheater which is surrounded by the Nymphaeum. Both are impressive on top of the mountain. The amphitheater is carved into the limestone. The stage is elevated. The acoustics allows low voices from the stage to be easily heard in the back rows. I'm looking forward to your play which will be scheduled for tomorrow night. We will have written announcements posted tonight in all public places. Riders will go out in the morning to make announcements in outlying areas. The amphitheater has room for several thousand spectators and the Governor expects a large crowd."

Several men walked across the bridge. They came around behind Sergio, Giuseppi and the soldiers who now were holding the reins to the horses. Giuseppi had his men move away so these men could get through. The first man said, "Welcome to Syracuse. My name is Mayor Tazio. Are you the group led by Thomas?"

Thomas smiled and said, "I'm Thomas. Let me introduce my companions. This is Centurion Baroni and these other men are our ship captains."

When Thomas had introduced the missionaries and ship captains, Tazio introduced Bishop Luca and High Priest Aristo. Bishop Luca said, "High Priest Aristo and I have a friendly relationship. That is why he is here with us to greet you. We both report to the governor and share our revenues with the Provence of Sicily."

High Priest Aristo stepped ahead of the others and said, "I wanted to meet you because you are the first to come here to put on a Christian play. You are protected and sponsored by the Roman military. I'm surprised that you are doing these plays at the same time Christians are being crucified in Rome under the decree of death if you are found to be a Christian. Obviously, not all Christians known to the Romans are being crucified. After all Bishop Luca is well known here in Syracuse. Having said these things, I welcome you to Syracuse. I will encourage my members to attend the play tomorrow night. At some point, I would be honored to give you a tour of my Temple of Apollo here on the Island of Ortiga."

"I am honored to meet you High Priest Aristo," Thomas said. "I would be delighted to accept your invitation to tour your Temple of Apollo. We enjoyed a tour of the Temple of Pythean Apollo in Gortyn Crete, recently. High Priest Hector gave us a wonderful history of Zeus, his family and his son Apollo. Thank you for your support of our play. I need to know what other events may be scheduled for us. When I learn this, I will send word to you to schedule the tour."

Bishop Luca walked up and said, "I too would like to welcome you to Syracuse. We've never seen or heard of a Christian play. I know all my members will want to attend."

Centurion Baroni said, "We appreciate your welcoming the missionaries. Centurion Sergio, where do we stay tonight and have there been any events scheduled for the night we arrive?"

Sergio walked in closer and said, "Governor Salvatore has invited you to the palace for refreshments and dinner later. He has guest rooms in the palace for four for tonight and tomorrow night. He suggested you invite two of your companions to also stay at the palace. We have arrangements for your other missionary companions and your ship captains for tonight at the fort. Principale Giuseppi will take care of them. I have brought the carriage to take you directly to the palace. The Governor invites Mayor Tazio, Bishop

Luca and High Priest Aristo along with their wives to dinner at the palace tonight to share in the welcome of the actors from Jerusalem. We will take Thomas and his guests to the palace and return to escort the three of you and your wives."

Thomas said, "Stephen and Mark, I would like you to go with Baroni and me. Drago, Tamir and Peter get your men organized for the night and go with Principale Giuseppi when you are ready."

The ship captains went off to give orders to their first mates and talk to their men. Sergio mounted his horse and Baroni, Thomas, Stephen and Mark entered the carriage. As they were seated, Thomas said, "I have never heard of a carriage before, but this is nice. It has a roof and has comfortable soft seats."

He turned and smiled saying, "Mark, I invited you to come with us this time because you will be the leader at the Island-of-Dreams once we find it. I want you to start assuming that leadership role. I know you have thought about it, but that time is coming. You need to deal with Romans directly once Stephen and I return to Jerusalem. Pardi will be a great help, but like he says, he has never given higher up Romans any orders before."

Once the carriage crossed the bridge it started to climb a hill, winding around several curves in the road, and then entered a flat area. They stopped and stepped out at the entrance to the palace. Sergio was ahead of them and showed them into the palace. On the right was a large room. Two officers came out and welcomed them. The two officers saluted.

Sergio said, "I would like to introduce Centurion Baroni from the Provence of Judaea. With him are Thomas and two of his companions, Stephen and Mark."

Thomas smiled. Sergio went on to say, "These are our senior officers here in Syracuse, Legatus Legionis Mario and Tribunus Laticlavius Renato."

Mario and Renato were tall with light brown hair and clean shaven faces. Mario had blue eyes and Renato had dark brooding brown eyes. Mario was handsome and smiling, but Renato had on a stern, but somewhat curious look on his face.

Mario looked the four of them over and said, "Governor Rufus in the Provence of Judaea sent word of you, Thomas, and your companions. You are an interesting visitor coming to us as a lead actor, but with your own ships and are accompanied by Centurion Baroni and his three ships. I understand one of the Principale officers from Judaea is retiring to join your group. Centurion Baroni, you have had the duty of providing security and traveling with Thomas. We have discussed your visit and will give it our utmost support. Does that surprise you?"

"I'm delighted, because I did not know what to expect," Baroni said. "We Romans can be somewhat unpredictable sometimes. Thank you for your warm and cordial welcome."

Renato relaxed a little and said, "Your visit gives me a good opportunity to become better known here, and to improve my position in this community. Governor Salvatore is a good friend of your Governor Rufus. Thomas, you are helping Governor Rufus catch a thorn in his side by the name of Hadar, who is helping the rebels. Yet here you are to put on a Christian play. Our Greek amphitheater will hold up to fifteen-thousand spectators. I doubt we will see that number, but you will get support from us, including Bishop Luca and High Priest Aristo. The mayor also has much influence in greater Syracuse. He is very supportive. I have never seen anything like this event. We are all curious about your trip, your approach to religious teachings and your Roman relationships. In the meantime, welcome to the palace. We will have refreshments. As soon as our other guests arrive and our wives are ready for dinner, we will meet in the dining hall. Right now the Governor and his wife are waiting for us on the terrace."

Sergio turned and led everyone out of the large room and into a hallway leading further into the palace. Two soldiers in dress uniform stood in front of a door, but stepped aside as Sergio approached. The door opened and Sergio marched through, leading everyone onto the terrace. Mario turned sideways and said, "Governor Salvatore and Lady Madelena, I would like to introduce Centurion Baroni, Thomas and two of his companions, Stephen and Mark. Men this is our governor and his wife."

The governor was middle-aged and his wife was several years younger. They made a handsome couple and both were smiling. Salvatore was clean shaven except for a well trimmed mustache. Thomas stepped ahead of Baroni and said, "I'm proud to meet you Governor and Lady Madelena. You have a wonderful city and a delightful home."

Salvatore smiled and said, "We have some time before dinner. May I offer a choice of wine and some excellent sliced cheeses? We have room to sit, visit and look out over the city and the Mediterranean. The sun will set before long. Our guests should arrive soon to meet you and enjoy the view and sunset."

Everyone selected their choice of wine and cheese. They sat in a circular setting with the Governor, his wife and the officers sitting with their backs to the view. Thomas was astounded at the treatment they were receiving and the incredible view.

The governor said, "Tell us about your trip coming here."

Thomas talked about the trip and the events in Crete. Baroni talked about the attack by Hadar's two ships and the ben Yaakov which is now the Palermo Vine. Their hosts applauded this tale. Stephen talked about their trip to Malta and the visit with Governor Pietro and Lady Caterina.

Everyone stood when a few women came out onto the terrace. Mario was smiling and said, "Please meet my wife, Lady Fabrizia, Renato's wife, Lady Anna, and Sergio's wife, Adriana."

The Governor introduced their visitors. The door opened and three couples walked out onto the terrace. Mayor Tazio said, "This is my wife, Laura, Luca's wife, Lady Donata and Aristo's wife, Lady Agnes." Thomas introduced his group.

As the sunset turned into a glow everyone stopped to watch the various shades of the red sky. Soon soldiers came out and lit torches around the terrace. A soldier in a unique formal uniform stepped out on the terrace. His white tunic was over the top of long pants. He said, "Ladies and gentlemen dinner will be served in the dining hall when everyone is seated. When you reach the table, look on the plates to locate your name. The names are written in Latin and Greek. If you need help just raise your hand."

The group had reached eighteen in number and they slowly walked into the dining hall. When everyone had located their name, the governor and his wife sat and everyone did the same. Servers started pouring wine in their goblets and serving dinner.

Lady Madelena leaned forward and said, "Thomas, you are a stranger and a Christian, but you seem quite at ease and comfortable here. I wish I could be as calm and collected as you are."

Governor Salvatore smiled and said, "My wife does not get to come to very many public dinners. I am new to it myself. You obviously have done this many times. I guess being an actor and all makes this easy for you."

"You must know how well you have treated me and my companions," Thomas said. "While you are right, I have done this a few times. All of the Roman Governors and officers we have met have treated me with the utmost respect. Each time I have prepared for the worst, but have been pleasantly surprised. I do feel comfortable. Maybe it is because Jesus is with me."

Mario leaned forward and said, "I understand you will go on from Sicily to find a specific island in the Mediterranean to build a Christian house of worship and a community. All of us would like to know how you have selected a specific island. There are many."

"My great-grandfather was Jesus' brother and an apostle," Thomas said. "After Jesus was crucified and resurrected, Apostle Thomas made a lot of money as a trader. He also had recorded conversations Jesus had with God during his ministry. The money he earned and the writings he made have been handed down to me. The island we are to find was first located by Jesus and his great-uncle, Joseph of Arimathea, and was noted on a map handed down to me. A few years ago, I had a dream or vision. In this dream, Jesus appeared to me on the island I am to find. He told me he and his great uncle had found it and while I was there I should look closely at it. He ordered me to find the island and build the house of worship with a vault to store Apostle Thomas's writings. Jesus told me terrible times are coming to Israel and we must leave to safely store records."

"I'm not a Christian, but I do know a little bit about it," Salvatore said. "What I have learned is that Jesus is the son of God and came to earth to save mankind. So what you are telling us is you met with Jesus who is the son of God and took orders from him."

"Yes, that is what happened," Thomas said. "And what you just told me is correct."

Lady Madelena leaned forward again and said, "If Jesus is the son of God, why did he let himself be crucified?"

Thomas smiled and leaned forward, "Jesus' primary reason for living the life he led was to save mankind. His death was prophesied by Jewish prophets, including many of the things he did and his violent death. Jesus was saving mankind from eternal death. You might ask why this was so?"

Thomas leaned back and continued, "We believe god created man and woman and named them Adam and Eve. He placed them in the Garden of Eden giving them eternal life. God made only one commandment which was not to partake of a specific fruit growing there. They were tempted and ate the forbidden fruit. God became angry and threw them out of the Garden of Eden and they lost eternal life for themselves and all of the generations of their descendents. This is the major sin all of us inherited."

Salvatore sat up and said, "Isn't this the sin that Jesus' death paid for?"

"Yes, his death was for our forgiveness," Thomas said. "Jesus and John the Baptist told us that in order for us to accept this forgiveness, we must be baptized."

"What happens when we are baptized?" Mario asked.

"When we are baptized all of your sins including Adam and Eve's sin is forgiven," Thomas said. "But your spirit is also reborn, inheriting again eternal life."

"Can you tell us other teachings of Jesus," Mayor Tazio asked.

Thomas went on eating, drinking and answering questions. He looked down the table to see Stephen talking with Bishop Luca and his wife, Lady Donata. Mark was engaged in a conversation with High Priest Aristo and his wife, Lady Agnes. He looked at Baroni who was in a conversation with Renato and his wife, Lady Anna. Sergio and his wife, Lady Adriana, were listening to and watching everything Baroni said.

The dinner plates were gathered and plates of sliced fruit, cheese and nuts were served. A sweet after-dinner wine was served in smaller goblets. Governor Salvatore stood up and all of the men stood. The governor picked up his new small goblet and said loudly, "I would like to propose a toast to religious peace tomorrow afternoon, when we hear what the missionaries tell us, our citizens and soldiers in the amphitheater."

Everyone took a sip and looked at Thomas who said, "I would like to propose a toast to the wonderful city of Syracuse, its citizens and the Romans who protect it."

Everyone said, "Cheers." They sipped their wine, but looked again to Thomas who said, "I would like to thank Governor Salvatore and his charming wife, Lady Madelena, for a wonderful evening with fine food and wine. Please toast them."

Again, more cheers and sipping. Salvatore sat down and so did the other men. The conversations around the table started again and went on for a while. Governor Salvatore and Lady Madelena stood and led everyone to the terrace. High Priest Aristo and his wife came over and he said, "This has been a delightful evening. I would like to remind you of my invitation for you and your missionary companions to visit the Tempio de Apollo in the morning after breakfast. I will meet you at the temple."

Lady Agnes smiled and said, "I will be at the temple with my husband tomorrow morning. I do not want to miss anything."

Bishop Luca, his wife Donata, Mayor Tazio and his wife Laura stopped Thomas. Lady Laura said, "I heard what you said about Jesus dying to forgive us for the sin of Adam and Eve. That was powerful and simple. I can't wait to hear what you and your companions will say tomorrow."

Lady Donata said, "I heard what you said about Jesus' death and saving us. My husband will learn a lot from you and your companions."

Bishop Luca smiled and said, "I have learned a lot tonight overhearing you, Mark and Stephen. We are very happy you are here for this visit and the play tomorrow."

All of the guests made their way out the front to wait for their carriage ride home. Governor Salvatore assigned one of his guards to lead Thomas, Stephen, Mark and Baroni to their bedrooms. Lady Madelena said, "We will see you in the early morning for breakfast. Have a good night's rest."

† Chapter 39 †

The Play in Syracuse
Friday, May 10, 125 A.D.

Thomas awoke as the early light of the dawn came through his window. He got up and went downstairs to the dining hall. Mario and Renato were drinking something steaming. Thomas sat and listened to them talk about military arrangements for the security at the play. Thomas asked, "Do all of you live here in the palace?"

Mario said, "All of us live here now. We are looking to find homes of our own. Renato, Sergio and I are new here. None of us have children and Governor Salvatore has been kind to let us stay here with our wives."

Baroni came in, sat down and said, "I arranged for Sergio, Thomas and I to have horses to ride. The carriage can hold only six men. I want your missionary companions to ride in the carriage."

Stephen and Mark sat down. "I heard that," Stephen said. "We get to ride in the stroller while you ride a horse. On second thought that is a good deal for us." He laughed.

When breakfast was over, Sergio and Baroni led Thomas, Stephen and Mark out the front entrance to the carriage. The other four missionary companions were there, along with a soldier holding the reins to three horses. Thomas and the officers mounted their horses and the missionaries boarded the carriage. Sergio went ahead with Baroni and Thomas following. The clatter of the horse's hooves and the rumble of the carriage wheels were steady until they passed over the bridge and stopped at the pagan temple of

Apollo. High Priest Aristo and Lady Agnes were standing in front of three other men.

The men on horseback dismounted and the missionaries alighted from the carriage. Aristo welcomed them. Mayor Tazio and his wife Lady Laura walked up, and Aristo started his tour. He said, "This temple was built by the Greeks and is over seven hundred years old. Please follow Agnes and me into the sanctuary."

When they were inside the temple sanctuary, candles and torches burned throughout the building. The special sacrifice pyramid was especially well lit. Aristo said, "High Priest Hector in Gortyn Crete told you the story of Zeus, his family, wives and children. I will not go over that now. I just wanted all of you to appreciate our temple and our worship services here. You have shown me and the followers of Apollo great courtesy by letting me show you our wonderful temple. I wish you well with your play today. Governor Salvatore tells me that a better understanding between followers of Apollo and Jesus can lead to less quarrels, arguments and fear among our people."

Thomas thanked Aristo and Agnes. Sergio led everyone back to the horses and carriage, across the bridge and to the palace. The fort was nearby. Sergio dismounted and said, "We will travel to the amphitheater this same way. We have two carriages. We will follow the governor, Mario and Renato and their wives in their carriage. My wife will go with other officers from the fort. Meet us back here after lunch."

Baroni, Thomas, Stephen and Mark went into the palace and out onto the terrace. Baroni requested a fire be built and ordered juice, cheese and nuts brought out to them. The four of them sat down to view the city below, the island and the Mediterranean. As they were enjoying themselves two servants came out and placed wood in the fireplace and lit a fire. The four of them got up to sit around the blazing fire. Two servants came out with treats.

They sat enjoying the fire and the treats. Ladies Madelena, Fabrizia, Anna and Adriana came out, dressed with boots and colorful blouses. They took seats around the fire and the servants brought out more treats.

Lady Fabrizia slid sideways to look Thomas in the eye and said, "Besides allowing us to again have eternal life, what are some other wonderful features Jesus taught?"

"For this life, he taught about living to love God and our neighbors. Jesus taught that he knew each of us in the beginning before we were born. He loves us, wants us to be full of joy and love him in return. He wants us to return to him and has created a process that can lead us back to him in eternal life."

Lady Madelena smiled and said, "All of these teachings are beautiful. Why did the Jews want Jesus killed? They should've listened to him."

"Jesus was winning the hearts of the poor people, the middleclass priesthood and other special groups in Israel," Thomas said. "Jesus also did away with sacrifices and taught the Law of Moses had become between his chosen people and him. The Jewish leadership felt threatened by his teachings, the introduction of baptism and elimination of sacrifices. The result was a fear of losing their livelihood and power. Their solution was to get the Romans to kill him. And they did."

Baroni said, "Jesus also advised the Jews to respect the laws of the Romans. He said this by asking what was on the Roman Denarii. It was pointed out that the Caesar was on the Denarii. He therefore said give to Caesar what is his and give to God what is his. Life for the Jews could have been so much better if Jesus had not been killed. On the other hand, Jesus lived and died as the Jewish priest of old had prophesied. He paid the price for us to be forgiven and have eternal life."

Baroni stood and said, "I hate to break up this serious sharing of religious beliefs, but we must leave now."

He led everyone out to the carriage stand. Sergio came riding his mount with reins to two horses in his hand. The horses were black and had silver trimmed saddles and bridles with lace hanging behind the saddles. The two carriages came up the lane. The three couples boarded the first carriage. The other missionaries walked up from the fort to join Stephen and Mark. The first carriage pulled forward and the missionaries boarded the second carriage.

The road led them to the top of the amphitheater and soldiers were lined on both sides of the lane. Sergio led Thomas and Baroni past the center above the main isle of the amphitheater. Thomas looked down on the amphitheater and could not believe what he was seeing. All of the seating was full.

Soldiers came to take the horses as Sergio, Baroni and Thomas dismounted. The three couples in the first carriage were stepping out while the missionaries in the second carriage were disembarking. There had been a rumble of people talking, but it became quiet. The three couples marched down the center isle led by Governor Salvatore and Lady Magdalena. Thomas and Baroni led the missionaries, but stayed back from the three couples. Before the three couples reached the fifth row, six soldiers stood and stepped out and stood at attention to allow the officers and their wives to enter. Lady Madelena went in last to save her husband's seat. The soldiers marched two by two to the stage followed by Governor Salvatore, Baroni, Thomas and the missionaries.

Mayor Tazio, High Priest Aristo and Bishop Luca stood with the governor. The missionaries scattered as usual around the stage. Thomas felt a little dizzy with the elevated platform, the drop off into the canyon behind him and so much sky. He walked up to the four men and shook their hands, then stood to the side. The governor shook hands with the bishop and the high priest, who went up the center aisle to join their wives. The mayor walked forward to the front of the stage. Thomas stood next to the governor and was shocked to see the audience completely filled the amphitheater with soldiers standing all around the caves at the top and down both sides. The top rows were also filled with soldiers. The audience was talking to one another creating a roar again.

Thomas walked along the stage with his arms in the air. Gradually, the audience quieted down and the mayor smiled at Thomas. The mayor introduced himself and cheering and clapping erupted. He said, "We are here this afternoon to experience a Christian play. They were sent here by Governor Rufus from the Roman Provence of Judaea. Our Governor Salvatore has accepted them and has sponsored this play with the support of Bishop Luca, High Priest Aristo and me. I would like to introduce you to Governor Salvatore who will say a few words and introduce the play."

Governor Salvatore stepped forward and said, "Welcome to this wonderful amphitheater built hundreds of years ago by the Greek people. I have been good friends with Governor Rufus in the Provence of Judaea. He met the men on the stage with me and highly recommended them to me to perform a play they have produced in several Judean cities and Gortyn in Crete. They tell me the play is done in a question and answer mode, which tells the story of the life, death and resurrection of Jesus in Judaea. During his life he brought the Good News. We will hear some of this as well. It is my hope that this play can remove suspicion about Christianity and shine the light on the truth. Regardless of your faith, I hope you enjoy this play. Now I present to you Thomas, the leader, who will introduce his companions."

The audience was quiet. The mayor and governor went up the center aisle to sit with their wives. When they sat down, talking erupted again. Thomas let them talk as he paced back and forth at the front of the stage.

When he reached the middle, he stopped and raised his arms. Gradually the audience quieted again. Lowering his arms, he shouted, "Welcome Syracuse."

More cheering and clapping erupted. Thomas raised his arms and shouted, "We love your city. Many of you have heard of Apostle Paul who over sixty years ago brought Christianity to the Roman Empire. He started Christian ecclesia in many locations, but I have to say, he never had the opportunity to speak to so many people in such a beautiful setting as we have here today. Let us begin."

"Was Jesus prophesied by the Jewish prophets?" Thomas asked, pointing to Stephen.

"Malachi was a Jewish prophet who wrote, 'Behold I send My messenger, and he will prepare the way before Me. And the Lord, whom you seek, will suddenly come to His temple, even the Messenger of the covenant, in whom you delight. Behold, He is coming says the Lord of hosts.'"[178]

"Was there another who prophesied Jesus?" Stephen said pointing to Mark.

"Yes, Isaiah was another Jewish prophet who prophesied, 'Who will prepare your way before you. The voice of one crying in the wilderness: Prepare the way of the Lord, Make His paths straight.[179]'"

"Mary was the name of Jesus' mother. Was she a virgin when she gave birth to Jesus?" Mark asked, pointing to David.

" Mary was a virgin and was betrothed to Joseph. The angel Gabriel was sent by God to Mary saying, *'Rejoice highly favored one, the Lord is with you: blessed are you among women! ...she was troubled at his saying, and considered what manner of greeting this was. Then the angel said to her, 'Do not be afraid, Mary, for you have found favor with God. And behold, you will conceive in your womb and bring forth a son and shall call his name Jesus. He will be great, and will be called the Son of the Highest; and the Lord God will give Him the throne of His father, David. And He will reign over the house of Jacob forever, and of His Kingdom there will be no end.' Then Mary said to the angel, 'How can this be, since I do not know a man?' The angel answered and said to her, 'The Holy Spirit will come upon you, and*

---

[178] Ibid, Malachi 3.1.
[179] Ibid, Isaiah 40.3, and Mathew 1: 2.

the power of the Highest will overshadow you; therefore, also, that Holy One who is to be born will be called the Son of God.'"[180]

"Was there someone who was born before Jesus, who would announce Him?" David asked Paz.

"Yes, 'There was a man sent from God whose name was John. This man came for a witness of the Light that all through him might believe. He was not that Light, but was sent to bear witness of that Light. That was the true Light which gives light to every man who comes into the world.'[181]

Paz looked around at the audience and said. "When the Jewish priests asked, 'Who are you?' He confessed and did not deny, but confessed, *'I am not the Christ.' And they asked him, 'What then? Are you Elijah? He said, 'I am not.' Are you the Prophet? And he answered, 'No.' ...What do you say about yourself? He said, 'I am the voice of one crying in the wilderness: Make straight the way of the Lord, as the prophet Isaiah said.'"[182]*

The questions and answers continued for some time. Then Thomas held both arms up, ran to the front of the stage and shouted, "We'll take a short break."

The missionaries ran into a tunnel and out to where they could take a break and relieve themselves. After about a quarter of an hour, they walked back onto the stage. They stood as the audience returned to their seats and everyone was seated again. Thomas started the questions again.

"What mattered most to Jesus in his teachings," Thomas asked, pointing to Ben.

"Apostle Paul said, 'Love means living the way God commanded us to live. As you have heard from the beginning, his command is this; Live a life of love,"[183] 'No matter what I say, what I believe, and what I do, I'm bankrupt without love.'"[184]

"Did Jesus have more to say about love?" Ben said, pointing to Stephen.

"Because God is love, the most important lesson he wants you to learn on earth is how to love. It is in loving that we are most like him, so love is

---

[180] Ibid, Luke 1: 28-35.

[181] Ibid, John 1:6-9.

[182] Ibid, John 1: 19-23.

[183] New Century Version Bible, Dallas: Word Bibles (1991), 2 John 1: 6.

[184] The Message Bible, Colorado Springs: Navpress (1993), 1 Corinthians 13: 3b.

the foundation of every command he has given us,"[185] "The whole law can be summed up in this one command: Love others as you love yourself."[186]

"What do the ten commandments have to say about relationships with people?" Stephen said, pointing to Thomas.

"Four of the Ten Commandments deal with our relationship to God and six deals with our relationship with people,"[187] Thomas said. *"This means two things: love God and love people. Jesus said, 'You must love the Lord your God with all your heart...' This is the first and greatest commandment. A second is equally important: 'Love your neighbor as yourself.' All the other commandments and all the demands of the prophets are based on these two commandments. "*[188]

"Did Jesus die and what did his death accomplish," Stephen asked, pointing to Ben.

""The Jewish prophet Isaiah foretold many, many years ago that the Messiah would come to live amongst us and die for us," Ben said, he told us. *"But he was wounded for our transgressions; he was bruised for our iniquities, the chastisement for our peace was upon him, and by His strips we are healed. We all, like sheep, have gone astray; we have turned, every one to his own way; and the Lord has laid on him the iniquity of us all."*[189]

Ben pointed to David. "What happened to Jesus?"

"Jesus was arrested and eventually brought before the Roman Governor Pontius Pilate, by Caiaphas, the Jewish priesthood leader," David said. "He and the others demanded the death of Jesus, but the Governor asked, *'What has this man done?'* The leaders told of his life and threat to Jewish leadership. They again requested Jesus to be put to death. They shouted, he claims to be the king of the Jews and therefore he can't be a friend of the Caesar. The Governor eventually washed his hands of Jesus' blood and consented. He sent Jesus to be flogged and presented Jesus in a purple robe and again the Jews demanded that he be put to death on a cross."

"Was Jesus killed?" David said pointing to Thomas.

---

[185] Ibid, Rick Warren, page 123.

[186] Living Bible, Wheaton Il: Tyndale House Publishers (1979), Galatians 6: 14.

[187] Ibid, Rick Warren, page 125.

[188] New Living Translation Bible, Wheaton Il: Tyndale House Publishers (1996), Mathew 22: 37-40.

[189] Ibid, Isaiah 53:5, 6.

"Jesus' flogging and his death on the cross were so terrible," Thomas said. "Jesus had a crown of thorns placed on his head as he dragged the cross up the hill. Jesus' wrists were nailed to the cross and a spike was driven through both of his feet into the cross. He experienced such agony as the cross was dropped in the hole in the ground. A sign was placed on Jesus. *'Here is the King of the Jews.'* What a mockery."

"YES, JESUS WAS KILLED," Thomas shouted. "What happened to Jesus after he died?"

Thomas asked, pointing to Ben who walked forward on the stage again. "Joseph of Arimathea negotiated with the Herod and Pilate to take down Jesus' body from the cross before the sun went down," he said. "A soldier was instructed to pierce Jesus' side and through his heart to be sure he was dead and then pull him down. His body was taken to a cave, a private tomb, where his body was washed and dressed in new linens. A large stone was then rolled in front of the cave entrance. A Roman Centurion was stationed outside the tomb with temple guards to stop anyone from entering the tomb without their knowledge. The governor and the Jewish priesthood were concerned Jesus' body would be stolen and his followers would claim that he had been resurrected. That is not the end of Jesus."

Ben stepped back a few steps. He looked around and breathed slowly. The audience was very quiet waiting for him to continue. Finally, he walked forward again.

"On the morning after the Sabbath, Mary Magdalene, the most significant woman in Jesus' life, came to the cave," Ben said. "She found the stone blown away, lying several cubits from the tomb. The Centurion was standing back in fear, the temple guards ran away and Jesus' body was gone."

Many oohs and ahs came from the audience.

"Jesus came to die for our sins," Ben said. "He died for our atonement. His death was a trade for our forgiveness and our redemption. After his resurrection, he later in the day met with his mother, Mary, and Mary Magdalene to ask them to arrange for the Apostles to be together the next day at sunset. He then left and returned the next day to see his Apostles. They each felt his healed side and holes in his wrists. His brother, Apostle

Thomas, was not at this first meeting and did not believe Jesus was alive.[190]He saw Jesus later and believed. "

Finally, Thomas asked Ben. "Why was Jesus killed?"

Ben shouted, "Jesus died for our sins. With his death and resurrection, we are saved and can receive eternal life."

Thomas ran to the front of the stage, jumped into the air and shouted, "BECAUSE OF JESUS WE ARE SAVED!"

The audience stood, clapping. The governor ran down the stairs and the missionaries stood half on each side of him. He held out both arms to each group and they bowed several times. He then shook hands with each missionary and then shouted, "Thank you, Syracuse."

Back at the palace, everyone expressed excitement about the performance, but they were exhausted. They said good night and retired to their rooms. Sleep came quickly for Thomas as he stretched out in bed.

---

[190] Ibid, John 20:28-29.

✝ Chapter 40 ✝

The Baptisms in Syracuse
Saturday, May 11, 125 A.D.

The three couples and their guests met in the dining hall at sunrise. The women were the first to start talking about the play. Each had the opinion that there would be large numbers of people wanting to become Christians. They felt the message was powerful. The presentation and support by the governor, mayor, bishop and high priest gave encouragement for conversion to Christianity.

Salvatore said, "I never expected to see over fifteen thousand people in the audience. It took my breath away when we got there. It was not until I stepped out of the carriage that I realized what was happening. The whole event will change Syracuse. I hope it is for the good."

Breakfast was served while they continued to talk. Governor Salvatore said, "Thomas, I was doing my friend, Governor Rufus a courtesy to let you perform your play here. You have six talented missionaries. By a show of hands, how many at this table are inclined to become Christians?"

Lady Madelena slowly raised her hand; then Mario and Lady Fabrizia raised theirs. Thomas looked at the others. The governor raised his hand; then Sergio and Lady Anna raised their hands. Renato and Lady Anna sat looking at everyone. Renato smiled and said, "Anna and I just came from Rome where we saw more than a dozen Christians crucified. We are afraid: Anna wants to think and pray about this. Fear is stopping us."

Everyone lowered their hands. Thomas smiled and said, "I completely understand your fear, yet those of you who raised your hands have addressed your fear. The decision can be made at any time; just remember the baptism saves your spirit for eternal life. But the heart of the matter is the Good News spreading throughout the Roman Empire. The time has come to bring peace and Christ's message of love to all people."

Salvatore looked around at everyone and smiled, saying, "Caesar Hadrian has taken a very different approach to Christianity. About fifteen years ago Pliny wrote to Trajan and Trajan took his advice to eliminate killing people for being just Christians. They would only be punished if it was documented they had committed some crime. He wrote to forbid hearsay evidence. Hadrian has honored the advice of Pliny and Trajan, but he has gone further. Suetonius was Pliny's secretary in Bithynia. He is now Hadrian's secretary and received a petition to take action against some local Christians. Hadrian was aroused less by the Christians than by their ill natured critics. He showed his anger at the critics when he wrote, '*And this, by Hercules, you shall pay special attention to, any of these persons, you shall sentence him to more severe penalties in proportion to his wickedness.*[191]

He looked around and said, "I'm less concerned about the danger of becoming a Christian with Hadrian's anger at critics of Christianity and his flexible attitude to blunt the criticizers. Renato and Anna you need not fear as much as you think."

As they were finishing breakfast, a soldier came in and whispered into the governor's ear. Salvatore said, "We have guests. Let's go to the terrace."

The governor led the way to the terrace and a bright morning. Thomas wandered around looking at flowers and wondering what would come next.

---

[191] Ibid, Anthony Everitt, page 218. (The emperor may have adopted a tolerant policy because he saw through the hysterical prejudice against the sect and understood that it was not a group of fanatical criminals who practiced cannibalism, but was in fact pacific and posed no serious political threat. Alternatively, we know that he was fascinated by religion, especially the kind concerned with spiritual experience and individual commitment, and this may have motivated his approach.)

He turned around as several people came out of the palace to the terrace. They were accompanied by twelve soldiers. Mayor Tazio and his wife led several men and women. Tazio walked up to the governor and said, "Good morning. I have come here with members of our town council. We have met with people from the various cities and districts that make up Syracuse. Every member came to see me early this morning, some before dawn. Apparently, many people are demanding they be baptized this morning while the missionaries are here. They all want to have eternal life and enjoy the love of Jesus."

The governor talked separately with each member of the counsel with the same message to him.

Bishop Luca finally said, "We have a high demand for baptism at a level I have never seen. I would propose three locations to perform baptisms today. The island of Ortiga has the Fountain of Arethusa and can be perfect for baptisms. The Ciane Springs where papyrus grows can accommodate many lines for baptisms. The river Arethusa is also a good location. As many here know, the river Arethusa goes underground and appears again in the Island of Ortiga in the Fountain of Arethusa."

Thomas said, "Apostle Paul would be proud of us, for he started the Christians here sixty-six years ago in a three day visit.[192] Much earlier in history, I understand Plato performed in the amphitheater. It was a pleasure yesterday to follow him. So now Bishop Luca, you have three locations to conduct baptisms. How many in your congregation can perform baptisms."

Bishop Luca's smile brightened. "I've met with my counsel who are outside now and six of us can assist you in the baptisms. I've ordained them over the past two years. With the seven missionaries and the six of us, I suggest we assign three missionaries and two of my men to the Fountain of Arethusa on the Island of Ortiga. I would like to see two missionaries and two of my men go to the Ciane Springs. That leaves two missionaries and two of my men to meet at the River Alpheus."

The governor looked to Thomas and said, "Can you do this for Syracuse?"

"We can do it for Jesus," Thomas said. "We can do it for Syracuse."

Sergio and Renato were the first to leave. Bishop Luca made assignments of locations with his six men. Everyone not riding in a carriage

---

[192] Ibid, Acts 26: 12.

left the terrace and went out of the palace together. Salvatore looked at Lady Anna and asked, "You and Renato were not going to be baptized this morning at breakfast. Have you changed your minds?"

"We were afraid, as we told everyone," Lady Anna said. "Your information on Hadrian's attitude softened our fear. Renato whispered to me when the bishop was talking. Let's just get baptized with everyone. I was surprised, but I decided we would do it. So we are ready."

Lady Madelena said, "Thomas, I assume you baptize women. If so, what should we wear?"

Thomas smiled and said, "Yes, we baptize women. You would wear a dress over underclothing. We will baptize you in your underclothing. Wear some discreet underclothing. I am sure there will be many other women. You will be good examples for them."

Thomas, with a surprised look, said, "No wonder the governor said this morning, This may change Syracuse! Let's go out to the carriage stand."

When they came out of the palace, soldiers were riding in formation in three groups. One group went down the lane towards Ortiga and the other two groups rode west. One group was following Stephen, Ben and the two local Christians. The other group was following Peter, Mark and two local Christians.

David said, "I can't believe this is happening so quickly. Jesus must be working very hard here to help all of these people get organized. I know he is helping you Thomas. You were decisive out on the terrace. But then again, so was the bishop, the mayor and the governor."

Thomas looked at Paz, David and Stephen and said, "Remind me later to tell everyone in our group what Governor Salvatore told his officers and wives at the breakfast table about Hadrian's attitude. Everyone will be delighted by what he told us."

The carriages pulled up to the stand and stopped. The men from Bishop Luca's group came out of the palace. Thomas said, "Let's board the second carriage."

As they boarded the carriage, the governor came out with Mario and the four wives to board the first carriage. Renato and Sergio rode up the lane and got in front of the first carriage. The rattle of the wheels changed when they went over the bridge. The soldiers had roped off an area to contain their horses and were surrounding the spring. Several soldiers were at the entrance.

Seagulls flew in and landed on the railings on the edge of Mediterranean. Pelicans swooped in and landed below the seagulls. Thomas announced, "The birds are here because the Holy Spirit is with us. Do not fear for this is normal."

The governor marched carefully around the spring to the Mediterranean side being careful of the pelicans and seagulls. He looked surprised and said, "The birds are a treat. This is a great day for Syracuse. I applaud your decision to be baptized today while the missionaries are here. We and our wives will be the first to be baptized. Honor us by watching us be saved."

Thomas, Paz, David and the two local men were let into the entrance and walked down to the spring. The governor, Mario, Renato, Sergio and their wives came down with several soldiers. Thomas announced, "David and I will baptize a couple at a time. Please remove your uniforms and dresses."

Having been warned of this procedure, the men removed their uniforms and handed them to the waiting soldiers. The women removed their dresses to reveal blouses and riding pants. Thomas smiled and announced Governor Salvatore and his wife, Lady Madelena will be the first. Thomas led the governor and David led Madelena. When they were waist deep in water, both kneeled down. The baptisms were done at the same time. When Thomas and David pulled them out of the water, the audience cheered. They walked back to the soldiers holding the uniforms and dresses. Salvatore and Madelena stood inside a circle of soldiers with their backs to them. They took towels and dried themselves and he changed into a dry tunic and put on his uniform. Madelena carried her dress.

Thomas announced, "We next have Legatus Legionis Mario and his wife, Lady Fabrizia."

They walked into the water and were baptized. They went back to do the same as Salvatore and Madelena. Thomas said, "Tribune Renato and his wife, Lady Anna, are next."

Renato and Anna walked hand in hand into the water and were baptized. They went back to do the same as Mario and Fabrizia. Thomas said, "Now we have Centurion Sergio and his wife, Lady Adriana."

Sergio and Adriana moved into the water and were quickly baptized. They walked back to do the same as Renato and Anna. The four couples walked up the steps and through the soldiers. When they reached the carriage, everyone stopped and turned around. Thomas followed them out to stand in front of the soldiers who held the crowd back. Governor Salvatore shouted, "WE HAVE BEEN SAVED. THOMAS, YOU CAN CONTINUE."

The four couples boarded the carriage, except for Renato and Sergio who mounted their horses that were held for them. They led the carriage across to the bridge with its wheels clacking over the stones. Thomas went back to the spring entrance and shouted, "We need to have everyone who wants to be baptized form five lines. Each line should come down the steps to the edge of the spring. There are five of us here including Ben, David, me and two of your citizen Christians. We will each perform a baptism at the same time four others are being done. Be prepared to remove any clothing you do not want to get wet. Have the person behind you hold any clothing and retrieve it when you return from your baptism."

The seagulls fluttered around and some were walking near the spring. The pelicans sat with their sides to the railing. They seemed insistent about staying during the baptisms. It was late afternoon when the last of the baptisms were completed. Thomas walked to the top of the stairs and raised his arms to stretch. All at once the seagulls flew away up the coast of the island. The pelicans stood and ran to fly away. The remaining crowd clapped and cheered as the last of the birds flew away.

One of the soldiers said, "The baptisms have taken more than half of the day. I counted the men and women baptized and there were three-hundred and twenty-two, plus eight for the governor, the officers and their wives."

Another soldier said, "Of those you baptized, eighty-eight were soldiers. Many of us standing guard want to be baptized, but we can wait for Bishop Luca and his men to baptize us. Thank you for what you have done here today."

Bishop Luca's men thanked Thomas and walked on across the bridge. The driver announced, "We will return to the palace now."

David looked at Thomas and Paz who were both wet and smiling. "I can't believe I baptized over sixty men and women today," he said. "I wonder what has happened at the Ciane Springs and the River Alpheus."

It wasn't cold, but the three of them were shivering when they reached the palace. Thomas stepped out when they arrived and the carriage continued on to the fort. He went to the entrance and the guards smiled at him and let him enter. In his room he changed into a dry robe and brushed his hair and beard. He lay on his bed on his back and went instantly to sleep. He awoke to voices in the hall. He got up to find Stephen and Mark walking towards their rooms. Both were wet and shivering.

Thomas grinned and said, "We baptized Salvatore, Mario, Renato, Sergio and their wives one couple at a time. After that we baptized another three-hundred and twenty-two. What happened at your location?"

Stephen smiled and said, "Sounds like you were quite successful. Ben and I went to the River Alpheus and I asked a soldier to count the number of men and women we baptize. When we were done, the four of us had baptized two-hundred and fifty-five. What a beautiful place that Ciane Springs is. That is the first time I have seen papyrus growing in the water."

Mark was shivering and said, "Next time, I am going to take an extra robe. Peter and I enjoyed an interesting ride to the River Alpheus. There were hundreds of people there, but only some wanted to be baptized. I also asked one of the soldiers to count the number of people we baptized. When we were done, I found the consensus was two-hundred and sixty-five were baptized of which one soldier said seventy three were soldiers."

"Both of you had great success," Thomas said. "I wish I could have seen those places. Now go get a dry robe on and I will meet you on the terrace,"

When he came out on the terrace, the four newly baptized couples were seated looking at the city below. Thomas sat down facing them.

Stephen and Mark came out ahead of two servants carrying honey cakes and goblets. A third servant came out carrying two amphoras. The third servant went over to the fire-pit and made a fire. Everyone sat eating cake and sipping their drink. When the fire was burning brightly, everyone went to sit by the fire.

Lady Madelena was looking into the fire and said, "I have been saved, but I feel the same."

Lady Fabrizia looked around and said, "I felt the love of Jesus today and I feel really mellow now. I'm really happy all of us were baptized."

Renato stared into the fire and said, "In spite of Hadrian's new attitude, we need to keep our baptisms to ourselves when other Roman officers come here or when we go to Rome. We have abandoned the state religion. I feel bad about keeping it secret because I would like to shout it to the world. I'm now a Christian, but I'm still afraid of our own people."

Thomas sighed and said, "We could all be killed tomorrow in an earthquake or a fire. At least we have the love of Jesus and the faith of an eternal life. Be careful if you must, but enjoy what we have found together. On the other hand, thank you, Salvatore. Your telling us about Hadrian's new attitude towards Christians this morning helps me greatly. The more I learn about him, the more I'm impressed with him."

A servant appeared and said, "We have a light dinner ready to serve in the dining hall."

Everyone left the fire and went into the palace to the dining hall. They talked about the enormity of the baptisms done in the three locations. Thomas prayed to thank Jesus for the baptisms and bless the food. When everyone was finished they went to their room.

✝ Chapter 41 ✝

Provence of Sicily to Govern
Sunday, May 12, 125 A.D.

Thomas slept soundly and awoke to sunlight streaming through his window. He got up, put on a fresh robe, packed his saddlebag and took it down by the palace entrance. He went into the dining hall. All four couples were seated with Baroni, Stephen and Mark. The governor said, "Sergio was at the fort early. The soldiers we had on duty while you were baptizing others yesterday have requested we set up a time for Bishop Luca to baptize them. It seems you have started a trend."

Thomas smiled and said, "I will not take all the credit. When we baptized all of you yesterday, I am sure every soldier in Syracuse knows about your baptisms by now. Of course, I think that's wonderful."

Breakfast was served. The food smelled great and the mood at the table was uplifting. Lady Madelena asked, "When will you try to leave?"

"We will go to the pier after breakfast," Thomas said, "Your husband says the best time to sail north through the narrows is after noon. If we sail from the pier at noon, we won't get to Palermo until after dark tonight. Tomorrow, we will sail to find the Island-of-Dreams. I do, however, hate to leave. I have enjoyed our stay with you. My companions have been treated very well at the fort. We are in your debt. The time on the terrace, gazing at the city and the fires, has been a treat. The dinners in here have been wonderful experiences. Thank you for your friendship and hospitality."

Governor Salvatore looked up and said, "Thomas and Baroni, you are going to search for the Island-of-Dreams. When you find it, you will leave Mark in charge of the construction. Thomas, you will travel to Gaul and Britain and then return to the Provence of Judaea. Baroni and his three ships will travel with you to protect you. Mark, you will have the Islander to travel back and forth to the mainland. Pardi will have the Palermo Vine. My concern is you will need protection from raiders coming by the island."

Thomas sat thinking and then said, Governor, do you have any solutions?'

Salvatore said, "Yes, your island will come under the protection of the Roman Provence of Sicily. We already do this with a number of islands around Sicily. I will send two hundred soldiers and three ships to be stationed on the island. They will help build a pier to station the ships. I'll also have them build a fort. They will be part of your protection. You will need to recruit at least two-hundred men to come out to live on the island to work on the construction and be armed to guard you. My men will train your recruits."

"I'm stunned that you are willing to do this," Thomas said.

"Thomas, I have the power, the resources and the desire to do it," he said. "I will send a courier with you to delivery my orders to the fort in Palermo. I will have him report to you and Baroni, at the Free Spirit no later than noon. In time I expect to make some financial gain for this effort from the Island-of-Dreams. I have a feeling there is more there than a site to build a house of worship. You'll give back to Sicily more than it will cost us, but don't worry about that now."

"I wonder if you're right. Thomas said, looking at Salvatore.

"Thomas, there is another subject that we need to talk about," Salvatore said. "Governor Rufus said in his package to me that you are his client in a Roman sense. I was startled by that comment. But now that I know you it makes sense. You do know what it means, don't you?"

"Yes, I do know the relationship between a client and a Patron," Thomas said. "I think it is a wonderful concept. I'm also a client of Governors Pietro and Stefano. These webs of relationships are a great Roman custom."

"Are you, Stephen and Mark ready to be my clients," Salvatore said. "I'm willing to take on the roll of Patron to all three of you, as well as your governor. These are in addition and separate from being a Christian."

"I'm delighted to be your client," Thomas said. "I'm also delighted to become a citizen in the Provence of Sicily."

Stephen, I want you to be my client in case something happens to Thomas," Salvatore said. "Mark, I want you to be my client because you are going to build the house of worship and the homes. You'll be the governor of the island. You'll report to me and my officers in regard to overseeing the island community."

Stephen and Mark agreed to be faithful clients of the governor. They both looked amazed at this development. They discussed the web of client relationships and the obligations they were assuming.

"Its settled then and I am pleased," said Salvatore.

"Before we leave, I have gold and silver bars with me on the Free Spirit that need to be deposited in the Bank of Rome. Could you assist me in this deposit? It will be easier for Mark and Pardi to access these funds to buy building materials, food, supplies and pay the men they recruit."

Salvatore smiled and said, "We have a branch of the Bank of Rome down the street from your ships. Centurion Sergio and I will meet you at the Free Spirit. Keep the carriage to take the gold and silver bars to the branch. I'll talk to them about giving you, Pardi and Mark authority to withdraw coin as both of you need it. We have branches all over the Roman Empire."

At the pier, all of the ship captains were busy with their crews, loading supplies from supply wagons from the pier. Baroni and the missionaries went to their ships to put their personal items away. Thomas stood talking to Peter when Tamir came up the gangplank. Tamir said, "Welcome back. I thought you should know that all of the men who now serve on these ships are Christians. Yesterday, Drago, Alonso, Bernardus and I led the men from all three ships over to the Fountain of Arethusa. You did not notice. We were in the two lines for the local Christians. Local citizens and soldiers were fighting to get in lines for Paz, David or you."

Thomas and Baroni gave Tamir a hug and turned to see Drago, Alonso and Bernardus walking onto the ship. Thomas said, "I hear you are Christians. Congratulations."

The Roman captains smiled and got hugs from Thomas and Baroni. Baroni said, "Since all of you are here. I want to tell you what Governor Salvatore is going to do. He will send two hundred soldiers and three ships from Palermo with us. The Island-of-Dreams will become part of the Provence of Sicily. The two hundred soldiers will help build a port and pier on the island. They will then at some point build a fort. Mark and Pardi will be responsible for recruiting men to move to the island to work on the construction and train to provide additional protection for the island. The soldiers stationed on the island will train the recruits in fighting skills."

A soldier walked up the gangplank and saluted, and then asked to see Centurion Baroni. He said, "I am a courier sent by Governor Salvatore to travel with you to Palermo. I have orders for Tribunus Laticlavius Lorenzo at the fort in Palermo. Governor Salvatore is waiting on the pier for Thomas."

Thomas took Stephen down to the cabin deck and pulled out the boxes with coins, as well as gold and silver bars. He took the gold and silver bars out placing four bars of gold and six bars of silver on the floor. He combined the coins in the second box and set it back where it had been. He then wrapped the four gold bars and six silver bars in towels. He and Stephen made five trips to carry the them to the carriage. Sergio got into the carriage with Thomas, Stephen, Mark and Baroni. The governor talked to the driver and got into the carriage.

The carriage rode a short distance and then Sergio and the governor got out. "We'll go make arrangements," Salvatore said. "Wait here."

Sergio said to the soldiers on horseback, "Men, stay here with the carriage."

They were gone a short time and returned with four men from the branch of the Bank of Rome who had a rolling cart. Mark and Stephen pulled the four gold and six silver bars out and placed them on the cart. The four men pulled the cart and the governor, Sergio, Thomas, Stephen, Mark and Baroni followed them into the building. The governor gave instructions for recording the gold and silver. The bars were weighed and receipts were prepared. Sergio explained to the men in the branch about the need for papers and authorization for those who could withdraw from the account. When they left Mark, Pardi, Stephen and Thomas had authority and papers to withdraw from the account. Everyone returned to the carriage and rode back to the ships. Mark, Stephen, Thomas and Baroni thanked the governor and said good bye.

The port workers released the lines to the five ships and pushed them back. Crews on each ship had their oars out to turn their ships to sail south out of Porto Grande. The Free Spirit took the lead. The ships turned around the tip of Ortiga and out into the Ionian Sea and turned to go north. The sails were pulled up and the wind caught them. Thomas was standing on the stern looking back at the other ships.

Joziah stepped up on the stern and Thomas said to him, "I understand you are now a Christian. Congratulations."

Joziah smiled. "I've never been happier. I feel free and have joined a community that I can help build. I wish the men who are on the Palermo Vine could have been here. We have four here on the Free Spirit and there are four on the Islander. So, eight of us are Christians. Three of the four on the Palermo Vine are still of the Jewish faith. We will work on them when we get to the Island-of-Dreams."

It was not long before the guards came around to hand out lunch and give everyone a goblet of juice. As they finished lunch they entered the Strait of Messina. The wind was strong against their backs. As they passed Cape Peloro off their port side the water became turbulent, but as they got further north the water calmed down. Peter had the sails altered and used the bar to turn the paddles to sail west.

Peter had Ben and Joziah stand in the bow to watch the ships they passed to be wary of the possibility of more of Hadar's ships. As the sun sailed further west the glare of the sun off the water ahead of them hurt their eyes.

The Free Spirit sailed straight ahead with the other ships behind them. Thomas and several others had taken a nap. He came up and soon everyone was on deck watching as they sailed into the Palermo pier next to the Palermo Vine. The other ships docked in a line. The workers at the pier got all five ships tied to the pier. The ship captains, missionaries and Baroni met on the pier.

Pardi and Micah walked off the Palermo Vine and greeted everyone. Pardi said, "I visited my family and I brought back ten barrels of wine and two-hundred grape vine starts. They were delighted with my plans. Two of my nephews dug up the vine starts and packed them in one wagon and the wine was packed in another wagon. We arrived this morning and packed everything in the Palermo Vine. The nephews are probably back home by now. I was right, my brothers and sisters want the family vineyard for themselves and are happy that I didn't stay. But they were very happy and helpful to me."

✝ Chapter 42 ✝

More Roman Ships in Palermo
Sunday, May 12, 125 A.D.

The Roman courier came off the Free Spirit and reported to Baroni, who said, "Thomas, we need to go with the courier to the fort to have the message delivered and meet with Tribune Lorenzo."

When they arrived at the lane to the fort commander's entrance, they were met by an officer who introduced himself as Centurion Dante. He was a few years younger than Baroni, but had several commission medals hanging from his neck. He was tall and handsome with hazzle eyes. They followed him into the officer's reception area. A man in a familiar purple stripped uniform was standing there talking to another Centurion officer. He introduced himself as Tribune Lorenzo. Dante introduced everyone to him.

The courier saluted and handed the order bag to Lorenzo, who invited everyone to sit. He opened the bag and pulled out the papers. He read them carefully, looked up and frowned. He then read the orders again. "Baroni, you were here a few days ago. I should have talked to you then, but you were late and left during the night. Now you are back with orders from Governor Salvatore. I have under my command enough soldiers and ships to fulfill the governor's orders. You and Thomas must have dinner with Centurion Dante and me tonight and tell us more about this island and your plans. My wife was planning to have dinner with me. She will be delighted to welcome you. Centurion Dante, you recently became a Christian. I'm giving this assignment to you. Here are the orders to read."

Centurion Dante read and reread the orders. He looked up and said, "We are going to help you find this island and protect it while you build homes and the Christian house of worship? Yes, I want to know more. I need to know a lot more."

Baroni, Thomas and Dante talked about the island and the orders from Jesus that Thomas received a few years earlier. When Thomas mentioned Joseph of Arimathea, Dante said, "I spent time in Britain. Everyone there talks about Joseph of Arimathea. All sorts of people claim kinship with him. His grandchildren still have the tin and lead business, selling to the Roman army and others."

The four of them went to a series of rooms with tables in each one. Lorenzo stopped at one room with a small table lit with torches and candles. A lady sat looking at them as they entered. Lorenzo said, "This is my wife Giorgetta. These men are Centurion Baroni and Thomas. Of course you know, Centurion Dante. Thomas is a Christian from the Provence of Judaea and Baroni is in charge of his protection."

Everyone sat down and Lorenzo whispered in his wife's ear. Lady Giorgetta had blue eyes, auburn hair and very white smooth skin. She looked to be in her late twenties and had a nice twinkle in her eyes. She smiled and said, "I understand you are going to search for an unoccupied island."

Thomas leaned forward and said, "Yes, I call it the Island-of-Dreams. It was shown to me by Jesus in a dream. Jesus and his great uncle, Joseph of Arimathea, found it on a voyage from Britain to Judaea about a hundred years ago."

"Dante, you have talked about Joseph of Arimathea from time to time," Lorenzo said. "You learned about him when you were stationed in Britain. Baroni has been all over the Roman Empire. But, Thomas, who are you?"

"I am the great-grandson of Apostle Thomas, Jesus' brother and one of his apostles."

"I thought Apostle Thomas went to India and was killed there," Lorenzo said. "I didn't know he had children. Can you tell us more?"

"Yes," Thomas said with a grin. "Apostle Thomas worked for his great uncle, Joseph of Arimathea before Jesus started his ministry. He was involved in the caravan routes to Edessa, Parthia, India, Israel and Egypt. When Joseph of Arimathea was run out of Israel, he turned the caravan route business over to Apostle Thomas. Before Jesus was crucified and resurrected, King Abgar of Edessa wrote a letter to Jesus saying, *"Abgar Ouchama to Jesus, the Good Physician Who has appeared in the country of Jerusalem, greeting: I have heard of Thee, and of Thy healing; that Thou dost not use medicines or roots, but by Thy word openest (the eyes) of the*

blind, makest the lame to walk, cleansest the lepers, makest the deaf to hear;
how by Thy word (also) Thou healest (sick) spirits and those who are
tormented with lunatic demons, and how, again, Thou raisest the dead to life.
And, learning the wonders that Thou doest, it was borne in upon me that (of
two things, one): either Thou hast come down from heaven, or else Thou art
the Son of God, who bringest all these things to pass. Wherefore I write to
Thee, and pray that thou wilt come to me, who adore Thee, and heal all the
ill that I suffer, according to the faith I have in Thee. I also learn that the
Jews murmur against Thee, and persecute Thee, that they seek to crucify
Thee, and to destroy Thee. I possess but one small city, but it is beautiful,
and large enough for us two to live in peace."

Jesus answered saying, '*Happy art thou who hast believed in Me, not*
having seen me, for it is written of me that those who shall see me shall not
believe in Me, and that those who shall not see Me shall believe in Me. As to
that which thou hast written, that I should come to thee, (behold) all that for
which I was sent here below is finished, and I ascend again to My Father
who sent Me, and when I shall have ascended to Him I will send thee one of
My disciples, who shall heal all thy sufferings, and shall give (thee) health
again, and shall convert all who are with thee unto life eternal. And thy city
shall be blessed forever, and the enemy shall never overcome it.'"[193]

"Thomas went to Edessa later on and made a bargain for a large
payment of gold from King Abgar conditioned on the king's healing.
Thomas then sent Thaddeus to do the healing. Thaddeus took the shroud that
Jesus was wrapped in when he was laid in the Garden Tomb by Joseph of
Arimathea. When the shroud was viewed by King Agbar, he was healed."

When Thomas sat back to take a breath, Lorenzo said, "Well, what
happened."

Thomas smiled and said, "The king then paid the gold to Apostle
Thomas on his next caravan route through Edessa. Thomas took part of the
gold back to Jerusalem and deposited the rest with a banker and lender in
Damascus. Thomas continued his caravan business for another twenty years.
When the apostles divided the world, Apostle Peter assigned Thomas to India
to preach Jesus' Good News. Thomas turned the caravan business, his
deposits from King Agbar and the profits from the caravan business over to
his oldest son. The son was instructed to use the gold and deposits to further

---

[193] New Advent's Catholic Encyclopedia, The Legend of Abgar.

the cause of Christianity. Thomas still did not want to go to India, but Jesus had a merchant kidnap him and was taken to India. Thomas preached for seventeen years in India establishing seven Christian ecclesiae before he was killed."

Thomas looked around the table and continued, "The gold, banker deposits, homes in Arimathea and Jerusalem and other wealth were handed down to me, along with Apostle Thomas's writings. Apostle Thomas left a note to his relatives to move the writings out of Jerusalem to a Mediterranean island. Jesus told me the same thing in the dream a few years ago. So now I'm doing what I have been instructed to do. I'm using the wealth Apostle Thomas passed down to me to further Christianity."

Lorenzo said, "That story explains how you can afford two ships. I guess the Palermo Vine at the pier is yours. I understand Principale Pardi has retired from the Roman army and will use the Palermo Vine to help with the vineyards and construction on this Island-of-Dreams."

"The Palermo Vine belongs to Thomas as a spoil of war," Baroni said. "Thomas captured the ship with his crew from both of his ships and the soldiers on Principale Drago's ship."

"All right, you have explained part of the story," Lorenzo said. "Now why did Governor Salvatore decide to give you further protection and claim the Island-of-Dreams as a possession of the Provence of Sicily? This is not new to us; we now manage a number of islands around Sicily. But why did he want to do this?"

Baroni looked at Lorenzo and Dante and said, "I've something to tell you, but I have to ask first. How supportive are you to Governor Salvatore? I mean how good of a friend are you to him?"

Lorenzo looked shocked at the question and said, "Whatever he has done, I will support him. He is my cousin. We grew up together. I would die in his defense. Tell me what has happened."

Baroni looked doubtful and said, "Thomas, tell Lorenzo what happened in Syracuse."

Thomas looked worried and said, "We were accepted in Syracuse by Governor Salvatore at the request of his friend, Governor Rufus in the Provence of Judea."

"Yes, Rufus and Salvatore are great friends," Lorenzo said. "As a matter of fact, Governor Rufus is also a good friend of mine. So what did Governor Rufus want Salvatore to do?"

"He wanted Salvatore to allow us to put on a Christian play," Thomas said. "And we did."

Baroni said, "The end result is we stayed with the governor, his wife, Lady Madelena, and three senior officers and their wives. Yesterday, Thomas and his companions baptized all four couples and a total of eight hundred and fifty people, including most of the men on Thomas's ships and mine."

"That is incredible!" Lorenzo exclaimed. "No wonder both of you were concerned about telling me this. You can be sure that Dante, Giorgetta and I will keep this to ourselves. Salvatore and the officers in Syracuse will have no cause to fear us telling anyone. That is a private matter."

Giorgetta said, "I hope to hear how you did all that in Syracuse. You must be very much like Jesus."

"No, I am only his servant," Thomas said. "Jesus is the son of God, but he told me he would help. Lorenzo, Salvatore told several of us yesterday at breakfast about Hadrian's attitude to get angrier at the critics of Christianity than at the Christians themselves.[194] He seems to like spiritual religions. You'll have to talk to him about this. He made his officers, wives and us less fearful to be a Christian."

As they finished their dinner, servants came in to remove the dinner plates and goblets. They returned with fruit, a sliced, aged cheese and a drink, Lorenzo called brandy. They sat and talked for a few hours about the rebels in Judaea and Hadar who is providing provisions for war to Simeon ben Kosiba. They talked about the visits to Gortyna Crete and Malta. The plays in Gortyn and Syracuse were discussed at length.

Finally, Lorenzo said, "Stay here tonight. We will meet for breakfast and discuss the equipment, building materials for the pier and supplies. Dante and I will meet early to finalize a list. I hope the Island-of-Dreams is still unoccupied. Otherwise we may need to remove those that are there."

Everyone said goodnight and Dante showed Baroni and Thomas to their rooms.

---

[194] Ibid, Anthony Everitt, page 218. (He (Hadrian) makes clear that detractors should put up proofs or shut up. He wrote, "I will not allow them simply to beg and shout. If there is evidence, the governor should hear it.)

<table><tr><td>✝</td><td>## Chapter 43</td><td>✝</td></tr></table>

Loading the Ships for the Trip
Monday, May 13, 125 A.D.

Thomas awoke to a knock on his door. When he opened the door, Baroni was standing there and said, "We need to talk to Lorenzo and Dante right away. We have a lot to do today."

They walked to the room where they had dinner the night before. Lorenzo and Dante were going over lists of tents, camping equipment, food and personal supplies. Lorenzo looked up, smiled and said, "Sit down. Dante and I went over a list of building materials for the pier and the beginnings of a fort. We just finished with the camping requirements, which include two large leather tents, one for Dante and his men and the man you leave in charge."

Dante looked up as Baroni and Thomas sat down. He said, "I was up early and went over to the pier and talked to Pardi and his captain, Micah. I then talked to Peter, Tamir, Drago, Alonso and Bernardus. I was able to get an accurate head count for tents, cots and other supplies everyone will need once we reach the island. I have included forty extra sets of everything. I have accounted for who will stay and who will not."

Dante looked up anxiously, and said, " I talked to Tamir and Mark. They said you plan to cut timber on the island to use to build homes. I'm taking additional wood cutting equipment because I will need it for the fort. We talked briefly about the house of worship. If you plan to build it out of stone, I can locate stone cutters and masons. The building site will need extensive work before the building can be started. Mark said you plan to build a rather large vault out of granite. We will examine the granite on the island for suitability. If it is not the best or too difficult to cut out, there are a number of locations to choose from for that type of stone."

"You have done a lot of preparing this morning," Thomas said. "With all this preparation, I hope we can find the island."

"We'll find it, never fear." Dante grinned and said, "I believe we can locate what we need for the trip, pack all of it into the ships and be ready to leave in the morning. I told Peter and Tamir that when they travel to recruit workers, I will go with them. We can leave Pardi to supervise security while we are gone."

Breakfast was served as they chatted about the various supplies and the men Dante would take with him. As they finished breakfast, Lorenzo said, "I was awake a lot last night, and so was Giorgetta. We could not get over the program you have been following. Your missionary success in Syracuse still stuns me. I can't wait to talk to Salvatore. Giorgetta and I considered Christianity when Dante converted. But we were afraid for ourselves. We must learn what Salvatore and his officers considered in their decisions. I want to hear more about what he knows about Hadrian's current views about Christians."

Baroni said, "I'm a Christian and it took some convincing for me. I'm happy with my decision and whatever happens, will be. What Salvatore told us is very good news."

Lorenzo looked puzzled and said, "You are aware that the Apollo religion is a huge source of income for Rome. Each temple raises considerable revenue and shares it with Rome through the local Roman province. Each of your congregations will need to contribute to Rome the same way to become a revenue source for Rome too. Salvatore will discuss this with you. I'm sure he has already discussed it with Bishop Luca."

"Thank you, Lorenzo," Thomas said. "What you are telling me is good to know. The Christian members will be asked to contribute to the support of the congregation. The bishop can pay some of that support to Rome, since each bishop will be a separate revenue source."

"Something Salvatore may not know is interesting. Caesar Hadrian has announced plans to build temples all over the empire. These temples will have no religious affiliation. Each temple will be available to those around the temple to use as their place of worship. I understand that many will be used by Christian congregations.[195] One is scheduled to be built here. I just received the order."

Baroni sighed and said, "Hadrian is becoming the most flexible Caesar regarding religion. Right now we should get back to the pier to see what we can do to help."

Thomas shook hands with Lorenzo and then he and Baroni walked back to the pier together. The weather was warm and windy. The walk was delightful with people busy and bustling about. They reached the pier, smelling the fish market nearby, and met the ships' captains and Pardi. They talked about Dante's visit in the early morning and were really impressed with him. Pardi said, "Dante is very organized and is one of the best men you could have found for this duty. He's a prize since he knows the islands around Sicily. Better yet, he knows most of the Balearic Islands. But only you, Thomas, can identify the Island-of-Dreams. Do you get chills when you think about the possibility there isn't an Island -of-Dreams?"

Thomas smiled and said, "Jesus is helping me. I'm his right hand and we will find it. I'm convinced, now that we have Dante. All of you need to do is go over your supplies and get a list of anything you need. Dante will get it for us. Do we need any canvas to protect the ships when we have them moored for stretches of time? Have you talked about taking chickens and goats with us? If we do, we may need pens or materials to build them. We'll need fresh eggs, chickens, vegetables and dried fruit. The goats can give us milk."

Dante arrived and said, "We need to walk down the pier to meet the captains of my ships. They have been loading, but most of it is yet to be put away."

---

[195] Ibid, Anthony Everitt, page 218. ("The Historia Augusta reports that Hadrian commissioned the building of temples throughout the empire without any divine images in them, and that it was thought they were dedicated to Christ. Apparently they came to be known as Hadrian's temples. It is difficult to be sure what to make of this: the story may simply be the product of authorial fantasy, but if there is anything to it, it is more likely to have been the emperor's general attempt to widen the scope of recognized or official worship than to single out any particular sect (rather as the Athenians did with their altar to the Unknown God). However, he could well have had Christianity in mind alongside other Salvationist and monotheistic creeds of the day.")

The six captains, Pardi, Mark, Thomas, Stephen and Baroni all followed Dante. They came to an area reserved for Roman ships stationed in Palermo. There were three ships with all kinds of material and camping gear in front of them. Dante saluted a soldier and said, "I want you to meet these men, but first find the other two captains."

The ship captain walked down the pier and came back with two soldiers following him. Dante said, "Meet Thomas, who owns the three ships. He is in charge of this adventure and is the head missionary. Oh yes, meet Stephen. He is Thomas' cousin and closest companion. He will introduce the other missionaries before we leave. Our captains are Principales Nino, Ilario and Rocco."

Thomas said, "Meet Centurion Baroni and Principales Drago, Alonso and Bernardus. The captains for the Free Spirit is Peter, the Islander is Tamir and the Palermo Vine is Micah. Also, this is Mark who will be in charge of construction of homes and the house of worship. He will also become the mayor of the island. Meet Pardi, who just retired as Principale from the Roman army. He will be using the Palermo Vine and Micah reports to him."

The captains of Dante's ships were short in stature, but had large powerful arms. What they didn't have in height was made up with their determined demeanor. Their uniforms and equipment were in superb condition. Thomas took an immediate liking for them.

Walking back to the Free Spirit, Mark and Pardi commented on their continued good fortune. Mark said, "I'm sure I will enjoy working with them. They appear to be no nonsense men. I like the idea of having them on my side in a fight."

Dante and Pardi went into the Palermo Vine. Some men came along the pier carrying lumber and boxes of brass couplings. They walked up to the Palermo Vine and set everything down. They went back down the pier. While everyone stood watching them, they returned with more building materials and set those down. By the time Dante and Pardi came out, the men had made four trips. Dante took the two men into the Palermo Vine to show them where to store what they had stacked in front on the pier.

Returning, Dante said, "Thomas, follow me back to my ships. I want to show you what we have brought. You're the only one who has seen this island. Maybe you will think of something we have missed."

While they were walking, Thomas said, "As I remember from the dream, the lower part of the island is about ten to twenty cubits above the Mediterranean, but the edge appears to go straight down. I think there is a cove below the stone outcropping. Maybe we can build a pier there. We will need to hack some stairs into the side of the hill. The rest of the island is sixty to a hundred feet above the Mediterranean with cliffs on three sides from what I could see."

Dante said, "I'm bringing chickens, ducks, rabbits and some goats. I know we still need to find the island, but we have to eat. This will give us some fresh eggs, milk and meat."

"We can take some on our ships," Thomas said. "Once we find the island, you'll need to come back for more animals and chickens. We should take fresh fruits and vegetables. Can we get a large amount of dried fruit such as raisins, nuts and dates?"

Dante showed Thomas the tents, cots, camping gear and crates of chickens and rabbits. There were several goats tied to a cleat in the pier. There were sacks of feed for the chickens, ducks and the goats. They went into each ship and went over what had been packed. There were crates of flour and hundreds of loaves of bread.

Dante said, "We will have over three hundred men with us and the bread will go fast. Feeding everyone on the island or where ever we stop will be the largest challenge. Once we find the island we will need to be creative until we can get gardens planted and bring in more animals and chickens. I'll get a man looking for the fresh fruits and vegetables. I know where we can get the dried fruit. Maybe Pardi and I can find a herd of sheep to buy. We may need to graze them on a nearby island. Can you supply us with enough gold and coin to get past the first year? I mean Governor Salvatore and Tribune Lorenzo will pay our costs, but you will have a large crew working when the buildings are started."

"Dante, you need not worry," Thomas said. "I have set up adequate resources for Mark and Pardi. You need to make sure they spend the sums wisely. What do you think of this adventure?"

"I think it is exciting," Dante said. "But why did Jesus choose an isolated island?"

Thomas looked puzzled and said, "No one has asked that question. I think Jesus has more to tell me. I'm doing what he requires and have faith he will tell me more."

Now Dante Looked puzzled and said, "Do you or anyone in your party have any idea where this Island-of-Dreams is? If you do, we should talk about it this afternoon."

Thomas brightened and said, "We have the records of Joseph of Arimathea. Baroni and Peter have looked at them early on, but did not know where it is. I would suggest we get all nine ship captains together and talk about what we know."

Dante smiled and said, "I'll bring Nino, Rocco and Ilario down to the Free Spirit. You have the other captains meet us there with Pardi and Baroni."

Thomas had the map drawn by Joseph of Arimathea. Baroni and Peter reviewed where they thought the island was. Dante said, "It looks like it is near one of three larger islands called Menorca, Mallorca and Ibiza. South of Menorca is the Isla Del Aire. North of Mallorca is Dragonera and south is Cabrera and Conillera. There are islands all around Ibiza. The island you are describing sounds like an island off the coast of Ibiza. But I can't remember where it is. This island has some periodic earthquake activity and is unoccupied. Most of the island is covered with forest. The north end is low to the water and flat. The forested area is high and covers a much larger area than the north end. It's called the Rock of Mahon. However, we should go to Menorca, so let's start there first."

Thomas asked, "Are there Roman facilities on the larger islands?"

"Yes, we have fortified a wall around the city of Ibiza," Dante said. "The Roman headquarters in Menorca is Mao and in Mallorca is Pollentia. Lorenzo will be amused when we lay claim to the Rock of Mahon. I'll walk back to the fort and see if he remembers who is in charge of each island."

Peter asked, "If we have to look at several islands, how long will it take us after we leave Palermo?"

"If the wind is right," Dante said, smiling. "Even looking at several other islands, it will take less than a week."

By sunset everything was loaded, everyone ate lightly and went to sleep.

✝ Chapter 44 ✝

Fighting Hadar and Pirate Ships
Tuesday, May 14, 125 A.D.

Thomas and Stephen were awakened by Peter talking to Ben on the top-deck. They went up and found half the men walking around, waiting for the dawn. Thomas said, "Did we decide who will lead this armada?"

Peter said, "Dante is our new leader. He knows these waters and wants to have his three ships lead. The rest of us will follow them. We will continue to be bait, but I doubt Hadar would have his ships go this far west. However, we may be surprised. When we are past the San Vito la Capo, Tamir will begin to sail the Islander north. Pardi will have the Palermo Vine follow us within eyesight. Drago will sail south of us."

Pardi came over with Micah from the Palermo Vine. Pardi was excited and said, "I just saw two ships sail out of here. Micah confirmed they were Hadar's ships. Both had Jewish menorahs on their sails. I don't know when they came in and whether they knew who we are. It was good our sails were down. We may have an encounter with them."

"They could have purchased goods for the rebels in Israel," Thomas said. "Or they could be after us. I'm glad we have protection. Let's warn everyone."

Pardi, Micah and Thomas went down the pier to warn the other ship captains.

When they returned to their ships, Ben shouted, "Dante's ships are leaving."

Peter bellowed to a port worker who ran over and released the lines. Thomas could hear shouts from the other ships that were now struggling to turn and leave the pier. The oarsmen were working hard pulling the Free Spirit out into the bay. Peter shouted to the soldiers to pull up the sails. The wind caught and the oarsmen put up the oars.

Thomas was up on the stern again, watching Tamir and the other ships. Ben and Stephen were in the bow appreciating how quickly Dante's ships were pulling away from them. The further west they sailed, the harder the wind blew. Peter turned the paddle bar over to Joziah and stepped up on the stern. He said, "Now I know why Dante's ships got ahead of us so quickly, but we are staying with them now. I hope this wind doesn't take us into a storm."

"I saw on the map that we'll sail past Sardinia," Thomas said. "I guess Tamir will see it, but we won't. What do you think?"

"Dante is taking us a little north so Tamir may need to sail towards us to avoid getting too close to Sardinia," Peter said. "When we get past Sardinia, we must sail north to Menorca. If we see him coming our way we'll sail to the south as well. I'm going to check the sundial before it gets cloudy."

The wind was whistling and howling. Thomas said, "Let's go down to the cabin to talk."

In their cabin, Baroni looked at Thomas and said, "I talked to Dante and Pardi yesterday and we were all puzzled. Dante talked about the Rock of Mahon as possibly being the Island-of-Dreams. It has the reputation of a taboo and bad luck, but it is thought to be inhabitable. Local people on Ibiza claim that it was pushed up out of the sea about seven hundred years ago. Those who have visited the island say the forest is new and has no dead tree trunks. It has undergone a birthing process and the locals fear it. Of course the Rock of Mahon may not be the Island-of-Dreams."

The ship gave a creaking sound. Thomas said, "I think we're turning. Let's go see."

When they got up on the top-deck, Baroni asked, "Peter, why are we turning?"

"I'm turning to go a little south, because there is a storm ahead of us," Peter said. "Tamir is also sailing towards us. I don't know if he sees Sardinia or wants to avoid the storm or both. Ben came back before you got here and said Dante's ships are sailing south, but they're in the storm now. Look south to see what Drago's ships are doing."

Baroni and Thomas stepped over to the port rail and gazed south. They saw Drago's ships now sailing straight west. Baroni said, "Peter, Drago's ships are going west and not going south anymore."

Some of the men were in the cabins asleep, but most were on deck watching the looming storm. Ben came back to the stern and said, "I think the storm is traveling northwest. Dante's ships are in the edge of the storm, but I can't tell if it is raining on them."

Peter said, "We'll go straight west. Men, adjust the sails back like they were before. Joziah let the side paddles go so the ship follows the wind."

Stephen hollered, "There are ships coming south and will pass right in front of us."

Everyone on deck stopped to gaze at the ships that Stephen saw. There were five ships.

Peter yelled over the wind, "That first ship is the Islander."

As the ships got closer, Ben screamed, "The first two have Jewish menorahs on their sails. The next two have skulls and crossbones on their sails. They must think that will scare everyone."

Baroni grimaced and said, "Hadar is doing business with pirates. Now they have resorted to stealing. That's not smart of them."

Stephen said, "Probably not, since they are being chased by three Roman ships and here comes Tamir."

Thomas grabbed the long pole with the red flag, stepped up on the stern and started waving it. The Hadar ships were out ahead of them now. Drago and his ships started sailing north to see what the red flag meant. Dante's ships had turned around and were sailing back towards them. The Hadar and pirate ships turned and were trying to sail into the wind. They were slowly side-slipping towards the Free Spirit. They could see that there were three Roman ships coming at them from the north, south and west.

Baroni said, "They've gotten into trouble here with all these Roman ships. They must think they can get away by coming our way."

Peter shouted, "We need to get armed."

Baroni shouted, "Peter is right. Go down and get bows, arrows and pitch. Bring your swords.

"Josiah, help us pull down the mainsail," Peter said. "Lower the other sails."

The Roman pursuit ships were sailing southeast in an effort to cut off the Hadar and pirate ships. Drago must have had the same idea for he was sailing northeast. The Palermo Vine had its sails down and came up along the starboard side of the Free Spirit. Pardi shouted, "Those Hadar and pirate ships are turning to sail southwest. They will sail right into Dante's ships."

The pursuit and Drago ships turned back to follow the direction of the fleeing ships.

Baroni shouted, "Pull up our sails, so we can pursue them."

The sails on both ships were pulled up and they sailed towards the fleeing ships. Pardi and Baroni had their men ready with swords, hanging onto the railings and holding bows and arrows. The fleeing ships were in disarray.

Drago's ships encountered the Hadar ships first firing flaming arrows from all three ships at them. Only the lead Hadar ship sent arrows back. Peter and Tamir came in behind the pirate ships, sending flaming arrows high into their sails and the decks. With their ships sails on fire, they lost momentum. This allowed Dante's three ships to come in from the west side, the pursuing Roman ships coming in from the north. All six Roman ships sent clouds of arrows at all four fleeing ships. Both pirate ships and one of the Hadar ships were on fire. The men on the burning ships were diving into the water. Most did not come up.

Drago's and Bernardus' ships came in from the south and threw grappling hooks over the lead Hadar ship that was not on fire. Peter pulled the Free Spirit up to the bow of Drago's ship and Tamir pulled the Islander up to the bow of Bernardus's ship on the other side. They threw grappling hooks. Thomas held his sword as he climbed over the railing. Several men did the same from the other ships. There were arrows stuck into the deck, railings, sail arms and the stern. Many men were lying dead or dying. There were buckets scattered about and empty rain barrels used to control the burning arrows. Thomas went to the stairs to the lower decks and shouted, "Come up or we will come down there and kill you."

Six men came up the stairs with their arms in the air. One man said, "Holy God. Are you Thomas? We tried to get you over by Crete. What happened to the ben Yaakov?"

Baroni shouted, "Are there any others below?"

Another man said, "There are more. They are crying and fearful to come up."

The fires were roaring on the three ships. One by one they sunk, as everyone watched.

Thomas shouted again from the top of the stairs, "Don't make us come and get you."

They waited. The first six young men were herded to the bow. Soon four crying young men came up the stairs with their arms up. Thomas walked over to them and realized they were no more than twelve to fourteen. From the bow, the first man to speak said, "We were all kidnapped in Gaza and forced to stay in the cabins below. There were several kidnap victims on the other ship."

Thomas said, "Let that man walk over to me."

The man was young and wore a tattered robe. He had long hair, but only had fuzz for a beard. His face was bruised and his nose had been broken. He held his arms in the air.

Thomas asked, "What is your name and how old are you? What happened to your face?"

"My name is Simon and I'm the oldest at seventeen. I tried to get away in Marsielles, but they caught me, beat me and broke my nose. Those men were animals. All of us are scared. What will you do with us?"

"Why did you think I was Thomas?"

"You were described to us and we were told you would be on the Free Spirit or the Islander. I saw the signs for both ships when I came up the stairs."

"Joziah said, "Thomas, I know Simon and these other young people. We've killed the bad men."

Thomas sat on the stern and said, "What now?

"Let me talk to Simon and the others while a new sail is raised and the dead men are removed," Joziah said. "I'd like to explain to them how lucky they are. I'll see if there are any problems."

"We should use the extra sail for the Palermo Vine," Joziah said. "We could raise it and take this ship with us. Peter has taught me enough to captain this ship. By the way this is the ben Yaakov II."

Stephen waved to Pardi on the Palermo Vine. He then yelled, "We need your extra sail."

Pardi had Micah float the Palermo Vine next to the Free Spirit. Four men brought the extra sail over the Free Spirit. They handed it to four men on the ben Yaakov II. Drago said, "We will assign five men from Bernardus's ship and five from mine to man this freighter. My first mate is Aldo and he will captain this ship, with Joziah taking the first mate duties."

Thomas said, "Simon and three of these youngest fellows will go to the Free Spirit. The other six will go three to the Islander and three to the

Palermo Vine. Joziah, you and I will straighten Simon's nose after we leave."

Dante shouted, "Is everything under control?"

Baroni shouted back, "We have a new sail going up and have the ship staffed. When we release this ship, lead us again. We'll all stay together the rest of the way.

As the Free Spirit took its grappling hooks off and got ready to go, one of the Roman ships that had pursued the Hadar and Pirate ships sailed over to hail Centurion Baroni. The captain shouted, "We could not have planned a better attack. I see you are claiming that ship that had the Jewish menorah on its sail. You got it, so it is yours. We have pursued them from Marsielles. They tried to steal from a Roman warehouse, but they did not succeed. Thank you and by the way, who are you?"

"I'm Centurion Baroni with orders from Governor Rufus of the Provence of Judaea and Governor Salvatore of the Provence of Sicily."

"Yes sir. We will report your action when we return to Marsielles."

Drago said, "When the men on the ben Yaakov II sent two waves of arrows, I yelled at my men to stay under their shields. Only one man was hit in his arm next to his elbow. He'll be all right. We were lucky."

Baroni said, "We haven't enough time to bag these bodies. Just throw them overboard."

Drago's men unceremoniously threw the dead crew from the ben Yaakov II over the bow into the Mediterranean. The arrows were dug out of the sail pole, the deck and the railings. Soon the men were transferred and the remaining grappling hooks removed. Thomas looked up at the red star with the grape vines on the ben Yaakov II. He sighed and said, "We will pray for the dead tonight."

The Free Spirit eased up to the starboard side of Dante's ship. Thomas yelled, "What is the plan now?"

Dante walked to the starboard side and said, "We must be just west of Sardinia. We'll start our search for the Island-of-Dreams in Menorca. I'll sail to the Port of Mahon to see if there are more Hadar ships. When we arrive, only two of my ships will enter the Harbor, everyone else should wait for us to return."

Dante's ships turned and sailed northwest with Drago's ships, Thomas's ships and the ben Yaakov II following them.

---

† Chapter 45 †

Searching for the Island
Wednesday, May 15, 125 A.D.

The wind had been blowing briskly for some time, but the water in the Mediterranean still had small swells. They had been sailing mostly with the wind and the ship sailed fairly smoothly. No one had gotten sick yet, even with the chase and the battle. As it neared mid-day, they sailed into the storm clouds. It rained with drops driving from the rear of the ship. Thomas and most of the men went down to the lower deck.

Stephen and Joziah held Simon while Thomas straightened his nose. Simon was tough but, couldn't help crying. Thomas placed small cloth wrapped pieces of wood on each side of Simon's straightened nose and took a strip of cloth and tied it around his head to hold the wood and keep Simon's nose straight. Thomas said, "Now lie down and take a nap. Try to leave your nose alone."

Joziah talked to the other fellows who were twelve and thirteen years old. They were grateful to be rescued. They both cried because they had friends on the other ship that burned and sank. Simon sat up and said, "They kept us locked in the cabins. We broke out when you yelled at us. I'm sure the fellows on the other ship were locked in their cabin and went down with it. We're lucky."

Ben came down and said, "Peter thinks the wind is dying down."

Thomas and Stephen returned to the main deck. The rain was now a drizzle. Peter was seated, looked up at Thomas and said, "Dante got ahead of us, but we are catching up to him. Take a look."

Thomas saw Dante's ships and said, "They've stopped. Their sails are down."

As the Free Spirit came closer to them, Thomas noticed that the Islander had sailed close to the starboard side of the Free Spirit. Several of the men on both ships shouted, "We can see land."

There was a large land mass and a bay ahead of Dante's ships. A flag was being waved on one of Dante's ships. Peter shouted, "That's a signal to talk."

The sails were pulled down and they gradually floated up to the port side of the Roman ship. Grappling hooks were thrown over both ships railings and the men on both ships pulled them together. Dante bounded over the railings and met Thomas, Baroni and Peter. "That was crazy back there," he said. "We've reached Menorca. This is the entrance to the port of Mahon. The city of Mao[196] surrounds the port. Principale Rocco and I will sail in his ship to dock at the pier. Principale Nino will sail in behind us and turn around and sail back out to you. If we see those two Hadar ships that were at Palermo, we'll come out for you. If they are not in there, when I return, we'll sail south to a small island I heard about."

Baroni said, "We'll sail a short distance south and wait there. We're in the ship traffic here."

Dante returned to Rocco's ship. The grappling hooks were removed and they sailed into the bay towards the port.

Peter sailed south past the entrance to the bay with everyone following. While they waited for Dante, Thomas had Peter sail the Free Spirit over next to the ben Yaakov II. They pulled the ships together and Thomas, Stephen, Ben and Baroni went over to tour the ship. Joziah met them and said, "On

---

[196] Author's note. The port and the city were named after the Carthagean general, Mahon Barca, a brother of Hannibal and Hasdrubal Barca. The general had two nick names. One was Mao the other was Mago. He is considered to be the inventor of Mayonnaise. Another fact, the port of Mahon is the deepest port in the Mediterranean.

deck two, there are boxes of arrows, bundles of spears and boxes of swords. Let me show you."

Joziah held a lantern and led them down through level one and into level two. They inspected the boxes and bundles of spears. They also found barrels of flour and corn. Thomas said, "This food will be welcome when we find the island. We also have weapons for our men as we hire them."

They returned to the top deck and saw Nino's ship sailing towards them. Thomas, Stephen and Ben returned to the Free Spirit as Nino climbed over the railing. Nino had big eyes and was clearly excited. He was not sure what to say, but Baroni finally said, "Tell us man what you saw."

Nino said, "Yes sir. When we went in past Dante's ship and began to turn around, I saw a sail on one ship go up as they left the pier. It had a Jewish Menorah on it. We stopped and watched four more pull up their sails with the Jewish Menorah displayed as they left. Dante was on the pier when they sailed past him. I pulled into the pier and asked Dante what I should do. He said we'll never catch them unless they sail into the rest of the ships. He told me to follow them to see where they go. Dante is right behind us."

Baroni said, "Well where did they go?"

"They sailed out of the bay and turned to go north," Nino said. "Dante heard that some ships were going to the Roman port of Pollentia on Mallorca. They will probably be there tonight, if they are the ones."

Peter had the ben Yaakov II pushed away from the Free Spirit. Everyone watched as Dante's ship pulled up to the Free Spirit. The wind had died down. Dante leaned over the railing and yelled at Nino to ask, "Which way did the Hadar ships sail?"

Nino shouted back, "They sailed north."

Dante shouted, "I think they are going to Mallorca and so are we. Just ahead of us is a very small island called Isla Del Aire. Thomas, be sure to keep an eye out. Follow us."

Peter sailed behind Dante's ship. The others sailed single file behind them along the coast of Menorca. Thomas watched Dante as he leaned over the railing and pointed at a flat rounded rectangular island. It was several hundred cubits long. "I see it, but it is not the Island-of-Dreams," Thomas shouted as he held his hand out with his thumb pointing down."

They continued on going northwest. It was getting late in the day when they spotted some land. Dante's ship sailed around a finger of land. Baroni said, "That's the northeast corner of Mallorca. There are two ridges coming off the main part of the island and stick out into the Mediterranean. We'll sail around the northern one and then sail southwest."

They sailed along the north coast of Mallorca and kept the shore in sight. As the sun went down, they came to an island close to the shore shaped like a long ridge with a peak at the highest point. Dante pulled into a shallow bay on Mallorca and dropped his anchor. All of the ships pulled in around the bay dropping their anchors as it became dark. There was no wind and the Mediterranean Sea was flat.

Dante leaned over the railing and asked, "Thomas did that island look familiar?"

Thomas leaned over the railing of the Free Spirit and said, "No, that island has a peak and no flat areas. It is not the Island-of-Dreams."

Dante said, "We'll sleep here on the ships tonight. Each ship should appoint two shifts of watchmen. At dawn in the morning, we'll leave and sail to the big bay of Mallorca and into the Port of Pollentia. While Nino and Rocco sail into the pier, Peter will sail down past the gulf and stop to wait for us. We can see if the Hadar ships are there. If they are we'll either take them or send for your help. If they're not, then we'll sail to the small islands on the south of Mallorca."

The plan was relayed from ship to ship. The men on each ship ate light dinners and went to sleep. Thomas, Peter, Stephen, Ben, Joziah, Simon and the younger boys prayed for their lost friends killed that day in the battle. Thomas then prayed for the other men who had died on each of the Hadar and pirate ships. They then went to sleep.

Thursday, May 16, 125 A.D.

Thomas got up when it was still dark and went up to the top-deck. He noticed each ship had a lighted torch for their guards. Peter sat looking at his maps under a bright torch. He looked up at Thomas and said, "Well we eliminated two islands yesterday. There are several islands south of Mallorca, but only two are big enough to be the Island-of-Dreams."

Thomas said, "I've always wondered why Joseph of Arimathea and Jesus found an island north of the route coming through the strait of the Rock of Gibraltar."

Stephen came up from his cabin and said, "I always wondered too, but I think they came from Marsielles. Didn't Joseph of Arimathea have a pack train from the Atlantic side of Gaul down to Marsielles?"

"You're right," Thomas said. "I thought they sailed from Britain. If they came from Marsielles, then that explains why they were up here. They were off the shipping lane from Marsielles, but he said they had problems with their ship. They must have been in a storm and got off course. But where were they?"

As the sky brightened in the east before sunrise, all of the ships pulled up their anchors. Using the oars the ships pulled away from the shore. The sails were raised in a gentle wind. Dante's ship led the way. They sailed past the Sa Dragonera Island and turned south. As the sun rose in the east, they came to the large Mallorca bay. Dante's ship turned and sailed into the bay with Nino's ship following him. Peter kept sailing until they were south of the bay with the coast in sight. All of the eight ships pulled their sails down to wait.

Thomas was putting a new strip of cloth around Simon's nose after he rinsed his face. "Your face and eyes are black and blue," Thomas said. "But I think your nose is healing. Does it feel any better?"

"Yes, but it was only yesterday morning when it got broken," Simon said. "I don't know how I will ever thank you for rescuing me and fixing my nose. It's amazing how things have changed for me in one day."

Thomas could hear shouting and went up to the top-deck. Rocco's and Nino's ships were sailing towards the Free Spirit. Dante and another soldier threw grappling hooks over the Free Spirit's railing and they pulled up tight. Dante came over to talk to Thomas and Baroni. "We docked at the pier and I talked to the pier manager. He said the five Hadar ships stopped for about an hour last night and left again. The manager said they were going to Cadiz in Iberia and sailed south. We won't see them today, unless they stopped somewhere. Let's go look at the two islands. The largest is called Cabrera and the smaller is Conillera. We'll encounter Conillera first. I will have Rocco wait when we get to it."

They sailed south following Dante in Rocco's ship. The sun was directly overhead when Rocco's ship pulled the sails down. The Free Spirit and the other ships pulled their sails down and everyone stared at this island called Conillera. Peter said, "We can see several islands, but the largest one here is that long rocky one. It has that funny bend in the island, but it does not appear to have any trees or fresh water. Thomas, what do you think?"

Thomas was looking back and forth from one end of the island to the other. He finally said, "It does not appear to be the Island-of-Dreams. Let's move on, but I will keep looking at it as we continue to sail."

They pulled the sails partially up and came along side of Dante's ship. Stephen leaned over the railing and shouted, "Thomas said this is not the Island-of-Dreams. Let's move on and we'll follow."

It was the middle of the afternoon when they came to Cabrera. There was a large bay and all of the ships sailed in after Dante checked it out and signaled for everyone to come in to drop anchor.

Everyone on the Free Spirit looked at Thomas who said, "This is a large island, but I'm not sure it looks right. I would like to climb to the top of that hill and look around. Let's lower the tender and go ashore."

Baroni yelled to Dante, "Thomas wants to hike up to the top of that hill and look around. Three of us will go with him."

Dante shouted back, "It's getting late, let's stay here tonight. Tomorrow we'll sail to the islands around Ibiza."

Thomas and Stephen lowered the tender on the Free Spirit into the water and Ben climbed down a rope with a paddle. Thomas, Stephen and Baroni went down into the tender and Ben paddled to the shore. Once they set foot on shore, Thomas set out hiking up the slope towards the top. The ground was very rocky with some small cedar and brush. When they reached the top and walked around Thomas said, "Cabrera Island is very rocky and has no pine trees. There may be fresh water someplace, but I have to say, this is not the Island-of-Dreams."

Baroni led the way back down the slope to the tender. The sun had gone down and the weather was calm with a nice breeze. They noticed the tender had floated about fifty paces out in the bay. Thomas swam for it and brought it to the shore. Ben paddled them back to the stern of the Free Spirit. Everyone climbed up over the stern. Thomas and Stephen pulled the tender up while Ben secured it.

Everyone stayed on their ships, ate a light dinner and went to bed with guards assigned on each ship. Baroni, Thomas, Stephen, Peter and Ben sat in their cabin drinking watered wine, discussing the islands they had visited. Thomas finished the discussion and said, "I wonder if we will encounter the five Hadar ships? That could be a real fight, but we have two-hundred and sixty soldiers."

They finished their drinks, put out the lamp and went to sleep.

Friday, May 17, 125 A.D.

The next morning they rowed out of the bay and set sail for Ibiza. Sitting on the stern eating bread and cheese, Thomas said, "I hope we find our island today. Maybe the Rock of Mahon is it. Dante says it's somewhere off the coast of Ibiza. I'm getting excited now."

The weather was nice, with blue skies and a good light wind picking up. Thomas enjoyed standing in the bow watching Dante's ship. The breeze felt glorious going through his hair and beard. Later Peter came up to him and said, "We may only see three islands today. I'm getting anxious. Otherwise, we'll need to look for some supplies. We have over three hundred men on ten ships. We don't have enough eggs or milk for more than a few men. We have eaten the fresh fruits and vegetables. We're working on the dried fruit, but we're going to need some fresh vegetables and fruit pretty soon."

Later in the afternoon, Ben shouted, "I see land and Dante's ship is pulling their sails down."

They were looking at a long narrow island with beautiful sandy beaches. There were other islands in the distance. Peter was looking at his maps and said, "There are three islands out there. The one we see in front of us is S' Espardell. It is unoccupied and with no trees."

Thomas said, "S' Espardell is beautiful, but it is not the Island-of-Dreams. Let's move on."

They sailed south to a much larger island. As they sailed up to it, Dante turned away and sailed east. There was an arm of the island he had to go around.

Baroni said, "Dante is going around this island. Peter, what is it called? Why are we going around it?"

Peter looked at his map and said, "This Island used to be considered part of Ibiza, but you Romans have given it the separate name of Formentera. The best place to drop anchor is on its west side."

They soon were following Dante's ship around the arm and sailed west. They passed a large bay and continued around the tip and sailed north. The island shore turned east and the sail on Dante's ship was lowered. They had their oars out and slowly stopped and dropped anchor. He had pulled into a wide bay. The Free Spirit pulled next to Dante's ship and dropped anchor. The other eight ships did the same. The tenders were lowered on all of the ships and four men from each ship paddled to the shore. The men pulled the tenders up on the sand. The ship captains, missionaries, Baroni and Pardi met as they were stretching their legs and getting used to standing on land again.

Thomas looked around and could see an island to the north almost connected to Formentera. There was an inland lake next to where they had landed. The island was flat with two flat hills south of them.

Dante looked at everyone and said, "We'll stop here for the night. Thomas, what do you think of this island? Isn't it beautiful?"

Everyone stared at Thomas who finally said, "This is the most beautiful place I have ever seen. I love it, but it is not the Island-of-Dreams. I almost wish it was. I'm getting tired of searching. These sandy beaches and warm weather makes me want to take my clothes off and go for a swim. But, why didn't we sail on?"

"We don't have enough time today to look at each of the islands on the west side of Ibiza. From what I remember none of the islands we pass after these three are likely to be the Island-of-Dreams. I'm now hoping your island is on the north coast of Ibiza. If it is, we will spend all day tomorrow before we get to the Rock of Mahon. I'm pretty sure I know where it is now and we'll make sure tomorrow."

Baroni said, "Well, we are here for the afternoon and the night. Drago and Rocco assign some men to gather all the wood they can find. Let's make five or six fire pits. I'm going to have a swim."

Men from each ship were assigned to bring in food supplies for dinner. Hectic activity started as the men learned of the plans for the afternoon and evening. Men on the ships took off most of their clothing and dove into the water. The Roman ships had two tenders each, which were bringing food and supplies. The missionaries, Pardi, Dante and Baroni were the first to swim. They came out of the water and put their clothing back on.

Thomas said, "I feel like a totally refreshed person. Let's hike around and look at the island some more."

They walked north to the tip of Formentera and gazed at the island further north. Dante said, "That island was recently named S' Espalmador. It has big mud baths and is much larger than S' Espardell."

Thomas smiled and said, "It is beautiful as well, but it is not the "Island-of-Dreams.""

"Well, we have had a good look at seven islands so far," Stephen said. "I guess we will continue to hear you say tomorrow, it is not the Island-of-Dreams. Maybe you should ask Jesus if we are getting close."

They walked south and went around the lake on the east side and continued onto a finger of land that went out into the Mediterranean. Thomas turned and walked west to the west shore. He stopped and looked around enjoying the view. Looking at everyone, he said, "It would take a few days to explore the rest of the island. Maybe we can do that another time. Let's go back and help set up for the fires and the food."

They spent the rest of the afternoon and early evening getting reorganized and secured after the swimming. They were ready to eat. Some of the corn has been used from the ben Yaakov II. Everyone enjoyed a change in the diet. They finished by enjoying some of Pardi's wine, but most of the soldiers drank a vinegar and water drink. All of the men returned back on board their ships with the tenders tied securely. Guards were stationed for the night and the rest of the men were asleep just after dark. It had been a challenging and deadly few days, but no one wanted to talk about it.

✝ Chapter 46 ✝

Finding the Island-of-Dreams
Saturday, May 18, 125 A.D.

During the night, Thomas dreamed he was on the Island-of-Dreams on the lower level. Jesus walked his way blinding him. When Thomas could see Him, Jesus said, *"You've been thorough in your search, but you'll find this island tomorrow. Right now look up the hill to the forest. It's beautiful. Where we are standing is where you will build the vault and the house of worship. Now let's walk to where you will land your ship. I know you are startled at your progress and support by the Romans. Don't be surprised. You have been learning their ways. There is more to come."*

Before daylight Thomas told Peter, Ben, Stephen and Baroni about his dream with Jesus. "He showed me where to build the house of worship and where to climb onto the island when we find it. He gave me another look at the island from the lower level. It gives me a good sense of what I will see when we get there. Now that I think about it, he didn't tell me where the island is, but he said we'll find it. We must trust Jesus."

As it started to get light, the anchor came up on Dante's ship. With shouting, oars being manned and anchors being pulled up, the ships turned and finally sailed northwest. Thomas stood on the deck on the starboard side and gazed at the west side of S' Espalmador. He turned to Baroni and Stephen and said, "I sure would not want to be around here in a storm. These islands would become invisible. I wonder how many ships have crashed and sunk around here."

They sailed for a few hours and came to a tall rock standing in the ocean. It had a peaked rocky ridge and a pyramid shaped rock lower than the tall rock. Peter said, "That Island west of us is called Es Vedra. It can't be the island."

"You're right," Thomas said. "It's not the Island-of-Dreams."

Everyone laughed and Peter gave the signal to move on. They had not even taken their sails down. They continued to maintain speed sailing along the coast of Ibiza. They were eating lunch when they saw two small islands of rock and then a larger long island next to a portion of Ibiza jutting out towards it. They sailed in closer and took down the sails to give them time for a closer look. It was a large island but flat and looked like it was shaped like a U. There were no trees.

Thomas stood gazing at it and finally said, "It doesn't have any trees. No, this isn't our island."

Peter gave the flag signal to sail to the next island. All the ships pulled up their sails and they continued on, turning northeast to keep the Ibiza shore visible. Earlier in the day the wind had picked up. It was now late afternoon when the coast of Ibiza disappeared and they sailed southeast. Soon they could see land again and Peter said, "That is a section of Ibiza jutting out from the main island."

They continued on and saw in the distance an island. They followed Dante's ship on a route taking them on the east side of the island. The north end was low with grass waving, but the south end was much larger and higher with vertical cliffs and green pines on the top of it. It looked perfect. They reached the south end of the island and turned west. The sails on Dante's ship came down. All the other ships did the same. Peter brought the Free Spirit up next to see Dante leaning over the railing.

Thomas yelled with great excitement, "This really could be the island."

Dante shouted, "Thank God, I was beginning to think it was a figment of your imagination. I would like our ten ships to proceed with the Free Spirit in the lead. This is the Rock of Mahon. Peter, you should sail to the Rock of Mahon now from its southwest side. Watch out for islets and shallow rocks. Sail up to the island where Thomas can climb on it to see if it is his island. Peter you should proceed ahead of us."

Thomas shouted, "Jesus showed me last night where to land."

They sailed west and then turned to sail north. Thomas was watching the high cliffs and water falling off one area into the Mediterranean. The wind was gentle as it was getting close to sunset. All of the ships were now fairly close to each other, following in a staggered line. Everyone was anxious to get on the island.

Peter continued to sail the Free Spirit north ahead of the others. To the starboard side of the Free Spirit, Thomas continued to look up at the rounded cliff. The men got their oars out.

Baroni said, "Look at this wonderful island. It's about a mile from Ibiza. It is protected here."

Thomas shouted, "It's larger than I thought it would be, but I believe it is our island. I'm so excited. I'll need to get on it and climb to the forest to be sure."

The island was majestic, sitting about a mile off the coast of Ibiza. It had a high cliff coming down to a shelf next to the water. There was grass on the hill and the lower part. The upper area was substantial and was dark green above the cliff walls.

As they got closer to the lower north end, they pulled the sails down, and stood gazing at the beauty of the island. Thomas shouted, with glee, "Pull the ship forward slowly."

He stood in the bow pointing to the corner where the lower portion of the island connected to the hill. They rowed along the shear walls of the larger part of the island on their starboard side watching for rocks. The shear walls were straight up with no beach or land at sea level. Thomas said, "Pull the ship up to that corner area. I think I can jump onto the shore there and dig my feet into the sloping hill. This really looks right."

There was a sloping dirt hill that stopped at the top of a rock wall going straight down. The men pulled the oars until the bow went over the vertical rock wall and the masthead dug into the dirt above. Peter dropped the anchor, but the men kept pulling on the oars to steady the Free Spirit. Thomas walked out to the end of the masthead and jumped up the dirt slope. He dug his sandals into the dirt with each step to keep from slipping. Gradually, he got to the top and stood up straight. He yelled, "This looks right so far. I'll climb to the forest and be right back."

While Thomas was gone, the Islander, Palermo Vine and the ben Yaakov II pulled up along the wall down from the Free Spirit. The six Roman ships sailed in to form two lines of three behind them, dropping their anchors. Ben said, "The water here is really calm. We're protected by this long high section of the island off our starboard side. The Island of Ibiza protects us from the west. We are protected from the north by the smaller part of the island ahead of us. It looks like we can have a pier along the shore in front of us. Temporarily to get started, we can float a pier along this wall until we can build the pier."

Baroni said to Peter and Stephen, "Have you ever seen anyone more relentless to find a certain island than Thomas?

Stephen smiled back and said, "Thomas was asked by Jesus to embark on an arduous undertaking. Thomas never wavered, but you're right he has been relentless. The other tasks Jesus wanted done will now be attacked with unending vigor by Thomas. You watch."

Thomas reappeared above them standing with the sky behind him. He jumped up and down then yelled, "This is it. We found it. This is the Island-of-Dreams and I am thrilled by it. It is just as Jesus showed me."

All of the men on the ten ships shouted and jumped up and down delighted they had finally found it. Everyone laughed and pointed at Thomas as he continued to dance and shout. His arms and robe were flapping as he danced at the skyline.

The sun was down and it was getting dark, when Thomas finally came down the hill part way and stopped to shout, "Stay on your ships tonight. We'll begin tomorrow after tonight's celebration."

The Islander was next to the Free Spirit, and Mark, Paz and David climbed over the railings. Thomas stepped on the masthead, walking along it, and jumped onto the ship. The seven missionaries hugged each other and yelled, "We found the island."

After everyone sang and partied late on all the ships, they were exhausted and went to bed. Thomas fell into a deep sleep. He dreamed he was on the island with Jesus again, who said, *"First, I'm pleased that you found the artifacts in the room in the cave in Jerusalem. The artifacts were made by Moses and God. I'm delighted you packed them with Apostle Thomas's writings and the temple records. No one knows of these artifacts and you must keep it that way. You developed more support and protection from the Romans as I instructed you to do. Now you have found the island".*

*****The End *****

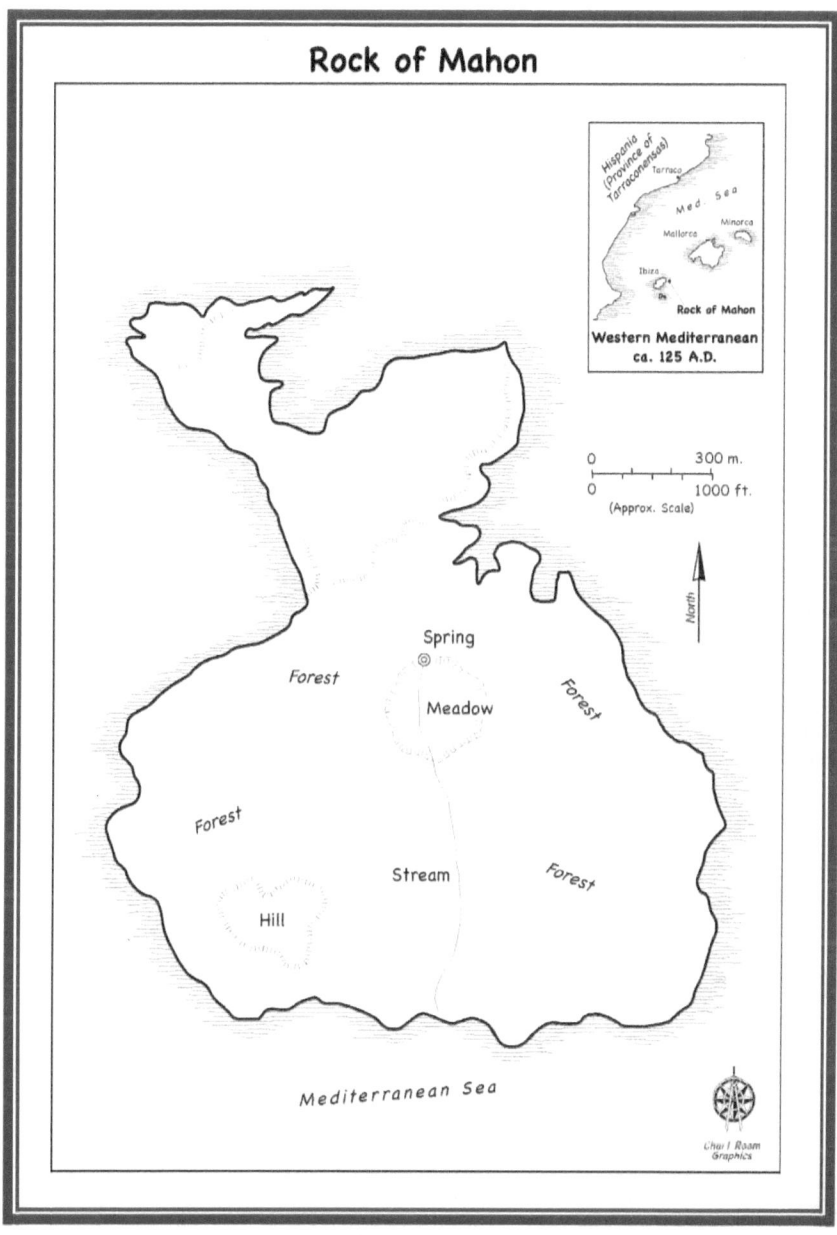

Thomas screamed, "We found the Island of Dreams."

Dante was amazed. The Island-of-Dreams is the Rock of Mahon.

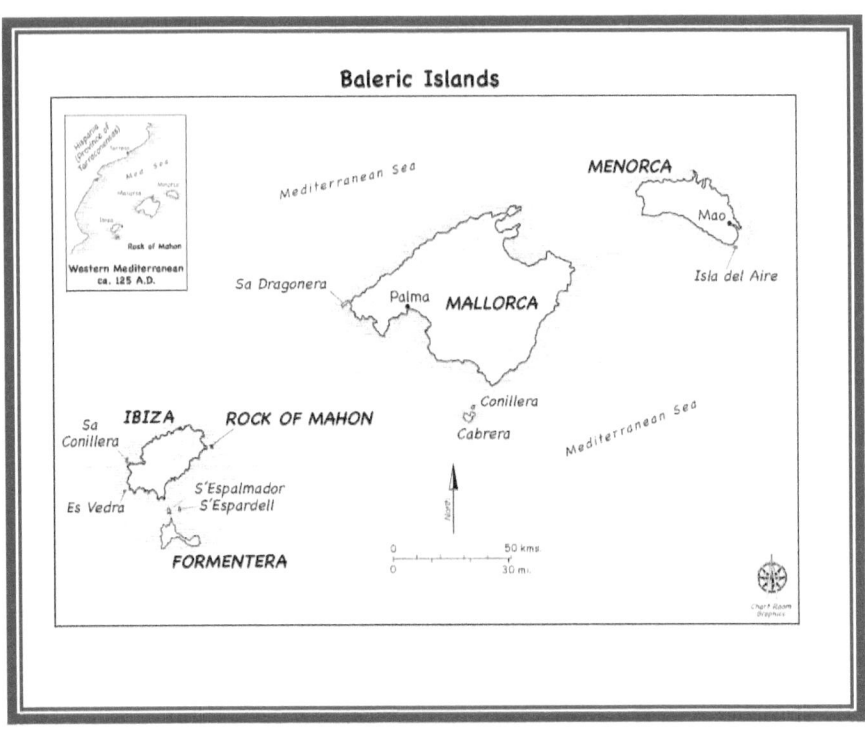

Historical Time Line

63 B.C. Pompey subdues Judea

37 B.C. Herod the Great gains full kingship of Judea ending the Hasmonean Dynasty

35 B.C. Herod rebuilds Hasmonean Fort into the new and larger Fortress Antonia

19-12 B.C. Herod enlarges temple mount and builds new Jewish temple (continues to 63 A.D.)

4 B.C. Herod the Great dies and Jesus Christ is born

30 A.D. Jesus Christ is crucified and resurrected; James the Just becomes Nasi of the Ecclesia

32 A.D. Deacon Stephen is martyred

32 A.D. The Pentecost and the spirit of God causes great numbers of conversions

36 A.D. Joseph of Arimathea and 12 members of the House of David are sent off from Caesarea with no oars or sails arriving, living making conversions in Gaul and Britain.

36 A.D. Joseph of Arimathea establishes the British church and the School of Avalon

36 A.D. Nazarene Ecclesia debate with Temple High Priests, arbitrated by Rabban Gamaliel.

41 A.D. Apostle James returns from 10 year mission to Spain and is beheaded

42 A.D. The Great Commission and the Apostles divide the world

42 A.D. Caesar Claudius issues edict to kill of all Christians, Druids and descendents of David

43 A.D. Caesar Claudius declares war on Britain

44 A.D. Apostle Peter makes visit to Rome and then flees from Roman persecution to Britain with Apostle Simon Zelotes

45 A.D. Claudius Caesar issues truce with Silurian family in Britain and invites them to come to Rome

55 A.D. Jonathon ben Ananas is killed by the Sicarii in Jerusalem

56 A.D. Apostle Paul makes his first visit to Rome

58 A.D. First Christian church above ground in Rome established in the Palace of the British

59 A.D. Most of the Royal British family is captured and taken to Rome

60 A.D. Boadicea war in Britain against the Roman legions killing more than 120,000 Romans

62 A.D. James the Just is Martyred by Ananas ben Ananas

66 A.D. Apostle Paul is beheaded in Rome and Apostle Peter is crucified upside down

Historical Time Line, Continued

62- 66 A.D. Christians flee Judea and especially Jerusalem to Pella led by Simeon ben Cleophas

66 A.D. Nero orders Gessius Florus in Jerusalem to confiscate silver from the Temple. Sicareans in Masada enter Jerusalem and lynch the Roman Garrison at Fort Antonia and Vespasian and son Titus are sent to subdue Judaea by Caesar Nero.

68 A.D. In spring, Nero commits suicide—Galba becomes Caesar and is lynched by his guard

69 A.D. Vespasian defeats Vitellius and Ortho to become Caesar in December

70 A.D. At the Passover, Titus arrives at gates to Jerusalem to find 24,000 Jewish soldiers, 600,000 Passover visitors and about 600,000 residents inside the walls of Jerusalem. The three factions of the Jewish army are in a civil war with each other.

70 A.D. Titus has destroyed Fortress Antonia and the Temple by August

70 A.D. By September more than 1,100,000 Jews died during Titus' siege of Jerusalem of which more than half died from famine caused by Jewish army units burning stored corn and other food and 97,000 are prisoners. Titus controls Jerusalem—Jewish artifacts are paraded and displayed in Rome.

74 A.D. Romans take Masada only to find all Sicareans had committed suicide

107 A.D. Crucifixion of Simeon ben Cleophas, age 120, Brother of Jesus and James the Just

115-117 A.D. Jewish Messiah revolt in Cyrene, Judea, Alexandria and Cyprus—250,000 people are killed in Cyprus and all Jews are expelled from Cyprus; all Greeks and Romans of more than 200,000 killed in Cyrene. Thousands killed in Alexandria and Judea.

117 A.D. Caesar Trajan dies and Hadrian becomes Caesar

118 A.D. JESUS' ISLAND OF DREAMS STARTS HERE

125 A.D. Thomas and Stephen begin effort to move Apostle Thomas' writings

132-136 A.D. Caesar Hadrian forbids castration and Jewish circumcision — Simeon ben Kosiba begins the formal messianic Bar Kokba war—Caesar Hadrian' forces destroy 985 Jewish Towns, 50 fortified cities, removes all Jews from Jerusalem and changes name to Aelia Capitolina and 580,000 Jews are killed

138 A.D. Caesar Hadrian dies and Antonius Pius becomes the new Caesar

Glossary of Selected Terms

Roman Titles:

Legatus Legionis These were the most important officers who commanded a legion of 2,000 or more soldiers. They were picked by the emperor from the senatorial class and had prior military experience as tribunes.

Tribunus Laticlavius These tribunes were usually young senators at the start of their public career. They wore broad purple strips on their tunic and were second in command of a legion. They may progress to the position of Legatus Legionis.

Centurion These men were in many cases recruited from the Roman knights or the city council members. Most had previously served as soldiers and non-commissioned officers (NCOs) in the legions or the praetorian cohorts. They usually commanded about eighty soldiers but may be assigned to various duties within the legion. Usually each legion had 59 or 60 Centurions.

Principale. These were non-commissioned officers who were numerous in a legion. There were nine levels of responsibility for Principales many of which had special duties. For this book I use the term Principale who would have been at the Optio level (one per Centurion or 59 per legion) and Tesserarius (Guard Commander with 59 per legion) as the Optio's second in command.

Nobilis Decurio. These were industrialist positions in the Roman Army. People in these positions were in charge of producing, shipping and delivering wheat, tin, lead, copper and other key supplies to the Roman warehouses.

Roman Drinks:

Alban. A preferred wine among upper classes. It provided several varieties of flavors, including very sweet, sweetish, rough and sharp. It was considered perfect if aged for fifteen years.

Calda. This drink was made with wine, water and spices. It was usually served warm or hot in the winter or cold mornings.

Chalybonium. This was a very fine wine produced near Damascus, Syria.

Chiam. This was likely the most prized Greek wine, with the best variety coming from Ariusium.

Falernian. This highly prized wine was mainly available to the upper classes. It was made from the Aminean grape originating near Naples but transferred to Mt. Falernus between Latium and Campania. This wine was best aged 10 to 20 years and usually had an alcohol content of 16%.

Lesbian. This was a Greek wine from the island of Lesbos and Mytilene. It was light, wholesome and had the natural taste of salt water.

Mareoticum. This was an Egyptian grape grown near Alexandria and was white, sweet, fragrant and light.

Mulsum. This drink used a common class wine and was sweetened with honey. It was often mixed with a large proportion of water.

Mustum. This drink was made from low quality grape juice with vinegar and drank fresh after pressing.

Passum. This was a raisin wine made from nearly dried grapes with the most prized produced in Crete.

Posca. This drink was made with vinegar like wine mixed with water to reduce the bitterness and consumed by soldiers and lower classes.

Taenioticum. This wine was produced in a long narrow sandy ridge near the western extremity of the Nile Delta in Egypt. It was aromatic, slightly astringent and of an oily consistency, which disappeared when it was mixed with water.

Tarraco. This was a Hispania white wine that was sweet and fruity produced in the Balearic isles.

Vinum Dulce. This was a sweet wholesome wine, made from dried grapes that were pressed in the heat of the day.

Vinum Diachytum. This was similar to Vinum Dulce but grapes were allowed to dry even more in the sun for longer periods of time. The wine was described as more 'luscious then Vinum Dulce.

Other words:

Amphorae. These were pottery produced storage containers of various sizes for storing wine, wine based sauces and other food items. They were sealed at the top with wax or pitch. Many had wood plugs that could be twisted at the top to pull them out of the wax or pitch. Wines were stored in this manner for fifteen to two hundred years. In 116 A. D. during Caesar Trajan's rule more than 100 million amphorae's were produced for a population of more than 50 million.

Ecclesia. This was an early word for church.

Nasi. Stands for president or head leader.

Providence. This word is looking to or preparation for the future provision. It describes a skill or wisdom in management or prudence or care or benevolent guidance of God or nature.

Superintendency. To act as superintendent of, direct, supervise or manage.

Zeukthrivai. A horizontal bar connecting to controls on each side of the ship to be a rudder to control a ship's turns.

Characters Encountered by Location

Arimathea Israel (118 A.D.)
Thomas, Age 18
Stephen, Age 17, Thomas' cousin
Uncle Cleophas and Aunt Ada
Grace, Ada's Handmaiden
Adam, Cleophas' Son
Gad, Cleophas' Son-in-Law
Carmel, Cleophas' Son-in-Law

Jerusalem Israel
David, Age 22
Paz, Age 20
Mark, Age 28
Tribunus Laticlavius Cerrone
Centurion Baroni
Principale Bardo
Principale Pardi
Ruth, Mayor's Wife
Nasi Judah Kyriakos
Rebecca, Widow
Neta, Head guard at Thomas Estate
Jacob and Amira, Neighbors
Mary, Ada's nurse
Leah, Ada's new handmaiden
Elizabeth, Leah's Assistant

Joppa Israel
Mayor Ezra
Peter, Age 28, Captain of Free Spirit
Ben, Age 18, the orphan
Tamir, Age 30, Captain of the Islander
Bishop Gamaliel
The boat manufacturer representative
The Inn Keeper and his wife
Centurion Markus
Principale Benito

Sebaste Israel (in Samaria)
Tribunus Laticlavius Pasquali
Centurion Felone
Centurion Natali (killed)
Principales Bataglia, Rizzo & Tyre
Caesarea Israel
Governor Quintus tenius Rufus
Legatus Legionis Dominic Mercelli
Tribunus Laticlavius Mascaro & Lady Lidia
Centurion Taccone
Bishop Ibrahim
Principales Guido, Paulus and Bagli

Island of Crete
Governor Stefano
Tribunus Laticlavius Flavio
Centurion Enrico
Principale Amedo
Roman Ship Captains:
Principale Drago, Alonso,
and Bernardus
Bishop Philip
Mayor Carsten
High Priest Hector

Island of Malta
Governor Pietro
Lady Caterina
Tribunus Laticlavius Nicolo
Centurion Filippo
Centurion Marco
Principale Matteo
Micah, Age 26, Captain
Joziah

Syracuse Sicily
Governor Salvatore
Lady Madelena
Legatus Legionis Mario
Lady Fabrizia, Mario's wife
Tribunus Laticlavius Renato
Lady Anna (Renato's Wife)
Centurion Sergio
Lady Adriana, Sergio's wife
Principale Giuseppi
Mayor Tazio
Lady Laura (Fazio's Wife)
Bishop Luca
Lady Donata (Luca's Wife)
High Priest Aristo
Lady Agnes

Palermo Sicily
Tribune Lorenzo
Lady Giorgetta
Centurion Dante
Principales Nino, Captain
Principale Ilario, Captain
Principale Rocco, Captain
Aldo, Roman captain
Simon, Survivor

Authors of Jesus' Island of Dreams
Stephen Thomas White

Stephen has brought Jesus' Island of Dreams to us from his many dreams about this island and the early missionary work. His exhaustive research, religious study and deep belief in the Christian message helps him to put the story into historical perspective. His footnotes connect with real places, people, and events as the story unfolds. He studied religion extensively in high school and through his college masters program. He continued to do research, experienced his dreams and went on to enjoy a successful business career. He is now fulfilling his obligation to tell this story. Look for future books in the Island of Dreams series with the next book entitled Jesus' Treasure Island. He lives in Arizona with his wife Laura.

Rev. Dr. Charles G. Jenkins, PhD. As a Presbyterian Minister, he brings his religious seminary training and his psychological graduate study along with his private practice experience. His in-depth research, teaching experience and worldwide travels bring insights to the historical events of the Good News of Jesus Christ for this adventurous book. He is native to Arizona and lives there with his wife Jean.

www.ingramcontent.com/pod-product-compliance
Lightning Source LLC
Chambersburg PA
CBHW021427240626
47153CB00001B/59